*read*iscover...

BooksMusic**Film** informa
Family history
Faxing**Games****Children's**

Please return or renew
avoid fines. It may be
in person. Please quo

Bletchley
Kingsto
MK Cer
Newp
Olne
Sto
We

Rue Amélie

Martin Lloyd

Queen Anne's Fan

First published in 2009 by Queen Anne's Fan
PO Box 883 • Canterbury • Kent • CT1 3WJ

© Copyright Martin Lloyd 2009

ISBN 9780 9547 1507 6

A CIP record of this book can be obtained from the British Library.

Set in New Baskerville 10 on 11pt.

Printed in England

Queen Anne's Fan

1

Paris in the 1970s

It all started the day I got the parking ticket. It was the last Tuesday of the month and I did not want to get out of bed. It was the day we collected from the girls.

I hated that kind of driving; crawling along the gutters of Pigalle at walking pace and ignoring the hooting of the traffic behind us.

I shaved at the sink and the morning sun crept around the courtyard to the chromium cage which the concierge had hung outside her window. Soon her brainless bird would start twittering. One day I would wring its neck.

There was half a bottle of milk in the fridge. I stood in my pyjamas at the open window for all the tenants to see and I drank it. What the hell! I could show them that life in a bedsit could be luxury.

Over the high roof tops came the lumbrous rumbling of Paris. Our quarter was quiet but it was hemmed in by the frenetic traffic of Les Invalides at one side and the colourful jostling of the Eiffel Tower at the other. Between the two poles, the seventh arrondissement slumbered on in undiscovered isolation. It was a village of its own.

I drained the plastic bottle, scooped up some water to give it weight, and threw it from the window. It thundered like a cannon shot, straight into the open garbage bin which the concierge was wheeling into the yard below me.

'*Connard!*' she shrieked. 'I suppose you think that's funny!'

I did, actually.

Out in the rue Amélie, Marguerite was washing the windows of her restaurant, the policeman with the large moustache and no chin was rocking on his heels outside the commissariat and two men in light raincoats were staring avidly into the dirty window of the printing shop opposite. I ignored them and walked down to the corner, not too fast and not too slow. I was still wearing my slippers. It was that kind of neighbourhood.

At the Café Clerc I ordered a big bowl of coffee and stole a croissant from the basket on the counter. Joanne was looking in the mirror and straightening her hair which was trying so bravely to be blond.

'And one croissant,' she added. 'Put your money on the zinc.'

Joanne was a businesswoman first and always.

'You've got a heart of ice,' I complained.

'You've got a purse of crumbs.' She held the bowl away from me until I had laid enough metal on the bar top. She turned away and I stole another croissant. 'Two croissants!' she called.

Joanne would see your breath on a boiled egg.

In the corner, Makele the Senegalese street sweeper was dreaming into his *kir*, scrawny black wrists protruding from his blue cloth overalls like some ju-ju doll. On the bench Pino was falling asleep over his coffee. He had just driven to Nice with a load of newspapers. Outside, the two raincoats were staring into the dry cleaners.

'Pino!' I called. He jerked awake. 'Have you seen those two pigeons before?' He screwed up his sagging eyes and pursed his lips.

'No. Friends of yours?'

'They seem to want to be.'

'They're not cops, anyway.'

That was the least of my worries. I would not have taken a studio-flat next to a police station if I had been afraid of the police, but I had rather hoped that it would be the last place that someone would think of looking for me. Perhaps they had tried everywhere else. I somehow thought not. They didn't look the tenacious types.

'Are you in trouble again?' Joanne moved the knight's helmet sugar bowl and polished the bar underneath. 'Why don't you get yourself a job?'

'I've got a job.'

'Driving Vincent around? Some job! Chuck it in and get a proper job. That pimp's no good. Get yourself a proper job.'

I grabbed her wrist a little too strongly.

'And would you marry me then?'

She wrenched it free with an insulting ease. Then she looked me straight in the eye.

'And if you gave up drinking, yes.'

That was the trouble with Joanne. You could never tell when she was joking.

'You old dishrag, I wouldn't have you. Can I use the phone?'

She switched on the meter. 'Who's paying?'

'Me.'

'What with? Drawing pins?'

'My money.'

'You haven't got any.'

'That's why I need to phone. I'm calling Vincent.'

'Does he owe you?'

'A bit.'

'How much?'

I paused and tried to look miserable. Underneath her hard crust I knew she had a heart of gold. I said 'Three weeks.' I thought she could afford that.

She sighed like a mother doting on a favourite child and opened the till. Her agile fingers prised up a bundle of ten franc notes and counted them one by one. Ninety francs. She picked out a telephone token from underneath and tossed it to me. 'Use the phone in the corner,' she said as she replaced the bundle in the till.

Vincent's phone rang and rang. At last an unshaven voice answered. It was Gaspard, Vincent's bodyguard. One metre ninety five and a face like an omelette. He usually sat in the front of the car with me and made lewd comments about the girls when he thought that Vincent could not hear. Vincent always heard and would poke him sharply between the shoulder blades with his stick. This would make Gaspard start and he would bang his head on the roof and then swear about the saucepan that he had to sit in. He really was very stupid. Vincent only kept him because he looked like a bodyguard and like me, he did not pay him much, if at all.

'Gaspard!'

'Who is it?'

'It's me, you fool.'

'The boss wants his car at ten o' clock.'

I said something rude about where the boss could put his car. I could imagine Gaspard clumsily clapping his fist over the earpiece in horror.

'Have you been paid Gaspard?'

'Yeah.'

'Oh. When were you paid?'

'When we went to Casino Harz.'

I remembered that job. It was not a gambling casino of course – all gambling in France was state run. It was an old *manoir* on the road to Compiègne with walled gardens and a kilometre long drive, but it had a restaurant and a band and a dance floor and about three lightbulbs to the hectare so that qualified it as a chic nightclub. Vincent had made me wait outside with the car like a real chauffeur. He had been there for four hours. I had sat there watching the rich and corruptible arriving in furs and jewels.

Four hours in the car with Gaspard is a life sentence with hard labour. Vincent had gone in bouncing, he had been pleased about something. One of his 'big deals' I had to suppose. But he had come out scowling and in a foul mood. Something had not gone as he had desired.

I never learned anything about it of course and Gaspard would have needed pictures and speech balloons to have grasped what was going on. I thought no more of it at the time. I had weathered all his 'big deals.' They usually ended in tears. We did not know it but this one was to end in more than that. But he had paid us, so that was something.

'But that was last month!' I pointed out. You have to point things out to Gaspard. 'So you have had nothing for three weeks like me?'

'Err... I did another job.' I could hear his brain cogs grinding through gristle. I couldn't wait for the jackpot.

'Never mind, never mind.' Then I wondered what Gaspard did when he ran out of money. It was not too much of a problem for me, I could always think of something, but Gaspard? 'Don't you run out of money?'

'You mean, when he doesn't pay us?'

'Yeah.'

'Yeah.'

'You mean you do run out of money?'

'Err... yeah.'

'Well what do you do then?'

'Me mum gives me some to tide me over. Oh the boss is here.' He fumbled the receiver over to Vincent.

'Has Gaspard told you when I want the car?'

'Yeah, ten o' clock.' I put on my bravado voice. 'But you won't get it unless I get paid. You owe me three weeks, Vincent.'

'It's "Monsieur Descamps" whilst you're on my staff.' His voice was like vinegar off a hot spoon.

'I don't work for nothing, Vincent.'

'You don't seem to understand that I've got overheads. It costs a lot of money to run a car like that. Now you get over here for ten o' clock or I'll send Gaspard around to persuade you.'

Nice man Vincent. You always knew where you stood with him. No ambiguity. I hung up and swaggered back to the bar.

'Well that certainly shook him up,' I said.

Joanne gave me a look that would curdle velvet.

'You great nun's fart,' was all she said.

The two raincoats followed me back up the street so I stopped at the door of the police station and read the notices pinned on the board. Echoing from inside came the staccato tacking of a one-fingered typewriter making mistakes. Someone swore.

'Chief in a bad mood?' I remarked to the policeman with no chin. He shrugged. He knew I didn't care. With a backward jerk of my head I indicated the two men. 'Yours?'

'What?'

'Are they yours?'

'Are what mine?'

'Those two men who've been following me.'

From the height of his doorstep he glanced lazily up and down the street. He did it nonchalantly so as not to arouse their suspicions. He did it well. His gaze fell back on me.

'Why don't you bugger off and annoy somebody else?'

I turned around. The street was empty.

The concierge collared me on my way back in. She was waving a piece of paper and the glint of victory enlivened her purple eyes and shivered in her double chins.

'It will give me great pleasure to throw you out!' she chortled.

I did not doubt her for one moment. She had the smug look of a fully-loaded cowboy when he knew that the baddie's gun was empty. 'And I will throw you out if you don't cough up what you owe to Madame Claire by midday tomorrow.'

'Ah, Madame Claire. And how is she? Still sprinkling ground glass on her pancakes?'

I rattled my finger nail along the cage like a machine gun, hoping the noise would give her bird a heart attack.

Madame Claire would throw me out. I washed my hands in the sink and wiped them dry on the net curtain. I would not be seeing it again, I guessed. I looked about the room. The peeling pink flowered wallpaper fading to beige; the lozenge-shaped wardrobe with the crooked door; the hissing geyser squatting over the earthenware sink; the woodwork painted brown. It was sordid. My strange elation at the prospect of abandoning it was only tempered by the realisation that I had nowhere to go. If only I had been kinder to Joanne. Too late to regret that now.

I saw the parking ticket flapping on the windscreen of the DS as I turned into the rue St. Dominique. I zipped it out with the flourish of a best selling novelist pulling his final sheet from the typewriter. *'Tow away requested 08.10'* it said. I screwed it up and dropped it to the pavement. I glanced up the street. No sign of the tow truck. One day my luck would run out.

As I put my key in the lock, two beige raincoats materialised in the chromium strip along the door and a pink hand closed over mine.

'I'll take that, Monsieur Descamps,' Shorty said. I weighed up whether it was worth telling them that they had got the wrong man. 'On behalf of Central Automobile Finance Syndicate I hereby formerly repossess this vehicle.' Lanky showed me the order. That bastard Vincent had defaulted on the hire purchase and had used my address to do it. 'Sign here,' he said. I signed *'V. Descamps'* with a flourish.

I decided not to put up a fight.

'Do you mind if I get my things out?'

Shorty looked at Lanky who nodded. They seemed relieved. I took Vincent's gloves from the dash, I had always liked them but I left them Gaspard's mints. There were only three left in the bag and one of those he had already partly sucked. As I straightened up, an orange-roofed tow truck turned in from the avenue.

'Time for a beer?' I nodded towards Jean-Marie's bar. I had not been in it for some time. They looked undecided. 'Oh come on, you owe me something. I could have cut up rough.'

'Bit early for beer,' Shorty said and locked the door with what had been my key. 'Have you got the duplicate?'

He dropped the key into his pocket. He was quite pleasant really. Lanky sucked on his moustache. The orange roof was crawling slowly nearer in the line of rush hour traffic.

'It's at the office. I'll send it to you.' I stepped towards the bar. 'Come in and write down your address for me.'

Shorty looked at Lanky who had stopped sucking on his moustache and was now rubbing his chin. Any minute now he would start scratching his head.

'We could have a coffee. No harm in that,' he said.

'Just a beer for me Jean-Marie.'

Jean-Marie wiped his hands on his black waistcoat and addressed Shorty.

'Are you with him?' He jabbed a spoon in my direction.

Shorty looked at me. 'Temporarily.'

'Who's paying?'

At last, Lanky scratched his head. 'We are,' he said grandly.

'That's alright then.' Jean-Marie gave me a look normally reserved for traffic wardens. 'His credit rating is just below Mexico's.'

Lanky looked at Shorty. 'We know.'

'I could sue you for defamation of character,' I threatened Jean-Marie. 'I've got two witnesses.'

'No you haven't,' Lanky said.

'Cheers then.' I blew the froth at Jean-Marie. He clenched his fists as his short fuse began to smoulder. Lanky and Shorty stiffened. In the mirror I could see across the street where the men from the orange lorry were smartly lowering the front of the DS onto their tow trolley. They don't waste their time, those guys. Perhaps I could get a job with them as a driver.

'If it wasn't for the presence of civilised company here I would push that glass down your throat,' Jean-Marie growled.

'Don't mind us,' Shorty said generously.

Behind them the tow truck sneezed twice on its brakes

as it tried to edge out into the unyielding line of traffic. Would you let a tow truck out from the kerb? Jean-Marie saw it and looked at me. I blinked back at him like an idiot. He grinned smugly and smiled to himself.

'What's the joke then *bougnat*?' I asked. I knew he hated me calling him that.

'You are Jo-Jo.' Then he laughed. 'The great tough Jo-Jo.' He introduced me to Lanky and Shorty. 'I give you, messieurs, the biggest cretin in the rue St Dominique.'

Lanky and Shorty shuffled nervously.

'Go on, amuse yourself,' I encouraged him. 'The laugh is always on you.'

'But not this time, cretin.' He theatrically looked out of the window. 'Is that your car being towed away?'.

Without looking up I shook my head. 'No.'

His face dropped in perplexity as Lanky slowly turned. '*Merde!*'

He nudged Shorty and then rushed out into the street. '*Merde!*'

Shorty wiped the coffee from his coat and rushed out after him. They watched the tail end of the DS disappearing down the street, stern down, like a speed boat. Then they ran.

'Seems like they don't want to pay for the drinks.' '*Merde!*'

Jean-Marie vaulted over the counter and chased after them. I drained my glass, selected two croissants and a boiled egg from the basket and ambled back towards the Café Clerc, trying to ignore the shouting of the brawling men and the hooting of the traffic. Hurrying down the street came two policemen from the commissariat, the one with no chin trying to button his jacket as he ran. I stepped respectfully aside.

'Why are you back?' Joanne asked.

'Makele!' I shouted.

'Jo-Jo!' Big black face, grinning like a piano.

I tossed him a croissant. 'Happy birthday.'

'Messi, Jo-Jo, messi.' He pushed it straight into his mouth with one finger.

'Can't you let a poor worker sleep?' Pino grumbled and then dropped his head to his arms again.

'Well?' Joanne wanted an explanation.

'You know, Jean-Marie's croissants are much better than yours.' I waggled the bitten end under her nose. Her nostrils flared. I recognised the warning too late.

'Will you answer me?' The room shifted ten centimetres to the left and my cheek stung from the slap. One of Joanne's slaps would sober up an archbishop. Two would canonise him. I concentrated on shelling my egg. It always makes my eyes water. With most people it is onions. Me, boiled eggs.

'I have just given away Vincent's motor car to those two nice gentlemen in the raincoats.'

'Of course. Knew I'd seen that type before. Finance company bailiffs,' Pino mumbled from somewhere under his armpit.

'Thanks for the warning.'

'My pleasure.'

'So you're out of work and broke?'

Joanne had this way of gilding life.

'I've still got my good looks.'

She silently swayed aside to uncover the mirror. I did not like what I saw. A brown-haired man of medium height with a face that would frighten nobody. Grey-green eyes sunken in sockets that were black shadowed from too little sleep and not enough food, a nose you could hang a hat on and a mouth which veered too easily to the sardonic. A wrinkled forehead above; a creased jaw below. And I was not yet forty.

'Jo-Jo got no *boulot?*' Makele lumbered up to the bar. His sunny black face was clouded with rain.

'You've got it, me old broom-shunter. Jo-Jo's got no *boulot.*'

'Makele take you to big bossman. He give you *boulot.*' His arm encircled my shoulders. To a Senegalese with no papers, having no job meant starvation. His concern should have touched me but I was too conceited.

Suddenly a ball of anguish shot through the sunlit doorway. 'They're after me!' it announced and dived for the dark corner. I silently unhooked Pino's workcoat from the wall and spread it over the crouching figure.

Pino raised his head momentarily and dropped it. Makele grinned. Joanne sighed heavily. It was going to be one of those days.

Martins the Portuguese. His full name was something like

13

Joachim Pele de Martins Silva but everyone called him Martins. In most respects he was the typical olive-skinned, black-haired peasant who had abandoned the fields of the Estrella for the bright lights. His stocky body had a wiriness about it which was not evident until you tried to move him out of the way. But by then it was too late.

Martins was mad. Not all the time, just occasionally. No-one could predict when it would be triggered off. Some said you could tell it in his eyes. They were black like coffee beans and never stopped for more than a second upon anything. Checking right and left, up and down, fearful. Three years playing hopscotch over land mines in Angola had made him a trifle irritable but the Portuguese army were not the caring type – they had just spat him out.

I looked around the bar. What a party! The matinal clientele of the Café Clerc consisted of a Senegalese road sweeper with a French vocabulary nudging double figures, a defrocked lawyer who delivered newspapers, a former driver and dogsbody for a small-time thug and a mad Portuguese limousine chauffeur. I then realised that the latter presented me with a glimmer of hope. When Martins came back to sanity he could put in a word for me with Voitures Verjat. I still had my *Grande Randonnée* licence somewhere, they would insist on seeing that. Getting a suit might be a problem. I could already see myself swishing along in one of their black Cadillacs with a rich widow cocooned in the back.

I took a step towards the quivering coat and my left ear was nearly torn from my head. Joanne had claws like a crab.

'Oh no you don't. He's got enough troubles without you adding your donation.' She was walking me ear-first to the door. I went with her. I hate to hit a woman. 'I don't want to see you in here until you have money and a job.'

This stung me a bit. Joanne could be purposefully unkind when she wanted.

'Why should I be different from the rest of your drop-out friends?' I hurled over my shoulder as I slunk down the pavement. A stale bread roll ricocheted off the back of my skull and made a noise like Fred Astaire in a sandpit as it exploded on the roof of a passing taxi.

I had one metro ticket left of an ancient *carnet* so I took the train to Barbès Rochechouart. I was going to ask Miro for a job. I had deduced that my term in Vincent's esteemed employ had come to maturity. Miro was a big-time thug. When he wanted a little job doing then he sometimes slipped it to Vincent. When this happened, Vincent would swagger about thinking he could roar like Al Capone. He couldn't; he just fizzed like Alka Seltzer.

Yes, I would ask Miro for a job. It was the right moment for me to move into the big time.

The train was fetid with hot, closely packed humans, rattling and banging against each other with studied unconcern. Before me swayed an elderly man in a rank smelling overcoat and a homburg. Red-rimmed eyes and dripping nose, and this was July. I turned away and looked at the tunnel wall wavering past. *'Dubo... Dubon... Dubonnet'* said the faded posters. The train strained up the slope from under the Seine and crawled into Concorde. All along the platform masses of brightly coloured and eager tourists stood, guide books in hand, ready to launch themselves into the Parisian folklore. As the doors banged open everybody in the carriage groaned silently and took a step backwards. I already had my back against the partition. I breathed in.

'Hallo Jo-Jo. What are you doing here?'

Henri. A lean *pied noir* with cadaverous eyes. A metro thief with a speciality.

'Hallo Henri. How's business?' I knew I was safe. My entire fortune amounted to the two twenty centime pieces in my pocket and the used metro ticket.

He shrugged. 'So, so. Soon be August.'

August. The holiday month.

'Going anywhere?'

'Might try Monte-Carlo this year. Did Nice last year but the cops are getting sharp since that conservative lot got in.'

'I had never realised how regional socio-politics impinged upon your trade.'

'You what?'

The train jolted off and he lurched against me. I smiled through my teeth and squeezed my hand at his throat, not quite playfully.

'Unless you're intending to leave me in credit, don't even think of it.'

'Honest Jo-Jo! On my mother's life. I overbalanced.' Then he looked at me queerly. 'You skint?'

'Down to the washers on my roller skates.'

He looked at me again and then his gaze drifted on.

'Customers. Must go.' He tapped me on the chest, about where my wallet would have been had I possessed one. 'See you again.' He began to worm his way down the carriage towards his victim – a foreign tourist with a summer skirt and a shoulder bag.

They had been excavating a new station at the Opera for as long as I cared to remember. Hacking down through the city subsoil, through the strata of centuries of primitve city sanitation. To counteract the stench the contractors were using a strawberry perfumed disinfectant. The result smelled like an enormous sweating brothel. The sickly stale odour permeated every tunnel, infused every stairway, percolated into every train. On windless days it could be smelled in the Opera building itself.

I tried breathing through my mouth and the smell stuck to my teeth like toffee. I could feel perspiration beginning to trickle down my spine. The workmen's yellow lightbulbs bobbed up and down past the windows as the train rolled past their festooned loops.

Strasbourg St.Denis, this is where I change. I nodded down the carriage to Henri but he was working. The girl was glancing pleadingly to the left and right in a gasping disbelief with Henri's carressing fingers between the buttons of her skirt and his other hand in her shoulder bag. What the hell! This was Paris. She could have stayed at home. At least she would enjoy some of it.

At Barbès Rochechouart I leaned against the pillar and watched the train rumbling off over the elevated section above me whilst I tried to think up a strategy to use with Miro. I gave it up and started watching the girls, jingling the two twenty centime coins in my pocket. A cheeky redhead in hot pants and thigh high boots shouted across to me.

'You prefer the cheap job then?'

I eyed her coolly. She wasn't one of Vincent's girls, that I was sure of. And this was not his patch. I sauntered over, fixing her with my eye. She squirmed uneasily and looked around.

'Emilie!' she called to a hag with a fag. Emilie glanced around, took stock of the situation with her forty years of street experience and returned to her lamp post.

'You're a bit new aren't you?' I said to her. 'I'm looking for Miro. You must be one of his girls.'

'Don't know what you mean. Are you a cop?'

'And naive with it. Just tell me where I can find him sweetie.'

'Don't know who you mean.'

I shrugged. 'I'll ask Emilie then.'

'Up that street. Big grey building on the left. Top floor.' She pouted.

'To show my unbounded gratitude, half of what I own is yours.' I flipped her one of my coins. She watched it roll into the gutter as I walked away.

It was a concrete office block. It must have been put up in the thirties. The street door was a double panel of iron and glass art deco. The vestibule was a sharp edged box of grey marble with a five pipe brass banister rail coiling up the stairwell and amber fluted glass lampshades on the walls. 'Top floor,' she had said. On the wall by the lift was a name board. I perused it. *'Mirovici Group – Floor Six'* that would be the one. It had never occurred to me to wonder what Miro's real name was. Mirovici. His father must have been a White Russian who had escaped during the 1917 Revolution.

I got out of the lift at the fifth floor for the good reason that it climbed no higher. From the landing window I could see across the rooftops of the city right down to the Seine and the Eiffel Tower; in the other direction, steep steps climbed in cobbled streets taking tourists up towards the Sacré Coeur.

My staircase to the sixth floor was of uniform grey stone. The notice on the door on the top landing said, *'Mirovici Group. Ring the bell and wait.'* I rang the bell and went in.

A gravelly voice grated, 'It says, *"ring the bell and wait."'*

The man slipped his feet from the table and, in one movement, rolled into an upright monolith of muscle to bar my progress through the ante-room.

'That's what I did.'

'And wait.' He prodded me in the chest with his fingers. It hurt but he was shorter than me so I did not hit him.

'I waited.' I gave him a witheringly superior look. 'It doesn't say how long to wait.' He hit me in the stomach.

The other door opened and Miro walked in. He glanced at me, doubled over.

'Who's this?' he asked.

'Some smartarse who can't read.'

'Nice shoes,' I said from my banana pose. I had not forgotten that I was trying to get a job out of this man.

'Show me his mug, Luc.'

The gorilla's hand grabbed a bunch of my hair and yanked me upright.

Rather than swagger about like the crook that he was, Miro liked to project the image of a Russian count. He had the figure and face for it. He was slim and dressed in an expensively cut grey suit with silk shirt cuffs held by mother-of-pearl links which matched his tie pin. To underline how the passage of time had dealt elegantly with him he proudly wore his thinning silver grey hair brushed straight back. His eyebrows, still dark and bushy, adopted a position on his forehead somewhere between scorn and pity. He was clean shaven and his perfect teeth shone with thousands of francs of dentistry.

The gunsight of his aquiline nose swung the hard blue eyes unerringly onto the target.

'Oh it's the driver for that idiot Descamps,' he remarked. 'Or should I say "business associate Descamps?" Where is he?'

'He's not here.'

'No Luc,' he restrained his door thug, 'don't stroke him again. You've had your fun for today.' Luc made a face which indicated that he could absorb a lot more enjoyment yet without satiation. 'Bring him in. He's making a delivery.'

This was news to me but I didn't show it. Luc pushed me through the doorway behind Miro. The office was straight from a Hollywood film set. The room was large, it occupied the entire top floor front of the building. The walls were lined with art deco walnut and the ceiling was illuminated by concealed lights. I expected to see a wall panel swing silently open and Edward G Robinson step in holding an automatic in his hand. On a podium at one end stood a massive wooden desk the size of a small Cadillac. Miro walked over and sat on a swivel chair behind it. I remained standing. I had to. There were no other chairs.

'I knew Descamps would realise that the job was too big for his tin pot outfit to handle.' Miro held out his palm. 'Well, hand them over,' he ordered.

'I haven't got them,' I stalled.

'Doesn't Descamps trust me?'

The innocent enquiry was outrageously impertinent. There was no doubt that Miro intended it to sound like a threat loaded with sinister malice. I wondered just what kind of business Vincent was getting himself into. If it involved trusting Miro, it was out of his league.

'Trust you?' I echoed. 'Not if he's got any sense.'

Miro stared at me for a second as if he had not heard. But I knew he had. His eyes went cruel. I didn't somehow think I was going to get a job today.

'Tell Descamps he's got a week to deliver it.'

'Tell him yourself. I don't work for him.'

I was definitely not going to get a job today.

'Since when?'

'Since this morning.'

'What are you wasting my time for? Throw him out.'

Luc shuffled forwards.

'I want a job,' I said.

Miro held up his hand. Luc stopped.

'You want a job?' I waited whilst he laughed. He showed me all his fillings. It looked like stocktaking day at Cartier's. 'A reject from that half-brained goat? Why should I give you a job? What can you do?'

'Drive.'

'So can my sixteen year old daughter.'

'Buses?'

'I don't take the bus.'

'Lorries? Artics? Bulldozers?'

He rearranged his silk tie. 'I don't own any bulldozers.'

'Tanks?'

'Throw him out.'

'Don't trouble yourself, Luc, I know the way.'

He troubled himself.

The redhead in the hot pants was still standing under the metro.

'O.K. chéri?' She grinned at me. 'Good business?'

'Buy yourself an ice cream.' I flipped the other twenty centime piece at her.

I crossed over the boulevard, thrust my hands into my pockets and threw myself into Pigalle. I would have to walk back to the rue Amélie. I had used my last metro ticket and had just thrown away my last coin. I could have done with a drink. I was still head down and pondering this lacuna when a woman's voice accosted me.

'Hello Jo-Jo. You're early this morning.' I looked up. It was Flore. One of Vincent's 'girls'. Henna'd hair, spangle top and miniskirt. 'Where's the old git? Too lazy to get out of the car?'

But I was not listening to her. I was looking at the envelope she was thrusting at me.

'Yeah, that's it.' My voice was vague. 'Lazy git.'

She switched her lilac plastic bag onto the other shoulder. 'You know Jo-Jo,' she jerked her head at the doorway behind her, 'as you're a bit early... I've always fancied you. One on the house?'

The nightmare vision of her wrinkled flesh unwrapping before my sensitive eyes jerked me to my senses. My fingers closed on the envelope and I pushed it into my pocket.

'Sorry Flore, can't stop. Another time perhaps.'

Like next century.

She shrugged. 'Another time then.'

As I walked on down the street, thoughts were pounding in my brain. Vincent could not get here for another hour at least. He had no car and no driver. I slipped into the patchy gloom of an awakening bar.

'Beer,' I said and pulled out the envelope, hiding it below the counter as I ripped it open and counted. Five hundred francs. I did not know how the levy was calculated or what the five hundred francs represented, I just knew that it was more than my month's rent. I tossed a hundred francs onto the counter.

'Haven't you got anything smaller?' The barman grimaced. I was probably his first customer. I shook my head. He scooped up the money. 'I'll go and see at the fruiterers. Don't go away,' he said, as if there were a danger of me walking off and forgetting my hundred francs.

'I'll tell you what – give me another beer before you go.'

It followed the first one down a treat. I sat up on the stool and tucked the four remaining notes into my sock. I watched a woman at a window in the building opposite brushing the knots from her hair. She was sitting in front of an oval mirror, tugging at tangles and talking to the unseen reflection of somebody behind her in the room. With each tug her bosom wobbled in her peignoir like schoolkids jostling in the queue.

The barman returned carrying a bag of oranges. 'Bloody Marie-Claire,' he muttered. 'Just wait till she wants a glass of water.' He scowled and slapped the change down before me.

'Cheer up.' I put my empty glass on the counter. 'Vitamin C is good for you.'

Roseanne, the short Lyonnaise with the long black hair, gave me her envelope with no more protest than a slightly quizzical look. I patted her bottom and she told me not to handle the goods if I wasn't buying. I sauntered away, tingling with the feel of the money in my pocket. When I got to the rue Victor Massé I thought Liliane was going to give me trouble.

'What do you want?' she asked. Her lipstick had left red marks on her teeth. She looked like Dracula's mother.

'What do you think?'

'Where's Vincent?'

'In the car.'

'Why isn't he here?' Her look was challenging.

'Do you want me to go and get him? He would be pleased to give an account of himself to you if you asked him nicely.'

She pinched her lips together and then pulled a plastic envelope from her purse. 'Ignorant peasant!' she said.

'I'll give him your message.'

'I meant you.'

I smiled magnificently and walked away. By the time that I had reached Estienne d'Orves I had five envelopes in my pocket and considered that honour had been satisfied. Vincent had owed me wages, now we were quits. As I walked along I carefully tore open the envelopes and discarded them. Now there was no proof of any wrongdoing. Just money. A little over two thousand francs.

I found Makele at the Madeleine, sweeping a tidal wave of water down the gutter with his besom.

'Jo-Jo!' His black face lit up and he gave me a hug. He stunk like a damp raincoat. I would never get used to the smell of Africans.

'Makele, pack up. We're going for a drink.'

Like a circus clown his great face dropped into an expression of heartboken regret that could have been interpreted by a blind man standing three streets away. He shook his head.

'Makele got no *fric*,' he said.

I pulled the bundle of notes to the edge of my pocket so that he could see them. 'Jo-Jo's got *fric*.'

'Jo-Jo got *fric*?' His eyes widened to the whites. He was giving me the full works. Any minute now he would start juggling melons.

'Come on. Where's your broom cupboard?'

With the toe of his sandal he kicked up the metal flap in the pavement and bent down and twisted the tap. The gush of water drizzled to a trickle. We shuffled to the green cylindrical tower at the street corner. The posters pasted around it were announcing the Winter Circus. He took out his key, opened the secret door in the column and stepped inside. Then he turned to give me his grand finale. From the blackness of the tower his teeth and eyes shone white just like the Banania advert. He propped up his broom and shook his jacket onto a peg. Then he stepped out into the sunlight in a torquoise and green shirt. I prayed that the colour would mellow after a few beers.

'I think we'll start over there.' I pointed at the nearest bar. 'And then we can work our way down to the river and find a bench.'

Makele grinned easily. He did not want to know where the money had come from. Its mere existence was sufficient for him.

'O.K. Jo-Jo. We drink.'

2

The horn was insistent and echoed strangely. After five short blasts it stopped. It sounded like a heavy lorry. I lay there thinking that it would probably run me over. I opened my eyes and gazed at the pretty patterns of light rippling on stone above me. The noise of the engine suddenly detonated as the stern of the barge came within the echo chamber of the bridge span. The light patterns jived and jigged madly and then disappeared as the bulk of the boat blocked out the light.

I turned my head gently. It was made of very precious glass and I did not want to break it. A bare brown foot twitched ten centimetres from my nose. Attached to it was the rest of Makele. He was stretched out on the cobbles, his mouth open, snoring. I could hear him even over the noise of the barge.

I sat up very carefully. I winced as the stern of the boat emerged into the sunlight and exploded into colour. Why did everything have to be so violent and vivid? I needed breakfast. I needed a drink and I needed to forget yesterday's binge. The latter would not be difficult, it was already slipping into a weak shandy of unknown faces, singing and drinking in different bars, each one a little lowlier than its predecessor.

I waggled Makele's foot. He snored louder. I bit his big toe. It tasted foul. I twisted it. He yelped something in African and jerked upright, his arms before him, ready to stab me with his fingers. His eyes rolled the complete circuit and then focused on me. He dropped his arms.

'OK Makele, OK,' I said quickly.

I reminded myself that these fellows came from a wilder place than Paris.

'Oh, Jo-Jo,' he said.

'Come on,' I said. 'Breakfast.'

We climbed up the worn stone steps to the street level. Makele took a deep breath at the top of the stairs and announced, 'Good drink with Jo-Jo last night eh?'

'Yeah, good drink,' I agreed and pushed him towards the bar at the corner of the square. 'Just a minute. Better freshen up.'

I brushed the sand from the seat of my trousers and smacked the back of Makele's shirt. The dust rose in puffs.

The bar was full of the lorry drivers delivering to the Bazar de L'Hotel de Ville. They arrive before Paris is awake, park by the unloading bay and then drink in the bar till the shop opens. We elbowed ourselves a place at the counter and ordered a couple of strong coffees. I grabbed a boiled egg and two croissants from the basket as it was passed down the bar to another customer. He gave me the evil eye. I shrugged. I found myself looking at my reflection in the mirror as I had done at Café Clerc. I did not need Joanne there to point out that I still looked like a loser. But now, of course, I had got money. I would show them. I would stroll in to the Café Clerc and order drinks for everyone and when the old dragon demanded to see my money I would suavely peel off a one hundred franc note from the bundle in my... I slid my hand discreetly into the other pocket. It was also empty. Pretending to scratch my chest, I felt in my shirt. Everything had gone. My clip of notes, my papers, my identity card. I had been cleaned out.

Makele caught my eye and grinned. He held up another croissant. 'Good grub Jo-Jo. Messi.'

I looked at the crumbs on the counter and at our two coffee cups. 'Back in a minute,' I said and jerked my head towards the toilets.

He nodded and the croissant went in to his cavernous gob in one movement. I ambled gently down the bar towards the tiled staircase and then slipped out of the door and turned sharply left. Keeping close to the buildings I walked around to the opposite side of the square. If I was going to walk home I might as well cross to the left bank now and save myself some footwork.

As I stood at the corner of the bridge I looked back at the bar. Makele was staring at me through the glass. I pulled my pockets out to show that they were empty, shrugged and walked off. He was big enough to look after himself.

Sometimes miracles happen. I managed to get back to my room without the concierge seeing me. I sat on the bed and eased off my shoes. My feet were throbbing. Paris pavements were hard. They were harder when you were too broke to stop at the bars on the way home. A fist suddenly crashed on my door.

'Monsieur LeBatard!' I jumped. It was the concierge.

'Are you trying to give me a heart attack? What do you want?'

'Open the door!'

'It's open. Just turn the handle,' I shouted and then added, 'I'm sure you've done it before.'

The door opened and she stood there in her voluminous flowered dress, huffing and puffing from the combined effort of the stairs and the knocking.

'I would invite you to sit down, but there's only the bed,' I leered at her.

She pulled her dress around her and huffed some more.

'Thought you would sneak past me did you?'

'Oh, were you there?' I enquired with mock innocence and massaged the sole of my foot.

'The rent,' she snapped. I started. 'Ha! I thought that would surprise you.'

I had just received a surprise, but it was not what she thought.

'How much do I owe?' I played for time.

'Three hundred and fifty francs. You know very well. And if you haven't got it...' She looked around my bedsit and her poached egg eyes sparkled in the frying pan of her face. '...and if you haven't got it, all this goes out on the pavement now. And you with it.'

I slipped my hand into my sock and absently rubbed the tendons at the back of my ankle.

'How much do you want?'

'All of it,' she managed to say without unlocking her teeth.

I pulled the fold of banknotes from my sock and snapped them open. I cracked each note with my fingers as I counted.

'One hundred, two hundred, three hundred, four hundred. I want fifty francs change and a written receipt.'

She snatched the money.

'I don't give receipts. What do you think I am?'

'Men of learning have been elected to the Académie française for trying to answer that question. Just bring me those fifty francs

25

and you won't have to talk to me for another month.'

'I'm not coming back up here. Collect it on your way out. On your way out to look for a job, you lazy tramp.'

It is wonderful how a little money can change a person's entire standing in society.

I washed and changed into clean clothes. I lugged my canvas bag across the street to the launderette, collecting the fifty francs from the claws of the concierge as I passed.

The woman in the launderette wore her sun-bleached hair tied up in a pea-green bandana. She looked like an unripe pineapple on a supermarket display.

'Can I leave these?' I dumped the bag on the tiles. 'No hurry for them.'

'Three francs forty.' She silently extended her hand, palm upwards. I handed her my fifty francs. She put it in the till and returned me forty. 'I'll keep the rest on account. You'll be broke next week but you'll still want your clothes washed.'

'Be my guest.'

As I left the launderette, the sight of the policeman standing on the doorstep of the commissariat reminded me that I had lost my i.d. card. I crossed the street.

'Yes?' the policeman said.

'I need to come in,' I said.

He did not move a centimetre.

'Why?' His suspicion was almost insolent.

I could see his point. Why anybody should volunteer to enter that gloomy den of grey-blue woodwork and blue-grey language I could not imagine.

'Business,' I said. 'I've been robbed.'

He stood aside. 'They won't believe you,' he observed. 'Who would rob you?'

I realised he was right. It would only complicate matters to say that I had been robbed. I would have to explain how it was that I had left Café Clerc in the morning with forty centimes and a metro ticket and had managed to drink myself into oblivion by nightfall. The man at the counter looked up from his newspaper.

'Yes?'

Not great conversationalists, these law enforcers.

'I've lost my i.d. card.'

He looked at me as if I had just recalled him from his month's leave. Now he would have to do some work. He scrabbled in some pigeon holes and then pulled out a form.

'Name?'

'LeBatard.' I looked at him, just daring him to say something. He thought better of it. It's not wise when the person is called 'The Bastard'. He's heard it all before and he is ready for you.

'First names?'

'Joel.'

'Date of birth?'

'Third May, 1933.'

'You look older.' He could not resist that.

'Thanks.'

'Place of birth? Oh shit, why am I doing this? Fill the bloody form in yourself.'

He flicked it across the counter and returned to his paper. I filled in the rest and slid it back to him. He tore off the duplicate, stamped it and flicked it back at me.

'Get a photo put on it.' He looked down at his paper.

'Any photo?'

He slowly lifted his head.

'What?'

'Any photo? I can put any photo on it? Bunch of flowers? Mont Blanc in the Spring?'

I like to get these things straightened out. Especially when a newspaper is more interesting than the person standing in front of you. The cop gazed at me, his thoughts apparent. They involved an engineer's vice and my genitals.

'Your photo,' he said quietly. 'Put your photo on it.'

He jerked his head to tell me to go. I went slowly, just to show him that I was not intimidated.

So Josef Sikorski was dead. I sat at the counter and ignored Joanne and the others whilst I read the paper. *'Died after a long struggle against illness'*. It was two columns for somebody who had been shunted off into a corner to get him out of the way after the Algerian War. Thank god that I had never reached the echelons in the army where jealousy and back stabbing held sway. *'The success that he brought to his peacetime appointment at the Ministry of Defence in reorganising the army pigeon post'* smacked to me, just a little, of snide waspishness. Never mind his record in Algeria, he was good with pigeons.

'Get me a *kir*,' I said to Joanne.

'You don't drink *kir*,' she said.

I put the money on the bar and said nothing. Josef had always stood me a *kir* before a difficult op.

She took the money and shrugged. I took the glass, slipped from my stool and toasted the mirror.

'*Mon colonel*,' I said. There was a stupid lump in my throat. I emptied the glass. Revolting. He had known I hated the stuff.

Joanne was standing staring at me.

'Are you sober?' she said.

I ignored her and returned to the paper. The funeral was at two o'clock tomorrow afternoon at a cemetery at St Maur. I suppose I must have been recalling old times or something because she had to tug at my sleeve to get my attention.

'Is that someone you knew?' she said. I turned the paper around for her. '*Colonel Josef Sikorski?*' she read.

I was quite surprised by what I said next.

'I think I'd like to go to his funeral.'

'You'll have to be sharp. It's at two o'clock.'

'Tomorrow afternoon,' I pointed out.

'That's yesterday's paper.' She looked up at the clock. 'You've got about three hours.'

'He's a real artist isn't he?' I pointed at Pino, dozing on his bench. 'He can deliver a Paris paper to Nice before five in the morning but Café Clerc doesn't get it until the following day.' I sighed. 'Oh anyway, I haven't got a suit. Not any more.'

Joanne looked at me. Up and down. As if calculating how many portions I would make. She lifted up the flap at the end of the bar and jerked her head at the staircase behind her.

'Go upstairs. The room on the left. Look in the wardrobe.'

It had been a daft idea to go to his funeral. I stood apart from the half dozen mourners and pulled the collar from my neck to allow the sweat to run down. I would have been better in my jeans. Hell, I would have been better in the nude. I held back a smirk as I imagined myself standing there stark naked. Joseph would not have minded. We had seen worse together. But the stuffed shirts around the grave would have had apoplexy. And the woman?

'What's so funny LeBatard?' a quiet voice said in my ear.

I turned. His fair wavy hair was now going grey, his blue eyes were watery behind steel-rimmed spectacles; a red face, corpulent body squeezed into a dark grey suit.

'You wouldn't understand, Reinhardt. 'You never did.'

'Try me.'

I ignored him.

'Is that your lot over there?' I said. I nodded towards three men with blue jowls and suits to match. They were holding their hats in front of them. Hats? Who the devil wore a hat nowadays?

'I'll introduce you afterwards,' he said.

'Don't bother. Who's the woman? Josef lost his missus years ago.'

It was his turn to ignore me. The woman stood looking into the grave. She was of medium height and wore a dark grey suit and black stockings. Her hair was tied back under her black hat with a black ribbon. Nobody would doubt that she was attending a funeral. Her shoulder bag was one of those with a designer's monogram tooled on it. It was also black. She glanced across at us through her veil for a second and then the priest closed his book.

'We didn't expect to meet you here,' Reinhardt said.

'It's a free country.'

'Not for people like you, *mon ami.*'

I turned and looked Reinhardt full in the face.

'It is a free country precisely because of people like me, Reinhardt. Your lot, Reinhardt, would have had us all in the ovens, Reinhardt.' I clicked my heels.

He clenched his teeth till his jaw went white.

'I've told you before, I'm from Alsace,' he hissed.

'Yeah, they all say that. Why don't you go back there?'

'I'll get you one day, LeBatard, don't you worry.'

I sucked my lip and gazed for a second at the earth being thrown onto the coffin. He turned away towards the others.

'Josef didn't like you either,' I added. I saw his back jerk as he resisted the reflex to turn and hit me. He succeeded, but then, I knew he would. He always got somebody else to do his heavy stuff.

'Why didn't you go with the others?' she said. She spoke from under her veil, her head still downcast. She had walked down the alley to me and I had not noticed. I suppose I had got to thinking about Josef again. I was standing there gazing and seeing nothing.

'I didn't come with them. I'm not with them.'

'Who are you with?'

'Nobody.' A nobody with nobody, I thought. 'What about you?'

'What about me?'

'You weren't with them either?' She shook her head. 'You knew Josef?'

'In a way,' she said. 'In a way. You?'

'We did some things together. In the army.'

She turned and pulled up her veil to look at me. She had plucked her eyebrows into a quizzical arch. Her eyes were dark, her nose, neat, her chin rounded. She had the face of a doll. A doll who played truant from the pram.

I fingered my sticky collar, then turned to the grave and saluted. 'With your permission, *mon colonel.*' I tugged off my tie and pushed it into the pocket of the jacket. I turned to the woman. 'And now I'm going to get a drink. Coming?'

She shrugged. 'Why not?'

We left the cemetery by the small wicket gate and crossed the street. This part of St Maur did not run to a brasserie. The corner shop was a tobacconist and bar. Vivid yellow tiles on the floor and stained wood panelling along the front of the counter which metamorphosed into the bar as it stretched towards the pinball machine.

I felt surreptitiously in my pocket and counted my money. The *patronne* was sitting at a table and reading a newspaper. She was a blousy fifty with red lips and green eye shadow. She ignored me but when she saw the woman she folded the paper, got up and went behind the bar.

'*Messieurs-dames?*' she said.

'What do you want to drink?' I asked the lady.

She pulled off her hat and dropped it onto the counter. She shook her hair free. It was brown, streaked with blond as if she had just come back from the Midi.

'Beer,' she said.

I ordered two beers. The *patronne* served us and went back to her newspaper. A fly droned in through the doorway, zig-zagged a reconnaissance of the shady room and then left. We stood side by side at the bar and drank our beer.

'So why were you smiling?' she asked me in the mirror.

I looked over my glass at her reflection.

'When?'

'In the cemetery. You were smiling before that man spoke to you.' She raised her eyebrows. I thought that if I told her the true answer they would stick on the ceiling.

'It was thinking of Josef. Things we did. Made me laugh.'

'Ah ha?' she said, still studying me in the mirror. She was unnerving me.

'My name's Joel.' I turned to her and held out my hand. 'Joel LeBatard.'

'How unfortunate,' she replied as she shook it. 'I'm Mathilde.'

'Mathilde...?' I said. She had told me nothing.

'Mathilde,' she repeated, then she shifted herself around to look at me in the flesh. 'So how often did you see... er Josef?'

That hesitation distracted me. Then it set me thinking. She had been on the point of saying something else.

'Rarely. In fact, not at all. Saw him a couple of times when I got out. Of the army,' I added. 'But it didn't work. Things weren't the same when we got back. We weren't the same people in Paris.'

'No,' she said, as if in reflection. Then she nodded to herself. 'You're right. Things weren't the same.'

'What about you? Close friend were you?' I did not think that she had been his mistress.

'You knew the men there?' She nodded through the window towards the graveyard.

I took a sip of my beer whilst I thought. She was not giving anything away. But she was asking a lot of questions.

'One of them,' I admitted. 'I knew one of them.'

'The one you spoke to?'

'He spoke to me first. I answered. His name's Reinhardt.'

'He didn't look very pleased with what you said.'

'Good,' I grunted and thought that she must have been doing a lot of peeking through that veil. Quite clever. See without being seen.

'What about the other men?' she asked.

'Don't know them. Reinhardt said they worked with him. He was probably telling the truth. He usually did if he thought it would make him look important.'

'You knew Reinhardt in the army, then?'

31

Time to turn the tables.

'Where did you know him from?' I asked.

'I don't know him.' She fiddled with her hat on the bar.

'You were talking to him. I saw you.'

She grinned slyly.

'He spoke to me first,' she said.

I shrugged as I put my money on the counter. It was too hot to play stupid word games with silly ladies no matter how pretty they were.

'Well I must go. Cheerio... Mathilde.' I said her name in insolent capitals and turned to the street. She stopped me with two words.

'Mathilde... Sikorski.'

She had a dark green Renault 4. On the gear lever she had tied one of those air fresheners coloured like a traffic light. It swung back and forth, pendulum style, as we lurched our way back to Paris. It irritated me. She was driving in high heels. I did not like that either. I am nervous of women who drive in high heels.

'I suppose I knew vaguely that Josef had a daughter.' I said this more to myself than to her.

She rammed the lever into third and roasted a red light.

'He only vaguely knew himself that he had a daughter. We didn't see him from one year to the next.'

I gazed out of the side window.

'The army was his life,' I said and the moment I had done so I knew that I had made a big mistake.

'We were his life. If he had wanted to spend his days playing soldiers then he should never have got married,' she snapped as we bounced off the centre island. *'Connard!'* she shrieked at a startled and inoffensive mobylette rider. The man glanced briefly at her, the resignation to injustice apparent in his eyes.

I said nothing. After all, she had just buried her father. A dame ought to be allowed to shout after that.

'Where shall I drop you?' she asked as we came into Paris.

'At the nearest Metro, if you like. I don't want to take you out of our way.'

'I don't mind.'

'Somewhere near the Invalides will do then.'

She raised her arched eyebrows again.

'Chic!'

'Not where I live.'

She drove on. Several times she looked as if she was going to say something but uttered nothing. When we got to the Place Vauban the traffic was pinched into one lane. Algerian workmen in blue overalls were ripping up the pavé as if they were gold ingots. That had been the start of all their trouble – thinking the streets of Paris were paved with gold. Double-parked on the corner a tipper truck of asphalt slowly steamed.

'*Eh merde!*' my driver said. She pulled up behind the Cityscope double deck tour bus and I watched the mini-skirted hostess run up and down the spiral staircase at the back. 'Why do they put windows on the stairs on those buses?' she asked.

'So that dirty old men like me can ogle the girl's legs.'

The hostess returned to the audio tape desk and punched a button on the console then she leaned her back against it. She was bleached blonde with black mascara laid heavily on her spiky eyelashes. She gazed blankly at us through the back door. Her face, two startled spiders in a haystack. I blew her a kiss.

'Oh, honestly! You men are all the same.'

The hostess waved and blew me a kiss. Then she formed her fingers into a pistol and shot me twice. I clapped my hand to my heart as the bus moved off.

'What was all that about?' she asked.

'That was Claudette. I used to drive for her.'

'You drove a Cityscope bus?' I nodded. 'I've always wondered what those girls actually do,' she said. 'How can they guide a coach from the back?'

'They don't. It's all recorded. They use tape cartridges like you get for the eight track stereo in cars, but bigger. Six languages. The hostess slots the cartridges into those letter box things on the front of the desk and starts them off. The driver has to follow a fixed route like a town bus and every time he gets to a tourist sight he presses a button which starts the tape cartridges. They splurge out their bit of commentary and then stop. He drives on to the next point and presses his button again. Robot driving like Pavlov's dog.

'How does the driver know when each commentary has finished?'

'He wears a headset like the passengers. I used to listen in Japanese when I did it.'

'Do you understand Japanese?'

'Not a word.'

'So how could you tell where you were on the tape?'

'I guessed.'

'Did you ever get it wrong?'

'Sometimes, but it didn't matter. Nobody knew. In fact, the Spanish tape is wrong anyway. If ever you watch a Cityscope bus going around the Place de la Bastille you will see most of the passengers looking at the column on their left whilst the Spaniards all look right, as the tape tells them to. They sit there wondering where the hell the monument is. Hah! Silly sods.'

'So what does the hostess have to do?'

'Not much. She listens in to the tapes to make sure that they have not broken or got stuck. She turns them over at half time. And she occasionally runs up and down the stairs to make old men like me very happy.'

'But you couldn't see her at the front,' she said smugly.

'No that's true.' I gazed idly at a bald man in a Mercedes picking his nose. 'It was a lousy job anyway.'

'So, you dove a tour bus.'

It was a non-engaged observation.

'For a while.' I glanced at the bus. It had a white roof. 'It was that bus I drove.'

'Really?' She pushed the gear lever into the dashboard. The stupid air freshener spun like a lime seed.

'That's why it's got a white roof.'

'Ah ha.' She was not interested. More reason to continue.

'It used to have a blue roof like the others.'

She blasted an old lady back onto the pavement with her horn and we lurched into the boulevard.

'But now it has a white roof,' she mocked me.

'Yeah, now it has a white roof.' She blew her breath noisily through her lips. 'For a while, it had no roof at all,' I continued.

'Why?'

'I took it through the underpass at the Etoile.'

'You...? But it's a double decker. It's too high.'

'It went in as a double decker, came out the other side as the biggest cabriolet in Paris.'

'What happened to the people on top?'

'The bus was empty.'

'That was lucky. It could have been awful.'

'Not lucky. I wouldn't have done it with passengers on board.'

She turned sideways in her seat and examined me with undisguised interest.

'Did you do it on purpose?'

With my left hand I steered her car away from the kerb. She did not notice.

'Of course.'

'What on earth for?'

'Short cut.'

'Is that supposed to be a joke?'

'The boss didn't think so. He never saw the funny side of anything. No sense of humour these capitalists.' I nodded towards the shady terrace of a corner café. 'You can drop me over there if you like.'

She bumped the car up onto the pavement and we bounced to a halt in a cloud of white dust under the trees.

I stretched over the seat and retrieved my jacket that I had thrown into the back. 'Thanks for the lift.' I held out my hand.

'Oh that's alright.' She shook my hand absently. 'Look, do you want to do a job for me? I'll pay you.'

This was where I had to take a stand. I could not accept charity from anybody. It's devastating for your self esteem if people see you as an unemployed layabout.

'Well,' I drawled. Gabin would have been proud of me. 'I don't know if I am...'

'You haven't got a job at the moment.' It was a statement, not a question. 'And you are broke.'

'Well I wouldn't say that—'

'You had to count your money in your pocket before you bought me a beer.' I opened my mouth to protest. 'At least, I hope that was what you were doing.'

'I am naturally careful with money. It's the way I was brought up.'

'And if your name is Joel LeBatard why does the name tape inside your jacket say, *Marc Antoine Dupleix?*'

'I am schizophrenic.'

'You are broke, out of work, in a borrowed suit and I am

offering you a job.'

'Why? You don't know me.'

'Perhaps that's why. Personal things are always better dealt with impersonally.'

'I should put your hat back on again. You've had a touch of the sun.'

'Please yourself.' She gazed through the windscreen. 'You were the only man at the funeral who smiled.'

'What do you want me to do? Dispose of a blackmailer? Empty a bank? Push a pimp in front of the metro? Collect your cat from the vet?'

Her dark eyes settled on me again as she appraised me. I returned her gaze evenly.

'Can you do all those things?' Her voice was careful.

I nodded thoughtfully. 'I'm no good with animals,' I said.

I gave her the telephone number of the Café Clerc and told her my secretary's name was Joanne.

I turned into the rue St Dominique. I cross the road now and walk down the pavement opposite Jean-Marie's bar. It saves unpleasantness. He never did get the cost of the drinks from the two bailiffs. As I passed the narrow entrance to the Passage Jean Nicot, an arm pulled me under the crumbling plaster of the archway. Not roughly, but with enough force to make me not want to argue. It was Gaspard, Vincent's bodyguard.

'Oh for Christ's sake, Gaspard, you nearly wrenched my arm off.'

'Look, Jo-Jo, this isn't personal,' he said. He was still holding my arm.

'Well what do you want?'

'Vincent is a bit upset.'

'Upset? What about?' I began to move my feet into a better position.

'You took the money from the girls.'

'Oh that!' I said. 'Does he want it? Where is he?' I looked around.

'He's back at the office. He told me I had to get the money or duff you up.'

So Gaspard was alone then. I knew I could run quicker than him.

'Charming! He didn't say, "get the money *and* duff him up" did he?' The question was a mistake. Gaspard started thinking. 'Look, let go of my arm and I'll give you his money.'

'No funny business Jo-Jo?'

'No funny business. Promise.'

'I don't like this job,' he confided suddenly. 'Me Mum said I ought to ask at La Samaritaine. They need chaps to unload the vans.'

'You'd be good at that. You like the physical stuff.'

'Not really,' he said. 'I don't like it. I'm just not very good at the other.'

'What, the thinking?'

'Yeah. That sort of thing.'

My arm was beginning to go numb. He was brutal in a gentle sort of way.

'Well let go of my arm and I'll give you Vincent's money. Then you can give it to him and tell him where to stick it.'

'No funny business?'

'I promised, didn't I?'

He released my arm. I lowered it gently and made a great show of rubbing the feeling back into it. He looked worried.

'That's better,' I said pleasantly and then laid a straight knock-out to his chin. It was like hitting a pillar box. Gaspard looked wide-eyed at me.

'You promised!' he accused me like a disappointed child, and lazily cuffed me with the back of his left hand.

And with that, the daylight went out.

3

The *thud, thud, thud,* gradually lightened to a *tack, tack, tack.* Uneven, a fumbled noise. It sounded familiar in parts. It was unpredictable yet somehow an ordered cadence. I had heard it before. The smell – warm and close yet airy and distant. Sweat and dust. Light began to appear. Bluey grey. A line at one edge. Vague shadows swinging across it as if anchored to the ground by one foot. Suddenly everything – the noise, the colour, the smell, lurched into focus at once.

For the second time that day, I was lying on my back looking at the ceiling. A car drove by outside, the noise of its passing lunging through an open outside door, its shadow fanning across the screen above me. A typewriter was clacking away.

'He's awake now. We can chuck him out,' a voice said.

'Get the quack to sign the papers to keep us in the clear,' another voice responded. 'We don't want him to get run over outside the door.'

'Why not?'

'Not outside the door.'

'Yeah, right.' A finger prodded me in the shoulder. 'Oi, you. Pain-in-the-arse. You can get up now.'

I slowly sat up on the bench and rubbed the back of my neck like they do in the films. Daft really. Gaspard had slapped me on the chin.

'Don't I get a glass of water?' I said to the cop.

'No. You're not going to puke up are you?'

'Your face usually has that effect does it?'

The cop stiffened. A short bald-headed man with a black moustache and a canvas holdall bustled into the ante-room.

'Can you give him something that will make his cock drop off if ever he comes near this place again, doc?' the cop said as he walked out.

The doctor's eyes twinkled. He sucked his cheek.

'Been upsetting our fine officers of law and order, have you?'

I was getting fed up with the whole palaver.

'Just give them their bit of paper, let me go and we'll all be happy.'

'Look at my finger,' he ordered.

I looked at his finger.

'Stick your tongue out.'

I stuck my tongue out.

'Shall I waggle my ears as well?' I asked.

'Can you?'

I waggled my ears. He signed the form and tugged it from the pad. It tore in half.

'That saves them the trouble of ripping it up after you've gone,' I said. 'What's the time?'

He pointed at the clock. It was just after six. I must have been out for a couple of hours. The cop with no chin came back in. He was swearing.

'The chief says I've got to file a bloody report.' He was disgusted. 'You!' He pointed a pen at me. 'Get up to the counter.'

'Thanks doc,' I said to the quack, 'I feel better already.'

I navigated shakily to the desk. The cop was struggling with carbon paper and coloured forms in multiple layers.

'I.d.card!' he snapped. I threw him the chit that he had issued me earlier. He unfolded it. 'This isn't valid.'

'You issued it.'

'It's got no photo.'

'It didn't have one on when you gave it to me.'

'I told you to get a photo on it.'

'Oh yes. It must have slipped my memory.'

'Don't try to be sarcastic.'

'I'm not trying, I'm succeeding.'

He gave me one of his looks. I quaked.

'Right. Tell me what happened.' He lined up his pen on the paper.

'I fell over.'

'That was after he hit you.'

'Who?'

'That donkey that Descamps uses.'

'Don't know what you're talking about.'

'You had an argument with him and he hit you. We've got two witnesses.'

I looked around the empty room. 'Where?'

'They'll testify when we need them.'

'I bet you believe in Santa Claus as well don't you?'

His knuckles whitened around the pen. His chief's voice boomed from the inner office. 'Chuck him out!' and then added, 'In front of a bus if there's one passing.'

That showed how out of touch he was. The buses don't come down our street.

As I turned in at the Café Clerc I bumped into Pino who was hurrying out in a haze of *pastis* to get the metro to the Paris Matin newspaper depot. He half turned.

'Oh, Gaspard was looking for you,' he said.

'He found me,' I replied, but he had gone.

I pulled up a stool to the bar and waited till Joanne deigned to look up from her account book. She glanced at the Ricard clock by the door and pushed a strand of hair from her face. She looked tired and haggard and I was far too sober to tell her.

'So, how was the funeral? Good fun?' she asked as she wiped the clean bar with a dirty cloth.

'Interesting. Met some interesting people. Have you got any aspirin?'

'So they were that interesting were they?' She pulled out her handbag from a low shelf. 'Your sidekick...'

'Gaspard?'

'Yes. He was looking for you.' She offered me the tablets as she rinsed a glass in the sink.

'Pino told me. I found him, thanks.' I reached for the aspirin. She made a sudden grab at my sleeve.

'Look at this!' she exclaimed. 'Is that how you repay kindness?'

I looked at the rent in the sleeve. I must have caught it on something as I fell. Suddenly I realised just how awful I felt.

'Look, don't you start on me. I've had just about enough for today.' I took the tablets and turned away. 'I'm going to bed. I'll bring the suit back tomorrow.'

'OK,' she shrugged. For once, she did not argue.

The sun was up. The concierge's bird was twittering and there was no milk in the fridge. But at least my rent was paid for one more month. I sat on my bed to think but it hurt too much so I packed up Joanne's suit and went to the bar for breakfast.

'I can get the lady in the launderette to repair the sleeve,' I said as I handed over my bundle. 'She does that sort of stuff.'

Joanne pulled a face and slid my coffee down the bar.

'Forget it. I shan't be using it and if you can't look after it then you won't be using it again.'

'It wasn't me, anyway, it was Gaspard.'

'Gaspard?'

'He duffed me up.'

'Gaspard?' The incredulity creased her forehead till it looked like an old seat cushion. 'You let yourself get duffed up by that great softy?'

'He's got hard bits on him.'

'Only between the ears. Why did he do it?'

'I don't think he meant to do it. It was a sort of mistake. Vincent sent him.'

'Fine way to treat an employee.'

'I'm not, since yesterday.'

'So Gaspard brought your severance pay then?'

'Sort of.'

She pulled the basket of croissants out of reach.

'Let's see your money before you get outside of any more of these.'

'I've been offered another job.' I pulled the basket back.

'Doing what?' She dragged the basket away and I snatched another croissant as she did so.

'Can't say.' I tapped the side of my nose. 'Hush, hush. Top secret.'

She snorted derisively.

'You? Keeping secrets? You couldn't keep warm.'

I looked around the bar. Makele signed to me with a pale palm chocolate hand then returned to the pictures in the newspaper. I took my cup and went over to his bench. He grinned at me.

'Good breakfast yesterday, Jo-Jo,' he said.

'Yeah, good breakfast.' I had last seen him staring at me from the bar across the street as I had showed him my empty pockets.

'No problem?'

His black face screwed up as he considered my question. Then he suddenly understood.

'Jo-Jo got no *fric.* Jo-Jo go to WC. Makele got no *fric.* Makele go to WC. No problem.' He shrugged his shoulders. Simple.

'No problem me ol' broom-shunter.' I slapped him on the shoulder. It was thin and bony under his overall.

The two youths in leather jackets who rode the despatch motorbikes turned in alarm from the pinball machine as Joanne snapped, 'His *what?*'

I looked up. She had the phone to her ear. With her other hand she was beckoning me with the concentration of a starving lion in Lent. 'He's just coming to the telephone, madame.' She clamped her hand over the mouthpiece. 'Secretary!' she hissed.

I took the handset. 'LeBatard,' I said.

'That really is a most unfortunate surname.' It was Mathilde Sikorski.

'It's the only one I've got. Some people think it fits.' I glanced at Joanne and added, 'Mademoiselle.' Joanne pretended not to hear but I saw her twitch her head. 'What can I do for you?'

'Would you help me?'

'Depends on what you want me to do.'

'Take my cat to the vet.'

'I said I was no good with animals.'

'That was a joke.'

'Should I laugh?'

'Please yourself.' Her voice was brittle and tired. Nervous. 'I want you to help me sort out Papa's stuff.'

It was the first time I had heard her call Josef, 'Papa'. I had sudden pangs of conscience and regret. This woman had just lost her father.

'Yeah, I'll do that for you.'

'Can you come to the flat? I don't feel like driving.'

'If you tell me where it is.'

'Just off the Avenue des Gobelins.' I looked at Joanne and waved writing fingers in the air. She handed me her order pad and her pen. ' It's number fifteen, rue Stresemann,' Mathilde continued. 'Flat three. It's on the second floor landing, left.'

I wrote it down and shielded my pen with my hand to annoy Joanne.

'What time?'

'In about an hour? Take a taxi. I'll pay.'

'I'll take a taxi then,' I repeated for Joanne's ears. 'I'll be there in an hour.' I tore the sheet off and handed the pad to Joanne. 'My new employer. She wasn't very impressed with my secretary.'

Joanne snatched the pad and clicked her fingers.

'Pen,' she snapped. 'You put it in your pocket.'

'I've got to look the part. This job is a step up.'

'Any job for you would be a step up.' She clicked her fingers again. I handed over the pen. 'There's a Prisunic at the corner. You can buy your own for sixty centimes.'

I think I impressed her with the taxi, though.

I had no intention of taking one. If Mathilde Sikorski was silly enough to refund me the fare then more fool her. I could hear the rumbling of a metro train under my feet so I sprinted to the exit stairs and forced my way against the grumbling humanity stumbling up into the daylight. I got my fingers on one of the spring doors before it slammed shut, much to the outrage of a flabby-faced matron dressed in a rusty brown sack.

'Monsieur, that is not the way in.'

No, but it saved me the cost of a ticket, so my taxi fare would be pure profit. I needed to make every franc I could. I knew that this flap with Mathilde Sikorski could only last a couple of days until she had got herself sorted out.

I did not know how wrong I would be.

'It's Lebatard,' I said into the doorphone. The latch buzzed and I pushed against the door. The stairs up to the first floor were white marble inlaid with black and the balustrade was panelled. From the first landing the stairs were carpeted and the balustrade, painted black iron. The carpet ran out at the second landing.

Mathilde Sikorski was standing with one of the double doors open. It was white ormolou wood with a chromium handle set horizontally at waist height. She was wearing a pair of faded blue jeans with deep turn ups and a loose cotton shirt with the sleeves rolled up. Her hair was tied back in a scarf and her feet were pushed into open sandals. She had red-painted toe-nails. I hate painted toe-nails.

'Come in,' she said.

I followed her. The hallway was rectangular but long which made it appear narrower than it was. The small crystal chandelier sparkled a reflection in the gilt framed mirror by the hallstand. Propped in the tray below was a jumble of umbrellas and sticks. The polished parquet creaked and cracked as only old parquet could as we walked towards the door at the other end. Mathilde Sikorski opened it and we were hit by the light and sounds of the street below which were flooding in through the two open windows. She walked across and pushed them closed, twisting the espagnolette with a quick flick of the wrist.

'I've been airing the flat but the traffic is so noisy.'

She stood and looked at me. I walked around the room. The rug in the middle appeared to be of decent quality but the colours were drab browns which just made it look dirty. The furniture was unremarkable. A sofa pulled in front of the television; a polished wooden table and four chairs at the far end by the matching sideboard; a bureau with a couple of framed photographs on top and an empty specimen vase in cheap glass; and two armchairs. The chair with the worn cloth on the arm had a small drinks table standing at its side. At the other end of the room the wall was covered with books on shelves, interspersed with untidy piles of magazines and the odd ornament.

Both the windows in the room had low railings fixed across them so that they could almost pretend to be balconies, but not quite. I crossed to them and gazed out. She watched me without speaking. I could see the tops of the trees in the Place d'Italie and the roofs of the buses as they turned across the square. I stared across at the building opposite. More windows. How many people living like this?

I turned back to the room. She was still watching me. I went to a door and opened it. A bedroom. Single bed, covers turned down, pyjamas lying on the pillow. A suitcase.

'My bedroom,' she said.

Her eyes followed me as I opened the door to the other room. Large wooden bedstead and bolster. Wrought iron reading lamp with a green shade, water carafe and glass on bedside table. Wardrobe with mirror against the far wall. I looked at Mathilde Sikorski. She was still watching me.

'This is not Josef's apartment,' I said.

She kept her gaze level. Challenging. Without a word she crossed the hall and pushed open the last door.

'The kitchen,' she said.

Veneered cupboards, breakfast dishes in a stainless steel sink, tiled work surfaces. On the floor were four cardboard boxes into which had been jammed empty wine bottles.

'OK.' I said, 'it's Josef's apartment. You've been tidying up.'

'Yes. What gave me away?' I had the feeling that she had been measuring me up for something.

'The water carafe by the bed. It would have been whisky. Malt.'

She looked at me and nodded. 'It was,' she said, and shut the door. We went into the salon and sat down. 'You knew Papa quite well then?'

'I told you. We were in the army together. Algeria. You get to know quickly which people you can trust in places like that.'

'People you can trust? Trust with what – the truth?'

'Something more important. Your life.'

'Did you kill anybody?'

'Probably. Why do you want to know?'

'Did Papa kill anybody?'

'Probably. Have you killed anybody?'

'Of course not.'

'What's your job?'

'I work for Mutual Assurance in Strasbourg.'

'Insurance companies don't generally like their employees killing people. We were soldiers. That's what soldiers do.'

'Did Papa like killing people?'

I looked at her. Sometimes people can get on your nerves. Her dark eyes were earnest. She was desperately searching for something but I had no idea what.

'Look, Miss Sikorski, I've come over in a taxi because you asked me to help you sort out some of your father's things. Just tell me what you want.'

'Oh yes, the taxi, how much was it?'

I made a quick calculation. 'Eight francs fifty.'

'Here's ten. That'll cover the tip.'

'I didn't give a tip,' I said. Honesty always pays.

'Keep it anyway.'

I put the money in my pocket. This was easy.

She was flicking at the catch on her bag. 'Look, sorry about the cross examination,' she said. I shrugged. 'The thing is, you knew Papa in a way that I didn't.'

'Forget it.'

'And that revolting man at his funeral started asking me questions.'

'What revolting man?'

'The one you were talking to.'

'Reinhardt? What was he asking you?'

She flapped her hand. 'Oh I don't know. Things like, "what was I going to do now?"'

'What has that got to do with him?'

'And he said that he would need to sort through Papa's papers. He said that there might be some official stuff in there that would have to be disposed of properly.'

'And is there?'

She turned away so that I could not see her eyes.

'I don't know.'

'You mean you looked but couldn't find anything.' She said nothing. 'What might he have had? He was only in the pigeon post. Anyway, what has it got to do with Reinhardt?'

'He gave me his card.' She searched in her bag. She was beginning to sniff. 'He said I should phone him at the ministry and arrange a time for him to come. He was very insistent.'

'What ministry?'

She read the card she had just picked out. 'Defence.' She handed it to me. 'He said he was an old friend.'

'Monsieur Max Reinhardt, Ministère de la Défense.' I knew the telephone number. It was the central switchboard.

'Well that tells us a lot doesn't it? I wonder what Reinhardt is interested in.' She was sniffing properly now. Into a screwed up paper tissue.

'He said he was a close friend of Papa's but he didn't even know his middle name.' The mumbled words were blurred by the tissue.

'Paul,' I answered automatically and with that, she burst into tears.

I cannot stand wailing women with painted toe-nails. They make me want to slap them or pour cold water over their heads. I got out of my chair and went into the kitchen. I poked about in the cupboards and found enough to make some camomile tea.

That would calm her down. And me. I brought in the tray and laid it on the table. She was convulsing in deep, quiet sobs, her tears dropping in great splashes onto the tops of her thighs and darkening her faded jeans. I sat next to her. Helpless. I should have told her that I was no good with crying women as well as animals.

'Look,' I began, and stretched out my arm. Suddenly she spun around and buried her head in my chest. She was wailing even louder now. I took a deep breath and held her whilst she grieved. I distracted myself by pulling faces at my reflection in the mirror. I was concocting a particularly inspired grimace, like an elephant pushed against a plate glass window when I noticed that she had stopped shaking. She pulled away from me.

'What are you doing?' Her voice was small but clear and controlled.

'Stress relief exercises.'

''Never seen that before.'

'They're Arabic. Designed for sandy places.' I waggled my ears. She smiled. 'Well that's better. It works for you.'

'Please excuse me, Monsieur le...' She shook her head in irritation. 'I can't keep calling you "Monsieur." What was your first name?'

'Joel. It still is.'

'Right Joel, you must call me Mathilde.'

'OK Mathilde.'

'Sorry about all that outburst. I'm still a bit upset.' She gulped again.

'It's natural.' I thought about Reinhardt. He was a nasty little ferret. He would not be sitting back and waiting for her to recover. 'Perhaps you ought to get me your father's papers and anything else you think Reinhardt might be interested in.' She looked at me, undecided. 'That's what you want from me isn't it? You don't need me to carry empty wine bottles down the stairs – you're younger than me.'

'I've got to trust you, haven't I?'

'Not in the slightest. I'm corrupted and deceitful and only doing it for the money.'

'I know. I was waiting at the window. I saw you coming out of the metro.'

'That's fine then. We know where we stand.'

She stared at me for an instant and then seemed to make up her mind. She got up.

'He kept most of his things in the bureau.' She dropped some split cardboard folders onto the table before me. 'It seems to be all papers and bills and receipts. A lot of it I don't understand. Most of it. There is some more stuff in a cupboard in here,' she said as she went into the bedroom.

Josef might have been a good soldier but he was no clerk. If I had been the sentimental kind of person I would no doubt have found some inverted emotional solace in ordering the witnesses of his life but I'm not. If he wanted to keep the guarantee for his electric kettle tucked into an envelope with his *Ancien Combattant* i.d. card then that was fine by me. I read, sorted and stacked whilst Mathilde continued to search in the cupboard. The little piles of papers grew in front of me. Letters from the bank. Demands from the Nicolas shop. Josef's life had rolled along on an overdraft of wine and whisky.

'Joel.' Mathilde's voice from the doorway sounded strained. I glanced up. The adrenalin shot through me like a bolt and from my sitting position I made a flat dive, my arms before me. I got one hand on the gun and another clamped on her wrist before she could react and then my momentum carried us crashing to the parquet in a skidding tangled heap. We lay there, both winded, gasping for breath. I could smell her perfume. I wondered if she could smell my fear.

'If you don't let go of my wrist my hand will drop off from lack of blood,' she said.

With my left arm I moved the pistol beyond her reach and then released her wrist.

'Just stay there whilst I get up,' I said. She looked at me, her eyes uncomprehending. I pulled myself up onto my elbows and eased my knees and hips. That floor had been hard and we had hit it solidly. I rubbed myself on my joints. 'OK,' I said. 'Your turn, but move slowly.'

'I can't do anything else. I think you've broken every bone in my body.' She sat up, not caring that her shirt had ripped open.

'You're lucky,' I said. 'The last person who pointed a Luger at me lived another eight seconds.' Her eyes grew wide. 'Don't ever, ever, do that again.'

'I was only showing it to you. I was going to ask you what I ought to do with it.'

'That is not the way to do it. If you ever find anything like that again, leave it where it is. Don't touch it. Ask me to come and look at it where it is. Understand?'

'Don't you think you are being just a bit melodramatic?'

I looked at her breasts and she gave her irritated shake of the head and pulled her shirt across her chest.

'Eight seconds,' I reminded her. 'That's all it took. And I didn't have a gun.'

'I still think you're being silly.'

I shrugged. Some people will not be told. I carefully picked up the pistol. It was an ex-Wehrmacht Luger, the nine millimetre model. I checked the magazine and breech. They were both empty. Although it was clean on the outside, inside it did not look as if it had been fired since VE day. The firing mechanism was stiff. The barrel was filthy. It was not a gun that Josef would have bothered with. It was a forgotten souvenir. She was leaning forward, watching me intently. Her unbuttoned shirt had gaped open again.

'It's not loaded,' I said.

She caught the direction of my glance. 'I will go and change my shirt.' Her voice was distinct. 'Sorry to spoil your enjoyment.'

'Who said I was enjoying it?'

She stopped at the bedroom door. 'Don't you ever try to be nice?' She disappeared into the bedroom without waiting for a reply.

OK. So it had been nice. But why should I tell her that?

'Where did you find the pistol?' I called out.

She came back in, tucking a shirt into her jeans. There was not much room for the shirt and she was slim.

'In a box at the back of the cupboard. There are some other things in there. I'll show you.'

I half expected to uncover a nest of grenades but it seemed that the box had been a repository for any object that Josef could not be bothered to dispose of differently. I shovelled some odd shoe laces and bolts and screws into one corner and piled up the treasures on the table.

'Those are army badges aren't they?' Mathilde picked up one of the bronze brooches.

'Cap badges.'

'Are they worth anything?'

'Possibly. There are people who collect these things. There's a shop in the arcade by the Gare St. Lazare that might take them.' I peered at one and tried to decipher the latin motto. 'I could find out.'

'Would you?'

I nodded and picked up the main object. 'But this is certainly worth money although I don't know how much.'

'It's Papa's old camera. I haven't seen it for years.'

'It's another battle souvenir.' I said. 'An old German Army Leica.'

'Is that why it is painted that horrible green?'

'Yes.'

'Is it a good camera? He was quite proud of it once. He was always taking photos of Maman and me.' She gulped and I could see that she was near to tears again.

'Oh yes it was a good camera in its day. One of the best. And I think I know just the man who will be interested in it. He's a professional photographer. He collects old cameras as well. I think they all do that. Jean-Marc would give me a good price for it. If you wanted me to sell it, of course.'

She nodded thoughtfully and said nothing. I wondered if she had heard me.

'What about the gun? Could you sell that?'

I put it back in the box and covered it with the shoe laces, scraps of wire and light bulbs.

'I might be able to but I'll leave it here for the moment. The last thing I need is to be picked up on the metro carrying a Luger.'

'Or in a taxi,' she added.

I thought that remark unnecessary. I sorted through the piles of papers on the table and held up one of my bundles.

'You can probably understand these things better than me.'

'Are they the insurance policies?' I nodded. 'I've looked at them already,' she said. 'They are worthless. They have all been redeemed.'

'Redeemed? Well I suppose you should know, it's your line of business.'

'Exactly.'

I sighed heavily. She was beginning to annoy me.

'Why don't you tell me what we are looking for, Miss Sikorski?'

She jumped. 'Looking for?'

I had obviously touched on a nerve.

'It's none of my business but who inherited?'

'As you say, it's none of your business.'

'So?'

'All Papa's estate comes to me. When the lawyers and the Tax have finished with it.'

'So why are we trying to sell cap badges?'

'What about the other piles of papers? What are they about? There is some army stuff there.'

'Those are his army pension papers; those are all bills, some still unpaid, mostly for wine and whisky; those are his identity cards – Veteran's Club ...' I picked up a matchbook and studied it. A high-heeled nude in a top hat was kicking silver stars into a champagne glass. It was from the Casino Harz. I showed it to Mathilde and raised my eyebrows.

'What?' she asked.

'Did he go to the Casino Harz often?'

'How should I know?'

'You are his daughter.'

'I live in Strasbourg. And anyway, he's old enough to... was old enough to....' She stopped and her eyes began to well with tears. They looked like olives in brine. 'What business is it with you what he did?'

'OK. Forget it. I just thought that it was not the type of joint he liked.'

'You know it?'

'From the outside.'

'They wouldn't let you in?' She gave a short smile. 'That must have hurt your pride.'

'I didn't even ask. That hurt their pride even more.'

I flipped the matchbook open. Somebody had written a telephone number on the inside. I put the matches in my pocket.

'What about this stuff?' She prodded a pile of cyclostyled sheets of yellowing paper.

'I'll look at it in a minute. I think it's mostly old copies of instructions from the office.'

'Do you think that would interest Reinhardt?'

Not in a million years. 'Yeah, possibly.'

She got up and went into the kitchen. I started to skim through the notices. They were of a banality that defied belief. Instructions on which electric light switches were to be left on overnight; notices advertising job vacancies in other departments; some pay slips from five years ago. I imagined Josef stuck for weeks on end, year in, year out, up on the sixth floor in offices converted from servants' quarters. Mansard roofs and sloping ceilings; the awful dirty beige official furniture, spending his day ordering bird seed and message canisters for pigeons. He hated pigeons. He had told me once that they were the absolute waste of time. They would fly straight at a gun and then they weren't worth the trouble of eating when you did shoot them. No wonder he had turned to the bottle.

Thinking of that, reminded me of the bottles. I went to the kitchen. Mathilde Sikorski was slicing *saucisson sec* onto a plate.

'Hungry?' she asked, and thrust a plate of bread and *saucisson* at me.

'Thirsty,' I said and looked pointedly at the boxes on the floor. 'Are they all empty?'

'Yes.'

'What about the whisky?' I took the plate.

'I poured it down the sink.'

'You–?'

'Have some fruit juice. Or is it too acid for you?'

'Proper drinks don't come in a carton.'

'Please yourself. That's all there is.'

She whisped past me and I followed her into the salon. We chewed the bread and sausage and looked at the pile of paper before us.

'There's not much more that I can do,' I said. 'I've put anything vaguely official in this pile here. You can show Reinhardt that. I'm sure he will be delighted to know which light switches need to be left on in the back office.' It was the kind of detail he would store away and use one day.

'You don't like him, do you?'

'I have reason to and anyway, the feeling's mutual. But what about you? You are not madly in love with him.'

'I'm not madly in love with anybody.'

We both jumped as the door bell buzzed.

'Christ!' I said. 'If I lived here I would discourage visitors.'

'You wouldn't need to.' She went to the interphone.

'Miss Sikorski?' a tinny voice said.

'Who is it?'

'It's Max Reinhardt. We met at your father's funeral.'

She turned to me and pulled a face.

'Come up.' She pressed the door release. 'Second floor.'

'He's not wasting his time. That is exactly like Reinhardt. Compassion always was a strong point with him.'

She walked through to the hall. The door opened and Reinhardt's voice echoed confidently down the corridor.

'Thank you for seeing me, Miss Sikorski. You remember at the funeral I mentioned that I might have to look through some of your father's papers and remove any of an official nature.'

'Yes, I recall you saying that. I cannot think what Papa might have had that would have required you to visit so promptly.'

The floor was creaking. The voices were getting nearer.

'It *is* the department's policy to check upon these things.' He emphasised the 'is' to distract attention from the reason for the policy. 'I shan't take much of your time.'

'Do please come through.' Mathilde Sikorski preceeded her visitor into the salon and gave me a wink. 'I believe you know Monsieur LeBatard?'

Reinhardt had been watching her bottom. He jerked as if he had been kicked in the face. I had often dreamed of kicking him in the face.

'LeBatard! What are you doing here?' he snapped.

'Hello Reinhardt.' I ignored his question but admired his insolence.

He turned to Mathilde. 'What's he doing here?'

'Why Monsieur Reinhardt, what a question! Does your enquiry extend to the visitors I have in my apartment?'

I beamed up at him. His face became puce.

'Forgive me mademoiselle,' he tried to excuse himself, 'but this man is no earthly good for you. Get rid of him. He is a crook and a layabout and a good for nothing. He is completely without honour.'

She showed him a chair and then eyed me thoughtfully.

'So you know him quite well then?' she said to Reinhardt. 'He told me he was corrupted and deceitful and only in this for the money.'

'He said that?' Reinhardt's voice became sharp. Any trace of unctuousness had disappeared. We did not understand at the time how Reinhardt's interpretation of Mathilde's remark would influence events.

'You know how honourable I am, Reinhardt. I wouldn't lie to a lady.'

'You would lie to your own grandmother.'

'I never had one.'

'Gentlemen, please!' Mathilde pleaded. 'What would you like to drink, Monsieur Reinhardt? I only have fruit juice,' she added.

Reinhardt pursed his lips and glowered at me.

'Nothing for me thank you, Miss Sikorski.'

'Fine.' She sat down.

I looked at her. She looked at Reinhardt. Reinhardt looked at the things on the table.

'An old camera,' he observed.

'Yes, Joel is going to try to sell it for me,' Mathilde said.

I was not particularly happy about her informing Reinhardt of my intentions but it was worth it to see the nasty smile twist his mouth when he said, 'Joel?'

She nodded across at me. 'Him,' she said.

'So we are on first names are we?' he said to me.

'We are. You're not. You will always be only "Reinhardt".'

He sucked on his tongue and looked at the camera again. Then he looked up at me. There was a meaning in there somewhere but I did not know what. He crossed the fingers of both hands before his stomach.

'So,' he began slowly, 'LeBatard is with you Miss Sikorski?'

She nodded pleasantly.

'He's just helping me sort out some of Papa's things.'

'Rather like you are, Reinhardt.' I indicated the piles of papers and cap badges on the table. 'Help yourself. That is what you came for isn't it?'

He nodded to himself then he looked at Mathilde Sikorski as he idly leafed through the papers. She waved a red-nailed hand at them.

'Is there anything there that you need to take away?'

'No I don't think so,' he said. 'Not here. Not now.' He was blaming me for something. He gave me one of his steely looks. I returned him a rusty one. 'You will regret your liaison with

LeBatard, mademoiselle.' His voice was quiet.

'Tell me why.'

He picked up the Leica and gently turned it over in his hands. He worked the shutter. 'He will cheat you.'

'He has as good as told me that already.'

'I would like to buy this camera, Miss Sikorski. How much would you like for it?'

This was new to me. Reinhardt interested in old cameras? Mathilde looked across at me.

'Well I don't know. Joel was going to sell it to a friend who deals in these things.'

'Five hundred francs,' he offered.

'It's a Leica, Reinhardt, not a Kodak Brownie,' I said. 'You're wasting your time. You can't afford it.'

He put the camera down and walked to the window.

'It's in a nice position, this apartment. It's yours now is it?' The question was casual. A bit too casual for my liking.

'It will be,' Mathilde said.

He began to wander around the room. There was something slightly menacing about the way that he assumed the right. He looked at books on the shelf. When he trailed his fingers over the bureau I could see that he was burning with curiosity as to its contents. He pointed to a door.

'And that is a bedroom?' He turned the handle. 'Ah, the kitchen,' he said to himself. 'Very neat. Very neat.'

Mathilde jumped up.

'The bedrooms are through here,' she said, and opened another door. 'Do have a look.' Sensible girl. Call his bluff.

Reinhardt glanced at her over the rim of his spectacles. He was assessing her. I could see his mind working. Was she stupid or was she involved?

'You've got a search warrant have you Reinhardt or are you just being an inquisitive boor?' I threw at him from the sofa.

He retreated behind his Germanic armour. He became distant and official.

'I can see that you have everything in hand, Miss Sikorski, I'm sorry to have bothered you. Thank you for your time.'

'Well I'm sorry you have been put to so much trouble over nothing monsieur.' She sounded quite desolate as she ushered him towards the door.

I heard the door click. I went to the window and watched him emerge into the street below me. He turned left and walked smartly up the street. Away from the metro and the buses and the taxis.

'That man gives me the creeps.' Mathilde flopped down onto the sofa. She picked up the camera. 'Why didn't you sell the camera? Five hundred francs is a lot of money. Is it worth more?'

'I've no idea how much it is worth. I just did not want Reinhardt to have Josef's camera.'

'I wonder why he wanted it? I suppose he was just testing us out.'

'Testing us out?'

What did she mean?

'Chains of command – you should know about those. He wanted to see who would make the decision on whether to sell. He wanted to know who was in charge.'

'I don't think Reinhardt is that clever. Anyway, it was me. I made the decision,' I added smugly.

'I am sure that Reinhardt is that clever but we fooled him didn't we?' She smiled at me. 'Because I am the one in charge.'

I had her ten francs in my pocket so I agreed with her.

4

Jean Marc was tall and thin. Like a poplar tree in the Dordogne.
He wore Nana Mouskouri spectacles. They made him look just
as idiotic as they did her. He let his hair grow long. It had been
the fashion when he had dropped out of university. And he always
wore a black leather jacket with a zip fastener up the front. He was
trying to convince us he was James Dean, not Mouskouri.

I had first come across him when he was doing the old street
photographer trick. You bought a Polaroid camera and then
hung around the tourist sites. When you spotted a target you
smiled and handed them a card. Whilst they read it you raised the
camera and snapped the strap buckle smartly against the back of
the case. It sounded just like the shutter. The card told them that
the photograph would cost twenty five francs. When they argued
you pointed out that they had wasted your film. Eventually they
either paid for the non-existent photo that they had never asked
for or they posed properly and then you stung them twenty five
francs for the picture anyway.

Jean Marc was no good at the job but he was ambitious. He
used it as a stepping stone. And he fancied himself as another
Cartier Bresson. In between tourist coaches he used to take
photographs of street scenes in the hope of selling them to
magazines. One day, when he was loafing about the Place de la
Concorde, he snapped a pigeon scoring a direct hit on the
Minister of Culture as he came out of the US Embassy. He sold it
to Paris Match – it went on the front cover – and with the
syndication fees, he set up his own studio. And I had told
Mathilde Sikorski that I would go there first thing in the morning.

But I was lying.

I came out of the metro exit in the booking hall at the Gare du Nord. I wandered onto the concourse and checked the ticket barrier. The *Grandes Lignes* was unmanned but the *Banlieue*, the Suburban, was guarded by a female gorilla in SNCF blue. Just my luck. Try the other barrier in the Cour de Départs. No better, it was unmanned but locked. I picked up a discarded transit note from the gutter and went back through the ancient black iron doors onto the concourse. I turned straight up the first platform on the right.

'Hey!' a voice challenged.

'Parcels!' I shouted and waved my piece of litter at the Checked Baggage Office. The man turned away. No point in making a fuss. I walked into the parcels office.

''Morning lads,' I said and walked across the tiled office and out through the opposite door onto the suburban platforms before they had even looked up. Easy when you know how.

I tried to reason things out on the journey to Pierrefitte but I was still no nearer my destination when I arrived. Mathilde Sikorski was looking for something in her father's possessions. That she had already searched was obvious. But she had found nothing. So she calls me in. Why me? Chance? Or because I was not with Reinhardt? She must be searching for something whose worth she had not been able to recognise but which she thought would be apparent to me. And then Reinhardt turns up on the doorstep with his bloated eyes and his red face and his story about looking through Josef's official papers which was about as subtle as a brick through Fabergé's window. So now we have two people looking for something. Were they both looking for the same thing, I wondered? Whatever it was, it was certainly not the camera. That was a red herring. Just another one of Reinhardt's subtleties.

I pulled the matchbook from my pocket, flipped it open and looked at the writing inside. I was going to ask my ex-employer, Vincent Descamps, why his telephone number was written in a Casino Harz matchbook found in Josef's flat. It would be, 'Good afternoon Monsieur Descamps, I'm making enquiries for a client.' Yes, he would hate that. I felt the ten franc note still intact in my pocket. 'A client who pays promptly,' I would add. He would probably ask Gaspard to duff me up again.

If he wasn't doing his mum's shopping.

Vincent's house was an undistinguished pavilion built in an anonymous suburban street. A low wall, a small tree in the front garden, a garage with brown concertina doors, concrete pantiles on the roof. The same as hundreds of other houses in the *quartier*. It was the ideal hideout for an international gangster – it would be the last type of place the forces of law and order would think of looking for him. But Vincent was not a jetsetting criminal – he was a small time crook and this was his home. This is where the police would find him straight away. They would catch him at breakfast like they did all the amateurs.

I pushed back the open gate. The rubber soles of my shoes squeaked on the red brick path. The moss was growing green at the foot of the concertina door, telling anybody with eyes in their head that the garage was not used for housing a car. I went around to the side door and then realised that I was now a visitor and not an employee. I should have rung the front door bell.

I raised my hand to rap on the glass but did not need to, for the door was already ajar. Careless that, leaving it open. Wouldn't do any harm to invite myself in. It would save the unpleasantness of Vincent putting his foot behind the door.

I paused to listen. Nearby, a bread van blew its strident horn and children shouted as they played in the street. But inside the house, all was quiet. No, not completely quiet. I could hear voices coming from the salon. I am not too squeamish about etiquette. I crept in and sidled down the corridor, standing ready to rapidly assume an, 'oh I was just going to knock,' pose. From the other side of the door I could hear Vincent being lambasted.

'You did what?'

'Well now the minister has seen them we'll have him on the hook,' Vincent inisted.

'You sent them to him? You sent them to him? You imbecile! I told you to wait until I had got it all set up.'

'But don't you see? He'll know they are just a taster – that we have got something more powerful.'

'Cretin!' The riposte was short and harsh. This man was angry. 'Imbecile! Now the minister knows we have them do you think he is sitting around on his arse waiting for you to contact him?'

'He doesn't know anything about us. I'm not that stupid. He doesn't know who we are. He has to wait for us to contact him. He'll be sweating.'

'So where are the originals?'

'I haven't got them yet.'

'You haven't got them yet.' The voice repeated the words with a menacing slowness. 'You send the only copies you have to the minister and you have nothing to back them up? Don't play with me Descamps. People who stand in my way get squashed. Just get them and we'll say no more about it.'

This was the kind of entertainment that I really appreciated – another thug putting pressure on Vincent. I thought of the sly way that he had used my address for the hire purchase on his car. He was unscrupulous. I screwed my head nearer to the door. This business sounded like an unpaid creditor coming to collect.

'But I haven't got them yet.'

'This was always way out of your league, Descamps.' The voice was scornful. 'Get me the originals and I might consider letting you out with your skin intact.'

'I've agreed to meet him at the club next Tuesday.'

'Ring him up and meet him tomorrow.'

'I can't. I don't know where he is.'

I was just beginning to think that the other voice sounded vaguely familiar when somebody wrenched my arm painfully up my back, pushed a foot behind my knees and pitched me headlong through the door into the room. My nose ground into the carpet.

'LeBatard!' Vincent shouted, 'what are you doing here?'

'Found him listening outside the door, Boss,' my unseen master of ceremonies announced. The voice sounded young. He landed a kick in my ribs just to show how grown-up he was.

I studied a pair of leather shoes level with my eyes. I had seen them before. Without looking up I knew the identity of Vincent's visitor – Mirovici. What the hell was he doing here?

'Good morning all.'

I started to get up but Miro's thug shoved my face down with his foot. The carpet smelled dusty.

'Well, well,' said Miro. He made it sound unpleasant. 'I don't think you hurt him. Kick him again, Paulo.'

'With pleasure, Boss.'

The shoe prodded the same spot on my rib cage.

'OK, that hurt,' I gasped and tried to get up again. He kicked my arm away and stood on my hand as I collapsed to the carpet.

I gritted my teeth. 'Enjoy it whilst you can, squirt,' I said. It was going to cost him dear one day but for the moment he just stood more heavily on my hand.

'It's that drunken toad who drives your car,' Mirovici observed to nobody in particular.

'Who used to drive his car,' I corrected him from my carpet. 'I am no longer on the payroll.'

'Oh yes. Since when?' Mirovici said.

'Since the bastard stopped paying me.'

Mirovici chuckled drily.

'What have you done with the car?' Vincent demanded.

I ignored him. My ribs were hurting and I was getting sick of looking at shoes. 'Miro, why don't you tell your ballet dancer to find some carpet to stand on? He'll damage his slippers.'

'And why should I?'

'I might cry if you don't.'

Mirovici chuckled again. 'It's always entertaining to deal with men who have absolutely no self respect – they are so compliant. All right Paulo, let him get up.'

'Sure Boss.'

The kid leaned his full weight on the foot and ground the shoe around before he lifted it. The blood began to flood back into my hand and make it throb. I got up slowly, allowing my hand to hang limply. He sneered at me. He was pale-skinned with fairish wavy hair and northern blue eyes. It made him look like a baby. He must have hated it.

'Bet you look good in your pink frilly tutu,' I said.

'Paulo,' Miro warned sharply but he was too late. The kid had moved towards me. I lashed out and the back of my dead hand knocked his face sideways in a humiliating slap. I had put as much power into it as I could, knowing that I would not feel a thing, and that the hand, being relaxed, would make stinging contact everywhere. I swung around and with my other hand I jabbed four fingers into his gut and wrenched upwards, nearly lifting him from his feet as I pushed the air from his lungs. He doubled over, crippled by the pain and gasping for oxygen. I straightened up and then gave him a gentle push. He toppled over. I crossed the room to a vacant easy chair and dusted down the cushion before I sat. It was brown vinyl. That was the kind of taste Vincent had.

Vincent was trying to work out what was going to happen next, his eyes flicking from side to side like a snake's tongue. Miro had sat through the little demonstration impassively.

'He'll be mad about that,' he observed.

I looked Miro straight in the cold, hooded eyes.

'That's where he goes wrong then, isn't it?'

He stared hard at me and then nodded slightly. 'Yes,' he said. Then he laughed. It was like icicles rattling in a bucket. 'You're right. Luc would never have fallen for that.'

'I would have done something different for Luc.' I still thought that there might be a chance of a job with Miro if I could prove myself tough enough. I nodded at the lad wheezing on the floor. 'Can't you afford a proper dog?'

'All right Paulo, don't make such a fuss,' Miro said, looking at me dispassionately, 'you'll get your revenge I promise you.'

I watched him crawl to a low chair and climb in. I was thinking as quickly as I could. Any minute now somebody was going to ask me what I was doing there.

'So what's the problem then Miro? Has Vincent not paid you either?'

Vincent choked on an angry objection as Miro turned to me and said, 'Perhaps LeBatard knows where he is?'

'He knows less than I do. He's never even met him.'

'Well I shall be the judge of that,' he said silkily. 'You can help out your boss–'

'My ex-boss,' I corrected.

'Quite. Your ex-boss who did not pay you.'

'Exactly. So why should I help him?'

Miro sucked on his teeth and considered whether to pull my fingernails out one by one.

'Perhaps you should help me,' he said.

'Same question.'

'Let me work on him boss,' the blue-eyed wonder wheezed from the corner.

'You just get your breath back Pauline,' I said. 'Your master might want his shoes licked.' He did not fall for it this time. He stayed put. He was learning.

'First of all, let's see if you know anything useful,' Miro said. 'And then I will consider how to pay you.'

'I already know your currency and I don't like the rate of exchange.'

Miro's steely eyes bored at me from under his hoods. Suddenly he snapped at Vincent, 'What is the man's name?'

Vincent jumped. 'He calls himself "Janus".'

'So,' Miro demanded, 'Do you know a man called Janus? Know where he lives?'

I blinked and tried to look nonchalant. 'Janus who?'

Miro sighed and looked expectantly at Vincent.

Vincent shrugged. 'I don't know any other name.'

I shook my head vaguely.

'The Janus that you took this pimp to see.' Miro pointed at Vincent. He was getting annoyed with me.

I looked at Vincent. 'When did I take you to see Janus?'

'I told you he didn't know anything,' Vincent said to Miro and then fell into my trap and added an explanation for me. 'When you took me to Casino Harz. I went to see this Janus.'

I silently registered the information as I shrugged at Miro. 'I stayed outside in the car.'

'What's happened to the car?' Vincent suddenly demanded.

I got up. I could see my way out.

'That's what I came to tell you. The finance company took it back. They were one creditor you should have paid.'

'And what about my money that you stole?'

'I drank it. Anyway Gaspard collected on that. Where is he by the way?'

Vincent looked uncomfortable.

'Oh he's... doing his mum's shopping.'

I could hear Miro laughing as I closed the door.

But I was not laughing.

I walked back to the station. I had to break into Mathilde Sikorski's ten franc note to buy a ticket. That hurt me.

I got out at the Gare du Nord and bought a sandwich at the stand on the corner then I walked down across the front of the Gare de L'Est to the Canal St. Martin. I stumbled down the cobbles at the side of the bridge and sat on an iron bollard to eat. I flicked loose stones into the green water whilst I ate.

I met a fireman once who told me about all the prams, bicycles and cars they had to dredge out of the canal every year. During the Algerian troubles it had been bodies, with their hands tied together. Never seemed to get into the papers.

I started to sort things out. I had gone to Vincent's because his telephone number was written on a Casino Harz matchbook in my pocket. A matchbook that I had found in Josef's flat.

When I had got to Pierrefitte, Miro had beem arguing with Vincent about something that Vincent had sent to the minister. This sounded like Miro muscling in on a job started by Vincent. A job that Miro claimed was too big for Vincent to handle

Then I remembered my visit to Miro's office. He had let me in because he had thought that I was making a delivery from Vincent. What did he think I was delivering? It must have been the same things. They both knew what they were but they weren't telling me. And because I had not delivered them, Miro had come collecting. Collecting something that Vincent had got from this chap called Janus whom he had met at the Casino Harz. The Casino Harz on the matchbook that had taken me out to Pierrefitte. I had gone full circle. But it was a circle of knowledge which kept me out. And those inside the circle had discovered that there was a piece missing. I needed to talk to Mathilde Sikorski but before I did that I needed to think.

And I needed a drink. I felt the camera in my pocket and remembered what I had promised Mathilde Sikorski I would do.

Two birds and one stone.

Jean Marc's studio was the top floor of a warehouse further down the canal. The five floors below him were empty. Derelict. He had bought the entire building. He was convinced that this area would become chic one day and then he would convert his concrete shell into luxury flats with canal views. It's good to have dreams. What an idiot! I took the goods lift up to the roof and there he was, stretched in a canvas chair, smoking a cigarette.

'Hey, Jo-Jo,' he cried as he jumped from the chair. 'How are you doing?'

'I can see you're not overworked. Business bad?'

'Couldn't be better,' he said as we shook hands. 'Come in and have a look at this.'

I followed him through the storm door into his studio. It was just one big room with two wooden shipping containers dropped into it. One served as his darkroom, the other was his bathroom. A square of carpet laid in the corner of the room denoted the bedroom. His bed, cupboards and chest of drawers stood around on it self consciously as if they had nowhere to flick their fag ash.

Jean Marc walked over to the fridge. It was squatting on the linoleum tiles that presumably designated the kitchen.

'Drink? Beer?'

'Got any whisky?'

He looked at me sharply and then smiled.

'Why not?' He poured a glass and handed it to me. 'Come and have a look at this.' I followed him over to a display board. 'What about those?'

I had seen them before. Three striking photographs of a snow covered mountainside in the morning light. Nothing seems amiss on the first one but on the second the avalanche has started and by the third it is in full swing. They were a remarkable sequence of images which had appeared in many of the important picture magazines.

'Very nice, but they are not yours. Some Jap took them.'

Jean Marc grinned good naturedly.

'Yeah, Takahashi. I didn't say they were mine.'

'But you wish they were?'

He put his head on one side, thoughtfully.

'I'm not so sure. Of course it was a terrific coup. He used a plate camera, you know? The old glass plate camera like that one over there.' He pointed at a polished wooden box with brass bezels protruding from one side.

'Why?'

'Perfectionist. You still get the best definition from a plate. Especially with modern coatings.'

'And he dragged that thing up the mountains?'

'So they say.'

'And stood around in twenty degrees of frost and waited for an avalanche?'

'Yeah. And when it came he was ready and quick enough to expose three plates in succession.'

'Is that difficult?'

'Not difficult but not easy if you are not prepared. And with gloves on,' he added.

I nodded and tried to look intelligent. I did not feel it.

'So what's all this stuff?' I pointed to a weird construction of plyboard and plaster of Paris.

'That's why I'm not so sure about the photos. Have you ever

heard of anamorphism?'

'Anna who?'

'It's not a girl. Anamorphism.'

'Can you drink it?'

'It's all about twisting something so that it appears just like a nonsensical mess but then when you look at it from a different angle, it all comes into focus. You've probably seen that painting at Versailles with the *memento mori* on it.' He nodded at me encouragingly. Did he really think I studied the pictures at Versailles? 'It looks like a smear of paint but if you glance at it as you go through the doorway, your view foreshortens all the distorted shapes and makes them into a skull.'

'Oh yeah, I vaguely remember the guides talking about something like that.' The trouble with Jean Marc was that he got too enthusiastic about things.

'Now look at this first photo.' He swung a light around to the photo pinned on the board. 'I was interested in those patchy shadows there.' He put his finger on the photo. 'I photographed that side of the mountain onto a slide and it's in that projector up there.' He pointed to a black monstrosity bolted to a shelf three metres up a stanchion.

'Dare I ask why?'

'I'm telling you. Right, this is a relief model of that side of the mountain.'

'Got any more whisky?'

He stopped and looked at me then he gave a sigh like the metro doors closing. 'You're not interested are you?'

'I'm thirsty.'

He switched off the light and we went back to the kitchen area.

'So what do you want?' he said.

I held out my glass. He had a short memory or perhaps he had just not been listening. Whilst he poured in more whisky I remembered why I had come.

'You collect cameras don't you?'

'Sort of. I've got some.'

'How much for this?' I pulled the Leica from my pocket. He turned it over in his hands and peered at bits of it. I was impressed. He looked as if he knew what it was.

'Well, it's genuine.' His smile was sort of wry. Surprised. As if he had expected the camera to be faulty in some way.

'Some naughty people have been known to paint these things up to look like old Wehrmacht issue but this one is real. Where did you get it?'

'It's not mine.'

'I didn't think it was.'

'I'm selling it for a friend.'

'Does he know you've got it?' I gave him one of my angry frowns. 'OK. I'm sorry. You have never been known to do anything dishonest in your life.'

'I never said that but I'm not a thief. And the owner's a she, not a he.' I liked saying that.

'What's she like in bed?'

'You'll have to ask her that. I'll put flowers on your grave every anniversary.'

'Two thousand francs.'

'Cash?'

'Be sensible. I haven't got that amount in the studio. If you can leave the camera with me I might be able to get you more for it.'

'How?'

'I don't want the thing myself but I know a chap who collects all military stuff. He knows sod-all about cameras so I reckon I could get two and half thousand for it if I guaranteed it was genuine.'

'Which it is.'

'Exactly.'

'Can't you give me half on deposit? If I go back to her with no camera and no money she'll get even more prickly.'

'What's the rush?'

'No rush.' I put the camera in my pocket and drained my glass. 'Thanks for the drink.'

'You're an awkward bugger sometimes.' He pulled out a bundle of notes and peeled off four five hundreds.

'That's two thousand,' I said. Good idea to remind him that I went to school. 'You said two thousand five hundred.'

'I said that I might get two and a half for it.' He pushed the money into my hand. 'If I do, we'll split the extra.'

'I'll remind you.'

'I don't doubt it. Now come and have a look at what I was trying to show you.'

He put his hand on my shoulder. Like a lamb to the slaughter

I followed him. Why does everything have to be so difficult?

He switched on his blasted projector and the snowy peak flooded across his plaster of Paris mountainside.

'Right this is the first slide,' he explained.

'Got any more whisky?'

'No. Pay attention. So Takahashi is across the other side of the valley and he has set up his camera on the tripod. Right?'

I looked at his eager schoolboy eyes magnified behind the lenses of those stupid spectacles.

'OK.,' I agreed. No sense in upsetting him.

'And he takes the photo. Nothing amiss. Just a nice mountain peak. Deserted in its majesty and all that crap.' He pushed his spectacles back up his nose and then flicked his hair back.

'You know, a short back and sides and contact lenses would make you into a different man. Almost handsome,' I added.

'Shut up will you? So Takahashi whips out the exposed plate and slips in a new one and caramba, an avalanche starts with no warning just after he opens the shutter.'

'You are jealous aren't you?'

'No, just extremely clever. Watch this. You can see that I have taken my slide of Takahashi's picture at a different angle. I turned it through about a hundred and ten degrees and then angled my camera at the inclination of the sun at the time that he took the photo.' I raised my eyebrows in surprise. 'Well as near as I could calculate. So this picture that I am projecting onto the shape of the mountain that I've built reproduces the light and shade conditions at the time.'

'You're serious about this aren't you?'

'And the shadows of the sun, as you can see, coincide as near as accuracy allows, with the crevices and peaks of the mountain.'

He adjusted the focus of the projector and then I could see what he meant. The model became a glowing, sunlit, snow-covered mountain, the three dimensional relief further enhanced by the superimposition of the colours and shadows.

'That's bloody good, that is. I've never seen anything like it.' I looked at him but he was grinning slyly.

'Nice try Jo-Jo, but we are not there yet. Just wait for the dénouement.' He pointed to the grey smudged shadows that he had tried to interest me in at the very beginning. 'Now it's time for you to use your brain. What is causing those shadows there?'

'It must be a bit of the mountain of course.'

'Show me which bit.'

I stepped up to the model, trying to keep out of the projector beam. 'Well I don't know. It's not that peak there because its shadow comes across there. And those lumps make those dark bits there.' I stopped. I was stumped. There was nothing on the mountain that could have caused those shadows. 'Something higher up?' I suggested.

'Higher than the top of the highest mountain in the range, you mean?' Jean Marc was grinning stupidly. He did look like Nana Mouskouri now but I did not tell him. He brought out a piece of stiff cardboard from behind his back and handed it to me. 'You'll need that,' he said. 'Hold it out over the mountain so that the shadows are projected on it.'

They always say you should humour lunatics and court bailiffs. I stuck the card into the beam of the projector and peered at the blob on it, wondering how long I was going to have to wait for the genie to come out of the lamp. Jean Marc was almost hugging himself with childish glee.

'Just tilt it slighty up at the far edge,' he said. I did so and the shadow shortened and became darker as it condensed into a sharper outline. 'A bit more. Now twist your wrist gently to your right.' I stared at the card. 'What have you got?' I was still staring. 'It should be an aeroplane,' he said.

It was. A two-engined job of some sort. I twisted the card the other way and the image slithered into a slurry of grey. I gently brought it back into focus again.

'That's anamorphism, you see. You can twist it in all directions but one and it is nonsense. Get it in the right angle and you have the picture.'

I think the whisky must have slowed me down a bit because I was just seeing the magic trick of the aeroplane appearing without considering its importance. But Jean Marc had got that all taped up.

'So, you see, he was not such a lucky photographer after all. He had got it all planned. He took the first plate as the plane approached. It dropped its grenades to start the snow slipping and he took the other plates. He also used three cameras.'

I gave the card another gyration to distort and refocus the shadow then I handed it back to him.

'You can't trust the Japanese,' I said. 'They think too much. What are you going to do about it?'

'I haven't decided. It seems a little petty to blow the gaffe but,' he grinned to himself, 'it would be rather satisfying.'

'Of course, you have never done any trick like this yourself have you?'

'Not my style. You know me Jo-Jo. Keep it under your hat though.'

'Sure. Sure. Anyway I don't know anybody clever enough to understand it.'

I walked down the canal to the Place de la République but the sight of the heaving masses pressing down the steps of the metro caused me to rethink my evening. I had two thousand francs in my pocket. Outside the Hotel Moderne Palace a knot of travellers was clustered around the luggage boot on a Skyways coach. The ginger-haired Irish girl who worked for Cosmos was frowning at a clipboard.

'Lost your pilgrims?'

She looked up, her green eyes startled. 'Oh you. I haven't goggled your slice for ages. Are you my jockey?'

She thought that she spoke the real Parisian *argot* but she missed every time.

'No. I'm not anybody's driver anymore. Lost your coach as well?'

'Probably stuck in traffic. I've only got two on this flight and they go in a taxi.'

'So why do you want a coach?'

She looked down at her clipboard.

'Fifteen coming in on the next.'

'That'll be hours yet. You know what Skyways is like. Fancy a drink?'

'I can't Jo-Jo, I'm working.' Her eyes were scanning luggage labels as the passengers staggered up onto the sidewalk with their luggage. 'Ah yes, there they are.' She walked briskly towards a middle-aged couple who were both wearing mustard. 'Mr and Mrs Corcoran?' she said. They nodded and soon all three were engrossed with directions for hotels.

'I'll be in Bertrand's' I called.

She waved a hand in irritation.

I walked up the steps and into the cool high-ceilinged vestibule of the Moderne Palace. I nodded at the concierge. He was leaning his elbows on the counter of his cubby hole and gazing morosely out at the light and the traffic swirling around the square.

'Is Bertrand open?'

'Who knows?' he replied lugubriously.

'Well, did he come into work today?'

'How can one tell?'

'Is he down there?'

'Could be. I think he sometimes sleeps there now.'

'Sorry I disturbed you.'

'You didn't.'

I turned sharp right and trotted down the stone steps which doubled back under the square. Bertrand's bar was a sombre cavern of muddy brown. The art deco wall lights reluctantly diffused their pink shadow onto carpetted walls and dull tables. The moquette was repeated on upholstered benches which huddled timidly in alcoves and behind screens. A tall fern-like plant in an enormous earthen pot lounged by the white pillar at the bottom of the stairs and tried to draw my attention to its neglect by wafting its yellowing fronds at me.

I ignored it. I can be tough with potted plants when needed.

Nobody really knew how Bertrand survived. His bar was a shambles, he was rude to his clientele when he was not downright insulting. He shuffled about behind the counter, mumbling to himself and singing disjointed snatches of boulevard *chansons*. Nothing went in the till, all money was thrust into one of the bulging pockets of his white jacket or into his trousers from which it occasionally dropped to be ignored on the floor. Any customer kind enough to point out this loss to him got a faceful of abuse. Some people said that Bertrand was a secret millionaire and held the major share stake in the hotel and that was why he could never be sacked. I didn't know about that. Others said that he had stumbled across some terrible secret and was blackmailing the director. Now that had to be rubbish. Nobody could blackmail a Parisian hotel director – they were never ashamed of anything they did.

Only the green glass shaded lamp above the bar was lighted. Bertrand stood below it, glowering malevolently at a young man and woman who were sitting in the cloying obscurity of an alcove in the corner. They were whispering to each other and it wasn't sweet nothings.

'*Salut* Bertrand.'

'What do you want?'

He flicked the bar with a glasscloth.

'Don't be so bloody rude, I'm not a customer. Give me a beer.'

He nodded to the street above. 'Working?'

'I don't drive Skyways anymore.'

He slapped the glass on the counter and the froth slopped onto the zinc. I sniffed.

'Something burning out there?'

'*Merde.*' He scuttled into the back room and blasted a few oaths around the walls. Then he reappeared with a bowl of soup in each hand. He kicked open the trap and lurched into the *salle*. The couple in the corner stopped whispering and watched in petrified amazement as he wavered towards them. He crashed the two dishes down onto the table. He did not spill a drop. Perhaps he had been concentrating when he had spilled my beer.

'But monsieur, there must be some mistake. We did not ask for soup!' the man protested.

'Shut up and eat!' Bertrand growled and turned away.

I thought for a moment that the young buck was going to make a stand of it but his dame steadied his arm on the table and he sat down again.

'But we didn't ask for soup.'

'You heard what I said,' Bertrand threw insolently over his shoulder. 'Eat it. Compliments of the house.'

The man looked at me for support. I shook my head slowly and turned back to my beer. It tasted good.

So did the second.

'How's business?' I said.

'What do you care?' He reached below the counter and pulled out a baguette. He snapped it into two pieces, showering me with crumbs.

'Thanks.'

'Sarcasm doesn't suit you.'

He kicked open the trap and launched out towards the alcove. The couple in the corner stared as he advanced upon them with a staff of bread in each hand.

'Oh sod it,' he said when he got half way across, 'I can't be bothered. Here's your bread,' he shouted and threw the two spears at them. The first landed between the two bowls and knocked the mustard pot onto the bench. The other hit the girl on the forehead. The man jumped up like a jack-in-the-box. He had black hair which was smeared down on his head with some dressing or other and his tie had a knot the size of a parking meter.

'Monsieur! I find your behaviour to be quite unacceptable. It's outrageous. It's—'

'Oh shut yer gob,' Bertrand snapped, 'we didn't ask for your opinion.'

'Oh, that really is the limit. That really is the limit!'

I could see that he was working himself up to scuff his suede shoes.

'Monsieur,' he turned his attention to me. 'I would ask you to bear witness that—'

'Put some more in that glass Bertrand. It's getting noisy in here.' I turned my back, leaned my elbows on the bar and watched the man in the mirror. Why were women attracted to squirts like that? He fizzled out finally and his girlfriend patted his arm and soothed his ruffled feathers.

'I've just been up to see Jean Marc,' I said.

'Oh yeah? He was a bright one, he was.'

'He still is. He tried to show me a trick with a projector. I didn't understand a thing.' Bertrand was looking at me, his mouth slightly open, lower lip wet. 'You'd better have a drink with me.' I pulled out one of Jean Marc's five hundred franc notes. Bertrand winced as if it smelled bad.

'Haven't you got anything bigger?'

Well at least he didn't ask me where I had got it.

'Straight through the gates I went. Zap.' He waved his arm and a glass crashed from the bar top. He ignored it. 'Cloud of white dust from my back wheel looked as if my arse was on fire.'

I had heard this story before. Back in the fifties Bertrand had been a motorbike rider for the *Canard Enchainé*. Sometimes he said it was *Le Figaro*. It depended on how he remembered it. This particular day he had been trying to get back to the news office with some photos that they needed in a hurry. So with the poor old photographer hanging onto his box of plates and camera with one hand, and onto Bertrand's belt with the other, they had wormed through the Paris traffic until it came to a standstill at the Louvre. There Bertrand had taken the bull by the horns and jumped his motorbike up onto the sidewalk and roared into the Tuileries Gardens.

'Which... which newspaper was it you were working for?'

Bertrand tried to fix his eyes on me and failed. They wavered about like flies in a bottle.

'Which newspaper? I've told you hundreds of times. The *Observateur.*'

The couple had left a long time ago. The man had tried to pay. Bertrand had told him to bugger off and not come back. Another satisfied customer. They had gone up the stairs, he, bristling with the final insult of not being allowed to pay for his girl's night out and she, glancing over her shoulder and wondering how good I would be in bed.

Well... everybody needs a dream from time to time.

'...down the stone steps with the cop running behind blowing his whistle. Bump, bump, bump, bump.'

'Yeah, I remember,' I said.

'Round the pond, all the nurses and kids runnning out of the way. It was like the Keystone Cops. Straight down the main alley, through the big gates and out into the Concorde. Ha!'

I had heard the story so many times before but it always made me laugh. I could see this little black terror zipping down the alley, raising a cloud of white dust as it slalomed through the park walkers and statues. The old ladies sitting on the benches at the side and feeding their stupid little dogs – I could see all their wigs being blown off as Bertrand swept by. My eyes were watering.

Then I suddenly straightened up.

Janus had got them, Vincent had had them. Miro wanted them. Reinhardt was looking for them. I raised my head from the bar. The rumbling street above was now quiet. I needed to talk to Mathilde Sikorski. Time to go.

'I'm going home Bertrand.'

'Bastard.'

'Cheerio.'

'Bastard.'

5

I sometimes think that I am a simple soul at heart. The sun was up and the concierge's bird was singing like a lark. There was still no milk in the fridge but, who cares? Today I could buy some fresh because... I had caught the gravy train. I was not sure where it was going nor at which station I would alight but I need not be greedy. When I had made my packet I could get off before the terminus and let the other passengers deal with all the welcomes on the arrival platform. I didn't need that kind of involvement.

'Have you put a photo on that i.d. declaration yet?' the chinless cop growled at me as I walked past.

'Yeah, it's a real beauty. Do you want to see?' I pretended to look in my shirt pocket.

'Bugger off,' he scowled.

Good work. Always keep on cordial terms with the local law. You never know when you might need their help in completing a crossword.

'Morning all,' I announced gaily to the Café Clerc.

'Here comes James Bond.' Joanne folded back her newspaper. 'What do you want?'

'Breakfast. Some bright, stimulating company. A Proustian discussion on the importance of lost time. Handmade silk shirts from the Rue Royale. An unopened bottle of Mouton Rothschild. An opened account at the Bank Rothschild. Health, wealth, a cottage in the country, a rich widow. Errgh.'

I had not noticed her rolling up the newspaper.

'There's your Légion d'Honneur.' She raised her arm again. 'It's traditional to do both shoulders.'

'Alright, Amazon, you've made your point.'
Thwack.
'That's for calling me Amazon.'

'It was a term of respect. Look,' I said quickly,' how much do I owe you on the slate?' I pulled out the slightly diminished two thousand francs.

'Don't be an idiot,' she said. 'I'm not ga-ga. You know damn well I would never give you credit.' I did know, but she had seen the money. 'What do you want? Coffee?'

I nodded and turned to lean on the bar. Makele waved at me from his table. I picked out a croissant and threw it to him. He rose and snatched it from the air like a big shiny black seal at the zoo catching herring. I should have felt guilty about that image, but I didn't. He had his croissant. I had my nice feeling. Before Joanne could restart World War 3 I tossed a ten franc note onto the counter.

'We're eating croissants,' I said.

'I noticed. Still got the job then?'

I glanced up at the Ricard clock. 'Another minute and we can celebrate its birthday. A whole twenty four hours.'

'If you make it.'

'Can I use your phone?'

She clattered my coffee down, pointed at her phone by the till and switched the meter on. 'Help yourself.'

Using the phone on the counter? I was going up in the world. I dialled Mathilde Sikorski's number. It rang unobtainable. I tried again. The same dead tone. I rang the operator. She tried the line. 'It's disconnected,' she snapped gleefully and cut me off. I put the phone down thoughtfully.

'You don't owe me for the phone.' Joanne looked at the meter. There was a tinge of resignation in her voice. 'But you would have owed me if we had laid that bet.'

'Technical fault,' I said, trying to convince myself that the gravy train had not just crashed into the buffers. 'I must go to work.' I drank my coffee, scooped up the change and then peeled off five ten franc notes and tucked them into Makele's pocket. 'Buy yourself a parrot.'

'Messi, Jo-Jo, Messi.' He grasped my hand in both of his and squeezed it like a toothpaste tube. It hurt.

It must have been still hurting when I got to the metro because before I could collect my thoughts I had paid money for a second class *carnet.* I really ought to check my pulse.

'Yes?'

Well it was still her voice on the doorphone.

'It's Joel Le Batard.'

'Good. Come on up.' The door buzzed me in.

She was standing in the doorway, a coffee cup in her hand. She was wearing those jeans with the thick turn ups and a tee shirt in green cotton.

'Do you know your phone doesn't work?' I said as she closed the door behind me.

'It does now. Did you try to call?'

'Yeah. From the bar. They all thought my job had finished. Cawing like crows in a cemetery, they were.' I laid it on a bit thick. She had given me a nasty shock, why shouldn't she suffer for a while?

'A chap from the PTT knocked on the door just after breakfast to tell me that it had been reported out of order. He fixed it no time at all.'

'Probably on piece rates.'

'How did you get on yesterday?' she handed me a cup of coffee. Those awful red-painted fingernails. 'What's the matter? Coffee smell bad?'

'No.'

'Why the wrinkled up nose and the grimace? More of your yoga?'

'No. I don't like nail varnish.'

She hung both hands in the air like cat's claws.

'That's so that the blood doesn't show.'

'Perhaps you should keep it on then. You might need it.'

'Oh,' she said sharply. 'Why?'

I pulled the bundle of notes out of my pocket. I swore silently because I had not taken the first precaution of separating some off for myself first. What was wrong with me this morning?

'I sold the camera.'

She came across and bounced onto the sofa beside me. Bits of her continued to bounce after she had stopped.

'How much for?' Her eyes were little girl's excitement.

'Well, I made a mistake.'

'What?' She sat back and looked at me shrewdly, wondering whether she was going to believe me or not.

'I took all the money out in one bundle instead of keeping

some back for myself.'

She grinned white teeth. 'It's my open and innocent nature. It entrances everybody.'

'It probably fools everybody,' I said. 'Jean Marc gave me two thousand francs.'

'Wow! That's good.' She lurched forward as if to kiss my cheek but stopped abruptly when I shrank back onto the arm. She frowned at me and then said, 'How much is left?'

I counted it out onto the table before her. 'Eighteen hundred and forty two francs and some shrapnel. I had some expenses,' I explained.

'Ah ha?'

'Metro.'

'No taxi?'

'Not this time. Sandwich. The rest of it I drank.'

'A hundred and twenty odd francs?'

'I was thirsty. Oh and I gave some of it to a Senegalese in the bar. He won't waste it. Unlike me.'

'So you're a charity now are you?'

'It's always easier with somebody else's money.'

She tugged out two five hundred franc notes from the pile. 'The rest is yours,' she said. 'So it was your money you gave away.' She got up to put the money in her purse. The cushion on the sofa slowly infilled the imprint of her bottom whilst I looked at the money. That could last me two months if I was careful. Two hours if I wasn't.

'Er... Thanks.'

She shrugged a pretty smile.

'I said I was going to pay you, so there you are.'

I scooped up the money and put it in my pocket.

'Right then,' I said as I stood up, 'job over.'

'Job over,' she repeated and walked me back down the hall. I followed her, watching her denim bottom just as Reinhardt had done. Reinhardt, treacherous Reinhardt. I could hear Vincent's cowardly pleadings, I could see Miro's cruel eyes. She held out her hand at the open door. I ignored it and slowly pushed the door shut.

'Job not over,' I said.

The parquet crackled behind me as she silently followed me back into the salon. I sat down.

'What is this all about?' She crossed her arms under her breasts and threw herself onto the sofa opposite.

'I was hoping you would tell me that. Oh, by the way, I should have told you that Jean Marc thought that he might be able to get another five hundred on the camera when he sells it on and if he does we are going to split it fifty-fifty.'

'Why bother telling me? Would I ever have found out?'

'No. Just to show you how untrustworthy I am.'

'You told me that at the beginning.'

'A reminder is always useful.'

'Is that all you wanted to tell me? I already knew you would cheat me.'

'But you didn't warn me how untrustworthy you were.'

'I am not untrustworthy,' she said through her teeth. Her voice was frigid, here eyes, splinters of anger.

'Good, then perhaps you will tell me why you really got me here and what you are really looking for and why you cannot find it?'

'I don't know what you mean.' She was tapping her fingers impatiently on her thigh.

'Sure?'

'Positive. And don't be so impertinent.'

'Perhaps I should tell you a thing or two little girl.'

'I told you not to be impertinent.'

'I am older than you. It's my prerogative. Let's begin with Reinhardt shall we?'

'Oh that horrible little man.'

'That horrible little man is a vicious, conniving, deceitful but ambitious agent of the Ministry of Defence. His section is one of those autonomous and anonymous security agencies that various politicians like to believe are there expressly to protect their valuable lives and, if needed, confound and perhaps shorten, the lives of their enemies. Perhaps that is what it was set up for, but Reinhardt runs it solely for the glorification and promotion of Reinhardt.'

'What has this got to do with me?'

'I didn't invite him to Jos... your father's funeral.'

'Neither did I.'

'But he was there.'

'Yes, he was there.'

I let that settle for a moment or two. She looked at me and unfolded her arms. The tee shirt filled and emptied a couple of times. I watched and waited.

'I suppose he was checking up on who knew Papa?'

'Your guess is as good as mine, probably better. But we know that it was more than that don't we?'

'How?'

'He came here searching for something.'

She bit her lip and looked down at her knees. She crossed her legs. 'Yes, he seemed to be searching.'

'What was he looking for, Miss Sikorski?'

She looked up sharply. 'Not "Mathilde" any more?'

'That was when I trusted you.'

'And you don't now?'

'I don't now.'

'Why not? Why not?'

'Tell me what he was looking for?'

'I can't,' she shouted. 'I don't know.'

'But you got me here with some treacle-story about sorting out Josef's affairs because you wanted me to find it for you, didn't you?'

'Yes, no, oh I don't know.' She burst into tears.

Jackpot! Just what I wanted – a hysterical weeping orphan. I watched her shoulders convulse as she pushed her face into the cushion. Sob, sob, sob. I waited. She sobbed some more. *Merde!* Why do I get myself into these situations? I suppose I had forgotten that she had just buried her father. Not very sensitive of me. I went across and sat next to her. I cautiously tapped her shoulder.

'Don't touch me,' she wriggled.

'Oh, who would want to?' I was exasperated. 'As you won't tell me anything, I will tell you what I know. All you've got to do is listen and sob at the important bits.'

'Crapule!' she said under her armpit.

Now that was more like it.

'Yesterday I did not go straight to Jean Marc's with the camera, I went to see my recent boss.'

'How recent?'

'He had just sacked me.'

'Why did you go to see him?'

'Because your father had written his telephone number on the inside of that Casino Harz bookmatch. I wanted to know why.'

'What was your boss's name?'

'Vincent Descamps.'

'Never heard of him.'

'Good. He is a small-time crook. Very small-time. When I got there he was entertaining a big-time crook.'

She stopped sniffing. 'Are all your employers bent?'

'Join the gang.'

She kicked me with her bare foot. But it still hurt.

'I listened outside the door for a while until... it was time to go in.'

'You got caught!' I saw a malicious eye glint wetly at me.

'The big-time crook is called Miro. He was coercing Vincent to hand something over to him. Something that Vincent had already had a sample of and had inadvisedly sent to a minister who was, "on the hook".'

She lifted her head and licked her lips. 'Now this is intriguing.'

'Yes, isn't it?' I agreed. 'So sit up and pay attention.' She stuck out her tongue and laid her head back down on the arm of the sofa. 'I said, "sit up"!' I gave her a sharp slap on the bottom. She bounced upright, her eyes blazing.

'How dare you!'

I easily caught both her flailing wrists and gripping them in one hand, forced them down into her lap. She tried to bite my hand. I slapped her face. She gasped.

'Have you finished?' I asked casually.

'You... you...'

'Oh that's utterly pathetic. At your age you should have a complete battery of oaths for occasions such as this. You are such an odious creature, I am sure this happens to you all the while.' She breathed hard through her nose till her nostrils went white. 'Now you look like the last runner in the Prix de l'Arc de Triomphe,' I taunted her. She said nothing. Another one who was learning. 'Good. Now, I am going to release your hands and you are going to listen carefully to what I am going to tell you. You are an intelligent girl and if you concentrate hard, you will surely learn something.' She began to wriggle her wrists. 'Oh, and by the way, if you try any more physical stuff I will give you an interestingly shaped bruise on such an embarrassing part of your body that you will stay indoors for a fortnight. Understand?'

She nodded tightly. Her eyebrows were so flat they made the letter M in Morse Code. I released her hands, watching her eyes all the while.

'You hurt me,' she said.

'Yes, I probably did, but that was nothing. The people you are getting mixed up with will break your legs, carve your face, smash your teeth, to get what they want. And you've got me mixed up with them now.' At last she was listening. Christ, it's difficult sometimes getting the youth of today to pay attention. 'Picture the scenario. Vincent, my ex-boss is quaking in his chair and protesting that he does not know where "they" are, nor the identity of the person who has them; Miro is inspecting him as you would something nasty on the sole of your shoe and deciding whether or not to rub it off.'

'And you?'

'Me?'

'Yes. Where are you in this picture of brotherly love?'

'I am lying face down on the carpet with a punk's foot grinding my hand into the foundations and the other kicking me in the ribs.'

'You're pretty tough with defenceless women though aren't you?'

'I wasn't even trying and you're not defenceless. Do you know anybody called "Janus"?' I watched her carefully. Her eyes did not flicker.

'Some god or other?' She pouted. 'Had two faces.'

'Most gods do.'

'Atheist as well? Is there no limit to your goodliness?'

'Try me one day.'

'So how did you get off the floor?'

'I talked my way out of it. I can be quite silver-tongued when I try.'

She snorted. I don't think she believed me.

'So what about Janus?'

'Vincent said that he had not got these things that Miro was threatening to pull his fingers off for but that "Janus" had got them.'

'And this Vincent and Miro, they are partners in crime?'

'They wouldn't trust each other further than they could spit.'

'How revolting.'

'Life's like that. One day Miro will get tired and Vincent will be found wheels up in the gutter.'

'These people don't sound very nice.'

'This is what I am trying to tell you. They are thugs, they are vicious, unscrupulous, cruel and we are in their way because you will not tell me what I am supposed to be looking for.'

'How are we in their way?'

'"Janus" was the radio code your father always used on ops. Whatever it is they want, your father had it. He showed some of it to Vincent.' I laughed. 'I probably drove Vincent there to collect it.'

'Where? The Casino Harz?'

I nodded. 'Because he does not have the necessary resources, Vincent proposes a partnership to Miro. I'm just guessing now, you understand? He shows some of the stuff to Miro and then sends it to the minister, without telling Miro. This is unfortunate because Miro, having seen the quality of it, considers that Vincent is too small to handle the business and decides to muscle in and take over. That is when he finds that Vincent has not got the stuff, and, as far as they know, cannot get it until next Tuesday when Vincent is due to meet this Janus again. Following so far?'

'I'm not stupid.'

'I've already told you that. I turn up at the point where Vincent is saying that he does not know where the stuff is. The two of them know what they are talking about but don't know the identity of the person who has got it; I am lying face down on the floor knowing who has got it but not what they are talking about.'

'In a bit of a pickle really, weren't you?'

'Yes and so are you. You have the unscrupulous head of an anonymous security section of the Ministry of Defence wanting to search your knickers and he knows where to find you, and a pair of thugs who would not stop at breaking us both into little pieces and who don't know you exist but who are going to find out pretty soon.'

'How?'

'Once Reinhardt has found them, he will tell them where you are. He will let them do all the dirty work then gallop in at the last minute on his white charger and carry the goods off to safety. So don't you think you ought to help me a little?'

I thought that would give her something to chew over. It need not worry me, of course. I had money in my pocket and I could walk out of that door. Or I could make some more coffee.

'I'll make some more coffee whilst you think it over.'

There were two suitcases by the bureau. I had not noticed them before. I set the coffee up and came back into the salon whilst it percolated. She was still sitting on the sofa. I hoped the picture I had painted would be sufficient. She saw me looking at the suitcases and jumped up.

Oh I forgot those,' she said. 'It occurred to me when I was cleaning out Papa's clothes and things. You are about his size and you're broke. It's all good labels. It would be daft giving it to charity or a hospital or something when you know somebody who could use it.' She swung a case up onto the dining table and clicked it open.

It was all good stuff and hardly worn at that. There was a couple of decent day suits, an evening suit, some nice shirts with crisp collars and cuffs. I turned over the patterned waistcoat and looked underneath.

'Um...' she faltered. 'Well I put those in anyway.... I don't know whether–'

'Men still wear underpants.'

'I'll take your word for it.'

'Do.' I looked in the other case. She was giving me a fortune in good clothes and I knew that I was not too proud to wear anything that fitted.

'Well?'

'Funny way for rewarding me for assaulting you.'

'Oh I'll get back at you another way, don't worry.'

'Thank you Miss Sikorski.'

'Still not "Mathilde"?'

'You haven't told me what I'm looking for.'

She sucked on her tongue and sorted in the cases. She pulled out a pair of slacks and a casual shirt.

'Go and put those on. Bathroom's over there. Then you can buy me lunch with some of your new wealth and I'll tell you all I know.'

I looked at myself in the bathroom mirror. Josef must have been nearly thirty years older than me but his taste in clothes had been young. I supposed he had had women. And he dressed up for the Casino Harz of course. I combed my hair back and washed my face. Not bad. Not bad.

She looked me up and down critically. Turning a circle around me, pulling at my shirt, tugging at my belt.

'You'll do,' she said. 'We'll go to the Italie on the square. They do a nice *menu du jour.*'

'Just a minute,' I said.

'What's the matter?' She was slipping her feet into her shoes.

'You don't think I'm taking you out with you dressed like that do you?'

'I beg your pardon?'

'Well look at you. Scrappy tee shirt and grubby jeans. Hair all over the place. I wouldn't be seen dead sitting in a restaurant with a woman dressed like that.'

'What?'

'Go and tidy yourself up girl. You look as if you've been rolling around on the floor. I'll give you two minutes.'

'You... you pig!'

'One minute and fifty seconds.'

The Italie was crowded with business lunchers throwing food down their throats. We managed to squeeze into a small table in the corner of the open-fronted pavement terrace. The noise of people talking and greeting easily drowned that of the traffic thundering around the Place d'Italie, and this suited us. In a very public, noisy place it is often easier to talk about private matters.

I finished my *filet de hareng*, sipped at my beer and watched her savouring her *oeuf dur mayonnaise*. She had changed into smart trousers which were made of some thin material which was all the rage and which waved in the breeze and clung to her legs when she walked. It is a good job that I have got no imagination. She had swapped her tee shirt for a simple blouse, into which she nearly fitted. She looked up suddenly.

'Was your fish OK?'

'Yes, fine thank you. How's your egg?'

'You weren't looking at that.' She grinned and straightened her back. I raised my eyes to the foliage on the plane trees. 'You prefer the blouse then?' she said.

'It is a lot smarter than the tee shirt.'

'Well you look a lot smarter too.'

'That's fine then. Steak or the rabbit?'

'Rabbit.'

'I don't actually know what we are looking for,' she admitted.

'Oh well done! I'm glad you waited till coffee to admit that I had fed you under false pretences.'

'Look Joel, are you serious about these nasty people?'

'Never more serious.'

'You don't look worried.'

'You don't know me well enough. I might be terrified.'

'You don't look it.'

'I was in Algeria with Josef. You know that. Did he ever talk about it?'

'No.'

'And I don't talk about it either. Nobody who was actually in the fighting talks about it. The noisy ones are the HQ staff who kept out of the way and telex operators who knew what was going on. Quite a lot of them survived.'

'If you are so tough, why were you smelling the carpet?'

'You have to know when to be beaten and when to preserve your strength. I got out of it. You wouldn't have done. You don't know when to give in. You would keep fighting and get yourself hurt. Really hurt.'

'You hurt me on the sofa.'

'Only your pride.

'Brute.'

'What are we looking for, Mathilde? Give me a clue.'

She sat back and fiddled with her teaspoon.

'Papa was a bit vague in his later years. I did not see him that often. Once or twice a year. He never came to Strasbourg, I always visited him here.'

'What do you mean, vague?'

'Well sometimes he just did not make sense because he was drunk most of the day, but when he was sober, one thing he kept coming back to was this thing about having prepared himself a good pension. An unofficial pension.'

'Look Mathilde, if you are worried that Josef might have been breaking the law, forget it. He almost certainly was. We were all on the fiddle. Selling stores, diverting supplies; one adjutant even invented a complete platoon.'

'He was like a terrrier with it though. It was something that he was certain would bring him wealth and security. "But they've got to be placed properly. Like dynamite," he used to say.'

'Any idea at all what he was talking about?' She shrugged. 'Or where he had put them?'

'None. You've seen the apartment. You've seen his papers. Was there anything there to worry a minister?'

'Nothing to worry a nun. It was just old office stuff. Gumph. Reinhardt looked at it, he didn't want it.'

'But how did he look at it?'

'What do you mean?'

'Can we get some idea of the size and shape of what he was looking for by the way he handled the pile of papers?'

'I see what you mean, but I can't really remember how he did it. But can we be certain that he knows exactly what he is looking for?'

'The minister must have told him,' she said.

'Not necessarily. Josef might have laid his hands on some compromising documents. The minister would merely tell Reinhardt that there had been a leak somewhere and order him to stop it. He would not want anybody extra knowing what had been compromised would he?'

'You mean, he would not trust his own security section?'

'No minister would trust a setup like Reinhardt's. It gets results because it does not officially exist – it can do what it likes. It only submits an account of its activities when pressed and ministers prefer it like that. If it cocks up, the minister can deny any knowledge of its operations.'

'So are we looking for some state secrets do you think?'

I gazed out at the square whilst I thought. The traffic was slowing down on our corner as it negotiated a *Compagnie des Eaux* van which had double-parked on the pedestrian crossing. The patrons were beginning to leave the terrace and hurry back to their offices. The old ladies with dogs had not begun to arrive yet.

'If it is state secrets, all parties will stop at nothing you realise that?' I looked at her frowning face. 'Why are we doing this?' I asked suddenly.

'What do you mean?'

'We suppose there is a lot of money to be had. Money that

Josef had hoped to cash in for his pension, right?'

'Right.'

'Well, is it worth it? Do you need lots of money? It's probably illegal. Is it worth risking your life for it?'

'But it should have been Papa's money. They are trying to muscle in on it, you said so.'

'Let's face it, if Josef had to choose Vincent as a go-between for the underworld, he must have been a bit rusty.'

'I don't know.'

'Vincent is a paper doll. He is a laughing stock.'

'You said he was dangerous.'

'Look, why can't we just say to Reinhardt, "tell us what you want, we will find it and give it to you and you keep the others off our back"?'

She stared at me. 'You're joking aren't you? I'm not giving that slimy creep anything. And neither are you.'

'I couldn't. I've got nothing to give.'

We walked back up the rue Stresemann, not quite arm in arm. I paused and looked up at the facade of number fifteen. All the windows of the second floor had balcony rails across them. I counted along from the stairwell and recognised the two windows of Josef's salon by the colour of the curtains. The building next door, number thirteen, had been built in a more flamboyant style and their rooms had real balconies, projecting part way over the street.

'What are you looking at?'

'I was just wondering why he bought a flat like this.'

'Who knows?' She shrugged. 'Easy for the metro, far enough out to be quiet. Hundreds of reasons.'

We went up. She sniffed as she opened the flat door.

'Coffee! You left the coffee on.'

'Sorry, I forgot.' I had been too worried about her trying to get me out of my clothes. Neuroses like that are good for my self esteem.

She came back in from the kitchen. 'There's no harm done. *Fumigation à la café*. Perhaps it will catch on. Are you going to take these clothes?' She pointed at the two suitcases. 'And what about those cap badges? Repeat the success you had with the camera and you could be wintering on the Cote d'Azur.'

I took the bag of cap badges. Well, you never know.

'Thanks very much for the clothes.'

She smiled. 'You find it difficult to say "thank you" don't you?'

I just gave her a look. I blame that sort of observation on the philosophy they study at university.

'Can I leave one suitcase here? I don't want to drag two cases around the metro. I'll collect it next time.'

'I can drive you over.'

What? In high heels? In that Renault 4? Not likely!

'No, don't trouble. I might stop for a drink on the way.'

'Yes, you might. Leave it here. It won't be in the way.' I looked at her and she looked back.

'So where are we?' I asked. 'What is going to happen next?'

'You tell me.'

'Well Miro and his thugs will find out next Tuesday that they have lost their contact.' She sucked in her lips and her eyes filled with tears again. I stood my ground. I really was brave. 'That gives us some time to try to discover what it was that Josef had for sale.'

'Then what do we do?' she sniffed.

'I've no idea, Mathilde, none whatsoever.'

I restocked my wardrobe and tied up all my cast-offs into an old sheet and dumped them straight in the garbage bin. No sentiment. This was the gravy train. You had to be dressed for it.

It was five o clock and I had not seen the inside of a bar for a couple of hours. I wandered around to the Café Clerc just to show Joanne that I was still employed. A black Cadillac was parked outside on the delivery bay. It sat there like an obscene slug on a stick of lettuce. Martins was standing in the middle of the bar and Joanne was brushing down his suit.

'Turn around,' Joanne coaxed.

He turned. Wordless. Black eyes expressionless. He would make a good Mafia hearse driver.

'There, you'll do.' She stood back, somehow fulfilled.

'*Merci madame.*' Martins gave a little bow.

'You look very smart,' she said to me as she eyed up my outfit. 'Nice clothes.'

'Goes with the job,' I said. 'The one you thought I had lost.'

'Early days, yet. You could still lose it.'

Joanne could deflate a Zeppelin.

'Job on tonight?' I asked Martins.

'Hotel Scribe for the Lido. Argentinians.'

'Not much driving but a lot of waiting around.'

He shrugged. 'The tips are good.'

'I bet they ask you to take them to a "special cabaret".'

Martins grinned. 'I know a few, don't worry. And I'll get commission from the doorman.'

Something was wrong in the café. I looked at Martins, tucking his order book back into his pocket; Joanne, now behind the bar. They both kept glancing into the corner of the bar. At Pino. Pino was sitting behind a glass of red wine. Nothing unusual about that. It would be either wine or *pastis*. He usually had a glass or two to fortify himself for the eighteen hundred kilometre high speed drive that he made five times a week, delivering the newspapers. But he had overdone it tonight.

'Hey Pino,' I called.

He lifted his head. His watery eyes were rimmed with red, his grey hair falling in untidy straggles across his glowing face. He was muttering something.

'Shouldn't you be getting ready?' I went over to him.

'Not going. Don't want to go.' His voice was slurred. 'They can't make me.' His head rolled. His eyes followed in the taxi behind. 'No more.'

'Pino!' I shook his head by the hair. 'Come on, wake up and get moving. You should be on your way to the press by now.'

'Oh go and pick flowers!' He shuffled to get up and fell backwards onto the bench. 'And you can pick flowers as well,' he shouted at Martins. He swept his arm around in a ragged arc. 'You can all go and pick flowers and stick them.'

I left him and went to the bar.

'Why did you let him get like this?'

For once in her life, Joanne looked guilty. I wished I'd had a camera.

'He was half cut when he came in. He's been drinking all day.'

'And who's been serving him?'

'I'm not his nursemaid.'

'Just his executioner. Look at him. He can't stand up, let alone drive. Why did you keep serving him?'

'It's my business. That is what I do. I run a bar, not a charity. If he can pay for a drink, I will give him one.'

'He'll never get another job after this.'

'He's adult and innoculated. It's his choice.'

'And then what do we do with him when he's out of work and broke?'

'He's not your family is he?'

'Is that all you care about?'

She slammed a tray onto the bar top.

'Look Jo-Jo, you are in no position to lecture me. What have you done with your life? Eh? You've had a job for twenty four hours and it goes to your head. I've been working my fingers to the bone since my old man walked out on me ten years ago. Do I care about Pino? No I don't. I don't care about Pino, or Makele, or Martins or Jo-Jo. I don't care about any of you. Nobody is looking after me.'

I could see her point but I didn't tell her. I never agree with an angry woman, it only encourages them. I went and inspected Pino. He looked disgusting.

'Where are your car keys Pino?'

'Not going. Don't want to do it.'

'Yeah, I heard you. Where are your car keys?'

'You're a pal, Jo-Jo.' He swung an arm approximately around my shoulders. 'Always said that. Jo-Jo's a pal. Always help a friend in need.'

'Where are the keys?' I started to tap his pockets. He burped.

'Keys are in the car,' he said suddenly. 'Always have to leave them there.'

Right. All I needed to know now was which car was his. I shook him upright and made him look at me.

'Pino, listen to me. I'll deliver your papers but I need to know which car is yours.'

''Course you do.'

'Well?'

'Always at the end. It's a grey one.'

'Idiot! They are all bloody grey! What's the number?'

'You can't miss it. It'll have *'Nice'* on the tailgate.' His head dropped to the table top. He was dead to the world.

I stood over him. I didn't want to spend the next twelve hours on the autoroute. I wanted to spend them in bed.

Joanne bustled up to me with a paper bag which she thrust into my hand.

'Sandwiches. You can eat on the way. There's a couple of bottles of beer in there but go carefully.'

'Thanks.'

'Martins!' She called him back from the doorway. 'If you're going to the Scribe you can drop Jo-Jo off at the Paris Matin depot. Hurry up, both of you.'

Martins nodded.

'Get in the back,' he said, 'or they'll know I'm giving you a lift.'

6

From the street I could see the Paris Matin cars backed up at the low end of the loading dock. They used the estate car version of the Citroen that I had driven for Vincent; their tailgates were raised like a line of saluting ss at Nurenberg.

I slipped in to the depot and loitered in the shadows for a few seconds to get the feel of the place. No newspapers were being loaded, the cars were still empty. Four men were kicking their heels at the far end by a drinks dispenser. They looked like drivers. I wandered over. One of them saw me approaching and said something and the others turned to watch. I felt like John Wayne strolling up the main street of Dead Gulch City. I decided to go in with six guns blazing.

'I'm Pino,' I said.

'No you're not,' the hairy one said.

'I am tonight.'

They looked at each other like teenagers at a dance.

'Godeau won't like it,' the fat one observed.

I shrugged unconcern. Almost on cue, Godeau arrived. He was bald and sweating in a leather-fronted apron.

'Another fifteen minutes they reckon. Has that runt Pino turned in yet?' Then he saw me. 'Who are you?'

'Says he's Pino,' the fat man said gleefully. Perhaps he liked watching people have heart attacks.

'*Merde, merde, merde!* Not again. That's it. That's it. He's out. I don't want him in here again.' Suddenly he stiffened as a man in shirt sleeves poked his head around the door.

'Everything ready, Godeau? No problems?'

'All's fine, Monsieur Brandt, fine.' He glowered at me. I kept quiet. I can be diplomatic upon occasions. The man glanced around the faces. The drivers returned expressions of choirboys who had innocently drunk the communion wine. Brandt's glance rested briefly on me. His eyebrows got together for a conference and then adjourned. He nodded and disappeared back behind the door.

Godeau sighed.

'Do you know the form?'

'Vaguely,' I said.

'Caramba!' His voice was sarcastic. 'Can you at least drive?'

I looked at him levelly. Why was I bothering?

'I can drive.'

'Do you know where you're going?'

'Nice. It's on the Cote d'Azur,' I added.

'Smart guy, eh?'

'Smart enough. Where exactly do you want these comics delivered to?'

'The wholesaler's are Nicoletti. Their distribution depot is behind the Gare du Sud.'

'Not Nice-Ville then?'

'No. The Gare du Sud is further up. Ask a policeman if you can't find it.'

'What about the péages on the autoroute?'

'What about them?'

'Who pays?'

'You do.'

'What with?'

'Try whatever you like but in my experience they only take francs.' He grinned maliciously at me. 'And if you want to know where the francs are, you will have to ask Pino, because the drivers draw them in advance.'

I did not need to ask Pino. I knew where the francs were. In Joanne's till. At this rate Mathilde Sikorski's eight hundred francs were not going to last me very long. Then I found myself grinning when I remembered what she had said. That if I repeated my success with the sale of the cap badges, I could be wintering on the Cote d'Azur. Little did she know that I would be there tomorrow morning.

I walked down the line of cars till I found the one with 'Nice' on the tailboard. I opened the passenger door and dropped Joanne's ration parcel onto the front seat. I glanced in the back.

The two rows of rear seats had been removed and the trim had been stripped out and the load platform lined with plyboard. Every gram they saved was extra payload. I sat in the driving seat and adjusted the squab to suit me. Most of the controls were familiar, those that were not would not be important. I pushed my head back and gazed through the windscreen at the blank wall opposite. My mind was empty. Too much had been happening to me in too short a time. And I needed a drink. It would have to be the bloody coffee machine.

As the coffee came down the chute a fork lift truck chugged out of the works and onto the dock.

'Forget coffee,' Godeau said. 'There's your stuff. Get loading.'

The truck dropped a pallet of bundled newspapers at my car and gingerly backed away. I think it was frightened of me. I lugged the first bundle from the top and jumped it into the back of the car. I turned for the second. The fat driver was shaking his head slowly.

'Not like that,' he said wearily. 'You won't get them in like that.'

I looked at the pallet again and realised that the entire load was for me.

'There must be a ton of newspapers there,' I complained

'Just under.' His glee knew no limits. He was one of those naturally cheerful people whom you always hope will fall under a bus. 'Now, do it this way. Open the back doors, right? Three bundles across, two down the side. Then load the rest from the tailgate for the first layer. Then repeat from the front for the second layer but reverse the pattern to make a bond. Right?'

'Right,' I said.

I would have some words to say to Pino when I saw him next and not many of them would have two syllables. I was nicely warmed up by the time that I squeezed the last bundle in under the roof.

'Just a minute,' Gleeful said. He pulled out a pocket knife and slit a string on the last bundle. He tugged out a handful of papers and gave them to me. I looked at them stupidly. What did I want with a handful of *Paris Matins?* I had got a car full of the wretched things. 'They are your armour. Put them on your front seat.'

'I can see that you are bursting to tell me why,' I said as I lifted Joanne's pack and dumped the papers on the seat.

'Oh, not really.'

I decided I would push him under that bus, I wouldn't wait for him to fall.

'Well suppose you tell me anyway. Just pretend that I don't know why.'

He sucked on his teeth and looked at me. I was praying that it would be one of the Berliet double deckers, fully loaded in the rush hour, on that lumpy pavé behind the Champ de Mars.

'You'll be breaking the speed limit all the way down.'

'Probably.'

'It's the only way.'

'So? Traffic cops are pretty rare at this time of night. They don't like the dark.'

'The traffic cops are all sitting warm and comfortable next to the girl who clocks your ticket at the péage. They don't even have to get out their motorbikes and chase after you, you come to them and present them with a ticket which tells them what time you went through the last péage and how far you have travelled since. They've got it made. So you hand out free newspapers all the way down, and you never get a ticket.'

There was more to this job than was obvious at first sight.

'Who pays it if I do?'

'Don't be an idiot. Whoever pays speeding tickets in France?'

'That's true.'

'Got a full tank?'

I turned on the ignition and waited whilst the gauge registered.

'Yeah.'

'You'll need it. When you get to Nice you have to fill up for the return journey. The wholesalers where you drop the papers, Nicoletti, have got a pump and they invoice direct to Paris.'

'That's nice of them.'

'It's to stop us fiddling the petrol money.'

'As if you would.'

He looked at me quizzically.

'Well, we used to,' he admitted. 'In the good old days.'

I could see Godeau's shiny head nodding down towards us.

'Look out, the boiled egg's coming.'

'What the hell are you waiting for?' he asked. 'That's a daily newspaper, not a monthly. Get moving.'

I started the engine.

'My compliments to your coiffeur,' I said and let in the clutch.

The car was heavy. Really heavy. The hydraulic suspension coped with it of course, that was why they used that model. No matter what you put in them they could still ride at the same height. But the weight had an obvious effect on the acceleration. There was none. At half past ten, many of the traffic lights on the side roads in Paris switch to flashing orange and the rule of the road reverts to the traditional priority from the right and pistols at dawn. I had still not adjusted to the appalling lack of speed when one of those poxy little handbags on wheels found me crawling across a junction in front of him. His vocabulary was poxy too.

Rather than navigate this bath tub around the city I cut straight to the Périphérique via the Seine and then floored the accelerator and waited for the pages on the calender to turn over. I lost momentum taking the curves in the underpass at the Porte d'Italie but the motor soon recovered and surprised me by pulling strongly up the two lane drag to the autoroute. Perhaps I was getting the idea. Only another five hours.

By the time I reached Orly I was doing one hundred and sixty and passing everything on the road, including a police patrol car that I noticed too late; but he was going home to bed so he left me alone. I held the accelerator on the floor and the car platformed out at a hundred and eighty.

Five hours. Five hours with my right foot going numb from the vibration of the floor. Five hours being jovial with policemen, poking newspapers into toll kiosks and spending Mathilde Sikorski's francs. My life was just a line of lane markers flicking towards me with hypnotic regularity; the cadence interrupted occasionally by the slower approach of tail lights then the sweep of my headlights along the side of a trailer, the roar of a truck engine and suddenly it was getting smaller again in my mirror. And still I drove on.

Midnight well behind me. Traffic was now sparse. I straight-lined the curves, passing from one lane to the next with no fear of upsetting anybody. Bridges flashed by ghostly grey, nearby buildings showed no lights. The engine droned a monotone. Lulling me, lulling me. *Thud, thud, thud*, the studs hammered under the wheels. I jerked my head up and gently eased the car back in line. You don't wrench the wheel at that speed.

At half past two I nearly died. Just south of Valence a milk tanker decided to use my lane to avoid some road works. At that time of the morning you don't look in your mirror. Why should you? You are alone in the world. And anyway, who is going to argue with twenty tons of milk? I pulled on the horn, turned up all my lights and stamped on the brake. The world before me exploded into bright yellow as the quartz-iodine lamps of the Citroen flooded the countryside for a kilometre around, the air horns shrieked like an express train and the brakes laid back and laughed at me. Stop the car? With this load? At this speed? We'll need written notice of that.

Red lights flickering on the truck. Deciding what to do. Did it matter? There would be no witnesses, and he's obviously speeding, whoever he is. Indecision.

The gap was narrowing quickly. I stamped back onto the accelerator, and shaved through in front of the truck. *Tack, tack, tack,* the plastic cones snatched at the wheel before flying away into the darkness. The truck driver vented his fright on his horn and his headlights. They were even more powerful than mine. Idiot! Him or me, I wondered?

I stopped at the next service station to get a grasp on life and drink a coffee. The restaurant was shut, all service was provided by a posse of vending machines loitering in the lobby. I stood there drinking a coffee made from syrup and felt very sorry for myself. No wonder Pino was drunk most of the time.

When I returned to the car I saw Joanne's pack and wolfed down a cheese sandwich and drank a bottle of warm beer – a combination guaranteed to give me indigestion for the next two hours. I rejoined the autoroute just behind that bloody milk tanker. And I drove on.

The road was turning eastwards now, parallel to the Mediterranean but miles from it. Already I could see the sky lightening at the horizon before me. I had the road to myself. How generous they were. I did not want it. I wanted to be in bed with a warm woman. Mathilde Sikorski perhaps? I'd rather bed a tiger. Joanne? No, she was Mathilde with brains and a machete. Why didn't I know any kind, cuddly, decent, sexy, compliant women? Oh, and with independent means. There must be some.

Although it was nearly daylight, Saturday morning Nice was not even thinking of waking up. I turned up to the Gare du Sud and wriggled about some back streets till I found Nicoletti. The depot door was shut so I rang the bell. I leaned against the shutters and waited. Across the road, the two men sitting in the bus shelter watched me. Nothing seemed to be moving behind the door. I rang the bell again. One of the men got up and walked across to me. He was short, dark and looked like a Corsican bandit; but then, everybody in Nice looked like a Corsican bandit. He held up a cigarette.

'Got a light?' he said.

I ignored him and glanced across at the man he had left in the shelter. He looked quickly away when he saw me.

'I said, "Got a light?".'

'I heard you.'

'Well?'

'I'm thinking about it.' I knew that there was a cigarette lighter in the car. 'What do you want?'

He slid the cigarette behind his left ear. 'Where's Pino?'

'Who's Pino?'

He pushed a thumbnail between his teeth and then sucked with his tongue. 'He agreed to take my old man back to Paris.'

I could have strangled Pino. The last thing I wanted was a pensioner for company on the return journey.

'Pino couldn't come. I'm his replacement.' I leaned on the bell again.

'Alright, alright, I'm here,' a voice grumbled from the other side of the door. 'Who is it?'

You mean, I could be a surprise?

'I'll give you three guesses and then I'll dump these comics in the harbour.'

The roller blind rattled up and when the storeman saw the car he waved me in. He was dressed in a blue overall: a thin man with thick-lensed glasses. I backed the car in and then got out. He peered short-sightedly at me.

'Who are you?' he said. 'Where's Pino?'

'That's what he wants to know.' I pointed at the bandit who had followed me in. The storeman looked at him.

'And who is he?'

In a flash of cruel inspiration I said, 'He's here to unload the papers.'

'Good, good.'

I lifted the tailgate and opened the back doors.

'Help yourself, mate. You don't want to leave your old man here do you?' I nodded at the shadow in the bus shelter. I thought my subtlety was dazzling. The bandit scowled at me and began to tug bundles of *Paris Matin* from the car. I sat in the driving seat and unwrapped Joanne's ration pack. I reckon I could be a manager if I tried.

It never takes as long to unload a car as it does to load it but I still had time for a leisurely sandwich and my second bottle of beer. Then the storeman took me to the pump and filled up my tank. I verified the number of litres and signed the chit, *'Brigitte Bardot'*. It would give the auditors a thrill. The man was still immobile in the bus shelter. The bandit was still hanging around outside, scowling.

'I won't forget that,' he said as I came out. It was supposed to be menacing.

'I don't suppose you will. It's probably the first honest sweat you've broken this year.'

As the roller blind rattled down half way behind us he waved to the bus shelter. The old man got up slowly and straightened his back. Then he picked his way carefully across the kerbs and pavings to reach us. He was wearing a beret and a beige raincoat with the collar turned up and a thin scarf was wrapped around his lower face. Just his eyes and forehead were visible. Brown eyes, watery, vague. Brown skin. Wrinkled forehead, silver hair. He was seventy if he was a day.

'Apparently you're coming to Paris with me,' I said, trying to be pleasant. I put out my hand. 'My name's Joel.'

A scrawny hand poked from his coat sleeve.

'Granddad.'

And that was the only word he ever said to me.

I am not much of a conversationalist and I spent some of the return journey thinking up rewards for Pino for foisting this passenger upon me but now that 'Granddad' was in the car with me, I contrarily wanted him to chat. If I had to have passengers, well then, they should provide some distraction for me. But he answered my questions with a grunt, pulled up his collar and turned his head away and went to sleep.

Saturday morning on the autoroute was quiet. Some local delivery traffic around Lyon at about seven. The car tore on. I hoped that my police immunity lasted for the return journey but just in case it didn't, I dropped my speed to one hundred and sixty. Without the load it was a different vehicle, quite pleasant. I glanced across at my companion. The scarf had dropped slightly revealing a curved scar on his cheek. The bandit had given me instructions as to where to hand over his old man when I got to Paris – Place de la Concorde on the Tuileries side. 'My cousin meeting him would recognise the car,' he assured me. I could believe that. It would not be difficult with *Paris Matin* emblazoned down each side.

I started to slow for the péage. My passenger woke up, gazed at the toll booths, pulled out his newspaper and tugged up his scarf . Quite a joke, I thought. I carry a ton of *Paris Matins* down to Nice and return with an old age pensioner and one copy of *Nice Soir*. Ah, the mysteries of commerce.

We cleared the booths and as I accelerated away I said, 'I'm stopping for the toilet at the next services. In about ten minutes time.' He grunted.

Granddad decided to stay in the car. I just hoped he was not incontinent. I took the keys and walked across to the toilet. The backs of my eyes were hot with fatigue. The sun was up now so the driving was easy but the night driving had taken its toll. I cursed Pino. I cursed Granddad and then I splashed some water on my face. It made my eyes sting with the dirt of my night travelling.

The cafe was bright and inviting. I glanced across at the car. Granddad was under his newspaper. No sense in disturbing him. I drank a *double express,* ate a croissant and flirted with the cheeky girl. The will to live began to flow back into me. Another three hours and I could be home in bed. Three hours. My head was beginning to buzz with tiredness. I took a shot of *pastis,* neat, and then walked back to the car as it burned its way to my stomach.

It was half past ten when my crackling eyes gratefully caught sight of the top of the obelisk of Luxor as we crossed the Pont de la Concorde. I swept to the side of the square by the gated entrance to the gardens.

'Here we are,' I said.

The old man pulled his scarf up against his face again. I had not realised that he was that frail. I had been lucky that he had not swallowed his birth certificate on the journey.

'Is that your family?'

He looked without recognition at a man who was approaching us from the shadow of the gateway. The Paris branch of the family obviously came from a different stock from the Meridional one. This man had an almost Nordic face, white, with a nose like the handle on a gas tap. The Paris section was also more affluent. He wore a silk tie for a start. He also walked with the gravity of those who believed themselves to be part of the ruling class, if there was such a thing in this egalitarian France.

He went straight to the passenger door, opened it and helped the old man out. I got out at the same time. He glanced across at me over the roof.

'*Merci monsieur,*' he said then he bent to something the old man said. 'No, don't trouble yourself,' he assured him, 'he's been paid.' He glanced across at me again as he steered the man away. '*Au revoir.*' He dismissed me.

So Pino had been paid for this as well? As I drove the car back to the depot I had a feeling that Pino would be keeping out of my way for a few days. I looked down at the *Nice Matin* that Granddad had left on the seat. That was all I had got out of the whole night's work. One bloody newspaper.

I took a taxi back to the rue Amélie. I decided that I was worth it and anyway I would add the fare to the bill that I was mentally charging up for Pino. The Saturday morning street was in full swing but the taxi driver had to wake me up.

'What number?'

'Drop me outside the commissariat.'

'As you like.' He made it sound as if I needed my head examined.

The cop with no chin watched me as I climbed from the cab.

'What were you doing in the back?' he asked.

'There was no room in the boot,' I said as I slammed the door. 'Don't you ever get birds nesting in that moustache?'

'Oh very funny, Lebatard.' He sounded my name with relish. 'Good name that – Lebatard.' I had heard it all before. It amused me about as much as the *Vache-qui-rit* poster.

'Salut Jo-Jo. You look rough.' Marguerite was washing her restaurant doorstep.

'Thanks. You'd know about people looking rough, with the food you serve them.' She swore and tried to slop dirty water onto my shoes. It slapped back in the bucket and burst over her apron. 'Grita's spilled the soup!' I called into the dark restaurant. 'Make another bucketful.'

As I entered my building the concierge glowered at me through her net curtains. She pulled open the door and thrust a couple of envelopes at me. 'Your mail. I would have given it to you last night but you didn't come in.'

'How do you know? Did you wait up all night for me? I might have gone out early this morning.'

She narrowed her pig eyes at me and shivered her chins.

'You didn't,' she said. 'I know.'

'Did you miss me?'

'Nobody would miss you.'

She was right but I was not going to agree with her. I took out my key and dragged it down the bars of the bird cage. The bird squawked and cowered in the far side.

''Morning, vulture.'

'And you leave my bird alone.'

'Sorry. Thought it was your husband.'

Bed. That was what I wanted. Thirty hours I had been awake. Wrestling with Mathilde; buying her lunch. Wrestling with problems. Buying time? Driving. Driving. Driving. The world was swimming before my fatigued eyes as I unlocked my door. My room welcomed me. The wardrobe was open, clothes thrown on the floor, the drawers upended on the bed. My few papers were scattered to the four corners. I checked the door lock. Scratch marks showed where it had been picked. But why leave the mess? It was not the professionalism that I would have expected of Reinhardt. Perhaps he was trying to tell me something. I was not listening. I did not care. I dragged the cover from the bed and dumped everything onto the floor. I pulled off my shoes. I lay down. I closed my eyes. Glorious.

It was early evening when I awoke. I felt as sour as the taste in my mouth. For a while I watched the snap changing pattern of light thrown onto my ceiling by the television belonging to the old biddy across the courtyard. Then I joined up the cracks in the grey plaster to make rivers, and carved animals from the damp stains by the window. I kept my eyes high. I did not want to look at the room made more squalid by the chaos of my life that I knew was still strewn about. Yeah, I liked that expression: 'the chaos of my life.' Who was I kidding? My life was not chaos. There was nothing in it for it to be chaotic. It was empty. Empty of purpose, empty of achievement, empty of acclaim. Empty of tenderness.

Pino. What would I not say to him when I saw him next? After five minutes of reflection, even I had run out of curses. He had drunk his péage money, drunk his passenger money and then sat back to let an idiot dive in to do the work. I could not fault him. I would have done the same in his place.

It only took me half an hour to clear up after Reinhardt's visit. It was not as if I had a mansion full of heirlooms to re-arrange. The clothes went into the wardrobe, the papers into the drawer and Annick's photograph back into its frame. That had been a touch of spite typical of Reinhardt and yet, Annick would not have cared a fig. The serene gaze from her eyes was a constant and painful reminder to me.

'He is a wise man who knows that a woman's opinion is worth nought; and yet he is a fool if he heeds it not.' That was Racine or Descartes or some other pompous pate-scratcher, I couldn't remember which. Perhaps it was me.

I sat on my bed looking at the photograph. Where was she now? It would be somewhere safe, with a person who cared for her... and showed it. Someone reliable.

I decided that first thing on Monday morning I would go looking for a job. But it was Saturday night so I dressed in something smart, courtesy of Mathilde Sikorski, and strode down the street like a strutting cock. I dined at the Madeleine on the boulevard where the waiter bowed low and discreetly below the light of the chandeliers and whispered, 'Sorry, Jo-Jo, need to see your money first,' as he handed me the menu. Oh yes, I was known in all the best places.

After dinner I walked back up the rue St. Dominique. When I reached the bright lights of the Ciné Dominique, I stopped before the posters. In the open foyer, Miriam was cashing up, her vast bosom wobbling as she flicked coins from the counter into her hand and then dropped them into the trays in the cash box.

'Good house?' I asked.

'Fair enough for a Saturday night.' She snapped the box shut and slid it into the safe under the desk. 'Jean Gabin always pulls them in.' I nodded vaguely. 'Do you want to see it?' She slammed the safe and switched off the foyer lights. 'Film started about ten minutes ago. There's space in the back row.'

I settled into the comforting dark; cocooned in a cohort of cinéphiles. The felt-lined door thudded gently behind me and in a waft of heavy perfume, Miriam dropped into the seat at the side of me. I put my arm around her and she leaned her head onto my shoulder. You see, somebody likes me.

Miriam rented a two-bed flat behind the Ecole Militaire. At ten o' clock on a Sunday morning you could walk from there to the rue Amélie without seeing another living soul. I almost managed it. Twenty metres from my door I saw three men in a black Renault 16. But they saw me first.

'Alright LeBatard, just move nice and easy.'

I do not like strangers poking hard things in my ribs and pretending that they have got a gun.

'You've been watching too many Westerns, *mon petit,*' I said. Then I stamped on his instep and elbowed him in the gut. I should have followed up with a punch to his jaw but the other two got to me first. They grabbed an arm each and twisted it back.

'Careful! Boss said not to mark him,' one reminded the other.

'I'll bloody mark him,' my first assailant promised.

'Lay off, Denis,' the driver warned. '"No marks, no cuts, no bruises," the boss said.'

'How kind of him,' I observed, 'but I'm not in the same union.' I crashed my shoe squarely into the driver's left knee.

'Bastard!' he said and twisted my arm harder.

'Well at least you've got my name right.' I gritted my teeth as discreetly as I could. Why give them the pleasure of knowing that they were hurting me?

'Get him in the car,' Denis grunted.

'What happens if I don't want to go?'

'Boss didn't say that we couldn't break your arms. He just said, "no marks, no cuts, no bruises".'

'And who is going to stop me from climbing out again? You

won't get three of us in the back of that car.'

I was wrong. And handcuffed. We drove down the rue Amélie, past the commissariat. They lifted a hand to the policeman; he saluted. That told me all I needed to know. The Renault lurched into the boulevard like a drunkard dancing on an escalator.

'How long has he held a licence?' I asked.

'Can't you shut him up?' the driver complained and thumped us through another gear change. The spring on a Renault clutch was as strong as a crocodile's jaws. His left knee must have been giving him agony. Hurrah.

'Better hood him up,' the driver suggested and darkness descended as they pulled a sack over my head and shoulders. It was made from a thick black cloth that smelled of rubber. It reminded me of the anti-gas capes in the army.

So, they did not want anybody to see me. I wondered why? The car accelerated down the boulevard and then tyre-shrieked into a side road. They were doing the full MGM job. Any minute now they would tell me they were going to take me for a ride.

'Rue des Mousssons? That's a stupid way to go on a Sunday,' I said as I heard the engine noise bouncing back at us from the narrow sides of the street. 'The barriers will be up for the market. You'll only have to back up when you get to the end.'

'He's right,' Denis admitted. 'You should take the next left.'

'Or turn here by the coiffeur and cut back to the boulevard,' I suggested from the obscurity of my sack. I was enjoying myself.

'*Merde!*' the driver shouted and we slithered to a halt. I could tell he had turned in his seat. 'How is he directing us? He's not supposed to know where he is. Can he see out of that bag?'

'Of course not.' Rough hands pulled the cloth tighter around me. 'He's only guessing.'

'Careful!' I said. 'No cuts, no marks, no bruises. Remember?'

'We had better take him for a ride.'

'At last! I thought you had forgotten the script,' I said, but I was thinking furiously. The purpose of the bag was not to preserve my anonymity but to stop me from seeing where I was being taken. I had no doubts as to who would be at my destination. The sinister aspect was that this was obviously an undercover operation involving undeclared premises. There would be no rules, no accountability and no explanations.

The car started up again. I concentrated hard. He took a sharp left; that would be the rue de l'Université. If the next turn was a wide right, that would be the Avenue Bosquet. I felt the car check slightly. Of course. There was a red light but he would jump it on a Sunday. We turned wide.

'Not saying so much now, smartarse. Lost your way?'

'You've just turned from the Avenue Rapp into the Avenue de la Bourdonnais. Call if you need any more help,' I said. I thought they might swallow that. I knew that we were in the Avenue Bosquet heading towards the Seine.

There was a sort of rustle of contentment. They thought they had fooled me. I had fooled them. But I still had to assimilate all the clues. Engine noise bouncing back from parked cars meant that we were in narrow streets; squealing tyres meant tarmac – it could be a bus lane; rumbling tyres was pavé. I needed to keep track of where we were but convince them that, really, I thought I was elsewhere.

We were still in avenues, not streets. Would they cross the Seine or turn along the quays on the left bank? A right turn, tyres squealing from the tarmac of the boulevard to the rumbling of the pavé. So it's not the bridge. We're staying this side of the river. Where was I supposed to think I was?

'Just passing in front of the Ecole Militaire,' I said. Someone grunted. 'I expect you'll turn down the Avenue de Sufferen.'

'Don't interrupt him,' the driver commanded. 'He might get us lost.' This was a veiled instruction to the others to keep quiet.

How I kept up the apparently inane chatter whilst driving two routes in my head with my eyes shut I cannot say. By the time that I had us driving past the Gare Montparnasse, I had recognised the noise of the brakes on an Air France coach as it squeaked down the ramp to the Invalides Aerogare and my suggestion that we were running alongside the cemetery on the boulevard Edgar Quinet would not have amused them had they known that I had heard the engine on the Bateau Mouche chugging under the Pont de la Concorde as we passed over the Seine.

Then the driver decided to amuse himself. I knew we had driven straight onto the Place de la Concorde towards the Rue Royale because I had felt the car nose into the dip in the pavé at the end of the bridge but suddenly I was thrown onto the jailer on my right as the car made a tight turn. Where would that be? Oh, of course, he was driving around the obelisk in the middle of the

Place de la Concorde. But he continued to turn. Round we went, again and again. I tried to count the turns; four and we would be pointing northwards again. But I suspected that he was driving out and back, across the square, inventing corners where there were none in order to confuse me.

'That's cheating,' I complained.

'All part of the game, old chap.'

'You'll get me lost if you carry on like that. How's the knee?'

'Bastard.'

Concentrate. He can come out of the Place how many ways? The Rue St Florentin I would recognise; it was narrow and I would hear the motor. The Rue Royale and the Champs Elysées were both wide but the turn into the former was tighter. He could go up the lane by the stamp market but on a Sunday we would be crawling. If he went back over the bridge, I would feel the bump. If he turned down onto the Quai des Tuileries would I hear the sound of the motor bouncing back from the wall on my left? I was not so sure.

'He's very quiet, Denis, do you think he's asleep?'

'I'm praying for your souls; it is Sunday. By the way, are you lot getting overtime for this? Is that why you're wasting time?'

He has turned right. A narrow street. We are off the pavé of the Place de la Concorde and onto tarmac. That must be the rue St Florentin. Unless we were already in the rue Royale, which is also cobbled. In which case he has turned into the rue St Honoré. So he could turn into the Place Vendome or... or.... I knew they had beaten me. I was lost.

'All right. I give in. You will have to find your own way from here.'

'We'll manage.'

They had beaten me. I must be getting old. I strained all my senses to pick up clues but they were scarce. Being transported in a black bag was confusing all my senses. I even began to question my orientation. Which way up was I? What was that smell? Sickly sweet; I had smelled it before. And then we dived underground. It was a car park. The tyres were squealing at walking pace on the smooth floor covering. The noise was closed in, then it stopped. The driver had switched off the motor.

'I should have known your outfit lived in the sewers.'

It was a valiant attempt at a witicism.

7

With my wrists linked before me by the handcuffs, I stumbled up concrete stairs. There was no smell of stale urine. This was not a public underground car park. I switched off my mind. I no longer felt any need to decipher clues.

'Take his bonnet off and let's see if we can stand the shock,' a familiar voice said.

I squinted as light suddenly flooded my world. It was coming from two fluorescent tubes in the ceiling. The room was square with no windows. The walls were lined with that board which is drilled with little holes; the board that government departments worldwide think is soundproof but is just about as effective as a glass anvil.

'Herr Reinhardt!' I snapped and clicked my heels.

He clenched his teeth, took a pace forwards and slapped my face hard. I could feel my cheek stinging but I did nothing. I had already scored a point.

'Naughty, naughty. Don't you remember – no cuts, no marks, no bruises?' I taunted.

'Oh I might just make an exception for you, LeBatard. Sit him down.'

I was pulled roughly into an upright chair with wooden arms. Those wooden arms were important. I watched as my captors chained my wrists to them. And my ankles to the cross bars.

'Are you worried I might pick at my spots?'

'You and I are going to have a little talk,' Reinhardt declared.

'I bet you try to frighten all your guests that way. What do you want me to do? Beg for mercy?'

'What a vaccuous idiot you always were. And you're not even funny.'

'At least I'm French.'

He flinched but did nothing. Two nil. I was doing well.

He turned to the others and jerked his head.

'All right you lot, out!'

They went. He walked around me, peering at me as if I were an exhibit in the Natural History Museum.

'Now listen to me, LeBatard. However much I might loathe you; however much of a complete and utter wastrel you might be; however clever you might think yourself; you have really stirred up the hornet's nest this time. By teaming up with Mathilde Sikorski you have got yourself into something far bigger than you could imagine. You are not big enough to handle this. You don't know the half of it.'

I don't know the tenth of it, I thought. How was I teaming up with Mathilde Sikorski? I thought back to Reinhardt's sudden arrival at Josef's flat and how his manner had changed when Mathilde had quoted me as saying that I was 'only in it for the money'. That had meant something to him. Had she said it on purpose? Had she known what the effect would be? What could she be up to that I didn't know about? Practically anything, I realised. Much as it hurt me, I decided to revert to honesty.

'I have absolutely no idea what you are talking about, Reinhardt.' I waggled my wrists. 'Be a good chap and take these cuffs off so that I can punch your face.'

'When I've finished with you, you won't be able to punch a metro ticket.'

'Oh very funny. I know you didn't think that one up by yourself. I've heard it before on a Fernand Reynaud tape.'

His smile was broad and downturned, like the radiator grille on a Simca Aronde. He pulled up a chair in front of me. In true cinema tradition he spun it around and sat on it to face me over the back. Perhaps he was scared that I might try to kick him in the crotch despite my bindings.

He was right.

'No matter how you try to collect, we'll trace it back to you,' he warned. 'You'll never live to enjoy it.'

'I wish I knew what you were talking about.'

Collect? Collect what? Are we talking about money? Was this the pension that Josef had prepared for himself?

'Ask your partner: Mathilde Sikorski.'

He sucked his lips in reflection. His musings annoyed me.

'You don't stand a chance, Reinhardt. You're not her type.' I saw no reason why he should enjoy his fantasies.

'And you are?'

I tried an enigmatic smile. I probably looked as if I had toothache. 'Reinhardt, why don't you just tell me what you want? It might save you a lot of time.'

'We'll get them eventually.'

'Jolly good. Can I go now?'

'We'll get them because you are going to tell me where they are.' The light tubes reflected in his spectacles like thick white eyebrows. I thought quickly. He does not know the vastness of my ignorance. He looked at me like a park keeper deciding whether I had paid for my chair. He flexed his fingers.

'You are not going to crack your finger joints are you?' I gave a shudder. 'I can't abide that.'

'Always the clown.' He shook his head and got up. 'I'll give you some time to think. Nobody knows you are here. You don't know where you are.'

'Now you're sounding like a philosopher.'

'I might come back in an hour. I might come back tomorrow.'

'Don't expect me to wait up for you.'

'You'll be here.'

'I might want to go to the toilet.'

'Tie a knot in it.'

Time passes slowly when you only have cream-painted sound board to look at. After a while the dots start to dance at the corner of your eye when you are not looking directly at them. You turn your head and they stop. Did that one move? There it goes, it did it again. Or is it just a fly?

I knew that there were other people in the building; I could detect vague mumblings of movement, but what they were doing and who they were, I had no way of knowing. Where was this place? It would not be at an official address, that, I was sure of. It would be one of those discreet outposts that the Ministry of Defence retains for occasional use as needed. Why worry? It did not matter where I was.

How long could I hide my ignorance? The longer I succeeded, the greater the chance I would have of tricking

Reinhardt into divulging information that would help me. Or help us, if I was including Mathilde Sikorski. Was I including her? Was she being straight with me or just using me to her own ends? She could be doing both, of course. She probably was.

The room was stuffy. I could do with a beer. I pulled at my manacles and managed only to bruise my wrists. I flexed my feet. The chair was screwed to the floor. What am I doing here?

'Reinhardt!' I shouted.

'You can shout as much as you like,' a tinny loudspeaker behind me said, 'nobody is listening.'

'I'm glad that you recognise that you are nobody.'

The speaker clicked off. Could I count that as three nil?

Two hours later, I was not so sure. My joints were stiffening, my mouth was as dry as Nefertiti's powder puff and my mind was churning. Reinhardt had given me plenty of time to think and I had not wanted it. Time to make a move.

'All right, Reinhardt, let's talk.'

'Monsieur Reinhardt is at lunch,' a minion's voice said over the speaker. 'I will give him your message when he returns.'

Very clever. I was pretty certain that Reinhardt was sitting next to the hidden announcer.

'No hurry,' I called, 'I haven't finished my coffee yet.'

That little quip cost me another hour's wait.

He picked up the chair and turned it around again. He was trying to hide a victorious smile, but not nearly hard enough.

'I didn't expect you to be reasonable,' he smirked. 'There is no point in appealing to an intellect–'

'You wouldn't know how to.'

'–when it is not there so I have to concentrate on the baser instincts.'

'Something you do know about.'

'Quite.'

'I can see that you are a busy man and I've got things to do as well. Why don't we jump the hors d'oeuvres and go straight for the *plat du jour?*'

'Excellent. So where are they?'

Merde. We were back to that again. Where were what? Perhaps I should try to look as if I knew what he meant and see if I could lead him on. He's only an Alsatian – they are not blessed with much imagination. I tried sucking on my teeth to show that I was weighing his request; my tongue stuck to the dry roof of my mouth and I nearly gagged.

'What about a drink?' I croaked. 'You can't ask me to talk with a dry mouth.'

'Water!' he called. One of his henchmen came through the door carrying a minute paper cup. 'Give him a sip.' He did. It nearly drowned me.

'Sorry,' he said. He was enjoying his revenge.

'That's enough. We don't want to soften him up.' Reinhardt watched the man leave. 'I suppose you made yourself difficult on the way here.'

'Not me. As quiet as a lamb, I was.'

'If you don't want to be a sacrificial lamb you had better start talking.'

Reinhardt must have been reading comic books.

'What do you want to know?'

He sighed theatrically. I watched his stomach. He had put on quite a bit of weight.

'Just tell us where they are and then you can go home and forget all about it.'

'What makes you think I know where they are?'

That stalled him for a second. Was that a flutter of indecision behind those steel-rimmed spectacles? And these things that I was supposed to know about – could they actually be people?

'You know where they are. And Miss Sikorski does.'

'How can you be so sure that we know?'

'Don't waste my time, LeBatard, we are sure.'

'In that case, find them yourself.'

'OK. You want to play the tough guy again. Be my guest. We'll show you how tough you are.'

He got up. The door closed. I was left looking at the panelled walls again. I had a premonition that the scoreboard was about to alter in his favour.

I started counting the dots on the wall but my eyes kept jogging up a line so I stopped. I tried twisting my head around to see if there was a camera with the loudspeaker behind me but I could not see. About half an hour later Reinhardt came back with another man who was carrying a bag and wearing a white coat.

'The doctor has come to examine you before the next stage. You see how concerned we are for your health.'

'You would do better examining that idiot's head,' I told the doctor. He ignored me. He wrapped the bladder on my arm and pumped it up to read my blood pressure.

'Good,' he said. He pushed up my shirt and listened to my heart and lungs. I did all the heavy breathing bit they always ask for. Reinhardt sat watching as if this were only the overture.

'He's got a healthy body,' the doctor said. 'Have you ever had surgery?' he asked me.

'Not really. Do you want to do some?'

'What's this scar from?'

'Appendix.'

'When was it taken out?'

'About fifteen years ago.'

'No surgery since? No general anaesthetics?'

'No.'

'Allergic to anything?'

'Only Reinhardt.'

'Penicillin?'

'No.'

'Diabetic? Fits or seizures?'

'I might have if you carry on asking me stupid questions.'

'Any heart problems? Palpitations?' I shook my head and gave him a look. 'Do you faint?'

'Only from hunger. When am I getting a meal?'

He straightened up and nodded to Reinhardt.

'Bring it in,' Reinhardt called through the door.

One of my abductors pushed into the room a chromium hospital trolley which rattled with equipment. The doctor attached one of those upside down bottles to a steel pylon and pushed a tube into it.

'Left forearm,' he said.

The attendant rolled up my left sleeve to uncover my forearm. Reinhardt's eyes were gleaming.

'Since you have decided not to co-operate and as we have the doctor here, we have decided to use a little persuasion.' I scanned the trolley for teeth pliers and things to stuff under my finger nails. 'We've found a new use for lysergic acid. You remember it's the stuff that the hippies call "LSD." They take it and see purple elephants and things.'

'That must be a relief to them.'

'And when they are hallucinating, they can be remarkably susceptible to suggestion. And garrulous.'

The attendant was dabbing my forearm with alcohol.

'Drugs are not my scene. I am too old for all that stuff.'

'We think the whole world will benefit from a little medical experiment.'

It was too ironic for words. But I managed to find some.

'Of course, doctor, I knew I had seen you before.' The doctor started in alarm. 'Medical experiments on prisoners? It was Auschwitz, wasn't it?' I nodded my head towards the door. 'I bet as soon as Reinhardt moved in he insisted they install gas out there, didn't he?'

'I don't like my patient, Mr Reinhardt.' His voice was cold and clinical.

'Nobody likes him,' Reinhardt reassured him, then the doctor jabbed the tube into my vein.

'Christ, you could have warned me! Are you trying to hurt me?'

The doctor said nothing. That was somehow sinister.

The attendant taped the tube to my forearm and the doctor connected the other end to the bottle.

'It's not pure LSD, of course,' Reinhardt explained. 'It's been cut with another little cocktail of things to help you along. And this apparatus allows us to monitor the dose, minute by minute if needed.' He pointed to the glass tap and tubes. 'Of course if you want to give in and just tell us, you could save us the expense of all these drugs.'

The doctor's finger hovered over the tap, mutely urging me to refuse. They wanted to do this. They wanted to. What are you supposed to do to counteract hallucination? Concentrate on a known fact so that you don't give anything away? But I don't know anything. What can I tell them? I don't know what they want. Think of something nice. Focus on something pleasant.

I shook my head slowly. 'Reinhardt, for the very last time, I have no idea what you want, nor where they might be, whatever or whoever they are. I have told you several times already. If you want to experiment upon me to satisfy your own pleasures, I can't stop you. But unless you kill me, I'll come after you. Pervert!'

'Unless we kill you? Now there's a real temptation.' He nodded to the doctor who turned the glass tap. A coldness began to seep into my arm. This was it then. Typical Reinhardt.

I had not seen them bring in the green and yellow lamps. When they started to flash them into my eyes I dodged my head about to try to evade the light. Then Reinhardt pushed his face up close to mine. It was a hideous face. Those steely spectacles snapped at me like mantraps and he puffed his cheeks out like a toad. How could he do that? Melting his face into a frying pan and grinning his teeth at me. Now I am up. Up in the air. Dizzy with speed. They have lifted me shoulder high and are waltzing me around the room, lurching hard into the corners and I can hear Reinhardt talking to me. Talking to me. Now there are purple and orange worms dancing out of his ears and they unleash the black ants from the walls. Think of something nice. Torrents of them rushing over me, crawling through my clothes, running in my hair. My hands are free and I beat them but still they come. The big white tent in the corner is flapping loose. I run to it and hide inside and pull the cords around me tightly; safe with something nice. Don't need any more photographs. Who wants photographs? I don't. High snowy peaks, mountains. Photographs of mountains and shadows of aeroplanes. Sliding down a mountain, snow splashing in my face, the world gone white. Not the photographs, it's the negatives. Negatives and positives. Plus and minus. Minus and plus. Plus is a big, red bloody crucifix and minus is a purple grin. Mathilde Sikorski? Why Mathilde Sikorski? Mathilde of the mountains. Big bouncing mountains leaping from her shirt. I can sing to you Mathilde, I can sing. I've got a lovely voice. You'd like it, but put those mountains away. Away with the luminous thermos flask and the glass snake. I'll sing about the negatives and the positives and why you must have them and what you must do with them. But I don't know the words give me a clue. A shiny yellow, slimy clue. I can see it creeping up the wall and flowering in a burst of ants. More ants. Black ants pelting at me. I'm positive about all the negatives and negative about all the positives. You were watching her bottom I saw you. Wriggling denim, blue and bumpy makes me go all hot and lumpy. Of course I've seen photographs. Jean Marc's got photographs. He's got hundreds of them. Snowy shadows and aeroplanes, those are your photographs. Can't trust the Japanese. What was his name? Kawasaki or Honda? Sounded like a motorbike but looked like an aeroplane. Ah, now you're being negative and I'm being positive. Cold arm again, must have left it outside the igloo. Do take that damn silly thing off your head. Can't stand painted fingernails, I've told you before. No, I lie, I've never told you. Perhaps I should. Oh no, not more ants...

Somebody was slapping my face but I did not really care. Oh all right, I'll open my eyes if you insist.

The doctor peered into my face then he straightened up.

'He's OK.'

I could have argued with his opinion but decided not to. There were no more orange worms, crawling ants or puddle faces but my eyes felt like cherries in a cocktail glass and my arms and legs were shivering. The tube had been taken out of my arm, all the equipment had disappeared and I was no longer shackled. I was obviously no threat to them now. Reinhardt was right, I could not have punched a metro ticket.

He was leaning against the table and looking at me, as if he were trying to make up his mind about something. My spirits rose slightly for he did not look smugly contented. I wanted to say something cutting but needed all my strength just to sit on the chair.

'You're a loser, LeBatard. An utter loser.' His disappointment had given way to disgust. He turned to the driver. 'Bag him up and dump him somewhere pretty, a long way from home.'

I watched the lights of the car as they disappeared down the deserted avenue. It had not occurred to me that it might be dark outside the bag as well as inside it. I looked around at the trees and focused on a solitary bench under a lamp. That would do for a start. I collapsed onto the seat and shivered with my whole stomach. Where was I? Did it matter? At least the world was no longer lunging at me in violent colours. A moth was fluttering in and out of the beam of the light. I watched it, waiting for it to turn into a bat, or a paper bag or a jet fighter.

But it was still just a moth. I tried to work out what I might have told Reinhardt but the modicum of reason that I formerly enjoyed, refused to function. I felt utterly washed up.

A convertible crawled slowly past on the opposite side of the road. The two girls looked at me. I looked back. They passed on. The story of my life. What was I doing here, on this planet? Where do the real people live?

'*Tu viens chéri?*'

The car had returned. I looked uncomprehendingly at the painted faces. I shivered again.

'I think he's ill,' the blonde said to the redhead.

'We'll go then.' She pushed the gear lever.

'No wait. We can't leave him like that. He looks ghastly.'

'He'll be no good to us then.'

'We ought to help him.'

'Nikki, just listen to the experience of an older woman...' But the blonde had opened the door. 'Nikki, be careful.'

She hobbled over to me on her high-heeled sandals and then bent to peer at my face. I blinked away any suggestion that her eyes would spin into orange snails, and looked back at her.

'Where am I?' I said.

'In the wood of course.'

In the wood. To a Parisian that could only mean the Bois de Boulogne. And if this was the Bois de Boulogne then it was obvious what two women in a convertible were doing; one was working, the other, riding shotgun.

'Nikki, come on, get back in the car. He's weird.'

'He's not well, Paulette, and he's no problem. Look at his clothes. It's decent stuff.'

'I don't care. He's probably on drugs. Get in the car.'

'What have you done to your wrists?' she asked.

I looked at them. They were marked where I must have struggled against the manacles.

'They tied me up.'

'Paulette, come and look at this.'

'I'm not getting out of the car.'

'We'll take you to the police.'

'It was they who tied me up.' It was not strictly true but I could not be bothered to make the distinction.

'You've escaped?'

'Nikki, get in the car!'

'No, they dumped me here.'

'Bastards!'

Prostitutes don't like the police either.

'Yeah, bastards.' I lifted my head and looked across at the redhead. She was older. Her hair was dyed. It would have been grey. 'Your friend is worried about you. You'd better go back.'

'Do you live near here?'

'In the Seventh.'

'That's miles away. How will you get home?'

'What time is it?'

'Where's your watch?'

'I don't wear one.' I had pawned it years ago.

'It's half past ten.'

I sighed heavily. Why was life like this?

'What's the nearest metro? Porte d'Auteuil?'

'Is Porte d'Auteuil the nearest metro?' the girl shouted to the redhead.

'Nikki, will you get in the car?'

'Paulette, where is the nearest metro?'

'It's the Porte Dauphine.' She pointed up the avenue. 'And it's that way. Now get in the car.'

'Oh that's good,' she said brightly. 'We're going your way. Come on.'

Paulette was about as trusting as a gypsy's dog. She did not think much of her friend's idea. The blonde sat in the back behind me and held a tyre lever in her hand.

'If he's any trouble Paulette, I'll bong him on the napper.'

'In the state I'm in love, you could knock me over with a sneeze.' I looked at the parcel shelf before me. 'Can I eat that apple?' I was half way through it before she assented. I ate the core and dropped the stalk over the side of the car. I wiped my mouth. I could feel a heavy stubble on my chin. 'It is Sunday night isn't it?' I asked. I was starving.

The driver glanced over her shoulder at the blonde and pulled a face. 'He gets out at the metro, Nikki.' She shot me a glance. 'It's Monday night.'

'Ah,' I said. 'That's why I'm hungry. I haven't eaten since yesterday morning.'

'*Merde,*' the blonde said. 'Look, they'll be a brasserie still open at the Porte Dauphine, we can–'

'Nikki! We leave him at the metro. That's it. Finish!'

8

One day, I vowed, I would wake up in a comfortable bed at a time of my choosing and not be startled into consciousness on a Himalayan mattress by the crash of garbage bins. I would lie gazing serenely at Renaissance cherubs beaming down at me from a frescoed ceiling; not screw my eyes up at a join-the-dots cracked plaster cartoon by Sempé.

I got up and studied my face in the mirror. Luckily, I've got a strong stomach. My eyes looked like the tail lights on a metro rake, disappearing into the grey tunnel of my face. I shaved carefully. It might not be much, but it's the only face I've got. What had I decided to do today? Oh yes, on Monday morning I was going to look for a job. Well, today is Tuesday. I lost Monday morning somewhere so that excuses me. Let's go to Café Clerc for a neat *pastis* and a stolen croissant. I felt in my pocket. Of course, I still have money. I don't need to steal a croissant.

'Where the hell have you been?' Joanne demanded. Then she saw my face. 'Christ, you look awful.'

'I feel worse. Give me a *pastis*.' I downed it in one gulp and saw the colour come back into my face. I pulled up a stool to the counter and nodded at the coffee machine. Joanne silently slid the basket of croissants over to me. It's nice being solvent. And so rare. I watched her hips shake from side to side as she wrestled with the chrome taps.

'Did Nice go off all right?' she asked.

Nice? Nice? I could hardly remember it. Then it came back to me. Pino, the bastard! I swung around.

'He's not here,' she said without looking. 'He's been lying low. Did he drop you in it?'

'And how. He drank the péage money and he drank the bunce

he was getting for bringing somebody's granddad up to Paris. I subsidized Paris Matin down the autoroute and nursemaided some mute fossil back up from Nice.' Joanne whistled. 'So he will be lying low for a while.'

'He ought to be out looking for another job,' she said as she put my coffee on the counter.

'Yes. So should I.'

'Oh I forgot, your...' She looked at me and then started her sentence again. 'She sounds quite young, your "boss".'

'Ah ha. What about her?'

'She rang a couple of times yesterday.'

'Any message?'

'No. Still got the job then?'

'As far as I know.'

'What have you done to your wrists?'

'All part of the job. I got hauled in for questioning.'

She gave me one of her exasperated looks.

'And I thought you were going straight. I suppose she is up to some sort of fiddle is she?'

'It's possible,' I said. 'It's quite probable.' She huffed at me. 'Can I phone? I've still got money.'

'Oh I can see that.' She pushed the phone over. 'You haven't pawned your clothes yet.'

'One has standards.'

'Mathilde Sikorski.'

'Mathilde, it's Joel.' I saw Joanne's eyebrows shoot up as she busied herself within earshot.

'Joel, I've been trying to get you. Where have you been?'

'Away. What do you want?'

'I've got something to show you. It was in the bookcase. I'm coming in to the centre of town. I've got to go to the Madeleine for some official stuff. Shall we meet near there?'

'Journier's? Big café on the corner?'

'With the red awning? Yes I know where you mean. I'll be there about 10.30.'

'I'll be waiting at a table outside.'

'Let's hope it doesn't rain. You know what women are like for keeping men waiting.'

'No and I hope I don't find out.'

It was a fine morning so I walked. Over the Pont de la Concorde where Reinhardt's thugs had finally confused me into submission. I even heard the *chug chug* of the Bateau Mouche again. That set me thinking. Where had they taken me? I should be able to work it out. How long had passed after we had hit the Concorde? Five minutes? Ten minutes? You can only travel a certain distance in that time. Then my logistical experience kicked in. The distance could be in any direction they chose, I did not know which. A five minute radius? A ten minute radius? In Paris? On a Sunday morning? I would not be surveying a block or two, it would be a matter of square kilometres. I could not search an urban area like that. It would take me the rest of my life.

Opposite the arcades on the rue de Rivoli the morning excursion coaches were filling up; the guides standing on the pavement checking tickets and pointing tourists to their coaches. Modern Paris in Spanish? Fifth coach along. Versailles and Fontainebleau? Right down the end, Jackie with the walkie-talkie will show you. Volkswagen microbuses were buzzing in from the hotels, squeezing between the coaches to deposit a handful of tourists, grabbing their next orders and then buzzing off again.

I watched for a minute or two. Down at the far end, by the agency I could see the top deck of the Cityscope double decker standing proud of the line of coach roofs. I could tell from where I stood that it was not the coach that I had decapitated. Still, no point in trying for a job at the agency. Daniel would not want me back. Another microbus nudged out of the rue d'Alger and crossed to the coaches. Now that was something I could do. Who supplied the microbuses? Perhaps I should try there? It required investigation, but for the moment I had a rendezvous with my current employer.

I chose a table just under the awning so that the sun would move around onto me. I ordered a coffee then changed the order for a beer. Why waste time with preliminaries? I emptied my mind of all reflection and torment and concentrated on what was sliding gently down my throat and what was parading before my eyes. Skirts had got shorter again. I approved.

'Cigarettes, matches, chewing gum, monsieur?'

The girl bounced saucily up to me. I looked at her tray and shook my head. She was probably a moonlighting student. Journier's had dressed her up in the caricature of short skirt and strapless bodice and put a bow in her hair. The customer saw lots of leg on the approach and lots of bosom above the tray and then purchased cigarettes that he did not smoke or matches that he did not want. I wondered what she offered to the ladies. She smiled frankly at my refusal and turned away, her briskness twirling the pleated fringe of her skirt and showing the backs of her thighs. She had the right idea. She would go far.

I sat back and waited. I drank beer and I waited. I waited and I drank beer. I watched the buses and taxis engaged in thrust and parry as they slalomed around the Greek temple of the Madeleine church. *'C'est magnifique mais ce n'est pas la gare,'* as some comic had put it. I watched the women strut past, noticing them perk up as they always do when they know they are being watched. And I waited and drank beer.

I saw Mathilde Sikorski some distance off. She was wearing a straight grey skirt and matching jacket, all very professional. I supposed that these were her working clothes for whenever she was doing whatever it was she did. Insurance wasn't it? As she walked, her eyes scanned the terrace of the café and her hair shook with each footfall. When I saw the height of her heels I understood why.

'Salut!' she said, then she caught sight of the empty beer glasses on the table and she frowned.

I raised my hand and she sat down, pulling the chair around to my side of the table so that she could also watch the traffic. Or the men, I suppose. She looked hard at me. I gazed serenely back.

'Am I late?' she asked, looking for my watch.

'How would I know?'

'Good God, what have you done to your wrists?' She caught my hand and twisted my forearm around. The abrasions still showed red and bruised.

'Reinhardt asked me some questions.' I pulled down the cuffs of Josef's silk shirt.

Her dark eyes opened wide. 'Did Reinhardt do that?'

'Not directly. I did it, struggling.'

'You said to me that Clever You always knew when to give in and that I would be the one to get hurt because I did not know when to surrender.'

'It doesn't hurt.'

'Oh good,' she said, and flicked my wrist with her finger.

I flinched. 'You great baby; it doesn't hurt.'

The waiter ambled along the line of tables behind us, almost as if he were going to ask her what she wanted to drink.

'I'll have a crème,' she threw over her shoulder.

'How did you know he was there?'

'Sixth sense. And that mirror.' She nodded at a pillar. 'So where were you?'

'You said I should winter on the Cote d'Azur so I went to Nice for the weekend.' I dropped my copy of *Nice Soir* in her lap. 'I brought you back a souvenir.'

'You're not lying?'

'Would I lie to you?'

'You know damn well you would.'

'And you would do the same to me. Probably already have. So now we've got the undying love and devotion sorted out, what is the news?'

'Just a minute. Tell me what Reinhardt wanted to know. What did he ask you?'

I gazed at the *'Eminence'* advert on the number 52 bus. It was trying to squeeze past the *Compagnie des Eaux* van which had parked with two wheels on the sidewalk.

'I don't know if I can tell you.'

'Oh well,' she snapped, 'if that is how far you trust me, then we are wasting our time altogether.'

'Not altogether. It's quite pleasant just sitting here in the sunshine, drinking beer.'

'It might be for you!' She stood up.

'Oh do sit down. Don't be so bloody prickly.'

'Don't you–'

'Shut up and sit down.' I nodded towards the figure of the waiter shambling towards us. 'Here comes your coffee.'

She glowered silently whilst the coffee was placed before her. The waiter glanced from her to me. I smiled up at him. 'Thanks,' I said. He looked away and wandered off. 'I can't tell you what Reinhardt wanted to know: I can't remember. They pumped me full of drugs to try to make me talk.'

She stared at me. 'You're joking! The old "truth drug" trick? You're making it up.'

'It was LSD actually.' I thought that little disclosure might win me some respect.

'Lsd won't hurt you, as long as you keep clear of balconies and windows. Did you feel you wanted to fly?'

'I thought I was flying at one point.'

'Yes, I always felt like that. That's how it gets you. You're all right as long as you don't actually try to fly. Lsd? Nothing to write home about.'

Now it was my turn to stare. 'How do you know?'

'University,' she shrugged. 'We all tried it. And cannabis. It's part of the education.' She looked at my surprised face. 'You're a bit behind the times.'

'Apparently so.'

She smiled quietly into her coffee cup, the corners of her mouth dimpling with impish malice.

'I bet you were a sight. Pompous Jo-Jo, riding a giraffe or some such thing.' She giggled. 'I wish I had been there.'

'Well if you had, perhaps you could have made yourself useful and taken notes or something.' I was short with her. 'It wasn't pure lsd.'

'That's always the problem, getting good grade stuff.'

'No, I mean they had mixed it with other chemicals.'

'Yeah, they adulterate it like that to make it go further but they still charge you the same price, you know. It's an awful racket.' She shook her head sadly.

'Look!' I said angrily, 'I'm not talking about some cissy student party with your long-haired boyfriends slouching around on giant bean bags smoking funny grass, this was an undercover operation where they tied me to the chair–'

'Kinky!'

'–and injected me with a cocktail of diabolical substances that completely altered my perspective on the whole world.'

'Yeah, of course, your metabolism is less able to cope with it the older you get. But still, there's hope for you yet if it gave you a new perspective on life.' I sensed that my jaw was working up and down on its own. I had run out of words and opinions. 'As you have been unable to add anything useful to our combined knowledge shall I show you what I found?'

I nodded. Mathilde was right. I had nothing I could add to our understanding of what was going on. She tugged a tattered envelope from her bag and handed it to me. I took out the folded sheet of paper and spread it out on the table top. It was some kind of document written in Arabic.

'What is it?' I asked.

'I've no idea.'

'Looks like a legal document. A will perhaps?'

'Could be.' She gazed out into the street. I thought she could have shown more interest.

'Where did you find it?'

'It was in the bookshelf. Hidden in a book.'

'Don't you think you are being a bit dramatic?' I was still seething from her trivial treatment of my horrific session with Reinhardt. 'I bet it wasn't hidden. Josef had probably just put it there to keep it flat. He was probably using it for a bookmark. It might have been nothing to do with him. Perhaps it was already in the book when he bought it.'

She sighed and dragged her eyes back from the traffic.

'Listen, when I said it was hidden in a book, that is what I meant. Papa had cut out the middle of the pages leaving the outsides intact to keep it looking like an ordinary book.'

I turned the paper over and studied the fiscal stamp at the bottom and tried to decipher the rubber stamps.

'What was the book?' I asked.

'Does it matter?'

'It does if you want me to believe you.' I was still annoyed with her.

'The Bible,' she said through gritted teeth. 'Satisfied?'

'I believe you.' I glanced past her to where the cigarette girl was leaning towards a client. 'It's almost worth rolling her a franc just to watch her bend down to pick it up,' I said.

'What?' She had been looking down the street again. She followed my gaze. 'Oh you men, you're all the same!'

'I'll take that as a compliment.'

'Idiot.' She caught the waiter's eye as he passed down the terrace. 'Have you got problems with your water?'

'What?' The waiter was nonplussed.

She nodded at the waterworks van.

'Problems with your water?'

The waiter glanced at the van.

'Nah, not us. Must be in the building above.' He jerked his head at the apartments. He started to move on.

'Was it there yesterday?'

'What?

'The waterworks van. Was it there yesterday?'

'Oh Christ, I don't know. Um, no. He turned up this morning, about an hour ago. OK?'

'Thank you,' she smiled at him. He scowled back.

'Do you fancy him?' I said. 'I didn't think much of your pick up line. At least I got a smile from the cigarette girl.'

'Cretin!'

'Well I can't sit here being complimented.' I stood up. 'I'm fed up with this game. I'm going to get a proper job.'

'Just sit down.' Her voice was quiet. I hadn't heard it like that before so I sat. Always ready for a new experience, me. 'Whilst you have been leching after girls young enough to be your daughter–'

'I never even winked at you.'

'I wasn't talking about me. In any case, I am far too old to be your daughter.'

'Thank Christ for that. I thought I was going to make an embarrassing discovery.'

'How many beers have you had?'

I counted the glasses. 'Six.'

'Oh, so you are still sober then.'

'And a *pastis* at breakfast.'

'One day I shall get you drunk to see if you make more sense that way.'

'You wouldn't be able to afford it.'

'I'd use your money,' she smirked. 'Just see if you can recall last week. You took me out to lunch at the brasserie at the corner of my street.'

'Yes I remember, you were quite amenable. Almost a different person.'

'That goes for you too.'

'But that was last Thursday. Since then I have had my bedsit turned upside down, I have driven to Nice and back in a day with a ton of newspapers and have been abducted by Reinhardt's thugs, tied to a chair, injected full of drugs and then dumped two days later in the Bois de Boulogne. Oh, and I went to the cinema.' I didn't think it necessary to drag Miriam into the discussion.

'What was the film?'

'*Remorques.* Jean Gabin. Before your time.'

'He plays a tug boat captain at Brest or Le Havre. Who was it who played the moll? Arletty?'

'I can't remember. You know I never look at women. What has this got to do with anything?'

'Nothing whatsoever,' she said, and looked directly into my face. 'Now keep looking this way until I have finished. I don't want you to give the game away. Do you remember that when we were sitting at the Place d'Italie, there was a *Compagnie des Eaux* van parked at the kerb?'

My eyes began to stray. She took my hands in hers on the table top. It stopped my attention from wandering in a dangerous direction. Rather ironic, that. Ten years earlier it would have started my attention wandering in a dangerous direction. I searched my memory.

'Can't say that I do.'

'It was parked on the crossing at the corner.'

'OK. If you say so. What of it?'

'Well, there is one parked on the pavement just here.'

'So? They've got problems.'

'Have you seen anybody get in or out of the van since you have been here?'

'No, but then I've been leching at teenagers haven't I?'

'Don't you think it strange that whenever we meet at a café a waterworks van turns up?'

I nearly turned my head but she squeezed my hands.

'Will you promise me to do that every time I try to look away? I like it. It reminds me of something that used to happen to me when I was handsome.'

'I will just have to risk your behaviour.' She sighed and released my hands. I blew her a kiss and turned on my chair.

I picked up my latest beer and held it to my face whilst I looked at the van. Then I put the glass down and stretched out my legs. She was absolutely right. Now I remembered. There had been a *Compagnie des Eaux* van at the Place d'Italie and it was just after Reinhardt had left us. And now there was one here.

I put my hand across and held hers on the table. I smiled into her face in as good an impression of affection as I could muster. She didn't quite recoil. I can be quite a good actor sometimes.

'There's a clever girl,' I said. 'I do remember. What you have to do now is ask me sweet little questions so that I can look into the distance whilst I contemplate tender answers.'

'What kind of questions?'

I turned back to face the street.

'That will do for a start,' I said as I allowed my gaze to settle abitrarily on the van. 'It looks pretty good. Quite authentic.'

'What does?'

I laughed easily and squeezed her hand.

'Why, the van of course.' I turned back towards the street, smiling contentedly and gave the van another good scrutiny. 'I'm trying to find out how they are using it.'

'I don't know what you mean.'

I glanced up at the roof whilst I appeared to consider this statement. 'Three aerials.' I pouted. 'That looks a bit greedy for a water company. I bet they are in contact with Reinhardt.'

'What are they doing?'

'Watching us, I expect.'

'I don't like the thought of that.' She folded up the paper and put it back in the envelope. 'How can they see us? The van's got no windows down the side.'

'That is what I am trying to work out. They might have people outside the van watching us and reporting in.'

'What would be the point of that?'

'Ah, wait a minute. I've got it.' I turned and took her hands as she had done mine. 'This is to keep you from slapping my face which is how our encounters usually end. Do keep smiling,' I said. 'You're supposed to be enjoying my company, remember?'

She threw me a beautiful smile which she somewhat spoiled by qualifying it with, 'I'd rather stick my head down the toilet.'

'Never mind, I thought you already had.' Her nails dug into my palms. I smiled bravely. 'They are using those spy-glass things that people put on their front doors. Do you know the type of thing that I mean? It looks like a little telescope set into the panel. All you see on the outside is a lens about the size of a button.'

'I haven't noticed any.'

'Look over my left shoulder. The dark blue letter *C* of *"Compagnie"*. At the bottom of the curve can you see a rivet?'

'Yes.'

'Well it isn't. The ones either side are rivets. That one is a lens.'

'Oh yes.'

'And the same with *"Eaux"*. Bottom of the letter *E*.'

'You're right.'

'I am sometimes.' I picked up her hand and kissed it.

'Why did you do that?'

'For the devilment of it; knowing that they were looking and you could not slap my face this time.'

'I'll save it for later.'

'Well, that's encouraging. At least you envisage a "later". What are we going to do about that?' I nodded at the envelope.

'We need to get it read by somebody.'

'Nestor.'

'What?'

'I've just thought of somebody: Nestor. He's a tour guide. He reads Arabic and Persian. He works just around the corner at the Cityscope agency. He'd cast an eye over it to give us an idea of what it says. I could go there...' I paused, thinking that I would probably not get over the threshold. 'Well, I could try to get hold of him. I know where he hangs out.'

She nodded slowly. Her hair bounced again. God knows what they spray on it nowadays.

'OK. Could you ask him about it? I've got to see some more narrow-minded civil servants in dusty offices.'

'Yes...' I faltered.

'What's the matter now?'

'I was looking at the cigarette girl.'

'Oh really!'

'*Mademoiselle!*' I called and then watched her as she flounced up to our table. She grinned when she realised I was looking. 'You know, you do that rather well,' I said.

'*Merci, monsieur.*' She bobbed and so did her bosom.

Mathilde scowled at me and then stared in surprise when I said, 'My companion would like some chewing gum. What have you got that is really chewy?'

The girl glanced unsurely at Mathilde. 'The spearmint is the normal stuff. I suppose the orange might be a bit more chewy.'

'Fine. I'll take the orange.' I paid her. 'And here's a franc for your wiggles.'

'*Merci beaucoup.*' She waltzed away, wiggling her hips and grinning at me in the mirror. I winked at her.

'Oh honestly!' Mathilde exclaimed.

'No harm done. She could make an old man very happy.'

'You're not an old man and you don't deserve that kind of

happiness.'

'I wasn't talking about me.' I unwrapped the gum and handed her two sticks. 'Get chewing,' I said.

'I didn't want the gum. You only ordered it so that you could ogle that girl's legs.'

'Right. Now I'm paying the price.' I masticated gingerly. 'It's revolting but it's got to be done.' I pushed the gum back at her.

'I don't like chewing gum,' she said firmly.

'I thought kids were always chewing the stuff. I can't see why you are making such a fuss.'

'I am not a kid.'

'I detest the muck,' I said, 'but I'm doing my duty.'

'It serves you right.'

'So you won't help me?'

'Certainly not.'

'The things I've done for you and you won't even chew some gum for me.'

'What things?'

'I am too much of a gentleman to embarrass you by listing them. God, this stuff is awful.' I put her sticks in my mouth as well.

'Good. I hope she was worth it.'

I looked her in the eyes as I masticated.

'I hope she is worth it,' I said. I laid down the money for her coffee on the table. 'Get ready to move smartly. I'll be back.'

I stood up and wandered down the pavement, chewing furiously. Then I turned and ambled back, pressing a plug of chewing gum onto each of the spy lenses of the van as I passed. Mathilde had followed my move. She jumped up as I returned.

'Let's go!' I grabbed her hand and dragged her clacking on her heels into the passage at the side of the café. We rattled through the gallery and burst out into the rue du Boissy d'Anglas, laughing like a couple of schoolkids.

'Your Monsieur Reinhardt will not be laughing,' she warned. Her eyes were sparkling.

'He would not have been in the van. That's too much like drudgery.' I tried to sound menacing. 'And he won't be laughing when I next meet him. Right,' I said briskly, 'plan of campaign.'

'Hang on a minute, let me put myself together.' With a swish she twisted her narrow skirt back around her waist. 'I didn't know when I got dressed this morning that you had athletics in mind.'

'You moved pretty quickly back there. Very impressive.'

'What are you looking at now?'

'I was just thinking what a small waist you have.'

She looked down and pulled her blouse together.

'Liar! You weren't looking at my waist.'

'They are part of your waist.'

'Is that all you think of?'

'Don't flatter yourself.' I held out my hand. 'Give me the document and I will go and find Nestor. I'm going in that direction anyway to see about a job.'

'Getting bored with my employment?'

'Not bored, no. I could never get bored whilst I run the risk of being kidnapped, drugged, beaten and locked up. But much as I enjoy it, it doesn't pay the rent. I need a proper job.'

'Something to keep you out of mischief?' She handed me the envelope.

'I'll go and find Nestor and ask him to read it for us. Just to decide whether it is worth translating properly. You go and do your business with your civil servants and then we'll meet this afternoon somewhere. What do you think of that?'

'Good idea. Four o' clock on the roof of La Samaritaine.'

'On the roof? In this heat?'

'They've got parasols.'

'But why on earth?'

'Because, you simple-minded man...' She tapped my nose with her index finger. '...Reinhardt will never get a waterworks van up four flights of stairs.'

'Yeah, good point.'

I stood inspecting the curve of her skirt as she walked away. She turned after a few paces and looked back at me.

'You're wasting your time if you're expecting a wiggle.'

'Pity,' I said. 'I'll use my imagination.'

'You do that.'

I walked past the Cityscope agency on the far side of the street, behind the cover of stationary coaches. When I saw the sandwich counter on the corner of the rue du 29 Juillet I remembered that all that I had eaten since breakfast was six glasses of beer and five sticks of chewing gum. I ordered a sandwich and waited for the morning excursion coaches to return to drop off the guides outside the agency. Soon I heard the muffled thudding of an exhaust brake as the first coach slowed for the guide to alight. I recognised her although all I could remember of her name was that it was Polish. She had a pale watery face, lots of wispy hair and an accent straight from the coal mines at Lens. She came into the bar, her head lowered over her purse as she counted her tips.

'Any good?' I asked.

She looked up.

'Oh hello Jo-Jo, long time no see. Yeah, not bad. Twenty five francs. Modern Paris in English only. Child's play. I was lucky. Marlise had to do it in Spanish and Italian and she got that Portuguese driver who smells.'

'How's Daniel?' I nodded towards the agency.

'Daniel? Oh he's up at the Opera office now. Jackie is in charge down here at Tuileries. He's a pain. Thinks he's the only man with a penis.'

'Well he's not.'

'Oh don't you start.' She snapped her purse shut. 'Zazie!' she shouted at the barman, 'give me a beer and a ham sandwich.'

'Wait your turn, Mophead!'

'And no mustard this time,' she added.

'I never put mustard in.'

'You did yesterday, unless the ham was off.'

'*Salope!*'

'*Cocu!*'

I grabbed my sandwich from its plate as soon as it arrived. I thought it important to immediately establish my proprietorship.

'Sorry to interrupt your slanging match,' I said. 'Have you seen Nestor today?'

'Nestor? Which one is he?'

'Old chap, silver hair, wears a blue jumper.'

'Older than you?'

'About two generations older.'

'Can't think who he is.' She nodded towards a girl in a red skirt who had just come in. 'Ask Marlise. She likes old men. Marlise!' she shouted, 'You like old men don't you?'

'Pervert!' the girl retorted. 'Zazie, give me a white wine and make sure it's cool.' She looked at me. 'I'm starving.'

I poked my sandwich at her.

'Thanks.' She twisted off the end. The barman winced.

'I bet that hurt,' he said.

'S'alright,' Marlise said, 'I'll put the end straight in my mouth and kiss it better.'

I swept the crumbs from the counter with my hand. I had forgotten the coarse repartee of the excursion guides.

'Do you know Nestor?' I asked her.

'Grey-haired buzzard, does Russian?'

'Yeah that's him.' I should have realised that he spoke Russian as well. 'Is he working today?'

'No, he's not worked for the last week. He had to go down to the Midi. He's got some family trouble.'

'Any idea when he'll be back?'

'Not a clue. I don't know him that well. It's not true what they say about me and old men.'

'Well that's a weight off my mind.'

She looked at me scornfully. 'You're not old.'

'Thanks.'

'You're prehistoric.'

As I walked down the rue de Rivoli, I decided that it was about time that I started to look after number one. Get a job, earn some money, drink some beer. Then I would not have to talk to Reinhardt or Miro or Mathilde or any other silly little girls.

The company that provided the microbuses had its depot out in Asnieres but their despatch office was in a little street behind the Palais Royal so I trudged along there and amused a toothless Algerian with my joke about wanting to drive a microbus. Did I have any experience? I've driven just about everything except a hearse. Did I know Paris? Yes, and the rue Sidi Ramdam. He didn't like being told which part of Algiers city he came from. Did I have a driving licence? Of course I've... *Merde!* It had been stolen with my i.d. card and I had not replaced it.

It was only when I was out in the street again that it occurred to me that I should have asked him to read Mathilde's document, always supposing that he could read Arabic, of course. Always supposing that he could read.

Mathilde was looking weary when I got to the roof of the Samaritaine. Her hair had lost a little of its spring and so had she. I suppose I could try to be a little more pleasant with her, after all, she was having to deal with loss. I could see some of that sadness in her eyes as she watched me approach.

'I've got you an orange juice,' she said. 'It's probably warm. I ordered it at four o'clock.'

'Am I late?'

'It's half past. That makes us evens,' she sighed.

I took her hand over the table and held it.

'I wasn't trying to get even,' I said. 'Tired?'

She looked down at the table and took her hand back.

'Fed up. Fed up with stupid, bigotted officials sitting pretty in guaranteed jobs. If I had the chance I'd go in there and stick an enema up the lot of them.'

'What have you been doing instead?'

'I've been shunted from floor to floor and from building to building. You wouldn't believe how complicated it is to die. I don't think I shall bother dying. It's makes too much work for those left behind.' She blew the air noisily out of her lungs. It wafted across me, warm and sweet with her tiredness. 'Not that I've got anybody to leave behind.'

'Nor me.'

We looked at each other without speaking. A group of Dutch tourists at a nearby table exploded into laughter as one of them fell from his chair. We ignored them. At length she said, 'Any luck with your guide chappie?'

I shook my head. 'He's out of town.'

'Did you get yourself a job?'

'I've already got one.'

'Thought you didn't like it.'

I looked at her, the tiredness creasing the corners of her eyes, the dejection. I recalled her bright eyes and the speed of her reactions that morning; the clattering recklessly through the arcade, holding hands and laughing like a couple of– Stop. Stop.

'I haven't finished it,' I said. 'I think my boss deserves a better service.'

'And will she get it?'

'I've just had a brilliant idea.'

'Oh yes?'

'Why don't we go somewhere and have some dinner? I only had a sandwich for lunch–'

'And six glasses of beer.'

'–and I don't suppose you ate properly either. Around the back streets hereabouts there's sure to be a little place that opens early .' She looked over at the Dutch tourists. Unsure. 'And I'll let you pay,' I added generously.

She smiled grimly. 'All right then. Come on.'

We walked side by side, slowly down the wide stairs, allowing the upward draft to cool us. When we got to the ground floor I saw one of those automatic photo booths and thought of the stupidity of not having replaced my driving licence. Then I remembered that the photograph was still missing on the police paper that they gave me at the commissariat. I felt in my pocket.

'Have you got a franc?'

'What for?'

I nodded at the machine. 'I need a photo for my i.d. card.'

'The machine needs two francs.'

'I've got one. Look.' I showed it to her. She silently dropped another alongside it. 'Thanks. Take it out of my wages.'

'Just a minute!' she stopped me as I pulled the curtain back. 'You don't think that I'm going to let you have your photograph taken looking like that do you?'

'What?'

'Turn around.' I turned. She reached up and pulled my collar straight.

'Now I know why you wear high heels.'

'Comb!'

'Me? A comb?'

She gave an exasperated sigh and fished in her bag and pulled out a long-handled pink affair.

'Stand still.' She dragged and fluffed the comb through my hair then leaned back to look at the effect. 'That's better. You know, with a little effort...'

I looked at her as I clambered into the cubicle. 'I'm not worth even that little effort,' I said, and pulled the curtain across.

When I emerged, I wandered off to look at umbrellas, leaving Mathilde to guard the machine and ensure that nobody stole my portraits when they were ejected down the chute. She joined me at the moment when I was fighting off three assailants with the point of my rapier.

'Oh do grow up!' she said. I put the umbrella back on the display and the shop assistant breathed a sigh of relief. 'Here are your photos. They will have to do.'

'Why are there only two? The machine takes four.'

'Because,' she said plainly, 'you only paid for two.'

It was whilst we were in the restaurant, waiting for the dessert that I had another brilliant idea.

'I need a couple of twenty centime pieces.'

'Haven't you got any money?' she asked as she opened her purse.

'It's all tied up in shares, government bonds and pineapple plantations.' I took the coins. 'Thanks, I'll be back.'

'Last time you said that to me you nearly dragged me out of my skirt down an alley.'

'Don't expect the same treatment this time.'

I went to the phone booth by the toilets. I rang the Café Clerc. Joanne answered.

'Yes?'

'Hello Beautiful.'

'Who is this?'

'Oh come on, how many people call you "Beautiful"?'

'Not nearly enough, Jo-Jo. What do you want?'

'Who's in tonight?'

'Usual crowd, Makele, Martins, a couple of bums from the other side of the boulevard, Pino.'

'He'll do. Call him to the phone but don't tell him it's me.'

Pino's voice rattled the receiver. 'Yeah, who is it?'

'It's Jo-Jo.'

'Ah, look...'

'Forget it. I want you to do me a favour. You owe me one Pino, don't you?'

'I haven't got any money, Jo-Jo, honest I haven't.'

'That makes two of us then. Just stay at the café, I'll be around in about an hour. I've got something I want you to look at. Professionally.'

'Professionally?'

'From the legal point of view.'

'You know I can't practise any more, Jo-Jo, you know I can't.'

'I'm not asking you to practise. I just need some of your knowledge. I'll see you in an hour. OK?'

'Yeah, I suppose so.'

'This little Renault of yours has four wheels. Most owners find that arrangement admirably suited to their needs. Can't you keep some of the wheels on the ground? You make me seasick.'

'Ooops' she said as she lurched the wrong side of a road island. 'You're not very brave are you?'

'On the contrary. Bravery is having the courage to persist in doing something which you know to be dangerous and which frightens you. Sitting in the passenger seat of your car qualifies on all counts.'

'Oh stop whining. This was your idea.'

'I would have gone by metro. By the way, thank you for dinner. You might be seeing it again.'

'If you're going to throw up, open the window.'

'If I could open the window, I'd shout for help. Turn right by the kiosk. Quick, there's a parking space on the boulevard. We can walk from here.'

It was only nine o' clock but the little streets of the seventh arrondissement were deserted. The lamps leered down at us from the facades of the buildings like hooded cobras ready to strike. It seemed natural to take Mathilde's arm. She did not complain.

'It's very quiet here,' she said as her heels echoed back from the walls.

'Oh yes, very quiet. It suits me.'

'And you've got all the shops you need.'

'Yes, there's the florist who sends out all my bouquets, and there's the launderette who gives me credit. I've even got my own police station.'

'How convenient,' she said but I felt her squirm under the salacious scrutiny of the cop standing on the doorstep. I just dared him to say something. Just something. I would have knocked him into the Fifteenth.

'Is this your café? It's a bit gloomy.' She stopped at the door. 'It says *"closed"*.'

'Somebody's turned the sign around. In you go.'

I pushed open the door for her and followed her in.

'Good God!' She jumped back into me. I grabbed her tightly.

'Just stand still,' I hissed. 'Stand still.'

The gun was pointing straight at us.

9

Icould feel the heavy thumping in her rib cage and the short anguished movements of her breathing.

'Stand still,' I whispered in her ear. I tried to sound reassuring. As if I had a plan of campaign. 'Don't move a muscle.'

The barrel of the gun was unwavering. A little black hole. A malignant eye fixed upon us. No sense in staring at it, I could not stop it from firing. I let my glance wander slowly around the bar. Opposite me, two strangers were sitting side by side, their hands on the table top, their eyes disbelieving. They were probably Joanne's two 'bums from across the boulevard.' I looked for Pino. He was at the back, rigidly grasping a glass of vin rouge. So much for him not having any money! Makele was on the bench by the wall. Big black wondering face, nervous white eyes that already knew what a gun could do, great black hands like a pair of ossified tarantulas. Joanne was rooted motionless behind the bar, her eyes weary with the resignation of somebody having to sit through the B movie again.

Mathilde was beginning to shake.

'You're doing alright kid,' I whispered.

Martins' black eyes were expressionless. His face was a mask. The gun in his hand was rock steady.

What a homecoming! I try to impress my boss with my friends and I get her shot by an Angolan war veteran who is languishing in the deepest despair of his latest *sandade*.

'Hello Martins.' No reaction. 'You know me, it's Jo-Jo. You gave me a lift in your limousine.' Talking to a blank wall. 'I've brought my friend, Mathilde, to see you.' Cold black marbles, unmoving in his face. I squeezed Mathilde reassuringly. She shivered. 'Say hello to Martins, Mathilde. He's my friend.'

She cleared her throat. His eyes flicked at the sound. She felt me tense up. My eyes were glued to the tendons on the back of his hand, trying to detect movement on the trigger finger.

'Just say hello, Mathilde.'

'Hello Martins.' Her voice started faintly but grew in strength. No reaction.

'Mathilde is Jo-Jo's friend, Martins. Jo-Jo is your friend.'

Christ, this was difficult. I never could understand psychology. I bet all these university students got lessons on it. When they weren't smoking stuff. Joanne's face was white, her hands were palm down on the bar. I checked. Everybody had their hands in view. Could he see mine, for God's sake? And Mathilde's? I had to hope so.

'Shall we be gentlemen and let Mathilde sit down?' The gun did not move, but his eyes did. Very slightly. 'Right, Mathilde,' I said in as pleasant a voice as I could muster, 'In a minute you are going to sit next to friend Makele on the bench there. Keep both your hands on your handbag, just as they are now and hold your handbag on the table top with both hands when you sit down. Say "yes" if you have understood.'

'I understand.'

'OK Martins, *mon pote*, Mathilde is going to sit next to Makele and I am going to stay right here by the door where you can see me and I shall not move a molecule.' The eyes flickered again. 'This is it,' I whispered and gave her a gentle shove. She tottered off on those stupid heels. I stood stock still whilst Martins tried to decide who was the greater risk. I felt his expressionless eyes settle back on me. I only felt them because I was looking at Mathilde's bottom. Taking the small steps in the tight skirt and high heels made her wiggle her hips just the way that she had told me she would not. Despite the situation I found myself grinning. If you are going to be shot by a paranoid schizophrenic you might as well go with a smile on your face.

I was still the target. It was time for the big gamble now that everybody was safe.

'Well I am going to get a beer, because I've got a throat like an empty cement bag.'

Holding my hands up level with my shoulders where Martins could see them, I gently turned my back on him and walked up to the bar. Joanne watched me approach with surprised eyes. I had no illusions about whether Martins would shoot a man in the back. He had been in Angola. Of course he would.

'Give me a beer Joanne. I'm parched.' She looked at me as if I were mad. Funny that. Compared to Martins, I held a first class degree in sanity.

'I can't. I've got no pressure. I was about to change the cylinder when....' She nodded at Martins.

Why does it always happen to me?

'Well give me a bottle from the shelf then, but keep your hands in view.' I could see Martins in the mirror. The gun was aimed at my back. I was still holding his attention.

'But I've only got Pinson's on the shelf and you never drink that.'

'I will today.'

'But you don't like it.'

For Christ's sake!

'I've changed my mind.'

'You said it was gnat's piss.'

Oh Jesus!

'Just give me one, OK?'

'If you insist,' she shrugged. 'But don't blame me if you don't like it.'

'I won't. I never blame you for anything.'

Not even for the gun in my back.

In the mirror I watched Martin's eyes swivel around to follow Joanne as she opened the bottle and poured the beer into my glass. I took the glass and turned and leaned casually on the bar as if I always drank with a madman's gun aimed straight at my gut.

'Cheers!' I drank that glass steadily to the end. It was the longest beer that I had ever drunk. And when I had finished it, I was still alive. Little things like that I find encouraging. Also, Martins' eyes were beginning to shift occasionally to the faces of the others in the room. We were getting somewhere. But the beer was still disgusting. 'Let's have some music.' I nodded at the wall behind the bar and said to Joanne, 'Get the guitar down.'

'It's dusty.'

'Well get me a cloth and I'll wipe it.'

She lifted the instrument down from its hook and muttered to herself as she cleaned it. I almost felt sorry for the trouble I was causing. I sat on a stool, pulled the guitar across my lap and picked at the strings to tune it. It was not far out but my fingers felt like sausages. The guitar was in better condition than I was.

'What shall I play?' I lifted my head from the frets to see the circle of faces. The two bums, gratefully grasping at the slender hope that they would not now be dying tonight in a seventh arrondissement café shoot-out; Makele, settling down in his seat with all the simple anticipation of a child about to be entertained; Pino, clutching his glass, wishing it would turn into Aladdin's lamp; Mathilde, just looking; Martins, watching. It was like Tuesday invitation nights at the Cave Rouge Montmartre all over again. 'Any requests?'

They just looked at me. You would think they had never seen a guitar before. I banged about with a fairly free-strumming version of *Lady be Good*. It was nothing like Django's rendition but it warmed up my fingers and it set their feet a-tapping. Progress at last. Martins' head was nodding slightly to the beat and his eyes were moving around the group, trying to identify who we were. But he still held the gun. I had no intention of trying to disarm him, he would have to do that himself.

It must have been my day for brainwaves because I had another one. I suddenly thought of the theme tune to *Jeux Interdits*. It was a soppy film that had made all Paris weep back in the 50s and for many years I had tried to master it as a guitar exercise. I knew I could never be a Narciso Yepes and it had been bloody difficult to play properly. Now I found myself having to paraphrase some of the fingerwork but the moment I began the lyrical tune I knew that I was on a winner. Martins was listening. Everybody was listening. In that darkened bar packed with anguish and twisted in tension, my pale-faced audience sat transfixed by the unashamed sentimentality of the notes.

The gun was wavering. This was how I was going to disarm him. I had no idea what the hell was going on in that tortured mind of his but at last the unfocussed blackness was fading from his eyes. As the final note died away and the darkness of silence began to close in he said,

'Again.'

Victory.

'OK Martins, I'll play it once more.'

He looked at me. 'Jo-Jo, he said.

He was coming back.

I played the tune again. Not a lot better because I was thinking and trying to remember the words of another song at the same time. When I reached the end he said, 'Again.'

'I'll play a different song, Martins.'

'Again,' he repeated.

Everybody was holding their breath. I ignored him and went straight into an Angolan war song that I knew. In Portuguese. I don't speak a word of Portuguese but you don't have to be able to speak a foreign language at all in order to sound fluent when you sing. It is just a matter of imitating sounds.

'*Oh menino negro, nao entra la ronda...*'

Don't ask me how I knew it because I could not for the life of me remember where I had learned it. Some barrack room, some bar, some brothel. It didn't matter. The effect was instantaneous. It was his language, he had fought in that war, and he could see the little black boy who was not allowed to play in the circle with the white children.

'*Oh menino negro, nao entra la ronda...*'

The gun sagged to the table top, the tears glistened in his black eyes.

'Jo-Jo.'

'Martins.'

'Jo-Jo.'

'Unload the gun, Martins, somebody might get hurt.' He looked at the gun as if he had just noticed it for the first time. 'Take the bullets out, Martins. You don't want to harm anybody.'

He cracked it open and emptied the magazine onto the table; the bullets bounced and rattled on the formica. I handed the guitar over the bar to Joanne. Martins watched unconcerned as I scooped up the ammunition and checked the gun.

'Stick all this in a drawer, will you? We'll get rid of it later.' I gave the lot to Joanne.

She sighed.

'Your beer's on me,' she said.

She had remembered that I had not paid for it.

'Thanks.' You have to know when to show your gratitude.

A buzz of hesitant conversation started up. Everybody was throwing anxious glances at Martins. He was looking back, bemused. He had no idea what was going on. I walked over and sat at his table.

MARTIN LLOYD

'You OK?' I asked.
'Sure, why ask?'
I pulled a face and raised my eyebrows.
'You've just given us all a fright. Bit of a turn.'
'A bit of a turn? Bad?' I nodded. 'I must go home.'
'You're not driving? I asked.
'No. Car's at the garage.'
'Shall we phone for Maria?'
He nodded thoughtfully. I took that as a 'yes'.

Maria was short, stout, dressed in black and very Portuguese.
She had lived with him for at least three years to my knowledge.
Her French was basic but she understood when I asked her where
the hell he had got the shooter.
'Shooter? He's got a shooter?'
'Not now, we've taken it. It's safely out of the way.'
'Don't give it back to him.' She was serious.
'I won't.' So was I.
We watched them leave. A normal couple homeward bound.
'What started him off?' I asked Joanne.
She looked at me as if I had just asked her to predict the
winning numbers on the *tiercé*.
'Who can tell?' She swept some empty glasses into the sink. 'I
was getting a new cylinder for the pump when suddenly he
produces this gun. You can guess the rest.'
'How long had you been sitting like that?'
'About twenty minutes but I liked your style, Jo-Jo; push the
woman in first.'
'Yeah, if he had shot my boss that would have solved all my
problems.' I felt too jaded to argue with her.
I could see Mathilde trying very hard to understand her
conversation with Makele. She was flinching every time he
touched her arm to emphasise his meaning. I went over.
'Good music, Jo-Jo. Makele like good music.'
'Thanks me old broom-shunter.' Mathilde turned around to
see me. 'You look annoyed,' I said to her.
'I am annoyed,' she snapped. 'When will you stop calling me
"kid"?'
It seemed that I could please no-one tonight. Unless they were
stark staring mad and toting a loaded gun.

'Yeah, OK. Sorry. Sorry about Martins as well.' She shrugged. 'He's usually all right but he sometimes has these funny turns.'

'They're not very funny, but quite revealing.' She put her head on one side. 'You've got a nice singing voice. What was the song?'

'It was an Angolan war song. About a black child having to stand and watch whilst the white children played. All very sentimental.'

'You sang in Portuguese.'

'Martins is Portuguese. The song is Portuguese. He fought in Angola. Simple really.'

'Simple,' she repeated. I could not fathom her manner. Some women make themselves obscure on purpose.

'I'm closing in fifteen minutes,' Joanne shouted. 'I've had enough of you lot for the rest of my life.'

I have always admired Joanne's commercial acumen. Then I remembered why we were here. I waved at Pino. He tried not to see me. I looked hard at him. He got up and reluctantly came over to us.

'This is Mademoiselle Sikorski, my employer,' I said.

'*Enchanté mademoiselle.*' Pino was a lot sober now than when we had come in. It's wonderful the improvement that a little pistol waving can generate.

I took out Mathilde's envelope.

'Sit down and look at this. We want to know what it is.'

He unfolded the paper. 'But it's all in bagpipe writing, I can't read that.'

'Can you not tell what it is? What type of document?' Mathilde asked.

'Well it's a legal paper of some sort.'

'Even we had worked that out.' I probably sounded a little sour. Mathilde poked a finger in my ribs.

'How do you know it's a legal document?' She leaned across the table. I looked at her waist again. Sort of.

'The layout. The format.'

'Any idea what it says?' I asked.

'I told you, Jo-Jo, I can't read that stuff.' He turned the paper over. 'But if you want to know what it says, why don't you ask Elie Frazier?'

'Who?' we said in unison.

'Elie Frazier.' He tapped the paper. 'He's an official translator.

Got his office somewhere around the rue du Renard, at the back of the Hotel de Ville. He must have supplied a translation of the document to somebody. Look, that's his mark. 'EF 4459'. That will be the number of his translation.'

'Will he have kept a copy?' Mathilde was surprised. 'Surely that's a breach of confidentiality?'

'He will deny that he has. But he will have done. They all do. Standard practice. You'll find his address in the Bottin.'

'Come on you lot, out!' Joanne started to switch off the few remaining lights.

We got up. I saw the two strangers making for the door.

'Oi! You two!' They stopped dead in their tracks. 'Nothing happened here tonight. Understand?' They looked at each other and then nodded. 'If Joanne loses her licence. I'll be straight round to see you. And I won't be carrying a guitar.'

They scuttled out. Joanne pushed me through the door behind them.

'Why don't you keep your big mouth shut, Jo-Jo?'

'So, you're a pretty popular guy?' Mathilde observed as we walked back to her car.

Yes, I was a pretty popular guy. About the only person I didn't upset tonight was Martins, and he would have shot me if I had. I suddenly felt tired. Perhaps it was the anticlimax. Perhaps it was the disappointment at finding myself still alive in this world. I was fed up with living out of a crummy bar, being doped, being broke and being threatened with guns. I felt in my pocket and pulled out her paper.

'Here's your document. You heard what Pino said. The translator has got an office in the rue du Renard. You can go round there tomorrow morning. I'm sure you could charm a copy of the translation out of him. Just wear that suit with those high heels and wiggle your bottom like you did in the café. Failing that, you could always pay him to translate it again.'

'Oh you're impossible. Now what's the matter?'

'Nothing. Here's your car. Get in it and go home. I've got a bed to go to.'

I stood watching her car as it bounced down the quiet boulevard. What was the matter with me? How the hell could I know?

The cop with no chin was not basking in the morning sun on the doorstep of the commissariat so I went in.

'Monsieur?' This cop had fair hair and was scratching his head with a pen. Showing off that he could write, I suppose.

'I've got these photographs to go on my form.' I laid them on the counter like a pair of rare stamps.

'Oh yes?' he said as he took my crumpled *récepissé*, 'I can do it now, it won't take long. Do you want to wait?'

Had this fellow been on a public relations course? What was wrong with him?

'No I'll come back in half an hour.' But as I turned to go, something caught my eye. 'On second thoughts, I'll wait.'

I wandered over to the notice board to read the 'wanted' notice. You don't often see these notices nowadays, what with the advances in television and newspapers and radio and such. They are quite a rarity. And it is even rarer to recognise one of the faces on the notice.

'Who's this villain?' I asked casually.

The cop banged his stamp down a couple of times and then looked up. 'Oh him, that's Mohammed El Assawi for what it's worth.'

'Why do you want him?'

'I don't want him and neither does the Police. He's an Algerian political agitator. Apparently.'

'What has he done?'

'In the last twenty five years? Sod all as far as I can make out but one of those trendy do-good organisations has invited him to talk at a convention they've organised. They've done it on purpose of course, to embarrass the government. They know he is banned. They just want to cause trouble.'

'We don't need to import foreigners to cause trouble. We've got enough of our own.'

'I heartily agree,' he said pleasantly and handed me my completed form. He folded his arms on the counter top and leaned on them. 'And I can't see the point in giving us notices like that.' He stabbed his pen at the notice board. 'This isn't Orly airport. He won't fly into the seventh arrondissement will he?'

'No, you're right there,' I agreed. I took my papers and walked out into the street.

No, Mohammed El Assawi would not fly into the seventh arrondissement. He would not fly into Orly or even sail into Marseille. No, he would fly to a country that would let in anybody, like Italy for example, and then cross into France on the land border at Vingtimille, near Nice. There, he would find some mug in a *Paris Matin* car who would drive him up to Paris and deliver him to the Place de la Concorde. He would be such a mug, he would do it for free.

Of course, Mohammed El Assawi would not actually declare that he was a political agitator, he would say he was somebody's grandfather. He probably was. And he would have to keep a scarf around his face to keep the chill and prying eyes out. And when we stopped at places where he would be looked at he would open his newspaper and hide behind that. But I had recognised the scar on his cheek.

I wondered if I could trade some points with Reinhardt by telling him that I knew where El Assawi was? But of course, I did not know. I had left him at the Concorde with a man with a nose like a gas tap. And I hadn't been paid. I wanted another chat with Pino.

I checked my money for breakfast. That reminded me that I needed a job. A proper job, not one playing amateur detective and fall guy to a young woman of deceitful designs and doubtful honesty, however attractive I might find her. Did I say that?

Joanne's face looked like yesterday's mayonnaise and I took the trouble to tell her so.

'Jo-Jo, you are about as funny as a miscarriage. And just as welcome.'

I put my money on the counter. It was the kind of language she understood.

'Coffee and two croissants. 'Nice to see that you are still in business then.'

'No thanks to you. You should have just let those two bums go last night. They were scared shitless. They would not have done anything. What do you think they know about café licensing? It would never have entered their heads to report me. But no, you have to be the great macho hero and throw your weight around.'

'Perhaps they'll think of prosecuting you for having no entertainment licence as well.'

'No chance of that. Nobody could claim that your squawking to a banjo was entertainment, however much your girlfriend seemed to like it.'

'I was talking about your gun-slinging circus act. And she is not my girlfriend, she is my boss.' Joanne grunted rudely. 'And if you want me to continue to be able to pay for my drinks, you'd do well to remember that. You were always nagging at me to get a decent job and when I do, you do your best to sabotage it. What's the matter with you?'

The skin on the mayonnaise cracked. She pushed the usual strands of hair back from her face.

'Sorry Jo-Jo. I didn't sleep very well.'

'You need a man in your bed.'

'Are you offering?' There was only scorn in her voice.

'No. I snore.' I bit into my croissant. It was better than usual. 'And who says that my boss liked my singing? This croissant is good,' I added for camouflage.

'I can recognise admiration in a woman's eyes, even if you can't,' she said. She glanced sideways at me. It was her attempt at coyness. She looked as if she had just discovered the clothes hanger in her dress.

'I don't look at women's eyes. They blink too much. Where did you get these croissants from?'

'That's a commercial secret, Jo-Jo, one that you will never discover because you will never get up early enough to find out.'

She was right. I gazed out at the slowly passing vehicles in the rue St Dominique. The whole world was up and working, all except me. And Pino, I had just remembered. I took my coffee over to his table and rattled his newspaper.

'Oh, hello Jo-Jo.'

He did not seem too pleased to see me so I decided on the psychological approach to throw him off balance.

'Thanks for your help last night.' He blinked at me. 'Mademoiselle Sikorski really appreciated it. She asked me to thank you.'

'Oh, right. Well that's all right, Jo-Jo, any time to help a pal.'

'Good. Tell me about my passenger the other morning.'

'Oh yeah. Sorry about him. I'd forgotten.'

'Or had you remembered and got cold feet?'

'No, honest Jo-Jo. It slipped my mind.'

'So, how much did they pay you?'

'Hundred francs.'

'Yeah and I breed hamsters. Try again.'

'Look, Jo-Jo, I haven't got any of it. It's all gone.'

'I'm sure it has. I'm not after the money, just the story. Where did you get "granddad" from?'

'A couple of weeks back a slimy little git collared me at the wholesalers in Nice. You know the place, it's near the–'

'I know exactly where they are.'

'Yes, of course you do. Well this fellow wanted me to take his grandfather up to Paris in the car. Easy money.'

'Very easy as it turned out. Why didn't he go by train?'

'Said he was too fragile. And it would take too long.'

'How much?'

'Five hundred.'

'Five hundred? I bet that's more than the Nice-Paris air fare.'

'Probably. Yeah.'

'Didn't you smell a rat?'

'Well I thought it was a lot of money but he said the old man could afford it. Why ask questions if you don't want the answers?' Life was simple for Pino. He had made it so simple that now he was out of a job again. 'Why are you worried anyway? He didn't cause you any trouble did he?'

I gave him one of my looks.

'Why ask questions if you don't want the answers?' I threw back at him. I thought that was quite clever.

'Jo-Jo!' Joanne was beckoning me to the phone. 'It's your girl-friend,' she said loudly across the uncovered handset.

'Thanks,' I said equally loudly. 'Now go and finish scrubbing the doorstep and I want to see my face in it.'

She huffed away down to the other end of the bar, annoyed that I had got the better of her and that she could not now listen to the phone call. It was Mathilde.

'I've been burgled.' She sounded jumpy. 'It's all a mess.'

'Why tell me?' I said. 'Have you called the police?'

'No.'

'Why not?'

'Can you come? I don't want to go back in there alone.'

I didn't understand that. 'What do you mean, "go back in there"? When did it happen?'

'Yesterday. Whilst we were in town. When I saw it I just turned around, went out, locked the door and left it.'

'No sign of a break in? No damage to the door?'

'No. That's what I don't like. They must have had a key.'

'Nothing to worry about then. It was only Reinhardt letting you know that he was still on the job and that you are still his favourite fantasy.'

'I don't want to be his fantasy, or anybody else's.'

'Where are you now then?'

'At a hotel on the Place d'Italie. I slept here.'

'Luxury?'

'Fleapit.'

'I hope their telephone kiosk is soundproof.'

'It doesn't matter, they don't understand French.'

I looked out again at the traffic in the rue St Dominique. It was clearing now. Soon, one of the motorcycle couriers would drop in for his first beer of the day. The postman would walk in whistling and throw a packet of bills on the counter and order a *pastis*. Martins was probably out there somewhere, black-eyed and black-suited, driving a black Cadillac in a black despair. Makele would be on a street corner, grinning on his broom, face turned upwards to the morning sun, just glad to be alive. And me...?

'Are you still there Joel?'

'Sorry. I was thinking.'

'What about?'

'Nothing.'

In the silence I could hear her breathing on the phone. I imagined her chest rising and falling.

'Joel, will you help me please? You are the only person I can turn to. I don't know anybody in Paris.'

'All right, all right, don't make a parcel of it. I'll come over.'

'Thank you.'

'Shall I come to the hotel? What's it called?'

'No, I don't want to stay in this dump a minute longer than necessary. Can you meet me at the Italie – the brasserie where you ogled my egg mayonnaise? Remember?'

'I know the place you mean but I don't remember the egg mayonnaise.'

'You never saw it.'

I suspected she was trying to make a point but it was either too obscure or too clever for my poor brain.

'I'll come as soon as I can. Get a magazine to read whilst you're waiting. One of those silly women's things.'

I replaced the receiver. Pino and Joanne were bent over the newspaper which was laid out at the other end of the counter. I slid up to them.

'Pino.' He looked up. 'Keep your eyes skinned, and you too,' I said to Joanne. 'I want to know if you notice anybody watching this place.'

'Not more bailiffs?' Pino grumbled.

'No, not bailiffs,'

Joanne looked at me. 'Are you getting into trouble again?' she said. 'Is it this Mathilde girl?'

'I don't know what I'm getting into and that's the truth.'

'Well, you be careful. Don't get out of your depth.'

'Oh, I can swim.'

'Not with concrete shoes.'

Always a barrel of fun, Joanne.

No wonder her old man left her.

10

As I was about to descend the metro steps at Latour Maubourg I saw a Cityscope coach driving around the back of the Invalides towards the Place Vauban. The guide was standing with her back to the windscreen, flapping a hand in the air as she gave her commentary. Wednesday. The Highlights of Art tour. That would suit me nicely.

I found the driver in the Café Vauban. He was drinking his free coffee whilst the group was being shown around Napoleon's tomb by his guide. I got a coffee and sat at his table. He looked at me.

'I know you, don't I?' he said and held out his hand.

'LeBatard,' I said as I shook it.

'Duchateau.'

'Who's your guide?'

'Marlise, the little German girl. I think she fancies me.'

'Oh yes, Marlise.' I remembered the guide in the red skirt who had come into the bar on the rue de Rivoli when I was looking for Nestor. 'Don't feel too smug if she does fancy you. She only goes for old men.'

'Suits me. I only go for young girls.'

'Well you're made for each other,' I laughed. 'Are you on the Highlights of Art tour?' He nodded. 'Can I hitch a lift? Have you got an empty seat?'

'Yeah, about fifteen. Where to?'

'You still go down past the Gobelins?'

'Yeah, we turn opposite to cut back to the boulevard.'

'That'll do fine.'

As it turned out, he decided that it would be easier to go right down to the Place d'Italie and turn there. He dropped me on the corner opposite the brasserie, his Setra hissing on its suspension as he paused for me to jump off. I waved from the pavement as Marlise blew me a kiss, the driver made me a rude sign and the passengers goggled.

Mathilde was at a table on the terrace, hiding behind a copy of *Marie-Claire* and an enormous pair of sunglasses. She was still wearing her business skirt and jacket.

'Do guides blow kisses to everybody?'

'To all the men,' I said as I sat down, and then added, 'Except the men guides. They blow kisses to the girls.'

'I didn't know there were any men guides. What were you doing in the coach?'

'I hitched a lift. I recognised the coach. I knew the tour came around this way.'

'You've driven it, presumably.'

'Presumably.'

'Do you want a coffee?'

'No, I've been drinking coffee all morning. Let's get on with the job.' I stood up. 'No sign of the waterworks van then?'

She shook her head as she rolled up her magazine. Her hair was looser now than yesterday. More natural, more human.

'What are you looking at?' she said.

'Your hair.'

'Oh it's a mess, I know. I'm sorry.' She put her hand to her head.

'I was just thinking how natural it looked. Not all stuck up like yesterday. And anyway, you've no need to apologise to me. I don't have a voice in how you look.'

She pushed the rolled magazine into her handbag, pursed her lips and made a point of saying nothing loudly.

We walked back up to the rue Stresemann. The sun was hot. Her pace was slow and weary. Another woman who had not slept well. Another woman who needed a man in her bed? Was I offering? I could imagine Mathilde's scorn; it would eclipse Joanne's a hundredfold.

At the door to the apartment she silently handed me the key. I inspected the lock plate. It was scratched and worn as any plate would be. Reinhardt's gang would have had a key to fit, I was sure. It would not have been an obstacle to them. I turned the key, pushed the door open and went in. Mathilde followed me down the corridor, following close behind me for protection. Hers, not mine.

I stood and looked at the mess in the salon. It was my bedsit on a larger scale. Cushions pulled from the sofa and easy chairs, contents of the bureau emptied out onto the floor, books and magazines from the bookshelf thrown into piles.

'Oh well, we've got some clearing up to do. Is there anything obviously missing?'

'I've no idea. I can hardly remember what was here in the first place.' She tugged vaguely at an antimacassar. 'You don't think it was burglars then?'

'No. This was a search, not a steal.' She followed me to the kitchen door. The cupboards had been emptied to the floor. 'That was just Reinhardt being spiteful,' I said. 'He was the same with me. Made as much mess as he could.' I pushed open her bedroom door. Her suitcase had been upended on the bed. 'And that is just Reinhardt being perverted,' I said. 'Do you really wear that?' Several rather delicate and expensive looking articles of lingerie effected in pastel shades of lace and silk had been spread out on the counterpain.

She squeezed past me, scooped them up and pushed them into her case as she righted it.

'If I do it's no concern of yours,' she snapped.

'You've gone a very pretty shade of red. Well, well, well,' I mused. 'To look at you, who would have thought it?'

'Idiot!' She elbowed me in the ribs as she went back into the salon. I watched her shoulders drop as she took stock of the mess.

'This is what we will do,' I said, 'You sit down here whilst I make us a tisane then I can start to put all this straight whilst you go and sort yourself out. You probably didn't sleep well and those were the clothes you wore yesterday.' I pushed her down into the chair. She offered no resistance.

It took me only a few minutes to put the things back into the kitchen cupboards because I was not hindered by knowing where they were supposed to live. When I carried the tea into the salon, Mathilde had kicked off her high heels and stretched her legs up onto the sofa.

'Thanks,' she smiled as she took the cup. She nodded at the mess. 'They were searching the books one at a time. That is why they are in piles – so that they did not mix up the unsearched with the searched.'

I could see what she meant.

'It would have taken them ages. They must have been certain they would not be disturbed.'

'They were. They knew exactly where I was and what I was doing. Remember? They were watching us from the waterworks van?'

'That's true. But you had the document with you. They must have seen it.'

'Probably not well enough to see what it was.'

'No, but it was obvious that you were showing it to me.' I looked back at the piles of books. 'Did you search all the other books after you had found the hollowed-out bible?'

'No. It didn't occur to me that there might be another one.'

'But it did to them.' I got up and started to carry the books back to the shelves, arranging them purely by size. 'Where is the bible?'

Mathilde poked about for a while.

'It's not here,' she said.

'So they've taken it with them. They find the bible with its secret hiding place... which is empty?' I glanced at her for confirmation. She nodded. 'And they decide to search all the shelves in case there are any others like it.'

'That does not advance us much does it?'

'I don't know. We don't know whether there were any other books with secrets. You didn't look, but they did.'

'Well I could not know that I was supposed to search every book,' she protested. 'It never occurred to me.'

'I wasn't saying that. It's just that if they did find another book, they would have taken it with them. And they would not have left a receipt.'

'No, I suppose not.'

She looked very small and frail.

'For all we know,' I continued, 'they may have found what they were looking for. That could be good news'

'How?'

'Well, they will leave us alone now. They will be satisfied.'

'Is that what you want? To be left alone?'

She was annoyed again. I could feel it. I sometimes get these flashes of second sight.

'It would make a pleasant change. And getting angry with me is not going to help in any way.'

'Why shouldn't I get angry? You said you would help me in all this and then you back out. What about Papa's money? His extra pension that he had saved? Who gets that?'

'You may already have it. But neither you nor I can read Arabic. As soon as we've got cleared up here, I think you should go and get that document translated. You never know, it might be a gold mine.'

She drew out the paper from her bag. 'Does that mean that Reinhardt is looking for this?' Her face clouded. 'What will he do to get it?'

I glanced at the weals on my wrists.

'Kill and all things less.'

'You keep it,' she thrust the document at me. 'I don't feel safe with it.'

'I don't want it.'

'Coward!'

'And anyway, you need to get it translated.'

'You'll have to come with me.'

'Perhaps.' I moved to the window and stood behind the net curtain and looked into the street below. Nobody was loitering on corners; all the parked vehicles were empty; there was no waterworks van. I scanned the windows in the building opposite, floor by floor, without seeing anything of note. 'Reinhardt seems to have lost interest in you. I can't see anybody watching.'

'It doesn't mean they're not there.' She put her tea cup down on the table, leaned back against the arm of the sofa and closed her eyes. Another five centimetres of her thighs slid out of her skirt. If she slipped any further she would be modelling her collection of lace for me.

'Why don't you go and freshen up whilst I finish this? You're distracting me.'

She opened her eyes. 'I'm not doing anything.'

'You've already done enough.' I nodded at the hem of her skirt. She looked down at her stockings.

'Oh really, you are the limit!' She tried to pull down her skirt and then gave up. 'I'll go and get changed.'

'You do that. You'll feel better afterwards.'

'Let's hope you do too.'

Now what did she mean by that?

To the drumming of the water in the shower I stacked books, filled drawers and reassembled chairs. Then I got some plates from the kitchen, raided the fridge and set out the beginnings of lunch on the table.

'Have you got any bread?' I called through the bathroom door.

'Not yet.'

'I'll go down and get some.'

The door rattled open in a flurry of steam. Mathilde pushed her head around the jamb.

'No, Joel, don't go. We'll get some later.'

'But we'll need some for lunch. It's already half past eleven, I'll be lucky if I get any at all.'

'No Joel, don't go. Don't leave me alone. Not here on my own.' The words tumbled out in a cascade. I went across to her.

'Look, the boulangerie is practically next door,' I said into her frightened eyes. 'Mathilde, I shall only be a minute. It's two floors down and two doors along.'

'But they've got a key. They might come back.'

She was really frightened.

'Well, put a towel around you or something and come and bolt the door behind me. You'll have to let me back up on the doorphone but don't unbolt this door till you are certain that it's me on the other side of it. OK?'

Her eyes searched my face. God knows what she was looking for. Eventually, she nodded.

She must have made me jittery. At the first floor landing an old lady passed me on her way up. I stood looking up the stairwell, watching her gnarled hand on the rail as it pulled her slowly up to the fourth floor.

Mathilde let me back in with a big smile. She was clean and fresh. She was wearing her faded jeans and a shirt. I didn't think it diplomatic to ask about what might be underneath. But she still had those awful painted toe-nails.

'Sorry about the fuss earlier.' She leaned forwards and bit the end of the crust. 'Come and have some lunch.'

'That's all right. I understand. It's never nice having uninvited strangers in your house.'

'And it came straight on top of the gun in the bar.' She shuddered. 'That was horrible. Seeing that gun barrel pointing at me, so definite and unaltering. I was terrified.'

'So was I.'

'Oh you were quite safe, tucked in behind me.'

'I was not tucked in behind you, I was being polite by allowing you to go through the doorway first. It's called "courtesy." You probably would not recognise it because your behaviour generally does not invite it.'

'Huh!' she said and broke a piece from the baguette. 'Sit down and eat.' She dug in the pot of rillettes with her knife. 'You didn't exactly leap in and disarm the man, did you?'

'You were in the way.'

'How convenient.'

'He would have shot you first.'

'And you were thinking of my safety.'

'Not in the least. The bullet would have gone through a slip of a girl like you and straight into me.'

'Beast.'

'Take it as a compliment on your figure.'

She looked at me challengingly.

'You're pretty brave when it is a "slip of a girl" holding the gun, aren't you?'

'I preferred you before when you were tired and hungry.' I sighed. 'What happened?'

'I had a rest and now I am eating.' She crunched a gherkin between her teeth.

'That's the trouble with kids: their power of recovery. One minute they are exhausted; they have a mouthful of food and they are up and firing on all cylinders again.'

'I am *not* a kid!' she shouted.

'Well stop behaving like one then.'

She looked down into her plate.

'I didn't like the gun. Not at all. It was ... it was so cold and intimidating. Divorced from the man holding it.'

'Right,' I said, 'Now we are getting somewhere. You are recognising your fears. What you need to do now is to decide whether you want to be on the wrong end of any more weapons.'

'What do you mean?'

'Is it really worth it? If this is the paper that Reinhardt is looking for you could just give it to him and you would never have to–'

'I am not–'

'Listen to me,' I shouted her down. 'We neither of us know what is in this paper do we?' She shook her head. 'So you could give it to Reinhardt and not know what, if anything, you have given up.'

'You're scared.'

'Of course I'm scared. So should you be. I don't want you to be harmed. I don't want to see you get hurt.'

'That's very chivalrous of you.'

'Mathilde.' She looked at me. 'Martins is not a bad or vicious person, he is just mad. We were lucky he did not pull the trigger. Reinhardt and the others are thugs. With them, there will be no luck involved. They will make the decision.'

'I know, I know,' she said. She picked up a carrot and fiddled it in the mayonnaise. 'It's a personal thing. Papa was probably a great soldier but he was a lousy father. Somehow, for me, this is a way of convincing myself that he was better than I had thought. This was something he was doing. I want it to bear fruit. It would mean a lot to me. Can you understand that?'

I looked at her pleading eyes.

'I suppose I can try,' I said. 'I can try.'

'So you're staying with me, then?' I pulled a face and nodded. 'No matter what it costs?'

Measure me up for the guillotine.

'No matter what it costs.'

'Good,' she said. 'We'll have a council of war when we've finished lunch but first of all, explain to me why when Martins holds a gun, you stand still, but when I hold a gun you jump on me and nearly rip my clothes off.'

'Is there an easier way to get your clothes off?'

'I'll ignore that. Give me a proper answer.'

'Martins knows how to hold a gun.'

'And I don't?'

'And you don't.'

'Show me. Get the gun and show me what you mean.' She nodded at her bedroom. 'It's in the bottom of the wardrobe where you put it.'

'I'm not going to be embarrassed by anything laid out on the bed am I?'

'You weren't embarrassed.'

She was right. I had been entertained.

I brought the gun back into the salon and checked it before her, showing her that it was empty of ordnance.

'This was how you held the gun,' I said, and waved it vaguely at the wall. 'This is how Martins held the gun.' It stopped dead still and aimed.

'Show me properly. Point it at me.'

'No. I don't want to point a gun at you, Mathilde. It's not a toy, it's a tool for a job.' I moved into the middle of the salon. 'Come and stand next to me and you can look in the mirror.'

She got up and came to me. She smelled of soap.

'What are you doing?' she said.

'Breathing exercises.'

'You were not. Your were sniffing. Do I smell bad?'

'Not bad, just clean. It's a nice smell, a clean woman.' She gave me one of those how-long-have-you-been-out-of-the-asylum looks. 'Here, take the gun, keep it pointing away from us, at the mirror.'

'Why? It's not loaded.'

'How do you know?'

'You showed me.'

'What do you know about guns? I could have loaded it without you even seeing. Always treat a gun as if it is loaded. It's good practice. It'll save somebody's life one day.'

'I had forgotten how heavy it was.'

'Well use two hands then. Look,' I stood behind her and stetched my arms along hers to place her hands on the gun. 'Are you right handed with a gun?'

'I've no idea.'

'Which eye would you use to aim with. Look along the top of the barrel there.'

She squinted.

'I would probably use my right eye.'

'OK.' I put her right index finger on the trigger. 'Now stretch your left index along the other side of the guard, like this.' I suddenly realised how close we were. Bits of her were touching me all the way down. 'Right, hold it like that,' I said, and stepped back. I could feel her eyes on me in the mirror.

'What do I do now?'

'Does that feel comfortable?'

'Not very.'

'Soften your shoulders. Relax your grip a little. You're not going to drop it. Is that better?'

'Yes.'

'Now aim at my reflection.' She hesitated.

'Is the safety catch on?'

'It doesn't have one. They did make a version where you had to squeeze the back of the grip to undo the safety, but not on this model. Go on, aim at my reflection. It's not as bad as what you wanted me to do to you.' She frowned and aimed straight at my forehead. I looked at the business end of the barrel. It's not a sight you ever really enjoy. 'You're lined right up on my brain. What little there is of it. How does that feel?'

'Horrible. How do you feel?'

'Quite safe. You would miss.'

'Why would I miss?' She turned. I automatically pushed the barrel back towards the mirror.

'The pistol pulls upwards as you fire and I would duck. The shot would go over my head. Now, if you really want to frighten me,' I put my hand on her arms and lowered them, 'you would aim about there.'

'And make a mess of your lunch.'

'Yes. At that level, I can't jump above the fire line; if the pistol pulls up as you shoot it will still find some target and if I dive to the floor you will hit me as I go down. It's the median point where you will always find something to hit.'

'The what? The median point? Where on earth do you pick up expressions like that?'

I took the gun from her hand. 'I read magazines at the launderette.' I went back into the bedroom and returned the gun to its hiding place at the bottom of the wardrobe. When I came back, she was standing sideways with her hand on her stomach, looking at her reflection in the mirror.

'Ha, caught you. Narcissist!'

She picked an orange from the fruit bowl and threw it at my head.

'Dessert!' she said.

I managed to catch it which annoyed her even more. I don't know what she was worried about, her stomach was flat and firm.

'Do you do any sport?' I asked, as I peeled the orange.

She picked out a banana, saw me looking at it, changed her mind and swapped it for an orange.

'I play badminton once a week with some friends at the office. I go swimming. I run up the stairs instead of using the lift. That's about all. Why do you ask?'

'I wondered how you kept in trim. You've got a good figure, but I expect you know that.'

'I exercise to make me feel good, not look good.'

'It's as good a reason as any.'

'Right!' she said, 'We'll go and get this translation.' I think I had embarrassed her. 'Where did your man say the office was?' She reached for the Bottin.

Elie Frazier rented a small office on the fourth floor in the rue du Renard, at the Hotel de Ville end. We got the metro direct to Chatelet and then walked. Anything rather than have her drive me. On the way, I went in to an office agency and got the document photocopied. Just in case anything happened. Then I walked her around the corner and abruptly reversed direction to check whether one of Reinhardt's monkeys was following us. We did not bump into anybody. There was still no waterworks van. The only excitement we enjoyed was nearly getting run down by a dumper truck full of earth as it carved the shortest route from Les Halles to the Périphérique. Those drivers must have been paid per load – they never took prisoners.

Elie Frazier answered the doorbell and took us three paces into a dingy anteroom. He was well into his sixties. He was short and hunchbacked. His skin was yellow, his eyes were black, his hair was white, his clothes were brown. He looked like the desert camouflage they put on our armoured personnel carriers.

'Madame? Monsieur?'

'I am Mademoiselle Sikorski,' Mathilde said. He shot an appraising glance at me which betrayed a quick intelligence beneath all that sand and camel dung. 'I believe you translated this document for my father.'

Elie Frazier took the document and shakily lodged a pair of gold pince-nez on his nose.

'Now let me see a bit.' He began to peruse the Arabic script. I just had that feeling that he was play acting. I flipped the corner over.

'It's got your mark on it there,' I pointed out. He tried not to show surprise, but failed.

'Ah yes, so it has.' He beamed at Mathilde but I could see a hard glint behind the lenses. 'Monsieur...?'

'This gentleman is my assistant,' Mathilde announced to stop me from giving my surname. Funny, giving my surname had never embarrassed me; her calling me "this gentleman" did.

'I see. How can I help you mademoiselle?'

'Do you have a translation of this document?'

'But I have translated it already.'

'Exactly. Do you have a copy of it?'

He fumbled around his nose with his handkerchief. Why did he need time to think? It was a straightforward question wasn't it?

'Do you not have the translation?' he asked.

'My father lost it.'

'Does he wish me to translate it again? It will incur another fee.'

'Her father's dead and you don't need another fee for a copy.'

He ignored me and inclined his head towards Mathilde.

'My sympathies mademoiselle.'

'Thank you.' She made a show of peering down demurely at her painted toe-nails then she looked up suddenly into his face. 'Can we discuss this?' She nodded at the door.

'Ah... er... Well of course.' He pushed open the double door behind him. 'Please step this way.' He ushered her towards the inner room whilst barring my passage with a scrawny arm. 'Principals only,' he said.

Mathilde casually put a hand to her neck. 'Naturally,' she said and gave me a look which told me to behave.

The door shut behind them.

It took her fifteen minutes to screw a copy of the translation out of Frazier. I had no idea how she had done it. He came out of his back room vowing to be at her service at any time in the future should she so require. She walked past me to the stairs. I followed like a puppy.

'Well?' I said when we hit the street.

'Well what?' She turned towards the metro.

'Have you got the translation?'

'Yes. No thanks to you. You don't always get what you want by being nasty to people. Sometimes it pays to be nice.'

'Obviously.' I looked at her. 'Do your shirt up.'

'What?'

'Reinhardt's fancies are showing.'

She looked down at where some of her satin was peeking out. She smiled at me as she closed the neck of her shirt.

'You look annoyed.'

'Are you surprised?' I was annoyed. I now recognised her sleight of hand on entering the room.

'It was only one button,' she said. 'That was as much as he needed.'

'It was probably as much as he could cope with.'

She shook her head in derision.

'Nothing happened. It's called feminine charm. Nothing to be jealous of.'

'I'm not jealous.'

'You've no reason to be. I've been nicer than that to you.'

'I've never noticed.'

'Liar.'

'And I've not asked you to be nice to me.'

'No, Joel, you have not. If I have been inadvertently nice to you at any time then it is down to my natural generosity and spontaneous good nature. It's just the way I am.' She shrugged and laughed.

'You underestimate the effect you can have on men.'

'Do I now?' She cocked her head on one side. 'You are an old fuddy duddy sometimes.'

I suppose she was paying me back for calling her a kid.

'So, what is the document. What does it say?'

She wheeled into the office agency.

'I'll give you a copy and then we can laugh together.'

I played roundabouts on a swivel chair whilst she worked the photocopier. She did not act as if she were handling state secrets. She gave me the papers.

'Don't read it yet,' she covered the text with her hand, 'we'll do it over a coffee. You can treat me.'

'Thanks. My wages are burning a hole in my pocket.'

'Are you skint already?'

'No. I was reminding you of my terms of employment.'

'Come on. We'll go over there.' She pointed to a café across the square. I recognised it.

'Um, not that one.'

'Wrong colour awning?'

'I still owe them for a breakfast. Well, two breakfasts actually.' She frowned up at me.

'Why did they give you a second breakfast when you had not paid for the first?'

'It was two breakfasts at once. Me and Makele. We had been on the razzle.' Her face hardened. 'All night.' She opened her mouth to say something. 'With stolen money,' I finished.

'Who stole it?'

'Who do you think?' I grinned.

'Who from?'

'My boss, Vincent. Or rather, I appropriated it from his girls.'

'His girls?'

'He's a pimp. Amongst other things.' She stopped and stared at me. 'You only have yourself to blame,' I pointed out. 'You took me without references.'

'I see,' she said shortly. 'Perhaps you overestimate the effect you have on women.'

'Never even thought about it.'

'Just as well. You'd be wasting your time.' She pointed to a small bar. 'We'll go in there.'

We sat in the gloom at the back and each read through the translation. It was obvious that she was already familiar with its contents. Elie Frazier must have been through it with her line by line. I bet he had taken his time. I imagined her, playing the innocent and leaning forwards to listen to him, aware that his quick black eyes were darting to the neck of her shirt. Bastard!

The document was full of Mohammeds and fathers of Mohammed and numbers of *piks* and yields in *kfiz* and 'by the grace of Allahs.' I read it through twice and sat back. Mathilde had already finished and was sipping her *citron pressé*. By no stretch of the imagination could Reinhardt be interested in this.

'It seems that your father bought an olive grove in Tunisia.'

'Yup,' she said. 'That's what Elie Frazier said it was.' She threw the yellowed document down onto the table. 'Near a place called Zarzis.'

'Where the hell is that?'

'Out in the bled, I expect.' She swirled the ice cube around her glass and grunted. 'I didn't even know he had been to Tunisia. Were you in Tunisia?'

'No, we were in Algeria. He would not have gone into Tunisia officially. But...'

'But?'

'Sometimes officers did slope off on intelligence sorties – unauthorised ferreting about, trying to discover supply lines and that sort of thing.'

'Spying?'

'If you like.'

'And on one of these trips he bought an olive grove?'

'Looks like it.'

'What with?'

'Misappropriated batallion funds probably.'

'Do you mean he stole the money?'

'No more than I stole the money from Vincent. He owed it to me.'

A sad lassitude suddenly invaded her. 'Let's go home.'

I bought a new cylinder lock at the ironmongers in the rue Stresemann and with the aid of Joseph's meagre toolkit I replaced the one fitted to the door of the flat. It would not stop Reinhardt but it might dispel some of Mathilde's fears.

'You need to put the key in the lock up the other way,' I showed her. 'And turn it in the opposite direction to the old one.' I handed her the keys.

She prised the old key from her bunch and fitted the new one. She went to the bureau and took out another keyring and performed the same operation. Then she handed it to me.

'You had better have a key as well.'

'Why?'

She ignored my question.

'That's the flat key and that's the street door key.'

'What's this one?' I shook the third key at her.

'No idea. It was on the keyring already. Looks like an office drawer key.'

'Probably his whisky cabinet.' I looked at the table. 'What have you been doing?'

'Looking at the atlas. Come and see.' She pointed at a dot on the map. 'Zarzis. It's on the coast.' I sighed. 'What's the matter?' she asked.

'At least Elie Frazier got one button.'

'Yes, but he was harmless.'

'And I'm not?'

'No. Just feckless.' I sat back. 'Now you're upset.'

'No, I was thinking of something entirely different. We ought to get a map or plan of where this olive grove is. It might in reality be a gold mine.'

'Where would we find a large scale plan of an obscure part of Tunisia?'

'It's not that obscure – the town is marked on your atlas and it is not a particularly comprehensive atlas.' She flicked her eyebrows up and down and pouted. 'Why don't we try the Colonial Cadastre at the National Archives? Tunisia was administered by France. We must have surveyed the settlement areas at the very least.'

She snapped the atlas shut.

'OK. We'll do it tomorrow.'

'Right. I'll go home then.'

'Stay and have something to eat,' she said quickly. 'I'll make an omelette or something.' Her look was intense. I could not fathom it out.

'I've got a better idea. We'll go down to the corner and let somebody else do the cooking.'

'OK,' she smiled. Then she stopped abruptly. 'Am I all right like this?' she asked. 'Jeans and shirt? Last time you complained.'

'Last time I was paying. It's your treat tonight. You can wear what you like. Makes no difference to me.'

And that did not seem to be what she wanted to hear either.

We ate at the Italie. We sat at the same table as before. The meal was nothing special but served its purpose. I had the egg mayonnaise this time and she had the tomato salad. We drank our coffee and watched the local residents making their way homeward as they clutched the fresh baguettes for their evening meal. Then a schoolgirl wandered along pulling a scraggy-looking dog away from the parked cars. Its tongue lolled out as if complaining that the day was still too hot for a walk. The traffic rumbled unceasingly around the square.

'So how far have we got then?' Mathilde asked. 'Last time we came here we were still trying to guess what Reinhardt was looking for.'

'We still are. He's not looking for an olive grove in Tunisia, that's for sure.'

'We don't know it is an olive grove for certain.'

'No, you're right. It could be a citrus plantation or a turnip field. Whatever it is I still don't think Reinhardt is interested in it.'

'What about Miro and his gang? Your ex-boss and that lot.'

'Yesterday, when Josef failed to turn up for the rendezvous, Vincent must have worked out that he had lost his contact. He will now be quaking with fear at the prospect of telling Miro that he cannot get hold of the things they want.'

'You said "things". In the plural.'

'That is what they talked about.'

'So it definitely is not the olive grove then.'

But I was not really listening. I was thinking that what would really suit us would be for Reinhardt to simply find whatever he was looking for without bothering us. Then Miro would not need to try to find us. And I could walk out and pick up my life where I had left it. If I could find where I had left it. I was sure I had put it down somewhere. It must have been in the cemetery at St Maur.

'Come on, time to go,' I said. 'You've got to be up early in the morning to go to look for that map.'

'What about you?'

'I thought I would have a day off.'

'Maybe there is something under the olive grove,' Mathilde suggested hopefully as we walked back. 'Minerals? Gold? Uranium? Or what about oil? They've got oil in Algeria. Do they have oil in Tunisia?'

'Yeah, olive oil.'

She glanced at the bill board as we passed a fleapit cinema.

'Ha! *Casablanca!* Can't get away from it.'

'Casablanca is in Morocco, not in Tunisia.'

Don't they learn anything at school?

'Have you ever been there?'

'Casablanca? No, but I've seen the film.'

I can prove that I am cultured when I have to.

'I haven't.'

'Not seen the film? Everybody has seen *Casablanca*. How old are you?'

'Twenty sevenish.'

'And you've never seen *Casablanca?*' She shook her head. 'Right,' I said. I took her arm and steered her across the street. 'I'll treat you, but you must behave.'

'God, it's in black and white.' The title blazed onto the screen as she struggled into the seat next to me.

'Of course it is,' I whispered, 'all the best films are. That was in the days when men were men.'

'And women were women?' she continued, *sotto voce.*

'Pay attention. And don't snore. Have a peppermint.' She put the sweet straight into her mouth.

'I didn't see you buy any sweets.'

'I didn't. I just found a loose one in the pocket of this jacket.'

She leaned aside and spat it rattling onto the wooden floor. A man two rows in front turned and shooshed at her. She jabbed me in the ribs. It was just like my first date.

I've always liked *Casablanca*. I like the honest acting. They use no artifice of nouveau realism to embroider their movements. Bogart isn't saying, 'look, I really am a bar owner'; he admits that he is acting the part but that does not detract in any way from the skill he employs in doing it. The dialogue is worth listening to as well. And it is funny and moving and dramatic and poignant and outrageously political. Yeah, I like *Casablanca*. How old did she say she was? Twenty seven? ish? And she has never seen it. Bah, kids of today. Brought up on television. Oh, I forgot. I mustn't keep calling her a kid.

But the kid was weeping on my shoulder so I put my arm around her. I remembered now. It's what you do.

'That was a good idea,' she said on the pavement. 'It was a lovely film. Really romantic.'

'Yeah I shall have to dry my shirt when I get home.'

'A girl is allowed to cry in the cinema.' She slipped her arm through mine. 'Will you walk me home?'

The full-leaved trees cast pools of darkness onto the sidewalk, the metal gratings glinting around their feet. The green cross at the pharmacy was flashing into the dress shop window, giving the mannequins a ghoulish complexion. We ambled along, in no hurry, it seemed, lost in our thoughts. I don't know what she was thinking; I hope she didn't know what I was thinking. A man on a mobylette wobbled precariously homeward. The bike seemed as drunk as he was.

'Well, here we are.' She turned to face me, her little doll's face serious. 'Do you know, that is the first time that somebody has walked me home?'

'Ever?'

'Ever.'

'I suppose your boyfriends all have cars, that's why.'

'It's not what they do have, it's what they don't have – manners.'

'I don't have manners. I'm just still in black and white.'

'When men were men.'

'Go on. Up the stairs.'

'Take me to the door. See me safely in Joel.'

She had not got rid of her fear. I pushed the timer on the light and we climbed the stairs. Thank goodness she did not decide to run up them. She fumbled with the key in the lock.

'It doesn't turn.'

'Turn it the other way, remember?' I put my hand on hers, twisted the key and pushed open the door. 'In you go.'

She hesitated. I sighed theatrically.

'You're a big girl now. Not afraid of the dark.' I switched on the light.

'Of course not.' She strode past me. 'Come on in, I'll make some coffee.'

Now it was my turn to hesitate.

'I mustn't stay long or I'll miss the last metro.'

I don't think she heard me. She pulled open the tall windows in the salon and then flipped the net curtains into the gap.

'It gets so stuffy in here.'

She went into the kitchen and made coffee.

'What are you reading?' she asked as she carried the tray in.

'One of your father's books from the shelf. It's a nineteenth century dictionary of applied and theoretical science.'

She looked over the page.

'Anamorphism? What's that?'

'It's a sort of optical illusion.' I closed the book, leaving the corner of the page turned over as I had found it.

'There's a breeze rising.' She nodded at the net curtains which were beginning to gently billow into the room.

We drank our coffee. The street was quiet. I could hear the footfalls of a lone walker padding along the sidewalk below me. I looked at the clock.

'I must—'

'Stay the night. Don't leave me here alone tonight. They might come back.'

'I've changed the lock.'

'They had a key, they can get another one. Stay just tonight. Look, you can sleep in Papa's room. I know there are a couple of pairs of pyjamas in the suitcase of clothes that you left on the bed.' I looked at her pleading eyes, her nervously twisting fingers. 'I'm scared, Joel.'

I can be a right mug sometimes.

Josef's taste in pyjamas was hideous, I left them in the case. Anyway it was too hot. I just stripped off and got into bed.

11

Suddenly I was awake. For a split second I wondered where I was till I saw the light from the street faintly glowing in the salon. I had left my bedroom door open expressly so that I could see it. Why was I awake? Then I knew. A shape moved stealthily in the doorway. Of course – the windows were still open in the salon. I shot out of that bed like a bishop from a brothel. Even I was impressed by my speed.

'Joel, it's me!' Mathilde shrieked as my hand closed on her neck. She flung her arms around me.

'For God's sake girl, what are you playing at? I nearly broke your spine.'

She clutched me hard.

'I couldn't sleep. I couldn't sleep,' she wailed in terror.

'All right, all right. Calm down.' I stroked her hair. She was shaking. 'Shhhh. Calm down. No harm done. But don't do that to me again.'

'No Joel.' She shivered.

'Nothing to be afraid of.' Her hair was soft, soft down to the nape of the neck. Her shoulders were smooth. 'Calm down.'

'I am calm.'

My fingers trailed gently down her spine.

Her voice was quieter. Under control.

'You're not wearing any clothes, Joel.'

A hand stroked down my shoulder blade and her breasts moved warm against my chest through her silk pyjamas.

'I don't in the summer.'

I could feel her heart beating. I could hear her little breaths.

'You're naked,' she whispered and I could tell that she was looking into my eyes when she added, 'and stiff.'

'That's what you do to me, Mathilde.' My hand slid slowly down to her buttocks.

'Often?'

I gently pressed her against my proof.

'Very often.' I kissed her forehead. She threw her arms up around my neck and pulled my mouth onto hers. I fought to get my tongue back.

'You want me don't you?' She was delighted to make the accusation. 'You want me.' She jerked as my body replied for me. 'You want me,' she hissed. I bit my lip. 'Say it,' she ordered. 'Say it. Say you want me.'

This will cost you LeBatard.

'I want you.'

I gasped as she raked her nails down my back. She ducked out of my shock-loosened arms and disappeared into the half shadows of the salon.

'You'll have to catch me first,' she challenged.

A naked man touting an erection does not throw himself without abandon into a chase around a gloomy room full of unfamiliar furniture. He applies some circumspection. Or he should. I charged through the doorway and cannoned painfully into the back of the sofa.

'Don't break it, I want to use it,' she called and I knew from her tone that she was not talking about the furniture.

Where did that voice come from? From behind the dark bulk of the armchair in the corner. I began to creep towards her. There was a sudden scrabble of movement. I raced around the chair, trod on something on the parquet and my feet slid from under me. I went down with a crash. I hurt my pride more than anything else. I angrily pulled up the treacherous cloth into a shaft of light. It was a silk pyjama jacket. Her head and shoulders bobbed above the sofa. She moved into a pool of brightness and wiggled her bare breasts at me.

'Reactions are a bit slow. How's your eyesight?' she teased.

'Right, my girl, you've asked for it.' I launched myself at the sofa. She flung up her hidden hand and I found myself fighting my way out of the pyjama trousers that she wrapped around my face as the sofa began to tip over. I skittered forwards onto the floor, suffocating in silk. I shook myself free and looked around quickly for any sign of her.

'You're not trying very hard,' she taunted as she ran the length of the room, the streetlight shafts flitting snapshots of bouncing breasts and swinging thighs.

I dropped into the matt shadow of the bureau and waited. 'Joel?' I inched along the cover of the upturned sofa, stalking the sentry. 'Joel?' Keep calling my pretty so that I know where you are. 'Joel?' I could see her ankle. It turned. 'Joel, where are you?' The extra words were all I needed. She squealed as my hand clamped on her calf. She shook her leg, she kicked. My other hand clamped above the first. I hauled myself up her, hand over hand, hand over knee, hand onto thigh. She writhed, she pulled and then my hand closed over her mound. She stopped struggling. Her breath came out in a long slow sigh. She looked down at me. She stood still.

'Oh don't you want me any more?' She put her hand to me. 'Oh yes you do.'

'Do you want me?' I asked. I could feel her answer in my hand. 'Yes.'

'Say it.' She clamped her mouth onto mine and rubbed her body against me everywhere that it could touch. She pulled her mouth away and her hot breath scoured down my neck. 'Say it,' I ordered.

'I want you.' Her voice was a growl. It raised the hair on my scalp. Without turning she swept the things from the demi-table behind her. They scattered and smashed on the floor. The curtains swirled net in the streetlight. 'Do it,' she hissed. She leaned her buttocks on the table and then her heels thudded into the small of my back, dragging me onto her. Where do they learn these gymnastics?

'I want you, I want you, I want you!' We were standing between the two open windows. I could see a vacant taxi waiting on the rank. I could smell the city night air wafting in through the wide open windows. 'I want you, I want you, I want you.' Her arms were pulling at my neck, matching the lunging of her pelvis. The table was thumping against the wall. She was gurgling and growling. I was probably saying something as well. Her heels began to beat a tattoo on my back and then she was shrieking like a metro whistle as her thighs convulsed around me.

She flopped onto my shoulder like a rag doll. We leaned into each other, welded as one, panting and holding tight. My eyes caught a movement in the block opposite.

'Don't move,' I whispered. 'There's a light gone on in the house across the street. They can see right in here if they look.'

'It was probably all the noise you were making.'

'Oh Christ, there's another light gone on. You've woken up the entire street.'

She began to giggle down in her belly then she stiffened and sunk her nails into my buttocks and her mouth into my shoulder, swallowing another wail as she climaxed again.

'Grrr that was good,' she said at last. 'That was a bonus.' She nibbled at my shoulder. 'What did you think of it?'

'It was... er... different.'

I had never done anything like it before in my life.

'Did you enjoy it? It was good fun wasn't it?'

'Good fun? All that running around?'

'Yes. Don't tell me that it didn't excite you. Sex should be fun, shouldn't it?'

'I had never really thought about it.' Sex was something that you just did until it happened. I peered cautiously out of the window. 'OK. The last of the lights has gone off now.'

She uncrossed her ankles and I lowered her feet to the floor. As I straightened up I ran my tongue up her belly and around her nipples. She drew in her breath through a gaping mouth.

'Oh!' she exclaimed as I swept her up into my arms. 'What are you doing?'

I carried her towards my bedroom and the large bed.

'I'm going to show you how to do it slowly. Very slowly.'

The windows were still open and now it was the morning sun and the street noises that were flooding in. I lay on my back and looked and listened whilst Mathilde slept on, her supple body wrapped and twisted half around me. And I thought, you are an idiot, Lebatard. Was the usual business going to start all over again? This was where they say, 'I could come and cook for you. I'll clean for you. I could iron your shirts.' They slip out of the bed quietly and the next thing you know is they are waking you up with a tray of steaming coffee and fresh bread and you give in.

'Were you going to say something?' a sleepy voice enquired from somewhere on my chest.

'Not a thing.'

'Good. Get me breakfast would you? I'm shagged out.'
I blame it on a university education.

Getting breakfast took longer than I had expected. First I had to restore the salon. It looked as if a whirlwind had hit it. I found a brush and managed to sweep up the remains of whatever had been on the table. I didn't think it was Limoges porcelain. In setting the furniture back I collected the components of Mathilde's nocturnal wardrobe.

'Make yourself decent,' I called and hurled the bundle through the bedroom doorway. I derived great satisfaction from seeing it wrap itself smartly around her head.

Mathilde sat back and picked a piece of bread crust from her bath robe.

'Was that the best you could do? Bread and jam?' she asked.

'And coffee.' I rattled the pot. It was the best that I intended to do. 'And you would not have got that if you hadn't have asked me so nicely.'

'What do you normally have for breakfast?'

Oh dear. Here it comes. And I was hoping that she would be different from the others.

'Why do you want to know?'

'To calculate how much extra effort you put into it.'

'None. You can check with Joanne next time you see her.'

'I will.'

'Now go and get dressed. We've got work to do.' She pouted at me and got up from the table.

'What shall I wear?'

'Whatever you can put on before ten o'clock,' I sighed, glancing at the clock. 'Today we've got to try to charm civil servants at the Cadastre Colonial.'

She poked her head from her bedroom and grinned.

'So something with buttons on?'

'Get on with it.' I jerked my head at the bedroom.

The Cadastre Colonial, as Mathilde discovered by consulting the Bottin, was right at the end of the rue Lecourbe near the Parc des Expositions. Like a lamb to the slaughter I followed her down to the boulevard to see if her car was still there. It was.

Covered with dust and looking no bigger than it had last time.

'Poxy little thing,' I muttered as I squeezed into the seat. 'Don't you ever clean it?'

'It's cleaner than your car,' she retorted and we screeched through the light as it changed.

'That light was a bit ripe. A lovely shade of red it was.'

'I'm colour blind.'

'Where are you going? Don't you know Paris?'

'Have you noticed the licence plate on the car? It's sixty seven. That's the département of the Bas Rhin. Strasbourg. How well do you know Strasbourg?'

'Never been there. It's where Reinhardt says he comes from. Turn left here. Go down to Denfert Rochereau then cut down the Avenue Leclerc to the Boulevards Extérieurs.'

'As if I knew. Idiot. Tell me when I get there.'

I have an inbred disgust of officialdom. Smug civil servants who are neither civil nor servile sitting fat-arsed on their pensions and pushing paper around all day.

We found the reference number of the plan we needed in a ledger and then a woman who looked as if she had not smiled since drinking sour milk at kindergarten gave us a form to fill in. It was all about confidentiality and public responsibility. We only wanted to look at a map. I let Mathilde fill it in. She was probably accustomed to doing things like that all day long in her office in Strasbourg. We handed it over and the woman sniffed at it as if she had never seen such a slip before in her life.

'Tunisia?' she scoffed with a mournful glee, 'that will take days to get.'

'We'll wait then.' Mathilde hauled her handbag up onto the counter and began to search in it. It was a challenge. Taking the conflict into the enemy's camp.

'Madame!'

'Mademoiselle,' Mathilde corrected sweetly.

'The counter,' the woman snapped.

'How kind of you,' she wilfully misunderstood and pulled out a small bag and emptied it onto the formica. Pots, tubs, tubes and phials of cosmetics bounced and rolled in all directions. 'One seldom has the time or the space to tidy one's handbag at home does one?' She smiled.

I turned to study a poster on the wall. I did not at that moment intend to buy any savings bonds at two and a half percent but you could never know when the information might come in useful.

Forty five minutes later a rattle in the pneumatic tube, scoring only three decibels less than a train on the elevated metro, suggested the arrival of our map. It had to be ours. Nobody else was waiting. Madame Sourmilk, however, was apparently so engrossed in her work that she did not hear it.

'Don't bother yourself, I'll get it,' Mathilde announced and banged the release button and began to pull up the hatch door. It was a brilliant move. Madame Sourmilk leaped from the chair as if it had suddenly groped her.

'That's my job, that's my responsibility,' she cried.

'Oh I could see you were busy.'

'One has many things to do. I am worked off my feet all day long. This place is a treadmill.' Her protestations mocked her as they echoed around the high ceilings of the empty room. She pulled out the cylinder and unrolled the map. She checked the docket with the reference number on the roll. 'Oh,' she remarked with ill-concealed disappointment, 'they've not made a mistake. It's what you asked for.'

'I was sure it would be,' Mathilde reassured her.

It was a large scale plan of a tract of land on the northern outskirts of Zarzis. I sat back and watched Mathilde eagerly scanning across the sheet to find the plot number that she had inherited. I don't know what she was seeing; romantic white buildings with domes and minarets; avenues of date palms and walled courtyards; mystic maidens with veiled faces swaying on mules and red-fezzed carpet salesmen calling out in the street? I was seeing acres of sand, flies, sun, filth and stench. If Mathilde persisted in her quest to prove that Josef had been a good father she courted the danger of establishing simply that he was a lousy real estate speculator.

'Here it is Joel. Come and look.'

I gave in to the childish enthusiasm in her eyes.

'Well, there you are then.' I probably sounded sententious but what do you say to somebody who is in ecstasies over their interpretation of an impersonal map? Perhaps she would be able to go through life without ever suffering the pain of discovering what it was that her father had left her. 'Is there anything marked in the plot?' Like a gold mine? Or a steelworks? Or a well, even?

'No, it's just that bit there, along the road. It has a cemetery on one side.'

'Useful.'

'What?'

'Quiet neighbours.'

'Closing in ten minutes,' Sourmilk piped happily. I expect she now had a three hour lunch break. She must be exhausted, poor lamb.

'Can I get a photocopy of this?' Mathilde asked.

'I regret, mademoiselle, the photocopier is broken.'

If she bubbled with any more contentment she would lay an egg.

'Hang on a minute,' I said. 'Don't surrender the map. I'll be back in two minutes.'

I skipped out into the street and into the Maison de la Presse before it too, closed for lunch. When I got back Sourmilk and Mathilde were engaged in a verbal tug of war so I unleashed my broadside.

'Gérard Dollberg says that we can have as much time as we like and if you wish to discuss it with him he will be going for lunch in ten minutes.'

Sourmilk stopped dead and stared at me.

'Monsieur Dollberg?' she asked, surprised.

'Well I call him "Gérard" but I expect he is "monsieur" to you.'

She relinquished the map. Mathilde was also staring at me. I was hoping she would not give the game away.

'Well I... I don't know,' Sourmilk stuttered. It must have been a shock for her to discover that the insignificant persons who had been interrupting her morning of frantic inactivity were actually bosom buddies with the director of her department. Almost as much of a shock as it would be to him when he found out.

'He's upstairs if you want to check. Meanwhile, we'll take a tracing as you are incapable of providing us with the official photocopying service that is advertised on the board.' I handed Mathilde the pad of tracing paper and the pencil that I had just bought. 'You've recorded her name, have you?'

Mathilde nodded, wide-eyed and then bent to the map.

We drank our coffee side by side on the terrace of the café on the corner and watched the cars and taxis queuing at the entrance to the Parc des Expositions. The Toy Exhibition was in its third day.

Mathilde's eyes were dancing and they were looking at me. It's a good job I'm tough or it might have affected me.

'How did you know Monsieur What's-his-name?' she asked.

'Ah well, I move in interesting circles you know.' She pulled a 'cut-the-crap' face. 'And when I went to the shop I saw a letter addressed to him lying in a pigeon hole.'

She was wearing a knee-length skirt in a light man-made material of some sort. It was patterned in small lozenges of navy blue, emerald green and white and lay close on her thighs. Her blouse was a matching navy blue and, I noticed parenthetically, that it had buttons.

'What are you looking at?' she smiled.

'What I cannot see.'

'Oh very philosophical.'

'No, just rude.' I smiled. 'But you have discovered something that you are just bursting to tell me.'

'How did you know?' I shrugged and said nothing. It is not wise to give too much away. 'The map we saw was the definitive land title map.' She took out her notebook and showed me the name of a company in the rue de Rivoli.

'What of it?' I said.

'They were the previous applicants to view that map. I saw it on the record sheet.'

'When?'

'Last year. And before that, nobody had looked at it for seventeen years. Why were they suddenly interested? And who are they?'

'We don't know they were interested in the bit you were looking at. How many plots were on that plan? Twenty? Thirty?'

'Not as many as that.'

'But even so.'

'It might be important.' She was insistent. 'We need to find out.'

'Mathilde,' I tried to make my voice gentle, 'Josef bought an olive grove.'

'Bauxite! Isn't that the stuff they make aluminium from?'

181

I nodded. 'I bet there's a load of bauxite under that soil.' She fiddled with the teaspoon on her saucer. 'Or tin... or coal... Something,' she whispered. 'There must be something.' Her eyes were wet.

'Come on then, finish your coffee and we'll go to the rue de Rivoli. It'll be like going home for me.'

Immobilier Grand Soleil had set up a sales office in a small shop under the arcades of the rue de Rivoli, at the Concorde end. I remembered it as a perfume shop but these places never last long. We stood before the window and gazed at the model countryside before us. Miniature chalets were spotted across a gently sloping park of green sward and date palm trees. A picturesque service road wound up and through the houses like a white snake. The model-maker had really gone to town. There was a little church and a public swimming pool and a selection of shops. It was idyllic looking. How he had the cheek to put so much green onto it I did not dare to wonder. Perhaps, like Mathilde, he claimed to be colour blind.

'Village Grand Soleil,' Mathilde read the board. 'Buy your own luxury chalet in our village development and enjoy all year sun in a French-speaking environment.' She looked sideways at me. 'What proportion of the population of Tunisia speak French then?'

'Ah, you miss the point. It's all to do with the meaning of words.'

'Semantics.'

'No, Jews have got nothing to do with it.' She sighed at me but I don't know why. 'I'll give you an illustration. There's a hotel up in the rue Victor Massé, near Pigalle.'

'I don't know it.' She looked pointedly at me. 'Why do you know it?'

She made it plain that she thought it was a *hotel de passe* – one used only by prostitutes, rooms by the hour and all that sort of thing.

'I used to deliver English tourists to it in my coach from the Gare du Nord. In the hotel reception the *patron* had nailed up a welcoming sign, *"English spoken here".*'

'So?'

'He didn't speak a word of English. He was from Carcassone.

Christ, you could hardly understand his French. His night porter was Jugoslav and his chambermaid was Portuguese. I asked the *patron* one day about the sign and he waved his arm around at the dining room. "What can you hear?" he said.'

'And what could you hear?'

'English being spoken. Everywhere in the hotel. None of the staff spoke it but all the guests did.'

She nodded her head slowly. 'I know a story about a polar bear that is almost as unfunny. I'll tell you it sometime. Come on. Look rich.,' She walked into the shop.

'Madame? Monsieur?' A well-oiled salesman advanced upon us. I waited for Mathilde to correct him with a 'mademoiselle' but she did not. Part of the plan, I suppose.

I have no idea where he had bought his suit but for once in my life I not only felt better dressed, but I was better dressed. Mathilde slipped her arm through mine. An effect which I somewhat marred by jumping as if she had just plugged me in to the mains.

'We would like to look at the details of the Village Grand Soleil,' she announced to my astonishment and to the salesman's delight. His eyes spun around like till flags.

'But certainly, madame, please come this way.' He laid out a house plan on the table. 'This is the design of the standard chalet. Entrance hall, living room–'

'We are not interested in the standard chalet.' Mathilde's voice was curt. I watched the salesman mentally add a few more thousand francs to his commission. 'Of course not madame.' He hurriedly scuffled the plan aside and delved in a box. 'This is the chalet *"grand standing."* Larger plot, larger living room, two extra bedrooms.' His finger flitted about the plan, dotting from feature to feature as Mathilde demanded to be shown them.

I stood back, wondering what her game was.

'No pool? Where would you put a swimming pool?' she asked haughtily. The salesman flicked back his greasy hair and made a vague stab. 'Only one garage?' she observed. 'How quaint.' He was beginning to sweat. 'Darling, how many cars would we take over?' It took me a second or two before I realised that she was talking to me.

'Only three, my pippet. We would leave the Bugatti in Monte Carlo.'

'Do show me on the site plan where the luxury villas are built.'
He was scurrying about like a fag end in a tornado.

'They are being built at this moment, madame.' He laid out a
site plan and pointed to several rectangles. 'At the top of the site,
here, here and here.'

I moved to stand next to Mathilde. I could smell her perfume.
I looked at the plan. It was an enlarged copy of the one we had
traced. I could feel her hip against me as she leaned across the
table. I looked quickly to see that all her buttons were done up.
Just checking. They were.

'So their gardens back onto this, what is it, a park?' she asked.

'It's an ancient, local, um... ethnic establishment madame.'

It was the bloody cemetery.

'But that's–' I stopped as Mathilde straightened up and her
heel leaned heavily on my foot.

'–delightful,' she finished. 'Such quiet neighbours, I expect.'
She threw a dazzling smile at the man. She had used my words. It
was a signal. She knew that it was the cemetery. 'And you have
managed to acquire all this land? How clever of you.'

'Well, we are specialists in the field, madame.'

'Now what about this road?' I asked. 'It looks like the main
road into town.'

'Yes, monsieur, it is the main road into Zarzis.'

'Does it carry much traffic.'

'Oh monsieur, this is Tunisia. An odd camel or two.'

He really thought we had straw in our hair.

'But if it got busy, say in a couple of year's time, is there an
alternative way out of the village?'

He rubbed his chin and studied the plan.

'Well, not really. We can't go that way because of the terrain
and that way is blocked by the cem... er... seminary. No, we would
have to come down to this road but I cannot see a problem there.'

I bet you can't. I turned to Mathilde, now that she had
released my foot.

'Well the decision is yours, my sugar. Just tell me how much
money you need.'

She looked at the man. He started.

'Oh, the luxury villa is two hundred and seventy five thousand
francs,' he announced breathlessly.

I gazed blandly at the wall opposite as if that amount of money meant nothing to me. It was the truth.

'And if we buy three? I expect we could negotiate a deal on that, could we not?' Mathilde continued naturally.

I looked at my nails. Spending money is such a bore.

'I...I... You would have to see Monsieur Palerme about that, madame, and he is not here today. May I take your details and ask him to call you?'

'May I take this?' She swept up the plan from the table. 'Just tell him the Comtesse de Ségur called.'

'*Oui madame*,' he whispered.

'Come along Charles.'

I wafted out behind her. If she was Countess, surely that made me a Count?

'Keep walking smoothly,' I said to her as we passed along under the arcades. 'He might be watching us. Must keep up appearances. No giggling or slapping each other on the back. And don't wiggle your bottom.'

'Jo-Jo!' I staggered as Marie-Hélène threw herself into my arms and kissed me hard on the mouth. 'You bastard,' she said as she broke free. 'You know I'm mad about you.'

'May I introduce the Comtesse de Ségur?' I indicated a startled Mathilde.

'Yeah and I'm Aristide Briand,' Marie Hélène said as she shook her hand. 'Comtesse de Ségur? The one who wrote *Les Malheurs de Sophie*?'

'The very same,' I assured her.

'She died in 1874.' Marie-Hélène laughed and slapped me hard on the back. She is a buxom girl who likes to wear her skirts short and her necklines low.

Mathilde had sidled into the cover of one of the pillars.

'Marie-Hélène is a guide,' I explained. 'She knows about these things.'

'I'm a bloody good guide aren't I, Jo-Jo? We made a good team didn't we?'

'We had our moments.'

'What are you doing now? Not driving?' She put her hand to her generous mouth. 'Oh, I forgot. The Cityscope!' She turned to Mathilde. 'He took the top off. Schhhiiiik.' She waved her hand like a knife blade. 'Now you see it, now you don't.'

'He told me.' Mathilde was struggling with her power of speech. Marie-Hélène has that effect upon people. 'Joel, I think we should be going.'

'Oh... Joel,' Marie-Hélène mimicked.

'Yeah, Joel. This lady is my employer.'

'Oh shit. I always put my foot it in it don't I?'

'Please don't trouble yourself, mademoiselle, it is of no consequence. But we really must be going. We have work to do.'

Mathilde walked off and I followed. I turned to wave to Marie-Hélène and she made a gesture which told me what she thought I ought to be doing with Mathilde.

So we still had something in common then.

I caught up with Mathilde just outside W. H. Smith's.

'Um...' I began.

'Don't bother.' Her voice was short. 'You could never excuse yourself.' She turned her disgust towards the shop window. 'Oh honestly! "Must keep up appearances" says you and the very next second you are pawing all over a girl.'

'I wasn't pawing her. I was fighting her off. There are not many ways to fight off a woman without touching her naughty bits.' I glanced across at her as she feigned interest in the display of books. 'It's quite nice for a man to have to fight off a woman. Good for his ego. I haven't seen you fighting off the men.'

'I do it more discreetly. Anyway, I've been dead for a hundred years.' She looked at me. 'Most of my suitors are ancient.'

'And paf!' I joked. But it still hurt. 'Come on, I'll buy you some lunch.'

'In a bookshop?' I heard her derision from the pavement as I walked into the shop. When I got to the stack of English newspapers I turned around. She was still standing there, smiling, as if I had lost my marbles. 'Are you coming or not?' I asked.

She rolled her eyes to the arcades and shrugged.

'I'll humour you.'

I took her upstairs to the tea room. She gazed around at the beams and the fussy dark wooden tables and the waitresses in black with white aprons and the blue and white china. I walked to the empty table by the potted plant and held a chair for her.

'Oh,' she said as she gracefully slid her bottom onto the polished mahogany, 'I didn't know they had a restaurant.'

'A tea room,' I corrected her. 'Others would have been more

discreet about their ignorance.' I sat down and she kicked my leg under the table. 'Oh we are still on speaking terms then are we?'

She pulled a face. I supposed that meant yes.

I knew about the tea room because of the guides. They come here to buy English books and then they go upstairs to drink tea, eat little cakes and try to chat up English boys. But the only people you ever find here are rich, faded Parisians trying to show how discreet and English they can be and middle-aged English tourists complaining more loudly than Parisians would about the high prices and the weak tea.

'Madame? Monsieur?'

'We'll have two of those.' I pointed to a phrase on the menu card.

'*Deux Welsh Rarebeet,*' the waitress confirmed and swirled off.

'I didn't know you could read English.' Mathilde looked just a little impressed.

'Well,' I said airily, 'working with foreigners all day long as I used to, you inevitably find languages rub off on you.'

'Ah ha,' she said. 'So what are we going to eat?'

'Oh it's rabbit. Done in the... er... Welsh way.' I nodded encouragingly at her. 'Wales is famous for its rabbit.'

'I never knew that. What exactly is the "Welsh way" of cooking rabbit?'

'Oh you'll see. You'll see. You'll like it.'

'Oh good,' she said eagerly. 'Just as long as it hasn't got *gratiné* cheese anywhere. I can't stomach that.'

Of course, she already knew, didn't she? What a stupid language. No wonder they can't spell 'Concorde'.

For a treat I let her choose the dessert.

'I think we should have another chat with Pino.' I tapped the plan folded on the table.

She looked at me above her coffee cup like the sun rising over the marshes.

'I suppose he is the nearest we know to a legal expert.'

'Oh you could get a proper opinion but it would cost you. Is it worth spending money on? Anyway, Pino still owes me for Nice.'

'Nice?'

'It was his job. He should have been doing it but I went instead.'

'Why?'

'He was drunk.'

'And you weren't?'

'Yeah, strange that. I'd never thought about it. Must be the effect you have on me. Sobering.' I paid up and we went down into the street. 'Now, do you remember where you parked the car?'

'Of course I do.'

'Damn. I was hoping we would have to walk.'

We crossed into the Tuileries garden. The sun glared blinding white on the sand. The little trees cast blobs of shade at their feet. At the far end of the garden, above the froth of green foliage, the tiled roofs of the Louvre glowed grey with a metallic heat like some great simmering charcoal furnace.

We threaded our zig-zag way through the alleys, grateful for the snippets of shade. Mathilde seemed involved in her thoughts. She was probably seeing the sprinkling fountains and blossoming orange trees around her villa in Zarzis.

'You don't look like a war hero,' she said.

That just shows what a lousy mind-reader I am.

'But you look like a countess.'

'But I'm not a countess.'

'Exactly. And I'm not a war hero. Appearances are deceptive.'

'You got a medal.'

'So did your father. So did Reinhardt for that matter. We all got medals. They gave them out like sweets at Sunday School. You got one for just being there. Anyway, I've lost it.'

'Lost it?'

'Pawned it. Years ago.'

'But it wasn't just a campaign medal was it? I've read the citation. "Rescuing two wounded colleagues whilst under fire. Selfless disregard of personal safety..."'

'Oh they make those stories up. They take them from a compendium. How do you know about all this? Where did you read the citation?'

'You told me at the beginning that you were corrupted and deceitful, so I decided to check up on you.

'It's a bit late for that now.'

'Oh I did it ages ago. Do I look like a fool?'

'I didn't say you looked like a fool. I said you looked like a countess. And I meant it.'

'You are funny sometimes.' We climbed the steps to the passerelle which leads over the Seine to the Gare d'Orsay. 'Why is there a bit missing in the middle of this bridge?'

'A barge came down stream on the winter flood and got jammed. We can still get across. They've put scaffolding over it. It's quite safe.'

'Well that's a relief. I don't think my insurance would cover me.'

'That would be embarrassing for you.' I glanced across to the left bank. 'Well your car is still there. Or at least the roof is.'

'You sound disappointed.'

'I am. I was hoping they would tow it away.'

'You don't convince me. You took great pride in showing me this secret place to park because it was unrestricted and nobody knew about it.'

'I must have a soft spot for you.'

'Yes,' she said, and kissed me on the cheek.

I should not let that sort of thing impress me.

But I knew that it did.

She drove twice around the block before she found a parking space. It was outside Jean-Marie's bar. I could see him polishing glasses and giving her the once-over with his lascivious eye. His other eye was dithering like a dog between dinners. He started angrily when he saw me get out of the car so I waved at him. He tried to say something rude with his fingers and forgot that he was holding a glass. I heard the smash from across the street. Poor old Jean-Marie. He did not improve.

The sidewalks in the rue St Dominique are narrow and every hard-elbowed, broad-hipped matron in the Seventh seemed to be steaming in the opposite direction. As we passed the end of the Passage Jean-Nicot I glanced quickly under the archway just in case Gaspard was waiting for me again. When we got to the Café Clerc, Mathilde stood aside.

'You go in first,' she said. 'I'll stay behind. The bullet would never go through you, you're too dense.'

'Oh stop fussing. A little bit of ordnance in your gut would give you a bit of weight.'

'Like you?' She jabbed her fingers painfully into my side.

'Ouch! Where did you learn to do that?'

'Playing badminton.'

'I thought it was a game for girls.'

'I play with the boys.'

Joanne was polishing glasses behind the bar. Is that what all bartenders do when they have no customers? She looked steadily at me as I walked in.

'You didn't go home last night,' she accused me.

'What's it got to do with you?'

Then she saw Mathilde behind me and realised how her remark could be interpreted. 'Madame,' she nodded. She looked embarrassed. That was rarer than a drinkable Beaujolais Nouveau and I savoured it accordingly. Mathilde smiled politely and did not correct her.

'How do you know I didn't come home last night?' I frowned at Joanne. Did I detect jealousy?

'Your concierge was in here asking about you. I think she was hoping you had cleared out so she could rent your room.'

'I'm surprised she bothered asking. Nosey old cow.' I leaned on the zinc and looked around the room full of beige vinyl seats. The bar looked like an empty chocolate box. With one chocolate hiding right in the corner.

'Pino!'

'Hallo Jo-Jo.'

'Have you eaten?'

'Yeah.'

'Fresh air,' Joanne grunted.

I put a ten franc note on the counter.

'Make him a cheese sandwich and bring it over.'

'You come and get it.'

'We're having a business meeting. And don't forget the change.'

We went over to Pino. He did not look drunk, just tired and dejected. Perhaps Joanne had taken my outburst to heart and had not been serving him as much alcohol. He stood up and shook hands.

'You remember Mademoiselle Sikorski don't you?' He bowed his head stiffly. 'We need your brain again.'

'My brain?' He spat a short laugh. 'My brain?' He looked about the room. 'I had one once.' His eyes fixed hungrily on the plate that Joanne was carrying towards him.

'Oh, don't let us interrupt your lunch, please,' Mathilde insisted. 'We'll have a coffee whilst you finish.' She slipped behind the neighbouring table. 'A crème for me please,' she said to Joanne.

'Certainly madame.' Joanne looked at me.

'Yeah, the same for me.'

'Please,' she reminded me.

'Please.'

Mathilde grinned all over her face. 'You ought to play badminton. You could pick up all kinds of tricks.'

I watched Pino as he chewed his way through the sandwich. I had a suspicion that it was yesterday's bread but he did not mention it. I looked at Mathilde. She smiled back, a simple smile. She was happy. She was doing something that she considered worthwhile.

Pino finished eating and brushed the crumbs to the floor. Joanne scowled at him but he was fearless now that he had food in his stomach. We showed him the plan of the chalet village and we compared it to Mathilde's tracing. There was no doubt. Immobilier Grand Soleil were going to drive a road straight through Mathilde's olive grove.

'Can we stop them?' she asked.

Why would you want to? I thought. Pino rubbed his chin.

'I need to read that translation again.' We sat quietly whilst he studied it.

'It is my property isn't it?' Mathilde insisted.

'Well, yes and no. The *figh* and the *amal* – the law and the jurisprudence in Tunisia, has a lot of French law in it but it still has its Arabic traditions. They've got five classes of land. Yours would need to be *melk*, that is, land not owing tribute or owned by community.' He picked a piece of bread from his teeth. 'But you would still need the *idjima* for it to be effective.'

'What is the *idjima?*' Mathilde asked.

Pino scratched his head.

'Well it's sort of the permission. No it's not really the permission, it's the agreement of the community.'

'And would that make it *melk?*'

'Oh it's that already. It's private land.' He tapped the paper. 'No doubt about that.'

191

'Do you know what you are talking about?' I asked. As far as I was concerned, Pino was a drunken bum who could not hold down a job. This display of knowledge was suspect to me.

'If you have nothing useful to add, keep quiet,' Mathilde snapped.

I kept quiet. I watched her hair swinging as she nodded at explanations. She was certainly getting my money's worth. I gazed out into the street. Occasional cars crawled lethargically past, looking for a parking space, looking for a turning; casual figures wandered aimlessly along the sidewalks with bored indifference.

Mathilde sat back in her seat. 'So,' she resumed, 'whoever holds this document, holds the title to the land?'

'Yes. It's a sort of bearer title deed. But in itself, that's not enough under the *sunna* – the sacred tradition, that is – to prove ownership.'

'What has to be done?'

'You justify ownership by physical possession of the land and you have to register that title at the local land court in Zarzis. To do both those things, you need to go to Tunisia.'

'Well that's cleared that up,' I observed as we walked back to the car. Finished and done with.

'I shall have to go to Tunisia. You heard what Pino said. The title needs to be lodged at the court.'

I stopped dead. 'Mathilde, it's just an olive grove.'

'It's not just an olive grove.' Her voice was angry. 'It's my olive grove.' She looked up at a *'Vacances 2000'* sign. 'This will do.'

It was the travel agency. I followed her in.

'How much is a return flight to Tunisia?'

The woman pulled a directory from a shelf behind her.

'To Tunis?'

'I suppose so. What's the cheapest?'

'When do you want to go?'

Mathilde looked at me. I shrugged. 'Don't ask me. I've got no opinion on this at all.'

'In a couple of weeks' time.'

They set about organising the ticket. I wandered over to the rack and pulled out a brochure of holidays in Martinique. It was full of grass huts, food grilled on the beach and girls with very small bikinis and very big–

'What are you looking at?' Mathilde asked.

'The blonde one in the blue bikini.' I showed her the photo.

'Oh, don't you ever change? Just for once, couldn't you–?'

'What?'

'Oh never mind. Come on.' I followed her from the shop.

'What are you going to do now?'

'All the important things that make up my life. Fill up the fridge. Go to the launderette. Behead a few statues in the church.'

She looked hard at me as if trying to make up her mind. Then she nodded. 'Right,' she said. She got in the car. 'The lady at the agency will ring me when the tickets are ready. You can pick them up for me, can't you?'

'At your service, madame.'

She looked me in the eyes. Still dark, still with those arched eyebrows. 'Mademoiselle,' she corrected clearly, then she put the car in gear.

'Just a minute,' I said. 'Why "tickets" in the plural?'

'Well you didn't think I'd be going on my own did you?'

She drove off.

I watched the world of Jacques Cousteau as it swirled and bubbled in the porthole. The manageress with the head like a pineapple was unloading one of the dryers at the back of the shop. Colours and shapes slopped and lunged against the soapy glass before me. They made more sense and showed more order than my world.

Why were we chasing about after this olive grove? So that Mathilde could prove to herself that Josef had been a good father to her? What was I doing in all this? I had joined the gravy train and had decided to stay on it whilst it ran. Surely we were trundling up a dead end with weeds in the track? There had been no waterworks van today. Nor yesterday. Nobody had tailed us. Nobody was watching. Nobody was interested. Reinhardt did not want this olive grove. Miro did not want it. We did not have what they wanted and Mathilde did not know what she had got. It was all getting very silly. There was nothing left in this for me except pain. I could hear the gravy train slowing down for the terminus.

Time to get my things together.

12

Annick smiled at me from the bedside table. The frame was still broken, I had wedged it together. One day Reinhardt would pay for that. Why was I feeling maudlin? I had lost Annick and it had been my fault. She would not have been happy with me no matter what she had thought. Was that the reason I was depressed? No, I remember now. Today is the day I get off the gravy train. That would involve another loss. What a martyr I would be. What an idiot.

I studied the screwed-up bundle of money on the table and tried unsuccessfully to calculate my total assets. I would have to get myself a job. I seemed to have been saying that ever since I had been engaged by Mademoiselle Sikorski. How would she deal with Reinhardt and Miro without me? Or would she have to deal with them? Had I not deduced that they, neither of them, were interested in the olive grove?

I kicked the bedclothes off, sat up and rubbed my stubble. It made a satisfying grating sound. Something was niggling in my mind. I rubbed some more. It still grated.

Reinhardt is not interested in the olive grove. His pigeons in the waterworks van must have seen Mathilde showing me the deed on the terrace of the café at the Madeleine. They could have taken it from us there and then but they had ignored it and Reinhardt had searched Mathilde's flat instead. So they were not interested in the deed. What about Miro and Vincent? They don't know that we have it. But are they looking for the same thing? Had Janus been playing true to his codename? A double game – one thing for Reinhardt and another for Miro and Vincent?

I got up. I knew one way to find out.

The notice on the door still said, *'Mirovici Group. Ring the bell and wait.'* I rang the bell and this time, I waited. Don't want to fluster Luc or that little, blue-eyed kid.

The door opened and Luc eyed me coldly.

'What do you want, Shitbag?'

Nice to know that he remembered me. 'Do you talk to all your employer's business associates like that?'

'You're not a business associate. You're a shitbag.' I jammed my foot in the door as he tried to close it. 'I'll count to three,' he threatened.

'Oh stop showing off. Just tell Miro that I'm here.'

'One.'

'You'll regret it if you don't.'

'Two.'

'You won't find another job at your age.'

'Three.' He crashed his heel down onto where my foot should have been, but I had moved too quickly for him.

'Temper, temper. Stamping your feet won't make you any quicker. You're too old for this job.' He slammed the door. 'I am going to walk down the stairs for the exercise,' I called through the door. 'If you can reach me before I leave the building, I'll tell Miro where he can find Janus.'

I walked down one floor to the fifth. This was as high as the lift reached. It was waiting where I had left it. I leaned in and sent it down empty to the street. When I got to the second floor I heard the lift motor start. Somebody was calling the lift up. I turned around and began to run up the stairs. It overtook me going up as I reached the third. I stopped on the fourth and waited for it to start its descent then I ran up to the sixth. Luc must have left in a hurry. The door was wide open. I walked in and shut it behind me. Just for the devilment, I dropped the catch.

I took quick stock of the ante-room and pulled Luc's chair out from behind his table. I opened the door to Miro's office and carried the chair in. No point in standing all the while. Miro was at his desk on the podium. He was hidden behind the *Wall Street Journal*. Just who was this supposed to impress? I suddenly thought how childish was his posturing. But I had not forgotten that children are the cruellest beings on earth.

He had not heard me, the carpet was too thick. I looked around the room. Business was obviously good. The bottle of

Johnny Walker was open so I poured myself a glass. Then I settled comfortably on my chair and waited. He rustled his paper. I sipped his whisky. It was Black Label, pretty good. A key rattled irritably in the door and then the handle shook.

'Sort that out Luc,' he called from behind his paper. Someone started thumping on the door.

'Boss!' Luc's voice was muffled by the thickness of the wood. Rather as mine must have been. Miro irritably laid down the paper and then he saw me. I was smiling and drinking his whisky. He looked quickly across to the door.

'How did you get in?' His voice cracked like a leather belt.

I gestured vaguely at the door. 'How else?'

He stared at me and tried to ignore the thumping.

'Where's Luc?'

'He's your thug, not mine.' Miro frowned at the vestibule. Luc had stopped knocking. 'Do you know? I think he's locked himself out. How careless.'

'Cretin!' Miro set his lips flat and grim. 'Let him in,' he said through his expensive teeth.

'I would not presume to such a task.' He skewered me with a scowl. It was pure venom. I would have quaked with terror had I been the impressionable kind. 'Do it yourself,' I said. I made my voice clear. 'And then I might tell you where you can find Janus.'

That shot went home. He stalked out. I could hear Luc getting a welcoming reception. He protested a lot. I took another sip at the whisky. It was improving by the minute.

They tumbled back into the room in a tangle of questions and accusations.

'I dunno boss, that bastard–'

'Well you've got the name right,' I called over my shoulder.

Miro restrained Luc with his arm. 'Another time,' he said. He walked back to his desk.

'Poor old Luc. I think he must be getting past it.' I turned briefly to him again, 'I hope you've got a good pension.' I don't think he appreciated my concern.

Miro sat with his finger on his lips, weighing me up.

'All right. You've had your fun. Where's Janus?'

I looked at my glass.

'Luc called me "Shitbag".' Miro blinked. 'Do you deal with shitbags or do you deal with business associates?'

Miro sat with his mouth open for a second then he wetted his thin lips.

'Luc, apologise to my business associate.'

'Yer what?'

'Apologise to Monsieur LeBatard.'

'Sorry.'

It did not sound very sincere but I smiled anyway.

'So you know where to find Janus?' Miro sounded dangerous again. I nodded. 'Well?' I pulled the photocopy of the title deed from my pocket and tossed it onto his desk. 'What's this?' he said.

'Is it important to you?' But I knew the answer already. He had no interest whatsoever in Mathilde's olive grove. It was something else that they were after.

He picked it up, glanced at it and tossed it back.

'Stop wasting time.'

'Shall I work on him boss?'

'Some businessman!' I said sourly. I stood up and finished my drink. I had learned what I wanted. Now I had to get out in one piece.

'Where is Janus?' Miro demanded.

'In St. Maur.'

'Where exactly?'

'I can tell you exactly where he is. And I can tell you that he will be of no use to you.'

'Let me be the judge of that.'

'Oh well, some people believe in spiritualism.' Miro started. 'Janus is in the cemetery. He is dead. They buried him a week last Wednesday.'

I walked to the door. Luc made to stop me. 'Ah, ah.' I tapped my chest. 'Business associate. Remember?'

'How do you know they buried him?' Miro would not give up.

'Because I went to the funeral.' I turned to Luc. 'I'll let myself out. It'll be less confusing for you.'

Down on the Boulevard Rochechouart a Saviem SC5 was sitting against the kerb with its engine running and the doors open. It is only a twenty eight seater but even so, the driver looked like a kid. Was I getting old? Suddenly I dived into the door-well and crouched behind the front bulkhead. The lad stared at me.

'Man in the lightweight suit,' I said. 'On the centre island.

About to cross the road. Can you see him?'

'Yes. What of him?'

'Tell me where he goes. I don't want him to see me.'

'Crawl right inside then – he might come down this sidewalk.' I scrabbled my way into the aisle. 'He's crossing the boulevard and going up the street you came down. He's out of sight now.'

I raised my head above the dashboard. The driver nodded at the road. I skipped out and stood at the corner. The man went in to Miro's block. I ran up the street and saw him get into the lift. I stood watching the jazzy orange lamps light in the art deco crescent above the lift. He went up to the fifth floor. I knew where he was going now. I walked back down to the boulevard. This had set me thinking. The coach was still there.

'Thanks,' I called through the door. 'It's too complicated to explain.'

The driver shrugged and smiled. 'There must be a woman in it then,' he laughed.

I was listening to the engine.

'What have you got in here?'

'Perkins. Petrol engine.'

'Petrol?'

'Yes. Bit expensive on fuel but goes like shit off a shovel. Are you driving?'

'Used to. Cityscope.'

'Those tourist double deckers? I could never do that. I would be terrified of going down an underpass like that driver did at the Etoile.'

I held out my hand. 'Lebatard,' I said. 'It was me.'

He laughed and then we shook hands solemnly.

'Which way are you going?'

'Gare du Nord,' I said.

'Hop in. I can go that way. Drop you on Magenta?'

'Thanks.'

Last time I took this train ride out to Pierrefitte I was trying to solve the mystery of why Josef had written Vincent's telephone number on a Casino Harz matchbook. The answer had not helped me much but because of it I was sitting on the train again and this time wondering why the man with the nose like a gas tap was calling on Miro.

Vincent was not pleased to see me. His shirt collar was undone; he was unshaven. His eyes were sunken and slow.

'Aren't you going to ask me in?'

'No. What for?' He had lost his cockiness.

'We've got things to discuss. I've been talking to Miro.'

He inspected me. I was apparently still functioning after a meeting with Miro. Nothing had been broken off. That impressed him. His hand dropped from the door handle. He shrugged and walked back down the hallway. I followed him in and closed the door.

'Not for me,' I said, nodding at the whisky glass in his hand, 'I've just been drinking Miro's Black Label.'

He looked me up and down. I was wearing Josef's clothes. He nodded, thoughtfully. 'You're doing alright then.' It was not a question, just a comment. He was strange. He did not look drunk but he was very subdued. 'I suppose you're working for Miro now then?'

I rapidly weighed up the chances of letting him believe his guess in order to see what information I could pump out of him but then my natural honesty won out.

'No. I'm working for Janus.'

'Bloody Janus,' he spat. 'Where was he on Tuesday? He was supposed to give them to me then.'

Them. In the plural. Not 'it'.

'He hasn't moved for over a week.' Well, it was not a lie. 'And did he promise that he was going to give them to you?'

'It was an understanding.' He dropped into a chair then he looked up hopefully. 'Have you got them? Have you brought them?'

I sat down and looked at the carpet where Miro's thug had held me under his shoe. 'What does Miro say about it?'

Vincent gazed out of the window at his neighbour's garden wall. 'He says he's taking it over. He sent Paulo around.'

'The blue-eyed kid? He must have enjoyed himself. I bet you put up a real fight. Where was Gaspard? Doing his mum's shopping again?'

'Haven't seen him for days. I think he's walked out on me.'

Now that was news. Gaspard hadn't the brains to walk out of a burning house.

'What did Miro want from you?' I asked.

'Nothing from me, now. He wants Janus. If he finds out that you know where Janus is, he'll get it out of you.'

'I've saved him the effort. You know I can't stand violence. I've just told him where Janus is.'

Vincent's sluggish eyes focussed on me as he digested this admission. 'So what are you doing here then?' His hand was trembling on the glass.

'Social call. Tell me why Miro is interested in Mohammed El Assawi.'

He sat up.

'El Assawi? Is he in Paris then? Has he arrived?'

'Oh yes, he's arrived. I drove him here myself.'

'You did?' I nodded. 'Has he met Janus?' Vincent was getting excited now. 'Janus insisted on it. He said that as soon as El Assawi arrived we needed to get hold of him. He would explain to El Assawi how to use the photographs.'

The photographs. Plural. That is what they are looking for. Photographs. I don't need to hang around any longer.

'Well all that is academic now isn't it?' I stood up.

'Why?'

'You haven't got the photographs?' He shook his head. 'And Miro hasn't got them? He shook his head again.

And neither has Janus and neither have we.

'So what is Janus going to do?' He was whining like a *deux chevaux* in first gear. 'I thought we had a deal.'

'He won't be doing anything now. We buried him a week last Wednesday.'

That was the second time that I had used that exit line in the same morning and it was still a knockout.

The train ground into the Gare du Nord and squealed to a halt. Already the workers were leaving Paris for the suburbs and an early start to the weekend. I wandered through the barrier and flicked my ticket straight into the bin. That was quite a novelty for me – having a ticket to be able to flick into a bin.

I fought my way out of the station against the homeward bound commuters and searched the traffic jam in the rue de Dunkerque for a useful roof. Dark blue and light blue? That would be a Brevière coach. He would not be going my way at this time of the afternoon. I stood back under the shade of the awning and watched Paris clog up. I had resigned myself to taking the metro when I saw the pale green nose of a Setra push gingerly out of the Cour des Arrivés. The driver was sweating in a company blazer and throwing short sentences over his shoulder at the person in the front seat. I walked across the front of the coach. The number on the registration plate was seventy six. Seine Maritime. Where would he be from? Rouen? No, it was Le Havre.

Make it short and make it tell.

'Smart material. S-150 with air conditioning,' I said through the open window. Now he knows I am a driver. 'Where are you making for?'

'I need to turn left,' he grunted.

'You can't. It's one way. You can turn when you get to Boulevard Magenta. Where are you taking them?' I nodded at the passengers.

'Hotel de Ville,' he said. A van behind him blew its horn. 'All right, all right, don't break my bollocks.'

The woman on the front seat put her hand to her mouth.

'You'll give her a heart attack if you carry on like that,' I warned him. 'Where's your guide?'

He pulled a disgusted face and indicated the offended matron. 'She hasn't been here since they lifted the tramways. She's about a hundred and twenty.' I glanced at the woman. 'It's all right. She's as deaf as a leg of mutton.'

'OK. I'll show you the way.'

I took him down the canal to the Bastille, sharp right into the rue Saint Antoine and up Rivoli to the Hotel de Ville. He died a thousand deaths for his paintwork but by the time I got off he would have given me his virgin daughter. The sun was still high in the sky. My shoes were good. I walked to the rue Amélie.

At the Café Clerc Joanne wore an enigmatic expression smeared on her face. 'You had a telephone call.' I moved to the counter. 'Your boss lady.'

'My employer.' I raised a hand to Makele. He blobbed a black finger on the word in the newspaper and once he was certain it would not escape, he waved with his other hand.

'B'jour Jo-Jo.' He bowed his head to the print and peeled back his finger to check that the word was still underneath.

My greeting probably cost him the sentence.

'Did she leave any message?' I asked as I lifted the receiver.

'I said you were out.' I dialled Mathilde's number. 'She asked me what you normally had for breakfast.'

'Get me a beer.' She did not move. 'Please.'

Mathilde Sikorski answered the telephone. I looked squarely into Joanne's face as she pulled at the pump. 'Whatever I can steal without the old dragon seeing,' I said into the phone.

'Ah, Joel. Yes, that is roughly what Madame Joanne said.'

Joanne slopped my beer onto the counter.

'So what did you want?' I asked Mathilde.

'Oh... nothing special.' She changed her tack. 'What have you been doing today?'

'Nothing special.' Two can play at that game. 'I'll come around tomorrow, about ten.' What I had to say to her, I needed to tell her like a man, face to face, not on the phone. I could not know it, but had I used the phone the story might have ended differently.

I gave the receiver back to Joanne. She looked at me hard and then placed it on the cradle. I drank my beer. Then I read the newspaper to Makele until it was time for bed.

Annick was still smiling in a cracked frame.

Bloody Reinhardt.

Bloody life.

'You look chic.' Mathilde tugged at my shirt collar to straighen it. It had not been crooked but we all know the conventions. She was wearing her jeans and almost wearing a blouse. I followed her down the hallway. Enjoy it whilst you can, loser.

'I've got some news for you,' I said bravely.

She sat on the sofa and left an inviting space beside her. I sat in the chair opposite. She pulled a face.

'I'm waiting,' she said. 'You do look serious.'

A car drove down the street. I could tell by the noise that it was a Citroen with duff hydraulics. Better get it over with.

'We've come to the end, Mathilde. There is nothing more I can do. Nothing more we can do.' She stared at me, saying nothing. That made it worse. 'It's been great fun despite all my moaning but this really is the end.'

'How do you know?' Her voice was like a little girl's.

I threw the photocopy of her deed onto the table.

'Nobody wants your olive grove Mathilde. Reinhardt doesn't want it, not Miro, not Vincent.'

She was biting her lip. She looked as if she was going to cry.

'How do you know?' It was a whisper.

'I went to see Miro yesterday.' She gazed steadily at me. 'And Vincent.'

'You went to see them? And offered them my olive grove?' She sat up straight. 'Without asking me? Who gave you permission?' She snatched up the photocopy. 'Who gave you the right?' She jumped up and stood over me. 'Who said you could do that?' She smacked me across the face with the paper.

I think I preferred her as the little girl.

'Listen...,'I began.

'Listen? Why should I listen to you? You've never even tried to help me. At every twist and every turn you've...' And then she was on me, punching, biting, scratching.

I'm not a naturally violent man and it is very difficult to defend yourself in a sitting position from a standing assailant. So I kicked her legs away. She went down onto her back and I rolled off the chair and held her flat whilst she flailed like a stranded beetle.

'Are you going to listen to me?' I said into flaming eyes.

'Not if you're giving in,' she said through her teeth.

I could feel the tension strumming through the body beneath me. I could smell her sweat.

'I gave in to you once.' I wound a hand in her hair and pulled her head taut. Then I kissed her. She stopped struggling and went slack. I can be a charmer when I try. I rolled off her and got up. 'I'll make us some coffee as you have neglected your duties as a hostess and then I will tell you what I have found out.'

She pushed herself up onto her elbows.

'What you have found out?' she echoed.

I looked at her, propped up with everything falling out of the front of her blouse. I shook my head.

'Can't you keep your clothes on?'

She looked down and pursed her lips.

'You're the first man who's complained.'

'Perhaps I'm old fashioned.'

She started to button up her shirt.

'Perhaps I like old fashioned men.'

'Are you going to listen to me now?' I asked. She nodded over her coffee cup. 'I know they are not interested in your olive grove because I know what they are looking for.'

'You do?' She put down her cup. 'What?'

'And I also know that we do not have it, or rather, them.'

'Them?'

'Photographs. Josef had photographs.' I glanced at her. She was going red in the face again. I just did not need her to burst into tears. 'I don't know what the photographs were of but I do know that we haven't found them.' I looked at her again as if seeking confirmation but really to make sure that she was not crying. She sucked her lip.

'How do you know they are looking for photographs?' She got up and began to wander around the room.

'It all ties in. The first time I visited Miro he thought I had come from Vincent. He asked me if I had brought "them".' She was pulling a cushion straight on the back of the sofa behind my head. 'Vincent told me yesterday that it was photographs that Janus was going to deliver.' Now she was by the windows, fiddling with the curtains. 'But he still does not know who Janus is. Only that he is dead.' Suddenly I remembered that I was talking about her father and that she had suffered the loss. 'Look I'm sorry.'

She wandered back and sat on the sofa beside me.

'No, it's me that's sorry.' She began to fiddle in her handbag. Any minute now the handkerchief would come out and we would be in the hysterical woman scene.

'And I have a vague idea that Reinhardt was mentioning photographs when they drugged me.'

'I'm sorry.'

'I get occasional flashes of the interrogation in my mind. I didn't like it much.' She was pulling the stuff out of her handbag. Why do women never keep handkerchiefs where they can find them? 'I've been having dreams.'

'Look Joel, I'm dreadfully sorry.'

'Oh don't worry. It's not your fault. I never did sleep well.' I laughed. 'Unless I was drunk. Anyway, the point is, have you noticed that since Reinhardt searched this flat he has left us alone? I think he found the photographs in another one of the books. Obviously he would not tell us but I think he found them.'

'I don't,' she said clearly. I sighed. Would she never give up?

'Look I'm sorry,' she said.

'Will you stop apologising?'

She was fiddling again. This is it. In a moment we'll have floods of tears. She stood up.

'I'll get you a drink Joel. You're going to need it.'

She dropped a set of photographs onto the sofa beside me.

It is not often that I am completely lost for words. I can usually say something. Even if it is only *'merde.'* I could feel my jaw working up and down but nothing was coming out. She pushed a glass into my hand.

'It's *pastis.* It's all I've got.'

I swallowed a slug neat. It probably burned but I hardly felt it. I picked up the photographs.

'So these are what they are looking for?'

'Judge for yourself.'

Five photographs, black and white snapshot size but sharp. I looked at each one in turn and then laid them out on the table in a sequence. They all showed the same view, taken looking into the tall double window of an imposing house. The windows were open. From the angle of the shots the camera must have been at a higher level in the building opposite. Possibly across the court-yard on the floor above. There was something bizarre about the furniture in the room. It was the library, or a study. A desk, heavy wooden chair. A filing cabinet? I looked from one to another of the pictures. I sensed that Mathilde was watching me from the chair opposite. A filing cabinet looked a bit... official. It was an office. I looked sharply at Mathilde.

'Josef's office was on the top floor wasn't it?'

'Yes, "a post amongst the pigeons for the pigeon post," he used to joke.'

'He took these photographs didn't he? With that Leica I sold? From his office window?'

'Probably. He had the camera with him often. He was always snapping at things.'

'Where did you find them? When did you find them?'

She took a deep breath.

'Don't get annoyed.' I didn't like the sound of that. 'They were in the hollowed-out book with the deed.'

'In the...? But you said... Why didn't you tell me?'

She looked down at her lap and fiddled with the hem of her shirt. She was flushed again.

'They are not very nice. I... I... didn't want to think that Papa... I was embarrassed. I think they are horrible.'

'So you put them in your handbag and kept quiet?' She nodded. 'So whilst I was being tortured by Reinhardt, you knew what he was looking for?'

'No, I didn't know, Joel, believe me, I didn't.' She threw the hair from her face with a jerk. 'Not until just now when you said that they were looking for photographs.'

'Why on earth didn't you tell me when you found them? Why did you keep them?'

'I didn't know what to do with them. I pushed them in my handbag to get them out of sight.' She shuddered. 'Do men really do that sort of thing to each other?'

'Some men do.' I put my hands behind my head and gazed at the ceiling. 'It must be blackmail, and one of them must be important.'

'They might both be important. It's difficult to see who they are. I didn't look too hard,' she added quickly.

'Have you got a magnifying glass?'

'Oh how could you!'

I clicked my fingers. 'Jean Marc,' I said. 'He has got all kinds of camera equipment. He could make enlargements of these. Then we would know.' I gathered them together and stood up. 'Are you coming?'

'Do we want to do this? Is this really what Papa has left me?'

'You don't know what he has left you until you get these pictures enlarged.'

'I don't want to see them again. They are disgusting.'

I stuffed the photos into my pocket.

'It's ironic isn't it? You get me in to find out what he had left you and shout and scream at me every time that I suggest that you let it drop and all the while you have got what we are looking for in your handbag and when I tell you this, you decide you're not interested any more.'

But my logic and rationale was obviously wasted.

'You go, Joel. I'll stay here.' She curled up her legs into the chair and hugged herself. 'I thought you came here to tell me it was all over.'

'I did.' She looked up. 'But it isn't.'

I closed the door gently behind me.

I think she was crying.

I was heartily glad to get out of the metro at the République. I came up at the corner of the rue du Faubourg du Temple just as a convoy of wedding cars charged across the square with all their horns blowing multiple counterpoint and their ribbons and bows dancing in the slipstream. I walked past the barracks to the canal and then I leaned on the railings on the bridge by the hotel de la Douane and watched a barge locking up out of the tunnel into the daylight. Children were playing in the sunlit garden and Saturday afternooners were lounging on the benches watching the cabin of the barge climb magically out of the trough. From this point southwards the canal was underground until it reached the Bastille. It used to be open air all the way but rioters found it too easy to use it as a defensive line so some time in the nineteenth century it was covered over. That was what one of the guides once told me. I don't always believe them.

Jean Marc had installed an intercom at his enormous cargo door entrance. I pressed the buzzer.

'Yeah?'

'It's LeBatard. Send the lift down and get the whisky out.' I pushed on the door and went in.

Jean Marc was out on the roof again, in the deck chair. In deference to the weather he had discarded his leather jacket. When I saw the design on his shirt I wished that he had not.

'Don't you ever do any work?' I asked.

'I could say the same to you, Jo-Jo.' He shook hands without getting up. 'I owe you two hundred and fifty francs. I sold that camera.'

'Keep it. I've got a job for you. Let's go inside.'

'Slave driver.'

'Well I can see that the whisky isn't out here.'

We clattered down the concrete stairs to his studio. It was refreshingly cool. But then, empty warehouses would be like that.

'What are you going to do in the winter? You'll freeze in here.'

'Oh I'll get a special assignment somewhere. Tahiti would be nice.' He nudged his Nana Mouskouri spectacles up his nose.

They slipped back down again. 'What have you got for me?'

'A thirst. Didn't you hear me?' I shuffled the photographs whilst he poured out the drink. 'I've got some prints that need enlarging.'

'Is that all? You can do that at the pharmacy. Have you brought the negatives?'

'I don't have them.'

'It's best taken from the negative.'

'You can do it without, can't you?'

'I can.' He took them from me. 'Are we going to worry about whether you have got the copyright?' He looked down. '*Merde!* I didn't know you were into that sort of thing Jo-Jo. Didn't expect that of you.'

'Don't be an idiot! We're just trying to find out who they are.'

'Not my taste.'

'Nor mine, but you can see now why I don't take them to the pharmacy.'

'Yeah. Quite. And I suppose we are not going to worry about copyright?' I shook my head. 'What's it for? Blackmail?'

'You don't want to know, Jean Marc. Don't ask questions. Just do me some bigger prints.'

'How many?'

'One of each. That works out at fifty francs per print. Good business.'

'OK.' He looked around at various bits of equipment. 'I can't do them straight away, I've got some things on the go. Be ready Monday.'

Why was he stalling? I tore a piece of paper from a pad on the table and wrote Mathilde's telephone number on it.

'If you have any problems, you can get me here.'

'Am I likely to have any problems?'

'That depends entirely upon you.'

That should make him think twice.

I decided to drop in to Bertrand's for a drink or two. It would be good to get out of the sun. As I approached the Moderne Palace my attention was caught by the activity outside the Skyways terminal in the ground floor of the hotel. It was just a waiting room and a baggage check-in. To call it a terminal was a bit cheeky but that was nothing compared to Skyways' effrontery when they assured their passengers that they would fly them from Paris to London. The London flight started in the Place de la République where they boarded a coach which took them seventy five kilometres to Beauvais airfield to find the plane. The plane then hopped over the Channel and, according to somebody who had done it, the moment it saw grass, it landed. And guess what was waiting for them in England? A bus to take them on a two hour journey to London.

The commotion was caused by that little Irish girl travel rep. who was waving her arms and shouting her invented argot at the station manager. She had the unnerving habit of standing between your feet to look up at you so that you were forever backing away and peering down your chest to talk to her.

'Oh the anguish! The anguish! How am I going to stack my pilgrims now?'

I winced. What did she think she was saying?

'Lovely day isn't it?' I declared.

She turned around, 'Oh you–'

I held up my hand to stop her.

'Don't start all that again. Just speak ordinary French,' I said. The station manager turned and silently shook hands with me. I had never had any trouble with him. He didn't have the energy. 'What's the problem?'

I saw his face lighten and the grip on my hand tightened.

'Ah, just the man. Do you want to earn a hundred francs?'

'Doing what?'

He jerked his head at the coach.

'Beauvais, with this lot. Company route.'

'On a Saturday? Are you mad? The Nationale One will be bumper to bumper with peasants trying to keep their tyres cool. Make it two hundred.'

'A hundred and fifty.'

'Done. When's the departure?' I took the money and rolled it straight into my pocket.

'Half an hour ago. All the bags are in the boot. Get moving.' I climbed into the coach and bounced up and down on the seat to test the spring. 'Everything works,' he assured me, 'this isn't a Paris outfit. Oh and by the way...'

I paused with my hand over the key.

'What?'

'You leave the coach in Beauvais. It sleeps at the airport and does the 13.30 down into Paris tomorrow.'

'Oh brilliant! How do I get home?'

'Bump a lift on the 022. It lands at eight thirty tonight. The coach leaves Beauvais at about nine.'

The first three hundred metres took five minutes. The traffic all wanted to go around the Place and along the Grands Boulevards. I needed to bulldoze a route through them to the Boulevard Magenta. I succeeded eventually and began the crawl out of Paris for the north.

I worked for those francs. 'Company route' meant that I had to stick to the standard route no matter what. The idea was that if I had a breakdown then the next coach up would see me and stop to help. It prevented me from taking short cuts or diversions to avoid jams. My prediction about the traffic was absolutely right with every wallowing Citroen and floundering Fiat that had ever hogged a white line, crawling along whilst the occupants agitated arms out of the windows to point out the scenery. The only time that they did not signal was when they were turning. I nearly shunted the first offender into a farmyard.

I pulled up outside the terminal at Tillé-Beauvais at ten minutes to six. The baggage was hauled off in no time at all and the passengers were herded through the checks and out onto the apron. They don't go in for all that 'ride in a bus around the airport' madness at Beauvais; here, the plane parks outside the window and you walk across the tarmac. If it is raining then you get wet.

It was a twin-engined turbo prop plane. It had Rolls Royce monogrammes on the engine cowls. Who says the English have no chic? I watched it from the window whilst it taxied, turned and took off with a solid confidence and then I knocked on the door of the Ops. room. A girl in uniform poked her head around the door.

'The keys to the coach for the 13.30 arrival tomorrow.' I dangled them in the air.

'Yes?' she said. 'So what?'

'Whoever drives the coach will need them.' She began to speak. 'And it won't be me.' I explained quickly. 'I was just helping out on this journey.'

'OK. I'll take them.' I dropped them into her hand.

'The flight that gets in at eight thirty is still on the mayfly is it? I need to cadge a lift down to Paris.'

'The 022? Yes that is still scheduled but it will be late.'

'How do you know?'

She nodded at the window behind me.

'It was late leaving. You should have got here earlier.'

'Have you only got one plane?'

'No. We've got three planes. We've only got one pilot at the moment.' She saw my disbelieving face. 'Air France have exactly the same problems.'

I thought her comment a little trite but I said nothing. I wandered back into the passenger area. The barman was pulling down the shutters. I persuaded him to make me a *croque-monsieur* and serve me three beers in a row. Then I took the whole lot through the emergency exit to the apron and installed myself on one of the chairs used by the crew. I was airside, in a restricted area and nobody cared a hoot.

I lounged in the late afternoon sun and drank beers whilst I watched a little red monoplane practice circuits and bumps and a tractor mow the grass alongside the runway. 'Air France have exactly the same problems,' my arse. The sun got cooler. My beers got warmer. This was the kind of life I could cope with.

At eight fifteen the girl in Ops still had no news and the barman had gone home because there were no more outward flights. A grizzled old tartar in green trousers began to swab the floor with dirty water. I suppose they have to get rid of it somehow. At a quarter to nine Ops still had no news and I began to wonder whether I should get a taxi into town and take the train. She put me straight on that idea by pointing out that the evening train to Paris had already gone.

At half past nine she said that the plane had 'gone tech.'

'Can they fix it?' I asked.

'They are trying.'

'Perhaps Air France could help. I'm sure they have the same problems.'

She did not think that was funny.

The little red monoplane had long gone to bed. The grass had all been mown. The lights were switched on only in my corner of the terminal. I was the only person there. At half past ten she came out of the Ops room with a red-faced man. He was obviously in charge whilst she did all the work. She switched off the office lights and locked the door behind her.

'The last flight is cancelled,' she called down the hall to me. 'You can go home now. I have to lock up.'

I liked her sense of humour. I scooped up a beer mat from the table and jammed it in the latch on the emergency exit door as I pulled it closed.

'Do you want a lift into town?' she asked. It was nothing more than a lift. There were only two cars in the car park.

'No, that's alright. I've got something arranged.'

I stood in the porch and watched their cars disappear down the approach road. They turned onto the main road. I put my fingers into the emergency doors and pulled them open.

Once my eyes had become accustomed to the gloom I dragged two of the benches together to make a bed and settled down for the night.

13

It was six o' clock on Sunday evening and I was dragging my feet down the rue Amélie. I had not slept well; the building had creaked and groaned as it had cooled down. I had breakfasted on what the barman had called, *'un hotdogue'* and the first coach down to Paris had been late leaving Beauvais. By the time I had arrived at the Skyways terminal at the République the station manager had made himself scarce. He would not catch me like that again. I had spent the afternoon at Bertrand's, drinking beer under the drumming wheels of the traffic in the Place de la République and listening to him abusing his customers.

There were three empty parking places outside the flats in the rue Amélie. Sunday night. They would fill up as soon as the locals had fought their way through the homeward bound traffic jams. Few people were in the street. I nodded at a dark-haired man going into the block of apartments. I vaguely knew him. I think he was an Argentine. He kept himself to himself. Marguerite's restaurant was closed and dark. She did not open until Tuesday.

I was nearly at my door when the man on duty outside the police post called me.

'Oi! Trouble! Come here, the chief wants you.'

'He can't have everything. Tell him he'll have to wait until Christmas just like the other kids.'

I buzzed the door open and stepped in to the dark passageway. The concierge's curtain twitched like a tramp on meths and then she lunged out of her box at me.

'The police are after you,' she squawked. 'They've been in twice already.'

'And all they found was you? What a disappointment that must have been for them.'

'They will take you away and lock you up like they should have done years ago.' She shook her shoulders in ecstasy and lumps of her body rolled around under her apron. She looked like a sackful of ferrets.

'You're just jealous. Only one person ever came after you and he's been paying for it ever since.'

'Ignard!' she shouted into the courtyard after me.

She probably did not know what it meant.

I was standing at the sink, washing off two day's grime when the knocks thudded at the door.

'It's open!' I called, and buried my face in a towel.

When I emerged the cop with no chin was standing in the doorway. He looked around the room taking in the faded curtains, the damp stains on the wall and the rickety furniture.

'Jesus! What a pig sty!'

'You must feel quite at home then. Have you come to scrub my back or just gawp?'

'The chief wants you. Now!'

'Is it urgent?' I dried myself very slowly. 'Or are you arresting me?'

'Stop arsing about and come. He wants to talk to you.'

I threw the towel onto the window rail.

'Oh well, that's different. If it's a request to assist our valiant police force in the execution of their arduous duties then I am only too willing. Lead the way, Maigret.'

The chief was the same one who had wanted me thrown out in front of a bus. I smiled angelically at him.

'I had forgotten what a pain you were,' he said. 'You know a chap called Fennec. We need you to identify him.'

'I've never heard of him.'

'Yes you have. You worked with him.'

'Fennec?'

'Gaspard Fennec.'

'Oh Gaspard! Yes I know him.' I had never asked myself what Gaspard's surname was. 'What's he done? Where is he?'

'He's fallen in the water. He's in the morgue.'

He must have seen the shock on my face because his smile was all satisfaction. 'Good. Come on, we'll take you.'

'Hold on. Why me? Why don't you ask his mother to identify him? She knows him better than anybody.'

'She's gaga. We sent somebody to give her the good news and he is still trying to get it through to her.'

'What about Descamps, his boss?'

'He's in custody.'

'What for?'

'I've no idea. Stop asking questions and get in the car.'

I waved both hands at the concierge and sat next to the driver to show her that I had not been manacled. I hope it spoiled her evening.

So Gaspard was dead? What had he been doing mucking about by the river? The great simpleton! He had probably been trying his hand at fishing. It was just the kind of stupid thing he would do. He hadn't walked out on Vincent after all. But why was Vincent in custody?

Call me a killjoy if you will but I have never liked morgues. I think it must be the atmosphere. It lacks the light spontaneity that I so cherish. The attendant flipped back the sheet. I looked at Gaspard's face and nodded. He took me to the witness book and gave me a pen. It had *'City Morgue'* printed on it. I bet they've never lost one yet.

'Did you know him well?' he asked. It was just a job to him.

'A workᴶmate, that's all. It's daft. It never occurred to me that he couldn't swim.'

'It wouldn't have helped him. He was dead before he hit the water – heart attack.' To me, that made it all the sillier. Gaspard was not even smart enough to get drowned. 'You sign your name here and put your address in that box.'

I wrote Mathilde's address in the box. It looked swankier. I thought Gaspard would appreciate that. I had always liked him in a funny sort of way. Even when he was beating me up he was only doing it because he had been told to. It was his job. It never occurred to him that it might hurt. He had no malice in him. And now he was on the slab. What had he achieved in his life? If I were on the slab in his place what would I have been proud of?

I put the pen in my pocket. I like to be a trend-setter.

They dropped me back at the police station. I walked straight to my door without a backward glance. I didn't thank them. They didn't thank me. The concierge poked her head out of her lodge and prepared a fusillade for me. I was in no mood for chitchat.

'If you utter so much as one syllable I'll push your fat face straight through that bird cage,' I threatened.

'Henri!' she squeaked. Her husband's head appeared under her left armpit.

'Monsieur!' he began.

'And you will follow close behind, rat face.'

I don't know why, but I've never got on well with concierges.

I was still thinking of Gaspard as I rattled up through the warehouse in Jean Marc's cargo lift. Monday morning. Everybody goes to work; those who have jobs that is. What would Gaspard have been doing now? Probably running some crooked little errand for Vincent. Who would do his mum's shopping now? Who would look after her? Not my problem. I clanged the gate back and stepped out.

'Where are you?' I called.

'Up here.' Jean Marc was standing on a girder, hiding behind the stanchion onto which he had bolted his old projector. 'I was just making sure that you were alone.'

'You've got some daft ideas. That long hair is addling your brain. Have you done the photos?'

He swung down to the floor in a couple of movements.

'Yeah,' he said carefully. 'I've done the best I can without negatives. They are fine definition prints, so that helps, and I've used high grade paper.' He hesitated then seemed to make up his mind. 'You'd better look at them.'

I did. 'Christ,' I said. 'That's Van der Leeuven isn't it?'

'Looks like it. A young Van der Leeuven. Taken about fifteen years ago I would judge from the clothes. I don't know who the other one is.'

'A close friend.'

'Very close,' he said drily. He shuffled the prints and slid them into an envelope. 'Well there you are. What are you going to do with them?' What was I going to do with them? I had no idea. Mathilde did not want to see them again. But you know what women are; fickle in decisions. 'It's blackmail, isn't it?' Jean Marc's voice was sharp.

'Well if it is, it's not me that's doing it. I just happen to have acquired the bloody photographs. God knows what I shall do with them now.'

'The minister would pay a lot.'

And when he said that I recalled what I had heard Vincent telling Miro whilst I was listening at the door; something about having 'sent them to the minister and now he would be on the hook.'

'No, that's not my sort of game,' I said thoughtfully.

'I'm pleased to hear it.' He looked at me and smiled. Then he dropped the original snapshots into the envelope. 'If you find any more family portraits, take them to your pharmacy. It will raise your status in the neighbourhood.'

'I'll bear that in mind.'

The metro groaned through the gallery above the platforms of the Gare d'Austerlitz and the train was bathed in a sunlit glow, tempered into a burnish by the glazing on the roof. The man perched on the *strapontin* opposite me frowned and looked away. I realised that I had started grinning at him. It was as if the sun had illuminated my route for me. I had just thought of what I was going to do. I was already on my way there. Another three stops and I would be in the Place d'Italie.

'It's Joel,' I said into the intercom. 'I'm coming up. I'll use my key.'

Mathilde was in her bath robe. Her hair was still damp from washing. She flicked it back. 'I tried to ring you,' she said. Her bare feet slapped on the wooden parquet. It reminded me of another time. Was it so long ago?

'I was away on a job. What did you want?'

She flopped onto the sofa.

'To talk. What have you got in the envelope?'

'The enlargements. I've just come from Jean Marc's.'

'I don't want to see them.' Her voice was hurried and tired in one. 'Have we learned anything?'

'One of them is a government minister; Van der Leeuven. He's the one who is—'

'Please!' She held up her hand. 'I don't need to know. I don't want to know.' I nodded. She was close to the edge of something. 'What do we do now?'

I looked at the clock. 'I'll tell you exactly what we do now.'

'What?'

'You go in there and get dressed and then I treat you to lunch at the Italie.'

She looked at me for an instant then she was girlish again. *'D'accord,'* she said and jumped up. 'Ooops!' she grinned and snatched at the errant panel of her robe.

OK. So I had seen it all before but a man can still appreciate a treat.

Whilst we jostled through the *menu du jour* with the rest of the working world we chatted about anything other than that what we knew we should have been discussing. She told me of her life in Strasbourg. Her job was interesting without being exciting; the workplace was convenient rather than comfortable; the social life was as hectic as she could wish. She loved to get into the Vosges and go walking. If I gave her more time she would talk herself back into her life as it had been before.

'What do you think of the locals?' I asked and nodded to the waiter for two coffees.

She pulled a face and her eyebrows disappeared under her streaked hair. 'A bit heavy. A bit... stolid.'

'They have that reputation. I can't judge, I've only met one.'

'Reinhardt,' she said.

'Where?' I quickly looked around.

'Idiot!' she laughed. 'I meant he was the only one you had met.'

I was glad she could laugh. She had startled me. Reinhardt's appearance at that moment would have upset my theory.

'Talking of your work, when do they expect you back?'

'I've phoned the office a couple of times. It's OK. My secretary can deal with most things for a while.'

'Your secretary?'

She looked at me levelly. 'Yes, my secretary. As a head of department I am allowed a secretary aren't I?'

'Well... of course. I just didn't know.'

'Oh, you thought that I was a junior claims clerk in the back office, did you?'

'No, I–'

'Yes you did. Men!' She did the 'disgusted' look.

'But you're only twenty seven.'

'I believe I said, "twenty sevenish".' There was mischief in her eyes now. 'You don't expect a woman to be accurate about her age do you? Anyway, I didn't think you would remember.'

'Neither did I.'

'So what job were you doing on Saturday?'

'Driving a coach to Beauvais.'

'Damn!' she said as a splash of coffee dripped from the bottom of her cup onto her blouse. Why Beauvais?'

'Oh, it's a boring story. It was where the coach had to go to and there was no driver and I happened to be in the wrong place at the right time.'

'But you got paid so your weekend wasn't too bad?'

'No, not too bad. Apart from having to identify Gaspard in the morgue on Sunday night. That wasn't much fun.'

She studied me hard.

'I can never tell when you're joking.'

'Neither could Gaspard but he won't have to try any longer. Life's a giggle isn't it? When I saw Vincent he was whining about nobody loving him and how Gaspard had walked out on him and all the while the poor sod was bobbing up and down in the water.'

'How can you say such things? That's horrible.'

'Yeah I know.' I laid my money on the bill. 'Come on, let's go.'

The first thing that I noticed when we got back was the envelope on the table. I knew it was causing offence where it was so I slid it into the bookcase. If I had my way, it would not stay there long.

'I'll change my blouse,' Mathilde said to nobody in particular.

'Do you need a hand?'

'No, nor an audience.' She went into the bedroom.

Pity. I was only trying to be helpful. There came a knock on the door. 'I'll go,' I called as I walked down the hall. 'It's probably the neighbour wanting to borrow a champagne bucket.'

But it was not. They hit me the moment the door opened. One in the face, one in the stomach. Before I could recover they had barged through the doorway and were dragging me backwards by the arms down the hall. I could taste blood in my mouth and my guts tied themselves into a knot of pain when I tried and failed to shout a warning to Mathilde. Miro ambled in behind them and placidly closed the door. I hung, gasping, between their arms whilst he surveyed the salon from the doorway.

'Get the chair from the bureau and sit him on it,' he commanded regally, 'and then we can have our little chat.' He was suave. He was composed. He was aristocratic.

My legs folded under me as they jammed the hard seat of the wooden chair against the back of my knees. I hurt everywhere but what pained me most was my mistake in dropping my guard. I should never have been so careless.

I watched Miro's leather shoes on the crescent of carpet in my vision whilst I recovered my breath. This was rapidly becoming a recurring motif in our relationship. Miro sat in the comfortable chair and his thugs, Luc and Paulo, stood behind me, one either side, just like they do in the movies.

'When you are ready, LeBatard. Take your time.' It was the voice of a poker player who held all the cards. Except that he did not. Otherwise he would not be here.

'You might as well come in and sit down,' I said at last. I don't like to shirk on hospitality. 'You could have left Lucky Luc and Pauline outside. They could play in the garden. It's quite safe.'

'Oh I promised them that this visit would give them the reward they have been waiting for.'

'I do hope so. I would hate to see Pauline cry again and of course Luc isn't getting any younger.'

'Can I hit him again boss?' Paulo was losing his self control. Miro shook his head.

'Now then LeBatard, you know why I'm here.'

'Tell me. I hate guessing games.'

'You can play it clever or play it stupid.'

'What's the difference?'

'Play it clever and you won't need much plastic surgery. Play it stupid and you'll be wearing an autoroute bridge as an overcoat.' His steel eyes smiled. His thousands of francs of dentistry glinted at me. This was the power he liked.

'Can I choose which autoroute? I don't want the A4.'

'Hit him.'

My head banged sideways as the blue-eyed kid punched my cheek. I could taste more blood in my mouth.

'All right, I'll take the A4 if you insist. Why don't you tell me what you want Miro, unless it's merely the sexual satisfaction of seeing me suffer?'

'Hit him.'

My head banged in the other direction as Luc took his turn. I sucked on my other cheek. I would have to lay off pimentos for a while.

'You've just proved my point,' I said. 'Whatever you want, you won't get it out of me like this. A tougher headcase than you has already tried and failed.' He frowned slightly. 'You're not the only one on this quest Miro.'

'Go on,' he said, 'whilst you've still got your tongue.'

'It's the photographs, isn't it?' I shook my head in despair. 'You should never have let Vincent send them to the minister.'

He looked at me. He was very still but I knew his mind was working. I needed mine to work quicker than his.

'That was Vincent's mistake,' he said. 'He dressed up that dolt of his in a hired postman's costume to make sure that the minister got the photographs himself.'

'I did not think that Vincent was that clever.' I could see that my remark had intrigued Miro. That was what I had intended. 'I hope he kept the receipt in the minister's handwriting. That would be very useful.' I smiled within when Miro's eyes betrayed that Vincent had not done so, and that Miro had not thought of the importance of it. Whatever airs he gave himself, he would be useless at poker. 'Anyway, that "dolt" won't be dressing up again. He's dead.'

'That was how we got your address.' He looked pleased with himself. 'The witness book.' He smiled.

I smiled back whilst my inner voice called me a lot of unchurchlike names. My sentimental salute to Gaspard had thrown Mathilde in jeopardy. Thank God she's had the sense to lie low in the bedroom. So far it has not occurred to Miro that I do not live here on my own. If I give him the photographs he will clear out and then I can let Reinhardt deal with him. I fancy seeing Miro on LSD.

'Oh I've never made a secret of my address. You merely had to ask, as a business associate,' I added. 'But of course, you came here as a thug.'

'And now you're leaving.' Mathilde's voice came hard and clear from the bedroom doorway. We all turned.

She was wearing her jeans and a khaki army shirt with pockets and epaulettes. She had a thick leather belt strapped around her waist and her feet were planted surely apart in stout black shoes. But what earned our respectful attention was the Luger that she was holding firmly in two hands, at head height, so that she could sight along the barrel at us.

'Stay just as you are everyone,' I warned. She was holding the gun confidently but I knew that it would soon be too heavy for her. Also, she was aiming too high. I sensed Paulo shifting his weight behind me. 'Freeze, Kiddo!' I snapped over my shoulder. 'She was taught to fire a pistol when she was four. With that gun, she will shoot your bollocks off before you've taken a second thought.' She lowered the barrel slightly, picking up the clue I had fed her about the median point. 'And there's eight pills in the bottle,' I said. 'You will all get a dose of medicine if you try anything.'

Miro's brain was working. He had dealt with situations like this before. He tried the charm.

'Madame.' His voice was mellifluous and condescending as he moved slightly in his chair.

'Shut it grandpa,' she snapped. 'And don't try the crap stunt about me leaving the safety catch on. This model doesn't have one.' Her voice was ice.

I had to give it to her. She had learned the words.

'It would give me great pleasure to see you on the slab next to Gaspard,' I said to Miro. His look was murderous. 'Another stupid move like that and I will.' I had to do something soon. They would try a concerted attack. And both she and I knew that the gun was empty. 'Right gentlemen, you heard what the lady said. You're leaving. Get up nice and slowly and walk down that hallway. And whilst you're doing it, just imagine what a nine millemetre slug feels like when it rips in through your spine and out through your gut.'

'Just one of you turn around and you'll all get it,' Mathilde added. 'One bullet goes through all three of you.'

I was not certain about that, never having seen it done, but I let it go. I watched them as they carefully made their way to the doorway of the salon. Miro's face was like stone; Luc was weighing up the odds; Paulo was still worried about what the Luger would do to his wedding tackle. They hesitated as they tried to decide who should go first. Perhaps they were calculating how far down the line the bullet would really stop. Then they shuffled down the hall.

'Keep going. Through the door and close it behind you.' I instructed. Miro took a last look at us before the door was pulled to. His eyes were hooded. He looked like a carrion-tearing eagle.

'I'll check the door,' I said to Mathilde. You check from the window that they go, all three.'

I bolted the door and listened to the steps on the stairs. When I came back into the salon Mathilde was grinning behind the safety of the curtain.

'There they go. They got a parking ticket,' she laughed. 'Serves them right.' She collapsed onto the sofa and dropped the gun at the side of her. She watched me whilst I took it straight into the bedroom and stowed it in its box of oddments. 'I'm glad that's over. A bit scary wasn't it?' she said when I came back into the room. I must have stared at her like an idiot. 'Oh, didn't you think so?' she asked.

'Scary?' She did not realise what she had just done. 'Weren't you afraid?' I said.

'Terrified.' She shrugged. 'But I didn't like what they were doing to you so I got the gun. I knew I couldn't hurt them because it wasn't loaded.' She pulled the shoes from her feet and stood up. 'You've cut your lip.'

'No I haven't. Somebody did it for me.' I dabbed at the inside of my cheek with my tongue.

'Just hold still whilst I get some of this blood off your face. Of course you would not have been hurt if you had not taunted them like an idiot. I don't know why you do it.'

I had done it to keep their attention. I did not want them sniffing around the apartment. Luckily, she had taken her handbag into the bedroom with her.

'If you didn't like what they were doing to me why did you take so long to come out with the gun?'

She stopped dabbing and looked at me in amazement.

'I had to get changed of course.'

'You had to get changed? Luc and Paulo were playing tennis with my head, Miro was promising to set me into the foundations of the autoroute and you had to get changed?'

'Of course. You have to dress for the occasion. Didn't I frighten them?'

'The gun frightened them.'

'And papa's belt and shirt. Oh it's such a bother trying to do up all those buttons and of course they fasten the other way on a man's shirt.'

'You only needed the gun.'

'Don't you understand men?' She shook her head in pity. 'If I had come out in a sexy short skirt and a low-cut blouse they would never have even looked at the gun.' She wiped my cheek. 'Would you have done?'

She did not need an answer. She knew she was right.

We stayed in for dinner. As the street gradually gained its evening quiet and the windows across the way began to glow with the light of families at table we started the discussing and the convincing. I was heartless and political, reminding her of the torture and assaults that I had been subjected to since I had been in her employ. She described in colourful, if inaccurate detail, the guns to which I had introduced her during the same period and enumerated the occasions upon which I had either insulted her or assaulted her. But she knew where I was leading.

'You don't want to see the photographs,' I said. 'I understand that. I don't particularly like them myself. But all the time you possess them you will be the target of an ever widening circle of admirers the likes of Reinhardt and of the imitation Russian count that you met today. There is one obvious way of putting an end to all this.'

'Give them to the minister?'

'Certainly not. You'd be behind bars quicker than blinking. Give them to Reinhardt. That would get him off our backs and we leave Reinhardt to deal with Miro. It would not be your problem. They've already got Vincent in custody, probably on suspicion of attempted blackmail. Do you want to be there as well?'

'He would not dare.'

Which world was she living in?

'Listen, you may have saved me some discomfort by swinging that pistol around–.'

'Good of you to recognise it.'

'–but you have made Miro into your enemy and that is never a good idea.'

She pulled her bare feet up onto the sofa. Red-nailed toes waving like a field of poppies.

'And how was it that Miro was able to find me? Tell me that. I believe you wrote my address down for him.'

I needed to try another approach.

'Where are the negatives?' I asked. She shrugged. 'Have you

told me the truth about what you found in the book?'

'Of course,' she said coldly.

'You didn't at first. You've not forgotten anything?'

'No.' She was getting angry.

'Not overlooked another envelope?'

'No.' Her teeth were gritted.

'First thing tomorrow we phone the number that Reinhardt gave you and arrange to hand over the photos.'

She fixed me with those dark eyes whilst she considered the proposal. She must have known what it meant.

'Then what?' she said.

'Then I go home. Job done.'

She slept all night curled around me like a serpent, tying me to her.

'Ministry of Defence.'

'Monsieur Max Reinhardt please.' I used my best telephone voice. It made Mathilde's eyebrows rise.

The phone clicked and then another voice said, 'Ministry of Defence.'

'Max Reinhardt please.'

I heard a *clunk* then the voice said, 'We don't have a Max Reinhardt.'

'I don't know the password. When will he be back?'

'I have told you, monsieur, there is nobody of that name working here.'

'Can I leave him a message?'

'Look, monsieur–'

'But you switched on the tape recorder. I heard you do it. Can't I leave him a message on that?'

The line went dead. I replaced the receiver.

'They don't want to know him.'

'You wouldn't get a job on our switchboard.' Mathilde frowned. 'We'll have to take the photographs to Reinhard. You've been to his office before. It's only a matter of finding it.' She picked up her car keys. 'Come on.'

'And how do you expect me to find the place? They covered my head. Are you proposing to drive me around Paris with my head in a sack?'

'If that is what turns you on, I'll try it.'

She pulled the parking ticket from the windscreen and dropped it to blow down the street.

'Don't you ever pay those things?' I asked as I did the sardine trick into the seat at the side of her.

'Don't be daft. They'll be another armistice as soon as the new government gets in. It happens every time.'

She probably did politics at university. She started the car and we lurched away from the kerb into the path of a delivery truck.

'I agree with him,' I said, pointing at the truck driver who was mouthing words at her.

'Oh, you've got your eyes open then?'

'I think I'll shut them again.'

'Where shall we start? Where are you sure you went?'

'Aim for the Concorde. I definitely went there but I ended up in an underground car park. A private park. Probably under a building.'

'That doesn't help me much. What was the last landmark you identified?'

'The Place de la Concorde. They drove me around it half a dozen times to make sure that I was lost before they took me to Reinhardt.'

'And how long after that did you stop?'

'Not long. I can't remember exactly.'

'Brilliant!' she muttered and winged a garbage bin.

I suppose she learned to drive in Strasbourg.

It was eleven o'clock and we were parked on the shady side of the rue Scribe. We had quartered the area as well as you can at that time on a Tuesday morning. We had looked for buildings with underground car parks. The whole idea was futile. The air was hot, the car was hot, I was hot. With the windows open, the sand and dust blew in from the enormous concrete hopper that was rattling away opposite, pouring concrete down into the guts of the metro system for some improvement or other. With the opportunist cheek of the regular commuter, three motorists had pulled away the red and white fencing which ran along the site and had parked their cars inside. They were covered with a fine layer of sand and cement dust. All it needed was a light shower and they would become statues.

'I'm going for a drink. Coming?' She looked at me as if I had said something indecent. 'I know a bar near here.'

'Now that does not surprise me.' She locked the car and followed me. I took her into the small streets around the back of the Opera House. 'I didn't know this part of Paris existed,' she said. 'Where are we going?'

'Charlie's Bar,' I said as I stepped from the narrow pavement to allow a lady to continue her way. She would have walked over me if I hadn't. She was wearing a light two-piece suit and her sandals were tapping on the pavement. I watched her pass. A good figure. Carried herself well. 'Now why can't you dress and walk like that?'

'Like what?' Mathilde snapped.

Why are women so sensitive?

I liked Charlie's Bar. It was sordid and not many people knew about it and those who did, didn't tell.

'LeBatard!' A voice hailed me from a table on the pavement. It was Simon. An unlucky coach driver.

'Laperche!' I shook hands with him. 'This is my boss.'

Mathilde gave him her hand.

'Madame.' He gave a little bow of his head.

'Mademoiselle,' she smiled. Now why did she think he needed to know that?

We sat. 'What are you drinking Simon?'

'No more for me Jo-Jo, I'm on the point of leaving. You've just missed Daniel.'

'Good.' We both laughed. 'Daniel works for the agency whose coach I decapitated,' I explained to Mathilde.

'And who do you work for, Monsieur Laperche?'

Simon looked at her as any man would I suppose. I was praying that he had a good answer.

'At the moment I am considering my options,' he smiled. 'Starvation or the Foreign Legion.'

'I'd go for starvation if I were you. You can wear what you like for that.' I ordered two beers from the old Moroccan who ran the bar.

'Actually, I'm off now to see about a job.' He stood up. 'Mademoiselle.' She smiled and gave him her hand again.

'A driving job?' I asked with reason. I had heard that he had been banned after the court case.

He looked squarely at me. 'Yes, a driving job.' He pulled his licence from his pocket and waved it at me.

'That's really good news, Simon. I'm pleased for you.'

'Thanks. Ciao Jo-Jo.'

I lifted my hand.

'What a nice man,' Mathilde said into her beer glass. 'A real gentleman.' She looked at me over the rim. 'Why can't you be like that?'

'Oh, shut up and drink your beer. I can't stand women who are smarter than me.'

'That must be a recurring problem for you.'

The sun had moved across the street by the time we returned to the rue Scribe. Then something stopped me. 'What's the matter?' she said.

I waved my hand irritably at her. I was thinking hard.

'That smell,' I said.

She wrinkled up her nose. 'What of it?'

'It's that strawberry-smelling disinfectant that they are pumping into the metro station at the Opera. It was the last thing I smelled before I met Reinhardt.'

We walked slowly to the car. She had left the window open and still nobody had stolen it.

'So his hideout is around here somewhere,' she said as she got in. 'I told you we could find it.'

'We haven't yet.' I slammed the door. 'But it must be near an entrance to the Opera metro station.'

'Or one of the metro building works. We can drive around and look at them all.' She pulled straight out into the street. I flinched and looked over her shoulder.

'Christ!' I said and ducked below the window line. I could feel the warmth of her breasts on my cheek.

'Joel! Not here! Not in the street!' The car lurched as she grabbed my hair and tried to pull my head out of her lap.

'That black Renault,' I said urgently into the thin cloth of her summer skirt.

'Stop it Joel.' She smacked my head. The car veered and a klaxon sounded behind us. 'People will see.'

'Listen woman! That black Renault. It's them!'

'Which black Renault?' She jerked her knee as she changed

gear and nearly pushed my adam's apple through my spine. 'How do you expect me to drive with your head up my skirt?'

'Have they gone past yet?'

'Oh *that* black car. That was the rude man who hooted at me. They turned left.'

I took a quick look then sat up.

'Well get after them woman!'

She spun the wheel, the tyres screeched and the car rolled with the corner.

'Don't start groping me again,' she warned as I fought my way back to my side of the car. 'I'm not in the mood.'

'There they are. Up there. Get after them.'

She had no need to take me so literally. Michel the Norman, driving the Cityscope double decker around the Opera, had stupidly thought that the green light meant that it was safe for him to continue. I slid the window open and waved my arm frantically to try to stop him as Mathilde accelerated hard through the red. I could have taken a brass rubbing of his radiator grill had I wanted to. He scowled as he recognised me. All I could offer him was a sickly grin. That would cost me a beer or two next time we met.

'There they go.' Mathilde slammed the gear lever into the dash and that stupid air freshener spun around on its string. 'This is fun, isn't it?'

Through the screen I just espied the tail of the Renault disappear up a side street and then my fingers were scrabbling blindly at the roof lining, looking for a purchase.

'You're wasting your effort,' Mathilde remarked as she hauled the wheel around and the horizon went vertical. 'This is the bog-standard model. It doesn't have grab handles.' The car tilted like Zizi Jeanmaire on the trapeze at the Casino de Paris. As it settled back, the short stab of a brake light ahead caught my eye and then was gone. We hurtled down the corridor of parked cars, Mathilde with her hair blowing in the breeze from the open windows and me, wondering how I got myself into these situations.

'Lost them,' she said as her foot came up off the gas.

'Stop!' I said at the same time.

The windscreen of a Renault 4 is a piece of flat glass. I can tell you that from the close inspection I made whilst unsticking my nose from it.

'Sorry!' she said, 'but you sounded in a hurry.'

I opened the door.

'They've just gone down there.' I pointed at the black grotto of an underground car park. 'I'll meet you at the Café de la Paix.'

I did not wait for an acknowledgment. I could hear tyres squealing on flooring. They were still going down. I ran across the road and plunged into the darkness.

14

I skittered in a crazy pasa-doble down the first flight of concrete steps without seeing them and then crashed painfully into the wall. Not stopping to catch my breath I bounced off and ran down to the floor below. I paused and listened. Nothing. The car must have gone to the level below this. Just as I was on the point of running down further, the light suddenly came on in the stairwell and below me a door banged. They were coming up.

I jumped through the door behind me and eased it silently back on its spring so that it was almost closed. I looked through the crack until I could see the tops of their heads nodding up the stairs then I knew that they were Reinhardt's thugs. I let the door close and stood in the darkness of the car park, waiting for them to go past. I could hear their shoes shuffling on the concrete steps and their arguing voices. For no real reason, I moved further into the gloom and crouched behind the first car in the lot. It was a silly precaution because the door was solid. They would not have seen me.

It was not a silly precaution. The door bounced open and the lights flickered on as the men's inane discussion about boxing boomed around the concrete chamber. I rapidly crawled to the back of the car, hoping to hide behind it but it was fender to the wall. They were almost passing the bonnet so I squeezed myself as far underneath the car as I could and prayed. They walked straight past without a glance. I judged their progress by the sound of their voices and then I got up on one knee and looked through the cars. They passed behind a van at the far end and everything went quiet. They had gone. Or were they waiting for me? I crept down the line of parked vehicles, ready to dive between them if needed. When I reached the van, I recognised it.

It was the waterworks van. I lay down and looked all around for feet. None. The place was empty.

I edged warily around the van and saw a simple wooden door in the corner. The type of door that was used on electrical switchgear cupboards. *'Electricité de France. Danger de Mort'* the sign warned me, *'415 volts'.* I gently tugged the door open and stood looking at the staircase leading upwards. Reinhardt certainly liked his Utilities – Water Works, Electricity Company. For him, life was just one big game of Monopoly. And I had landed on *'Chance'.* With my luck I would pick the *'Go to Jail'* card.

I was half way up the stairs when the light went out. I stopped and waited. Gradually my eyes became accustomed to a grey gloom. I continued carefully towards it and found the light leaking from another door. They had left it to slam on the spring but it had caught on the latch. I grabbed it to prevent it from closing fully. I paused and took a breath but there was no point in reflection. I knew what I was going to do. I opened the door and made an entrance. It was the dog-leg end of a corridor; fluorescent lights in the tiled ceiling, cream-painted walls, stained green carpet. I knew where I was. I had just walked in through the back door of Reinhardt's hideout. Now that would upset him.

I could hear the two henchman still talking about boxing; nearer to me a typewriter was rattling. I brushed down my clothes and rounded the corner in a businesslike manner. The middle-aged typist looked up and gawped as I passed her door. I heard the urgent squeal of her chair on the floor as she began her belated effort to intercept me. It did not worry me; with her bulk she would move about as fast as the Arc de Triomphe. The driver whom I had kicked in the knee was leaning back in his chair facing the doorway with his feet on the desk. He saw me first. His eyes went wide. I loved it.

'Merde!' he exclaimed and tangled his foot in the telephone cord as he tried to drag his legs off the table. The apparatus crashed to the ground and exploded like a grenade. Splinters of black bakelite shot into the four corners of the room. His mate turned around in alarm.

'Merde!' he said as he saw me.

I leaned casually against the door jamb as the typist puffed up behind me.

'Merde!' she said.

'You've got quite a vocabulary when you put your minds to it. Not exactly the Académie française though is it?' I observed. 'But you could probably write scripts for the Théatre Guignol if you pooled your talent.'

'What the devil are you doing here?' the driver said as he struggled to untwist the flex from his shoe. 'How did you get in?'

'Usual way – charm and intelligence.'

'He came up the back,' the typist gasped. 'I couldn't stop him.'

'Reinhardt would not have been pleased if you had.' I spoke to the driver. 'When you have finished your knitting get Reinhardt on the phone would you? Tell him I'm here. I've got something for him.'

'He's not here,' his mate said. 'He's out.'

'Oh shit, the bloody phone's broken.' The driver was now trying to slot discs of metal back into the handset.

'Much as I enjoy your company I'm not going to wait for him.' I pulled up a chair and sat against the desk. 'Give me a bit of paper.'

'Please!' the driver said. He looked as if he were juggling with a squashed tortoise.

'It's your career, not mine. I don't care. How's the knee?'

'Bastard!' He dumped the shell of plastic and wires on the desk in front of him and tore a sheet from the pad and threw it across to me.

I wrote Reinhardt a short love letter, telling him what I thought of him and his team and making a gift to him of all the photographs that we possessed – the originals and the enlargements. I told him truthfully that we had no idea where the negatives were. I was pretty certain that he had found them when he had searched Josef's books. As an afterthought, I suggested that he pay Mirovici a visit. I owed Miro that favour. That's what friends are for.

I took the envelope from my pocket and slipped the sheet inside with the photographs, and with that, a great feeling of relief flowed through me. The thing was done. Reinhardt had no more reason to dog my life. He had got what he was looking for and it was something that Mathilde and I neither needed nor wanted. Everybody was happy. They watched me silently as I sealed the envelope.

'Give me the Scotch.' I pointed to the roll of adhesive tape.

I signed three times along the edges of the envelope and then covered the signatures with the clear tape. 'Just in case you get tempted to peek inside.' I harboured no fear that the signatures would be used as evidence; they would never have got Sophia Loren into court. I stood up. 'Give this envelope to Reinhardt when he comes in and tell him he can get off our backs now.' The driver took it and turned it over suspiciously. 'Don't worry, it's not going to explode. At any rate, not in the sense that you understand it.'

'And Reinhardt wants this?' he asked.

'More than a blue-eyed virgin with blonde pig tails. It's what he's been looking for all his life. He'll be so pleased he'll probably kiss you.'

'Just a minute,' the other one said, 'what are we going to tell Reinhardt about how you got in here?'

'I'll leave that to your imagination.'

'How did you get here?'

I threw him a look of withering scorn. 'Did you really think that by putting a sack over my head you would get me lost?' They looked saucer-eyed at each other. 'I knew where I was all the time.' Sometimes a lie can be so rewarding.

'Might as well kick him out of the front door,' the driver said to the typist. 'He won't be coming back.'

She shrugged. 'Follow me.' She waddled off down the corridor towards the other end.

As I followed her I glanced through the open doorway of another room. The doctor who had so kindly ministered to me under Reinhardt's direction was standing there with his back to me. He was taking off his shoe with one hand; with the other he was gripping the edge of an open security cupboard to help his balance. Its door was heavy steel, reinforced, flame and tamper proof and the hinges were well oiled. Once you start moving a door like that, four fingers in the gap are not going to stop it. Without the Arc de Triomphe even realising what was happening, I took a step into the room and swung my foot as hard as I could. The slab of steel slammed with a satisfying crunch. I heard a gasp and no more. I hoped he had fainted on the spot.

The Arc de Triomphe turned at the end.

'What's keeping you?'

'Sorry.' I skipped forward. 'Thought I saw a chap I knew.'

She pulled out a key on a length of chain. I dared not postulate what she had attached it to. She unlocked the door and motioned me out onto the landing.

'Don't bother to call me a taxi,' I said. 'I'll walk.'

'Just bugger off, will you?'

A light breeze was teasing at the hem of Mathilde's skirt as she sat on the terrace of the Café de la Paix. She was drinking something cool-looking. Serge, the waiter from Pam-Pam's Bar next door was leaning on the partition and playing with his silver tray as he tried to interest her in conversation. Her face lit up and he thought he had made a conquest. Strange, she was looking at me.

'Joel, did you find him?' she asked.

Serge turned a sour face at me.

'LeBatard. I might have known. Some guys have all the luck.' He retreated to his own terrace.

'Some guys have all the looks,' I laughed back at him. 'This lady is my employer.'

He said nothing but pulled at the socket of his eye with one finger to show how little he believed me. I sat down next to Mathilde and gazed across the Place de l'Opéra.

'Success?' she asked.

'He wasn't there but I saw his henchmen.'

'You found his hideout?' I nodded. 'I said you would. I knew it.' Her fist was tight in her lap. 'Did you get rid of the– ?'

'Yes, I slipped a little note into the envelope with them. A bit of explanation.'

'I hope it wasn't rude.' I shook my head. 'Good.' Her fingers tapped the table. 'So that's that then!'

'Yes. That's that.' We watched the traffic coagulating around the square. 'What's the time?'

'Twenty past.'

'Thought it must be about that. Michel's late.' I nodded at the Cityscope double decker. 'He should be in the Place Vendome by now. I bet he skips the loop around the Opera and goes straight down the Rue Royale.'

'You miss the coaches don't you?' She was picking at the hem of her skirt.

'There's not many of those around now.' I pointed at an

open-platformed bus. 'No, not really. I miss the money.'

'Yes, we ought to come to some agreement over that.' She opened her handbag. 'Now, I think I said I would pay–'

'Oh forget it! I'll put it down to experience.' The Cityscope burbled past us to turn down the Rue Royale. 'I was right. That makes a change, for once.'

'No, I asked you to help me and I said I would pay you.'

'Well, perhaps you already have. We said lots of things. Anyway, it's all over now. Done.'

She was still fidgeting with her bag. I was hoping that if she was going to pull anything out, it would not be another envelope full of photographs. 'You know, there's something I still don't understand,' she said.

'I don't understand most of it. I've stopped trying.'

'Why did Papa take the photographs in the first place?'

'He was probably fiddling about with his camera. He would have had plenty of spare time in the office.'

'So, having taken them, why did he keep them?'

'Well, it wasn't for titillation, I can tell you that.'

'And it couldn't have been for blackmail.'

'Why not? That was the obvious reason.'

'But they must have been taken at least ten years ago. Van der Leeuven was nobody ten years ago. Did Papa keep them in the hope that the people on the photographs would become famous later? It doesn't make sense.'

'Do you always try to make sense out of the world?'

'Yes.' She turned deep eyes upon me. 'Don't you?'

'I used to. I stopped when teenage girls began screaming at Johnny Halliday.' I brushed some more of the car park dust from my trousers. 'I hope you didn't scream at him.'

'I was too young.' She looked across the square and added quietly, 'I am too young.' She sat up briskly. 'You've got stuff at home. Come back for lunch. I've got salmon.'

She was very quiet on the drive to the rue Stresemann and I did not comment once upon her driving.

I was packing the clothes back into Josef's other suitcase – the one I had left at the flat. I pressed the pyjamas in on top although I would never wear them. It would save Mathilde from having to dispose of them. Or lend them to another overnight visitor.

All through lunch she had twisted the events into knots in an attempt to disprove the inevitable interpretation that Josef had quite simply kept the photographs for prurient amusement. It was then that I had remembered about the Algerian that I had brought up from Nice. I had told her how I had found out that he was a veteran political agitator and that Josef had told Vincent that he was important to the affair. Not a clever move. She had angrily accused me of holding back on her and deceiving her. Given the speed at which events had unfurled I thought it was astonishing that I had remembered such a minor detail at all. I remarked that if somebody was guilty of holding back it was definitely not me. Another bad move. She had immediately burst into tears. I let her cry. It does them good.

She did not know any of her father's Algerian friends, if indeed he had any. I repeated that it made no sense to me and I was fed up from looking. And that was where we were.

I snapped the catches down on the suitcase lid and lifted it to the floor.

'It's for you,' Mathilde said from the doorway.

'What is?'

'The telephone. A man asking for Joel LeBatard.'

'Here? Who knows I am here? It's not Reinhardt is it?' She shook a sad head. 'OK. I'll come.'

'Jo-Jo?' It was Jean Marc, the photographer. 'You said I could phone you there.'

I unhooked the extra earpiece and waved it at Mathilde. She pushed back her hair to put it to her ear.

'No that's fine,' I replied. 'What do you want?'

'Who answered the phone? Was that the siren you were talking about? The one who is prickly?' Mathilde kicked my ankle. 'She sounded quite sexy.'

'You wouldn't know. You lot use your eyes not your ears.' I stuck out my tongue at her. 'What do you want?'

'Those photographs—'

'Oh that is all done and finished, Jean Marc. Thanks for your help but it's all over and we are pleased that it is.'

'No Jo-Jo, listen. You might want to know this.'

I sometimes get this feeling of dread. I had got it now.

'What?'

'I copied one of them.'

Mathilde gasped.

'You did what?' I said. 'What for?'

'It was something about it. I've been fiddling with it.'

'You idiot, Jean Marc. You have no idea what you are dealing with. Get rid of it. Burn it.'

'Jo-Jo listen, you need to see it. It's absolute dynamite.'

'Jean Marc...'

'Come and see it,' he insisted. 'Then you decide.' Mathilde was staring at me, waiting for an answer. 'Jo-Jo?'

'Give me a minute, I'm thinking. It's patently not an activity you are familiar with.' I looked at Mathilde. She stood up, picked her car keys from her bag and waved them at me. I thought of Reinhardt and his Monopoly game. I had so nearly got right around the board. But I always seemed to lose everything on that last bloody tax square between the Avenue des Champs Elysées and the Rue de la Paix. 'OK, I'll come over. But I think you're an idiot.'

Not as big an idiot as me, though.

Jean Marc's warehouse was standing proud and empty in the blazing sun, sneering at the green water of the Canal St Martin from its blank, dirty windows. Mathilde stopped on the quay and craned her neck to look up at it through the narrow windscreen.

'And this is where he lives?'

'Lives, works and–'

She frowned sharply at me as I swallowed the crudeness of the unspoken third verb.

'Don't be childish.'

'I was going to say "fishes".' I pointed at the straggle of drab men hunched at the end of their silent rods.

'Liar.'

Her spirits had perked up since Jean Marc's phone call. Almost as if she had a reason for wanting this business to drag on and on.

'Come on,' I said. 'Don't be such a school marm.'

She followed me across the road. The eyes of all the men followed her. The one that got away. Jean Marc's street door was open but I buzzed his intercom and waited. No sense in climbing five floors if you can ride in the lift.

'Which floor is his?' Mathilde looked curiously at the

tattered remnants of ancient workshop notices still clinging to the bare concrete walls.

'All of them.' I pressed the buzzer again. 'He bought the whole building. He thinks he's going to make his fortune one day by converting it into trendy flats.'

'Smart man. He probably will.'

'He's just not smart enough to send the lift down for us. He's probably out on the roof, sunning himself. Come on, we'll have to go up the stairs.'

'To the roof?'

'To the roof, and don't forget, I am an old man. Don't embarrass me with your fitness by running up them.'

I do not know what Mathilde expected to find at the top but we were both disagreeably surprised.

'Ah, LeBatard and Miss Sikorski,' Reinhardt said. 'Do come in.' He divided a portion of his smile into a leer for Mathilde. 'I think we've finished. We are just going.'

Jean Marc was handcuffed and standing between two of Reinhardt's goons. His hair was even more untidy than before. I picked up his Nana Mouskouri spectacles from the floor and walked over to him.

'Hello Jo-Jo.' He spoke with difficulty through his swelling lips.

'You idiot!' I put his glasses on his nose. 'All I asked you to do was make some enlargements.' He lifted his shoulders in mock contrition. The goons tensed up at his movement. 'Has Reinhardt got all your prints now?'

He looked me hard in the eyes. 'Every print I made.'

There was a meaning there but it escaped me.

'So what do you want Jean Marc for?' I said to Reinhardt. 'You've made a mess of his studio, you've got all the prints. Did you get my envelope?'

I could tell from his smug, bloated face that he had.

'I said you would lose out, LeBatard.' His insolent scrutiny crept up Mathilde, starting at her red toenails, up her legs, thighs, pelvis, breasts, face to her hair. 'I warned you, Miss Sikorski, that LeBatard would be bad for you.'

'Yes you did.' Her cheeks were red, her voice was colourless. He smiled again. He was mentally deflowering her there and then. I felt my hands tighten. 'Leave it,' Mathilde looked at me. 'Just leave it.'

'You could have saved yourselves all this trouble if you had given me the photographs in the beginning.'

'You could have saved yourself the trouble of drugging me if you had told me what you were looking for, but you had to play the inscrutable Alsatian didn't you? Or was it because you enjoyed it?' I wondered whether I ought to tell him that Mathilde had been carrying the photos around in her handbag all the while. Just to see if he had a sense of humour. 'Pervert!' I threw at him.

He jerked his thumb at Jean Marc. 'Put him in the car.'

'Jo-Jo!' Jean Marc called as he was led to the lift, 'hang on here for a bit will you? Anna will come. You remember Anna?' he insisted. 'You know – the avalanche. Tell her to try about fifty eight degrees will you? Do me a favour.'

I shrugged.

'Fifty eight degrees. OK.' It meant nothing to me.

'Mademoiselle,' Reinhardt gave a mocking bow as he retired. Mathilde turned towards one of the windows and ignored him. 'Loser!' he hissed at me.

'Just don't walk in front of my car, pervert.'

He crashed the lattice gate across and grinned happily.

'You'll never own one, loser.'

'I never did like that man,' Mathilde said.

I poked around in the cupboard and pulled out Jean Marc's whisky.

'We'll have to share a glass,' I said as I re-righted one of his low chairs.

'What are you doing?'

I sat down. 'Waiting for Anna to come so that I can tell her... whatever it was.'

'Fifty eight degrees.'

'Yeah, that's it.' I swallowed the whisky. It was the nicest thing that had happened to me all day.

Mathilde was pacing about the floor and tapping her fingers together. 'There's something weird about this.'

'About what?' I poured out another glassful. 'You're missing a great whisky.'

'Reinhardt didn't act surprised when we turned up. Almost as if he was expecting us. And why was he here?'

'To get the photographs that Jean Marc had copied.'

'How did he know about them? Who told him? Did you? Did Jean Marc ring him up?'

'Of course not. Jean Marc did not even know Reinhardt existed until he turned up to redesign his studio for him.' I tipped my head back and let the liquor trickle slowly down my throat. This was what I was designed for.

'We are not doing any good here. Shall we go? Do you want a lift?'

'I've got to stay for Anna.' I poured out a third glass. Mathilde wanted me to make sense of the world. This was how I made sense of the world.

'But when is she supposed to arrive?'

'Don't know. Don't care. I said I would wait. Jealous?'

She snatched up her car keys. 'You can be so infuriating.' She strode angrily to the stairs. There was a tear on her cheek. So she was jealous then.

I listened to the slapping of her shoes as she ran down the stairs. That's no proof of fitness. Anybody can run down five floors. I wondered what this Anna was like? I stretched out my legs and tried to conjure up her image. I gazed for inspiration at the black girders above me but all I saw was Mathilde. Perhaps I needed more whisky.

I jumped at the shriek of a barge siren from the canal. I was still in the chair. I must have dozed off. I looked at Jean Marc's clock. It advertised Kodak photographic paper and told me that I had been waiting for an hour and a half. I felt on the floor at the side of the chair for the whisky bottle. It was empty. Well, you can't blame me for that. If Jean Marc expects me to wait for this woman then the least he can do is to provide some hospitality.

Where was this bloody Anna that I was supposed to be waiting for? And how was it that Jean Marc thought I knew her? What had he said? Something like, 'we were talking about her and the avalanches'. Well, I don't remember that. The only woman he had mentioned was Mathilde, in a roundabout way. He had been utterly engrossed like a schoolboy with his discovery about the mountain and that trick with the projector. I looked up. It was still there, a black dusty hunk clinging to the girder three metres up like some tree-climbing predator ready to pounce. I recalled his excited eyes behind those spectacles as he had tried to get me to make the blob into the shadow of an aeroplane. Pretty clever stuff. What was the word he had used? Anamorphism, that was it.

I sat up. My head swam. I fought through it. She had arrived. This was the Anna I was supposed to be meeting. Anamorphism. I got out of the chair and waited a second or two for the horizon to settle down. What had Jean Marc been doing? I looked up at the projector but that would not have been any use. You cannot put a print in a projector.

Has Reinhardt got all your prints? 'Every print I made,' Jean Marc had said and had looked a meaning into my eyes as he had said it. Every print I made... but not every slide. Jean Marc could have taken a slide copy of the print. I looked up at the dusty black lump. And if he had, that is where it would be.

How did he get up there? Find a ladder. No, think. Think. You don't need to go to the picture, make the picture come to you. Switch the projector on. I stumbled around the pillar, tracing the cable down and around and under until I found the switch. The lens lit white and the fan whirred. There is too much sunlight. The curtain. That big black curtain. Drag it across, cut out the sun. I looked at the enormous glowing trapezium which now appeared on the floor, jazzing across the furniture. Even in its distortion I could see that it was one of Josef's photographs.

I hunted around for something to use as a screen. Jean Marc had used a piece of white cardboard but I could not find it. Eventually I discovered an offcut panel of laminate from his work surface. I manoeuvred it into the beam and twisted it to the correct angle to focus the image. The photograph condensed there before me. The windows opened into the room; I could see the desk, Van der Leeuwen and his friend. But this was no longer a snapshot, it was now one metre across. I dragged a crate over and propped up the screen, wedging it at that angle. I stepped back and looked at it. What had Jean Marc discovered? I needed another whisky but he only had orange juice. I shoved my chair around so that I could study the slide in comfort and I sat and sipped orange juice. It was disgusting; worse than the picture.

Josef had taken this photograph from his office, several floors higher across the courtyard. He could see right into the room. The furniture was foreshortened and distorted from that angle. I studied the pattern on the carpet. I looked for evidence of a third person. I tried to identify the papers on the desk but I failed.

The projector fan whirred on. I cast my mind back to the avalanche and the mountain. What had been of paramount significance was that when the mountain had been in sharp focus, the point of interest had not. That was anamorphism. I began to quarter the image, from top left to bottom right. I could see nothing in the room resembling the elongated smear of the aeroplane on the mountain. The light fitting hanging on chains, the framed map on the wall; my eyes crawled painfully across the board centimetre by centimetre. The natural fuzziness created by the gross enlargement of the slide made the identification of detail arduous. The whisky did not help any either.

I sat back and rubbed my eyes to refocus them. I could have done with Mathilde to help me. She was pretty smart. She would have spotted it in an instant. I gazed back at the picture again. The trouble was that a portion of the room was hidden by the two great windows which had been opened inwards. Anybody or anything could have been secreted behind either one of those screens. And you could not see through them, of course, because of the reflections on the glass. The reflections on the glass. I bounded out of the chair and feinted like a boxer with the beam as it threw a shadow of my head onto the very part that I wanted to study closer: bleary, stretched reflections.

I squatted below the beam and grasped the board. Which way should I tilt it? Fifty eight degrees Jean Marc had said but that was surely guesswork and anyway it was useless without an azimuth bearing. Think back to your Physics. Angle of incidence equals angle of reflection. The camera was pointing down, so the board needs to be tilted up. The reflections darkened into firmer blobs, but they were still indistinct. Because the window is also at an angle. How on earth do I calculate a tangent? Trial and error. I twisted my wrist gently and the blobs moved out of focus. Little by little I nudged my wrist back in the other direction until the image was as crisp as it would ever be. I stared at it. Jean Marc was right. It was dynamite. I now knew why they wanted the Algerian. He would know how to use this.

Judging the angles by eye, I calculated that Josef's camera had picked up an activity that had been taking place in the far corner of the courtyard, in a recess hidden from view. Safely hidden from everybody's view, they had thought. A man was kneeling on the ground. An Algerian. Just like the hundreds that had been hauled off the streets of Paris during the 'unrest' as the government had called it. He was bending forwards; partly because his hands were bound behind his back and partly because an officer in army uniform was pressing the barrel of a service revolver to the back of his head. He was being executed.

I stared and stared. What about the other photographs? Did they show the sequence of the execution? Did they reveal identities? I let the board slip. The tragic scene dissolved into grey blurs. Reinhardt had the photographs; we would never know the answers.

Did Josef know about this? Yes, of course he did. He had looked up anamorphism in that old reference book; he had turned down the corner of the page. Josef Sikorski had not been dreaming of bringing down a minister. This would bring down the entire government. The Algerian, El-Assawi, would still have the contacts. Once he had got these pictures into the Press and on television – all the foreign channels would love it – France would be a pariah.

Of course we had all heard the rumours. Everybody had. Algerians disappearing from police cells; tenants dragged out of lodging houses, never to be seen again. We all knew somebody who had been told by somebody else who had learned it from a secure source but, somehow, the official investigations had dismissed all the rumours as fabrication. They could find no grain of evidence.

The evidence was whirring away, three metres above my head. I threw the switch and it disappeared, the light, extinguished. I walked down the cold concrete stairs to the street and banged the door shut. I needed some fresh air.

I needed a drink.

It was only a ten minute walk to Bertrand's.

15

The cracks were still forging their haphazard destinies across my ceiling like the veins in a slab of marble. The window was open onto the courtyard. I tried to ignore the increasing hum of the city's machinery running, promising a busy day. Paris was up and doing. Even the concierge's bird was letting fly an occasional squawk.

I could remember no details of my visit to Bertrand's bar, just pale impressions wafting about my brain like clouds of steam in a shower. I had a feeling that down in that sombre cavern of brown and potted plants, Bertrand and I had been devastatingly rude to every one of his customers. The vague memory did not upset me unduly. It would worry Bertrand not one jot and his customers would have loved it.

I turned my thumping head away from the sun and the glaring, unshuttered window but the day insisted. I got up and washed my face in cold water. I looked at my reflection in the mirror. I supposed that I was unemployed again.

Out in the rue Amélie the sun had already staggered sharp black shadows across the facades; shutters looked like carrot graters, doorways like guillotines.

'Lovely morning,' the fair-haired cop said from the doorstep of the police station. 'Going to be another scorcher.' This bloke was unreal. Didn't he know the proper form for police officers? Where was the scowl? Where was the sneer? 'Bit of a sadness with your mate, the other day.' He pushed out his bottom lip and nodded to himself.

It occurred to me that I had no idea where Gaspard had fallen in.

'Which part of the river was he found in?' I asked.

'Now that I could not say.' He sucked his lip back in and then jerked his head. 'Come in and I'll look at the day sheet.'

Inside the station, the sunlight was struggling through the frosted glass and dribbling thinly down the grey-blue walls. It was a chilly place. The cop slipped behind the counter.

'Sunday, wasn't it?' he said and threw back the sheets of the day book. Whilst he read, I studied the notice board. Mohammed El Assawi was still on the poster. 'No, it doesn't say. The City Morgue might know.'

'No matter. What about this chap?' I tapped the poster. 'Who do I tell if I see him?'

'I'd thank you not to tell me.' He pulled a face as he scrabbled a hardback file from a shelf behind him. 'Do you think you might come across him then?' He still had his face turned down as he flipped the papers in the file but his eyes were sharp on me.

'You never know,' I said airily. 'I get about.'

'You would tell us in the first instance.' He put his finger on a notice in the file. 'But the circular came from the Gendarmerie.'

'Not your lot then?' Paris city police were the responsibility of the Ministry of the Interior. The Gendarmerie, which policed the rest of the country, came under the Ministry of Defence. Just like Reinhardt did. I leaned over the counter. 'Who's this chap?' I pointed at a photograph on the circular.

'You're not supposed to be looking at this file,' the cop complained. 'It's confidential. That bloke's the one causing all the trouble. Antoine de Guingamps – the founder of 'Patriots for Peace'. Too much money and too little sense. He invited El Assawi over in the first place. He only did it to cause a fuss. We're not interested in him.'

Perhaps you should be, I thought, as I looked at the man with a nose like a gas tap. I had seen him going in to Miro's. Here he had been photographed coming out of the Casino Harz. Josef went regularly to the Casino Harz, and so, apparently, did de Guingamps. I had taken Vincent there. It all linked up. That was where the deal had been done.

'You look rough,' Joanne was gleeful. 'True love getting you down?'

'More likely your poisonous coffee.'

'So you don't want breakfast?'

'And two croissants.' I waved a hand at Makele.

'B'jour Jo-Jo.' Good old Makele. Perhaps I should be sweeping streets. Nothing complicated, just a bundle of twigs and litres of fresh air.

'Where's Pino?'

Joanne smacked my coffee cup onto the counter. 'Rungis.'

'What's he doing there?'

'Working.'

'Working? What the...?' Luckily I was not drinking from the cup. If I had been I would have given her a shampoo.

'He's been there since four this morning. Driving for the fruiterers down the street.'

'It must have been that cheese sandwich I bought him. The thought of living on food like that for the rest of his life moved him to greater things.' I pulled the newspaper across and looked at the crossword. 'Who was it who wrote *Les Grandes Espérances*? Shakespeare?' I counted the squares. 'No, it doesn't fit.'

'It was the other English one.' She tugged on a strand of hair and pulled her head sideways whilst she reflected. Perhaps she thought it gave her a studious air; she looked as if she was straightening her wig. 'Deekeens,' she said at last.

I counted the squares. 'No, that doesn't fit either.'

'Smart pen,' she nodded at the *'City Morgue'* logo. 'Cheerful.'

'You didn't hear about Gaspard then?' She stopped polishing and shook her head. 'He fell in the river. Kaput.'

Her face sagged like one of Madame Claire's crepes.

'Poor bugger. What was he doing down by the river?'

'That's what I thought.' And thinking it again, I decided to do something about it. 'Can I use the phone?' She slid it across the counter. I dialled the number printed on my pen.

'City Morgue,' the voice replied. It was the attendant who had been on duty when I had seen Gaspard.

'I came in on Sunday to identify a body.'

'Oh yes?'

'Gaspard.' I could not remember Gaspard's surname. 'He fell in the river.'

'I remember. Fennec.'

'Yeah, that's him.'

'You didn't walk off with my pen did you?'

'Me? No, not me.'

'We have to sign for those pens. They're not presents.'

'Can you tell me where they found him?'

'Some people think we are a charity.'

'Must be very trying for you. What about Fennec?'

'Hang on.' I could hear muttering and the sound of papers being swished about. It was probably one of those tape recordings they put on to entertain you whilst you are waiting. 'Here it is. He wasn't in the river. He was in the Mare Saint James. '

'The Mare Saint James? Where the hell is that?'

'Neuilly. In the wood of course.' In the wood. The Bois de Boulogne. 'Was there anything else?' he asked.

'Yeah, just a minute.' My brain was racing. It was too much of a coincidence. 'Is er... Is he still there?'

'Who?'

'Gaspard. Fennec. You've still got the body?'

'He's not due out till tomorrow.'

'Could you do me a favour?' Before he could refuse I said, 'Look at his left forearm. Or the back of his hand.'

'Why?'

'Look for a wound. Like the type made when they put a tube in your arm in hospital.'

'Why should I bother? He died of a heart attack and fell in the water.'

'But what caused the heart attack? Did they analyse his blood?'

'Oh Christ I don't know.'

'Well will you look? Look at his arm.' I was pushing him hard. Joanne was staring at me. I could feel him wavering. 'Please.'

'Oh all right.'

'I'll hang on.' I jumped as he dropped the receiver to the desk.

'What's all this about then?' Joanne asked. 'It must be something important. You said "please".'

'I've got a hunch. I hope I am wrong.'

We waited. A car droned slowly by in the rue St. Dominique. A striped awning lifted slowly in the breeze and then sank back, exhausted with the effort. The telephone receiver clonked again.

'Yeah, there's a puncture wound on the back of his left hand. Satisfied?'

I put the receiver down. 'The bastard!'

Great big lumbering Gaspard had had a dicky heart. Who would have thought it? Not Reinhardt obviously. They strap him to the chair, stick the tube in, turn on the taps and blam, his heart gives out. An embarrassment, no more. What shall we do with the body, boss? Oh, chuck it in a pond somewhere.

'So?' Joanne asked.

I pulled a handful of loose metal from my pocket.

'How much do I owe you?'

'Ho, ho!' Joanne picked out Mathilde's keys from the coins. 'Monsieur has a safe deposit at Le Comptoir has he? Things are looking up.' She was holding the third key on Mathilde's keyring.

'What?' I stared at it.

'You can't fool me. I spent four years on the front desk down at Denfert Rochereau before they changed it. This was the new key they brought in with the electronic door and the cameras.'

'Don't know what you're talking about.'

She jangled the key like a Latino rumba player. 'It has three sets of tines on it. It will open the front door, the vault door and your box.' She turned the key sideways and inspected it. 'And your box number is H 221, in case you've forgotten it. Don't lose it, there is only one.' She returned the key with a grin.

I looked at the key. 'But it says *"8 BBA"*.'

'Letters are numbers and numbers are letters. You know as well as I do.'

I tried to look affluent and conspiratorial at the same time. 'Keep it under your hat.' I winked.

'Something in your eye?'

I stepped jauntily into the street but my mind was staggering with the speed of developments. Josef had photographed an Algerian being executed. Reinhardt had killed Gaspard. I would make him pay for that one day. Josef had a safe deposit box with only one key. And I had the key.

As the train rattled to Denfert Rochereau I looked at the key again. It was anonymous apart from the code stamped on it. H 221, I reminded myself. Fancy Joanne knowing all that! What I had not bothered to ask her of course, was where exactly the premises of Le Comptoir were situated.

I got off at Denfert Rochereau and stood outside the metro and watched the traffic pounding over the pavé of the Place whilst I thought how stupid I was. Then the postman came out of the tobacconist's behind me. Le Comptoir? It's that red door over there, mate.

A red-framed door as anonymous as the key. The panels in it were glazed with that fireproof stuff with wire mesh in it. The door frame was serious steel. Being the shy, retiring chap that I am I have never liked the fame and limelight of the stage and that camera up there in the porch made me feel nervous. But I had to act as if I knew where I was. I pulled out Mathilde's bunch of keys and slotted the third key into the lock. Joanne was right. The bolts on the door slid back with an electronic *'schlick'*. I went in.

The place was eerie. There were no pictures on the walls of the corridor, no notices or instructions. When I did meet a human being we startled each other. He came scurrying around the corner with a brown paper parcel under his arm. A man looking more like a receiver of stolen goods I could not imagine.

'Pardon.'

'Pardon.'

What a polite fraternity the criminal world is. I turned into another corridor, under another camera. Here were vault doors marked with letters. I walked to the door marked *'H'* and tried my key again. It swung wide open. This was magic. It clicked shut behind me. I looked at the line of boxes stretching down both sides of the room before me. Miniature steel doors set into a wall of steel. This installation must have cost a fortune. I was alone in the room. That suited me. I walked down to box 221. No time for sentiment, this was the final test. The key snicked into the lock like a cartridge in a breech. I took a breath and pulled the door open. A featureless grey cube yawned emptily at me. Nothing. A mocking void. Was this Josef's last joke? The air conditioning hissed at me. The lights stared unblinkingly down.

Suddenly I heard a key in the door and two men walked in. They were both wearing suits. The shorter man's suit fitted him. They looked at me and then the taller man started towards me. I swung Joseph's door shut and pocketed the key.

'My employer would like you to wait outside,' he informed me. His accent was Corsican.

'Well your employer is going to be disappointed then.' The man stiffened and scratched his black curly hair whilst he decided whether or not to show me his knife. I saved him from early baldness. 'Because I am not waiting, I'm leaving.'

I gave his boss the evil eye as I walked past. It always worries them in case you are higher up than them in the organisation and they should have recognised you.

I sat on the terrace of a bar and watched the traffic whirling around. So many busy people. And me? Well, I had nothing to do. I could take the keys back to Mathilde and tell her about my discovery. She would love the irony. An old Renault Frégate saloon lumbered by, the suited man sitting upright in the back, the taller one driving. They had to play the part. It was their destiny. Sartre would have expounded on that subject with great glee. What had Josef kept in the safe deposit box? I knew what the answer should be – the negatives. So why hadn't he? And where were they? Was some other thug or agent going to jump on me from a great height? No, Josef had withdrawn the negatives ready to make the trade at the next meeting. He had temporarily lodged them in one of his hollowed-out books and that was where Reinhardt had found them. That was the answer. End of story.

I chucked some money on the table and walked back towards the metro. It was only two stops to the Place d'Italie. I would go and drop off Mathilde's keys. End of story. So why was I fitting that key back in the red door? *Schlick*. The camera swivelled as I walked down the corridor. I did not meet a man with a brown paper parcel this time, nor a pair of part-time mafiosi. Door H, *schlick*. The vault was deserted. I counted down to Josef's box. The key still opened it. It was still empty. I crouched down and peered right in to make sure. I pushed my hand to the very back and swept the empty steel. Still nothing.

I stood up and looked about me. What was in all these boxes? Deeds? Cash? Jewels? I frowned down at the open door. Why was my box empty? I put my hand in again and waved it about so that I could convince Mathilde. As an afterthought I turned my hand palm uppermost and stroked my fingers along the underside of the top. There was something up there, taped out of sight. I pulled at the tape. Without looking further, I put the envelope straight into my pocket, closed the door and walked out.

It had to be the negatives. It had to be. But I was not going to check under these cameras, nor out in the street. I followed an old lady into the post office at the corner and stood at one of the writing desks and fiddled around with some postal forms. Nobody was even remotely interested in me. I slit open the envelope and looked in. The negatives were covered in talcum powder. I puffed it out and then sneezed. The powder settled in a cloudy snow on the desk. Removing nothing from the envelope, I flipped through the contents. There was no doubt. These were the negatives.

I should have felt elated I suppose but I didn't, I felt suddenly threatened. Reinhardt would kill to get these. It would earn him reward and recognition by saving the minister from a scandal. Miro would kill for these because he could see the commercial potential. The man with a nose like a gas tap, de Guingamps, would not sully his hands but he had not seen the photographs and did not know their potential. He was supposed to get them to El Assawi and El Assawi did not want money, he wanted revenge.

Me? I just wanted a quiet life on a desert island with a nympho-maniac beauty queen whose father owned a brewery. Failing that I went to the phone booth and rang Mathilde.

'I've got them,' I said.

'Got what?'

'The negatives.'

'Joel, listen-'

I could tell that she was excited but I interrupted her. 'I found them in a-'

'Joel, don't say any more. Be quiet.'

'But don't you want to-'

'Shut your mouth,' she snapped. 'You had better get over here as quickly as you can.'

'But-'

'Shut it. We need to talk. Take a taxi. And really take a taxi. Don't cheat this time.'

She hung up. That was not quite the reception that I had envisaged. She could be quite hurtful when she put her mind to it. A 'thank you' might have been nice.

I followed her order and grabbed a taxi from the rank outside.

'Ten francs if you can get me to the rue Stresemann in less than five minutes,' I urged him.

The driver turned a bloated eye on me as he juggled the column lever into gear. 'I don't do that kind of driving,' he said. 'Anyway, I don't know where the rue Stresemann is.

I threw myself back into the seat as he followed my direction and performed a tyre-screeching U-turn across the boulevard. And it was a diesel-engined Peugeot 404. Lino Ventura never has these problems.

Mathilde was watching for me at the window. She waved her arm, urging me to hurry. I ran up the stairs two at a time. Was this what she had said she did to keep fit? I must be getting old. She was wearing her light-coloured trousers and a violent red blouse. It matched her toenails.

'Go right through,' she said.

The windows were wide open in the main room, the net curtains hung limply in the air, barely filtering the street noise from below. I sat in the armchair. She sat on the sofa. She crossed her legs and her sandal jerked up and down.

'What did you do after I left you yesterday?' she said. So that was it. 'Did this Anna turn up?'

'In a manner of speaking.'

'Did she have the negatives?'

'No, I found them elsewhere, but Anna was very helpful.'

'I see.' Curt. Crisp.

'Aren't you going to ask me what she was like?'

'If she had been attractive you would have told me already. If I have to ask you, then you will make up an answer. It won't be true.' Her foot was still jerking up and down angrily.

'Well, I've got them.' I threw the envelope onto the table between us. She barely glanced at it. 'You'll never guess where they were.' She looked at me, waiting for an answer. She was jittery. I made her wait.

'Well, where were they?'

I jangled the key in front of her eyes. 'In Josef's deposit box, just down the road. They have been sitting there all the while.'

'So they were not in my handbag then?' she snapped.

'I did not say that they were.'

'But you thought it.'

I shrugged. 'You've got previous.'

'How did you find them?'

'Joanne recognised the key. She used to work at the safe deposit company. She told me all that I needed to know.'

'Did you pull out her fingernails?'

'I used my charm. Something you distinctly lacked when you spoke to me just now on the phone. What was all that about?'

Her answer came at me out of the blue.

'I think my phone is bugged.'

I stared at her. 'Why on earth do you think that?'

'That was why I had to be rude to you to make you shut up. Somebody might have been listening.'

'I assumed you were carving a new image for yourself. It's the modern fashion amongst the youth of today.'

'Idiot! I'm being serious. Think back to that meeting we had in the café at the Madeleine.'

'When you were jealous of the cigarette girl?'

She shook her head testily. 'I phoned you at the Café Clerc and we arranged to meet. By the time we got there Reinhardt had got the waterworks van set up to watch us. Was that just luck?' She looked hard at me with those dark eyes and arched eyebrows. I nodded at her to continue. 'And he took the opportunity to search the flat, knowing exactly where both of us would be.'

'Yeah, that's true.' She was making me think.

'Yesterday your mate the photographer phones you here to say that he has kept one of the photographs. We go straight to see him and Reinhardt is already there. Another coincidence, or is somebody tapping my phone? Can Reinhardt do that?'

'Not officially, because he does not exist, officially.'

'How is it done officially?'

'They duplicate your line at the exchange and run it into whichever department has got the warrant. There is a naughty way. They can put a micro switch affair into your handset but they would need access to your phone to do that and Reinhardt did not go anywhere near the phone when he came here.'

'That's true. And when they searched the flat they already knew that we were not there.' She looked across at me. 'So the phone had already been bugged by then.'

'If it was bugged.'

'What other explanation is there? He's not psychic. He knows what we are doing.'

She was sending me around in circles. Did it matter now if her phone was bugged? Reinhardt had got the photographs. He was satisfied that we did not have the negatives. Except that–

'The telephone engineer!' She suddenly sat upright. I waited for the buttons on her blouse to pop. 'Don't you remember? The day after Reinhardt saw you here, my phone went on the blink and they sent an engineer to repair it.'

We both stood up. I was beginning to tingle. Just like I used to before a raid.

'If you're right, then Reinhardt knows the negatives are here.'

'Because you told him on the phone.'

'I told you on the phone. The point is, he will now be on his way to get them.' I scooped up the envelope from the table and slipped it into my pocket. 'I must get them away.'

'Why?' she asked from the window. 'I thought you wanted him to have them. You said it would solve all our problems.' Dare I try to explain to her about anamorphism and the execution of Algerians? Did I have the time? 'Anyway, you're too late.' She nodded down at the street. 'He's just getting out of his car.'

We both jumped as a thundering thud shuddered the door. I was confused. If Reinhardt was still getting out of his car, who was at the door?

I ran down the hall to bolt the door. It resounded with a second blow and the point of a steel bar wriggled through and prised the top panel into splinters. Through the gap I could see the Luc's contorted grin as he prepared another jab and behind him, the cold slab of Miro's face as he adjusted his silk tie. This was the system of negotiation that Miro enjoyed the most.

'Go back into the salon!' I shouted to Mathilde. She was standing in the doorway with her fist in her mouth. I ran back towards her, thinking as I did so that we were trapped. There was only one way in and out of this flat. Miro was breaking down the door and presumably unknown to him, Reinhardt was on his way up. Such superb timing – it promised to be quite a party.

'What do we do? What do we do?' Mathilde asked and then screamed as another section of the door splintered.

'The window.' I pushed her to the furthest opening. I had a snapshot of the facade in my mind. I realised that I had subconsciously checked the exits on my first visit. So, I was not completely senile then. That was nice. 'Get over the rail and climb across the gap to the balcony on the next building.' She looked at me, unsure. It was a two storey drop to the street. 'Keep going along from balcony to balcony, to the fire escape at the corner.'

'I... I don't think I can.' She was frightened.

Another crash resounded from the hallway. 'Go on!' I pushed her. 'It's less dangerous than badminton.'

'What about you?' She swung a leg over the rail.

'Don't worry about me. I'll try to delay them.' I did not wait to see her response. If I was to hold up Miro and his gang I needed to get working. I ran back down the hallway and was met by the sight of Luc stepping through the wreckage of the door. I skidded to a stop, scooped up the vase of flowers from the table and hurled it at his head. An explosion of water and porcelain. I followed it with the table for good measure and then retreated back up the corridor. I slammed the salon door and turned the key. That would hold him for about five seconds. I upended the sofa and skidded it across the door. Quick look around. The room was empty. Just the net curtain showed where Mathilde had escaped. I needed to give her more time. The sofa shook as Luc shouldered the door. Plaster dropped from the frame. With a crash, the point of the steel bar stabbed through the wood. It wrenched sideways and the panel split. Luc's face appeared in the space. His hair was wet and plastered from the vase. He looked displeased and I sensed that he would blame me.

I searched wildly around me for a weapon. Think, LeBatard, think! The old trick with the gun would not work a second time. I jerked the table lamp from the wall socket with one hand and wrenched the flex from the lamp with the other. I swung the heavy lamp at his head but he swept it aside with his bar. Behind him, Miro was becoming impatient. I still had the electric flex in my hand. The torn wire ends gleamed bright copper. I splayed them apart like a fork and thudded the plug back into the electric socket. Just in time. Luc lunged the bar through the door and I laid the live wires onto it. There was a sharp crack and a flash. Luc's mouth showed all teeth whilst 220 volts shuddered through his sodden torso. The bar jerked backwards from his muscle contraction. Miro ducked but not quickly enough. It smacked into his jaw. I did not wait to count the fillings.

'LeBatard!' It was Reinhardt's voice. It came from the landing behind them. Well, this mess I would leave him to sort out. I ran to the window. Mathilde was three balconies along, stretching across another drop. The crowd which had gathered in the street below was pointing and watching her. Good. She would distract them. I climbed over the rail and decided to go straight down.

'The camera will be in one of the buildings opposite,' a loud voice explained. 'We won't see it from here.'

Camera? What camera? Did they think this was cinema? Some people have no grasp of reality. I gripped the concrete floor of the balcony with one hand and the bottom of the rail with the other.

'And that's Belmondo's double,' the know-all voice said as I dangled there. 'I've seen him before. He did all the stunts in *The Man from Rio.*'

Belmondo! Did he honestly think I looked like Belmondo? That bug-eyed gargoyle! I angrily jerked my body outwards and then let it swing back towards the balcony below. When I let go, I heard a gasp from the crowd but I was concentrating on my landing zone. I hit the target plumb centre and plunged feet first straight through the seat of a rattan sofa, bringing down the washing line as I did so. As I staggered amongst the flower pots, trying to kick my way out of wickerwork and damp pillow cases I heard a comment floating up from the street.

'Must be another comedy, then.'

I gritted my teeth and gave a final vicious lunge at the furniture. Comedy indeed! I swung down over the rail and dropped the last storey to the ground. The pavement came up with a bang. Yes, I was getting old. A paratrooper should have been more flexible than that.

I bounced up and looked around. The crowd parted eagerly to enjoy my next death-defying stunt. Reinhardt's black Renault was standing empty by the *porte cochère*. Half the public were watching me whilst the other half followed Mathilde's bottom as it wriggled onto the fire escape at the corner. With those eyes on me I felt stupidly self conscious. I realised that I had no plan, excepting escape. I paused for an instant. The door of a metallic gold Volvo saloon opened before me and Paulo scrambled out. It was the kind of timing that you could only achieve after a dozen takes and here I was, doing it in one. Paulo had seen Mathilde and he was going to intercept her. He had not seen me. He never did. I clipped him smartly behind the ear and toppled him headfirst into the fruiterer's stand. His unconscious body sprawled, purple-socked into the peaches. Well, if they wanted cinema, let's give it to them.

I jumped into the Volvo and started the engine. Mathilde was down to the pavement and the crowd were applauding her. What do I know about Volvos? They are built like tanks and have thirty centimetres of empty metal back and front to cushion you in a crash. Unlike Renaults. I slammed the lever into reverse, spun the wheels and reversed the saloon full speed into the front of

Reinhardt's car. His black slug bumped backwards up onto the bonnet of the car behind in a satisfying concerto of tinkling glass and crumpling metal.

'Joel! Joel!' It was Mathilde running down the pavement towards me. And yes, they were bouncing out of her blouse and yes, the spectators were loving it. She reached my window as I pushed the lever into first gear. 'Where are you going?' She ran around to the passenger door. 'Take me with you!'

Where was I going? I had not thought. I could hear the police two-tones getting nearer. Where was I going? Where had I been? Nowhere. All this time I had got nowhere. Where was I going? I was going back to the beginning.

'I'm going to see Josef!' I yelled. The door handle was torn from her grasp as I let in the clutch. The Volvo shot away from the kerb, dragging the fender of Reinhardt's Renault for thirty metres along the street before casting it aside.

Calm down LeBatard, calm down. You are in another street now and they do not know who you are. Drive like everybody else and you will be invisible. Just another well-dressed Parisian driving a flash car with a dent in the bodywork. Exactly like every third car you see in Paris.

So this was Miro's limousine was it? The leather seat was cool, despite the heat. I fiddled with the switches. The radio aerial climbed skywards from the front wing, then a blast of cold air hit me. Air conditioning? He really did like his luxury. I found a decent radio station and sat back in comfort to enjoy a relaxed ride out to St Maur.

The square by the church was unchanged. The doorway of the tobacconist's on the corner was a black hole of shade. Was it really only two weeks ago that I had looked in the mirror of the bar to talk to the girl with the veil? And look where it had got me.

The heavy-foliaged trees cast pools of shade around the square. I gleefully ran the Volvo the length of the cemetery wall, grinning happily as the stonework ground off the wing mirror, the rubbing strips and most of the paint. I got out and left the keys in the lock. It would give the kids of the neighbourhood something to play with. They could always buy matches from the tobacconist's.

I pushed open the wicket gate and walked slowly up the path

to Josef's grave. I stood before it. The earth was crumbling white and dry. Josef. *Mon Colonel*. You were going to topple the government that had betrayed you in Algeria. Others had tried. You might have succeeded. But they are not the same people, *Mon Colonel*. Your judgment was diluted by whisky and wine and distorted by sickness and solitude. Perhaps I should have visited occasionally. We could have gone out for a glass or two, reminisced about old times. Perhaps your daughter could have looked after you more; perhaps you would not let her.

I took the negatives from my pocket. The envelope came out with the Casino Harz matchbook tucked into it. I looked up at the sky; it was blue and cloudless. A crow drifted across from one tree top to another. A train horn sounded a few blocks away; a car swerved into the square, its tyres squealing on the hot asphalt.

'*Mon Colonel.*' I saluted.

Using that Casino Harz matchbook seemed like Providence and Destiny all rolled into one. They burned with a yellow flame, giving off a whitish smoke. I lit the next negative from the dying flame of its predecessor and dropped the blackened scrolls to the grave, one by one. Finish. End of story. I turned to await Reinhardt and Mathilde who were hurrying up the path. Reinhard's face was red and he was puffing. It was probably because of Mathilde's driving. I nearly felt sympathy for him.

'LeBatard!'

I ignored him.

'Are you OK?' I asked Mathilde. There were grubby scuff marks on her trousers. She looked hard at me and nodded. 'Well button your shirt up then.'

She hissed like a Japanese tour guide. I don't think she liked what I had said.

'LeBatard, give them over.' Reinhardt's podgy hand was stretched out towards me, his eyes watery behind the steel rims of his glasses. Too many restaurant meals whilst I went hungry. Too many four star hotels whilst I slept on four-legged benches.

'Give them to him Joel.' She looked tired. 'Do as he says.'

'Oh, so we do what Reinhardt says now, do we? Where are all those fine words you had about fighting for your father's memory then?'

'*Salaud!*' she swore.

Reinhardt looked pleased. I wiped the smile from his face.

'I burned them.' I poked the ashes with my toe. 'You can have what's left.' I watched his smile turn to a sickly grin.

'You burned them?' He snapped. 'What the devil for?'

'We didn't want them and if you had been the last person on Earth, Josef would have eaten them rather than have handed them over to you.'

'I see.' His voice was short. I don't think he believed me.

'So that's that then,' Mathilde said. 'It's all over.' She turned towards the gate.

I shrugged. I had known it before she had. In my best cinema drawl I said, 'We'll always have Paris.'

'You're no Humphrey Bogart,' she shouted over her shoulder.

'Well you're no Ingrid Bergman, either,' I threw back.

Reinhardt's sweating face was screwed into a conflicting distortion of disappointment and glee.

'You burned them?' He was desparate for confirmation but a triumphant malice gleamed in his eyes as he watched Mathilde walk out of my life. She unlatched the gate and disappeared behind the wall. She did not look back.

'Yes, I burned them. I suppose she was right when she said that you had bugged her telephone?'

'Smarter than you, LeBatard, smarter than you.'

'Everybody seems to have been smarter than me.' Now the trick question. 'How did you get on to Gaspard?'

'Ah, that was easy. They hired a postman's uniform for him to deliver the photographs. There are not that many theatrical costumiers in Paris.'

'Pity about his heart,' I said quietly.

Reinhardt's head jerked when he realised he had been tricked. No imagination, these Alsatians, no imagination. My first punch landed with a *clang* exactly on the stroke of one o' clock.

Just like a bloody cartoon.

16

Grey water was swirling down the gutters of the rue Amélie; the dust of summer days being washed to the Seine. The sky sagged sodden between the rooftops, dull with heavy cloud and immobile, featureless. A cool clamminess was creeping into my shoes. Josef's clothes were good but his footwear had never been my size. He had small feet. I had never noticed. All that time together and I had never noticed how small his feet were.

'Call this summer?' the cop with no chin remarked as I hopped across a puddle. He was standing in the commissariat doorway. For some reason he was trying to be pleasant. I took no notice of him. The manageress at the launderette opposite tapped on the window and held aloft my bag of laundry. I waved to her. I would collect it on my way back from breakfast.

'Lousy weather,' Joanne grunted as she slammed levers on the coffee machine. 'I wonder what he makes of it all?' She jerked her head at Makele. He was gazing like a child at the beads of rain as they trickled down the glass door.

'When it rains in Africa, it really rains. To him, this is just slight humidity.' I reached for the basket of croissants. Joanne pulled it out of reach. That movement seemed, kind of familiar. It hearkened back to the bad old days when I had no job.

'Sorry Jo-Jo, you owe me three days.'

'When have I ever let you down?'

'Every time, Jo-Jo, every time.' There was a knowing sadness in her eyes. I pulled the fifty franc note from my pocket and threw it onto the counter. I knew, and she guessed, that it was my last. She took it to the till.

'And take for two croissants,' I said, pulling the basket back towards me.

'We haven't seen your young lady recently.' The observation

261

was casual but she was watching me in the mirror.

'My employer,' I said and then added, 'My ex-employer.'

'Sacked for being late?' Joanne had the subtlety of a sumo wrestler. 'Kicked out for stealing the butter?' She put my change down and flicked her fading hair from her eyes. I left the money untended on the zinc just to show her the depth of my disdain for the material aspects of life.

'No job lasts for ever.'

'Yours never get started.'

'This was a short contract.'

'You can have an apple.' She thrust the fruit at me. 'Pino brings them back from Rungis for free. Go on,' she urged, 'it's healthy. It'll give you some vitamins. These last few days you've been walking alongside your shoes.'

I took the apple and scooped up the money. Philosophy is fine when you have dry feet. The doorway darkened for a second and suddenly Martins was at the bar, the raindrops glinting sharp on his dark jacket.

'Bonjour Martins,' Joanne greeted him. 'The usual?'

'Madame.' He gave her a short stiff bow. All very sober and correct. And schizophrenic. 'Jo-Jo.' He raised his glass to me. I raised my cup. I am not proud. After all, the man had once nearly shot me.

I pulled the newspaper over. Now that Pino was no longer working for Paris Matin we got the daily paper on time. It didn't make the crossword any easier though.

'Funny business down at St Maur the other week.' Joanne was still following my reactions in the mirror.

'Oh yeah?' I frowned at the clues.

'That man found beaten up in the cemetery. The papers reckoned that he was some secret agent or other. That's why there's been no follow up.'

'Oh yeah?'

Reinhardt had been in no state to talk when I had finished with him and when he does talk it will not be to the press. He will just bide his time and then come after me. And now I had nothing I could threaten him with. Perhaps I should have killed him like he had Gaspard. After all, Reinhardt was unofficial. He did not exist.

'Didn't you go to St Maur for that funeral?'

I looked up from my toils. She was working hard at this. Martins was following the interrogation. So was Makele, as best he could. No doubt it would get reported back to Pino. The café was pursuing its investigation.

'Yes. What of it? St Maur has a cemetery. The place is full of graves.'

'And did you hear what happend to Mirovici? Got his face smashed in.'

'It could only be an improvement.'

'Didn't Vincent do business with Mirovici?'

'If he did it didn't help him.' I tapped the newpaper. ' He's up in court tomorrow. "Demanding money with menaces".'

'Vincent? Demanding money with menaces? He couldn't threaten a rabbit. Do all your employers end up in court?'

I paused whilst an image of Mathilde flashed across my mind. Joanne noticed and smiled quietly to herself, the cow.

'No, not all my employers. They usually deserve what they get though.'

I was in credit by thirty centimes at the launderette so I got a smile from the manageress when she handed me my bag. The concierge was looking over the screen as I went through into the courtyard. She had left me alone since I had shouted at her. I could almost feel sorry for her. I must be going soft. I dumped the laundry on the unmade bed and ignored it.

Rue Amélie.

Here I was and here I would stay. A failure who would only grasp at the opportunity when he was certain that it had gone. A man who was attractive to the wrong sort of woman. The type who saw in him qualities that he could not find. A woman who was convinced that he was already something which he knew he would never be. Would I still be here in ten years time – hanging on month by month in a squalid bedsit?

This was crushing self pity. Action plan, LeBatard, action plan! You need a meal. What can you pawn or sell? I pulled open the drawer and the answer was there before me – the cap badges that Mathilde had given me. I stuffed them into my pocket and walked up to the boulevard de La Tour Maubourg. I was just in time to catch the morning Historical Paris as it was pulling away from Les Invalides. I rapped smartly on the side of the coach. The doors hissed open. The guide was Marie-Hélène who had scandalised Mathilde by jumping on me in the rue de Rivoli. She was sitting sideways on the guide seat looking down the coach as she delivered her commentary in English. The driver studied me suspiciously.

'Jo-Jo!' Marie-Hélène turned. 'How's the Comtesse de Ségur?' She guffawed. No refinement, Marie Hélène, just plain boisterous good humour. The tourists all craned their necks politely to see who she was talking to. She pointed at the driver. 'This is Patrick. Hop in.'

'LeBatard.' I leaned across Marie-Hélène and shook hands.

'Aah.' The light of realisation flitted into his eyes. Somebody else who had heard of me.

'Can I cadge a lift to St. Lazare?'

'Of course you can,' Marie Hélène said. 'St Augustin is the nearest we go. Will that do?' I glanced for confirmation from the driver who looked uncertain. 'Don't worry Patrick, I'll make it worth your while.'

His eyes flicked an interrogative at me. I gave him an imperceptible nod. Marie-Hélène's generosity was well known in the agency. If he did not know that he must be very new. I sat on the step and tried to ignore her meaty thighs each time they slapped me on the cheek. She was a lot of girl and not much of it was in her clothes.

It had stopped raining when they dropped me by the Eglise St Augustin. The pavements were washed clean, the sand around the trees was parted in rivulets and patched with puddles. I walked along to the Gare St Lazare. I remembered that there was a chap in the arcade near the station who bought and sold this type of thing.

'Tu viens chéri?' The invitation came from a blonde under a clear plastic umbrella shaped like a bell. She looked like an anatomical specimen in a medical school. 'Oh, it's you!' she exclaimed. 'The man in the wood.'

I stopped and stared at her. Then I recalled the two prostitutes who had picked me up in the Bois de Boulogne. I laughed.

'Yes it's me and I'm still broke. How's business?'

She pouted. 'They're all afraid of the rain. What about you? Did you get even with the swine who beat you up?'

'Do you read the papers?'

'Not really. I watch the TV.'

'The "Mystery Man" in the cemetery of St Maur?' Her hand flew to her mouth in surprise. 'Yes, I got even with him.'

'Wow! Was that your gang?'

'No. It was me. On my own.'

'A real man, eh?' She appraised me with a grin. 'Look, I'm not doing anything at the moment. Do you fancy a beer?'

'Another time, *chérie*, I've got a job to do and you've got rent to pay.' I could feel her eyes watching me as I walked to the arcade. I did not need to put a spring in my step, it was already there. A real man.

An hour later I was walking back down the rue St Dominique. The old chap in the shop had given me two hundred francs for the badges and he had obviously thought that he had got a bargain. I didn't mind. I had only been only expecting fifty. I had no idea these things had any value.

Jean-Marie was standing behind his bar, gazing at the steaming pavement. I waved to him. He waved back before he had realised who I was then he gave up trying to scowl and grinned instead. No hard feelings in the seventh arrondissement.

Mathilde's final taunt, 'You're no Humphrey Bogart!' was still running through my mind. No. It was Mathilde that was running through my mind. Well, this is not Casablanca, it's... I stopped and looked at the *'Vacances 2000'* sign swinging above me. It's Tunisia, land of sun, sand and opportunity. I pushed open the door.

'Monsieur?'

'I've come to collect two air tickets for Mademoiselle Sikorski.'

She swivelled on her chair to the cupboard behind her.

'Ah yes, here we are. Just in time. Paris-Tunis-Paris open-dated returns, departure from Orly, tomorrow at ten o' clock. In the names of Sikorski and,' she frowned, 'LeBatard,' she eventually said bravely. It cost her a blush.

I suddenly had one of those flashes of inspiration for which I am justly renowned. I could do with some more pocket money and I did not need two tickets.

'Mademoiselle Sikorski does not need her ticket. I am going to act on her behalf. She asked me to get a refund for her please.'

'Oh, so you just want the one in the name of... um...' The poor woman was torturing herself.

'Yes, just my ticket.'

'OK.' She slid the booklet across the desk. 'There will be a handling charge for cancellation. I think it's about three percent. I'll look it up.'

'Yeah, that's fine.' I could afford to be generous.

'Ah, but Mademoiselle Sikorski paid on her *carte bleue*. I will have to refund her through her account. I can't do it in cash.'

'What?'

'She bought them on credit. We are not allowed to make refunds in cash on credit purchases. But don't worry,' she added, 'I can assure her that it will appear on her next bank statement.'

Well, it had been worth a try and when Mathilde finds out at the end of the month, my failure will make her laugh which is more than my successes ever did.

I went home and packed. It did not take long. Then I dined at a fish restaurant in the rue de l'Université. It was the nearest I had ever got to higher education.

It was the last Tuesday of the month and the sun was shining.

I used to hate Tuesday mornings. It was the day we collected from the girls. I would not be doing that anymore. My passport was dog-eared but still valid. The airline ticket was tucked into it. My bag was stuffed with Josef's best clothes; the concierge would think it was my laundry. I took a last look at the room and then locked the door.

In the courtyard the sun was sparkling on the bird cage. I flipped a cod liver oil capsule through the bars. The stupid bird attacked it with short, sharp pecks. Good. By lunchtime it should have the squits like a fire hose. The concierge's eyes appeared at the window like over-ripe figs in a paper bag. I blew her a kiss. She nearly bit a chunk out of the screen.

I pondered whether to reclaim my thirty centimes credit at the launderette but decided to be magnanimous. At the street corner I took the big iron doorkey from my pocket and held it dangling above the grating. 'Madame Claire, you never repaired the leaking window and I asked you three times. My money was good. When you got it.' I released the key and watched as it plummeted into the black slime with a rewarding *gloup*. No going back now.

In the rue St Dominique people were moving with a purpose. It is called the rush hour. It was not a movement I had ever subscribed to. Its earnestness always frightened me. I slid my bag to the foot of the counter at the Café Clerc and drank my coffee. Pino was sitting in the corner huddled over a glass of red wine.

'That was a great apple I had yesterday,' I called. 'Fresher than your newspapers ever were.'

'Make the best of it, you won't see any more,' he muttered.

'He put the truck through a shop window,' Joanne said. 'Normal service has been resumed.'

'His jobs last even less time than mine,' I complained. 'But you don't nag at him.' I pushed my empty cup back.

'Perhaps it's because I think you could do better if you tried.' She nodded towards Pino. 'Unlike him. Anyway, you're up early. Going somewhere?' She looked at me and then she stood still like a statue as it hit her. 'You're going aren't you Jo-Jo?' she whispered. Her eyes began to fill. 'You're leaving the rue Amélie.'

'Pastures anew, as they say.' I did not need a weeping Joanne. What was wrong with her? She should have been pleased to see the back of me. 'It was great fun but adventure calls me.' I picked up my bag and walked out. She stared after me.

I strode briskly down the street and across the esplanade to the air terminal at the Invalides. There, I paid my six francs for the privilege of riding behind a uniformed chauffeur, complete with peaked cap, in the Air France coach to Orly. Up the ramp into the daylight we charged, paused at the top with a hiss on the brakes to intimidate the traffic and then lunged into the gap we had made. I sat back and watched Paris recede. That was where Mathilde had dropped me when she had brought me back from Josef's funeral. Denfert Rochereau, the red door of Le Comptoir still as secretive. Yes, I was leaving it all behind.

The coach got caught in the slow moving traffic on the Autoroute du Sud. I could hear the driver talking over the radio with the other coaches on the run. I didn't mind what he did as long as he got me there in time. We reversed into the bay at nine thirty five. I was up and ready to alight but he was in no hurry to open the doors. First things first. Gear in neutral, parking brake on, cap straight on head. These drivers really think they are the bubbles in the champagne.

I clattered down the steps and into the terminal. My flight was being called as I crossed the concourse. A crowd of black-haired North Africans were milling around the check-in desk making it a tangle of bundles and bed sheets, sacking and rope.

'For the ten o'clock to Tunis?' I called over the heads to the check-in clerk. He pushed aside a wizened old man with one hand and waved me up to the front with the other.

'Just one bag?' I nodded. 'Put it on the scales.' My bag looked quite refined amongst the disparate bundles as it wobbled through the rubber slats and into the darkness of the baggage belt system. The check-in clerk said that the plane was about a third full. He allocated me a window-seat towards the back. 'Go straight to the gate. The flight is boarding now.' He waved me towards the escalators. 'No time for shopping.'

That was the last thought in my mind so why did I glance towards the newspaper rack as I hurried to the gate? *'Mystery Man of St Maur talks,'* ran the headline. What the hell had Reinhardt said? And who to? I needed to know. I yanked the paper out of the rack and then dropped it like a rotten oyster. I was ten minutes away from escape. I did not need to know anything. I only needed to get on that plane. I just had to hope that the Customs officers had not read the paper.

I was the last passenger to embark. The hostess pointed me in the direction of my seat. The sexes were unofficially segregated on the plane. A handful of women wrapped in their black burkhas were sitting at the front, the men were further back. I nodded at a prosperous looking European couple as I passed. They acknowledged me as of the same race but not the same class. I buried myself in my seat by the window and silently begged the crew to shut the door and back the plane off the stand.

We waited. It was time to leave but we were still here. It must be something important, time costs money at an airport. Were they waiting for a police officer to come on board and ask for Joel LeBatard? Could they react that quickly? Of course they couldn't. I was frightening myself with a lurid imagination. It would take them days to check through the embarkation records. Wouldn't it? I dumped my jacket on the empty seat at the side of me. We still waited. Then the steward suddenly stiffened and went to the door. I could see the fringe of a figure standing in the doorway. It was a man in uniform with a peaked cap.

I was trapped and I was sweating. I looked around the cabin. Should I go and hide in the toilet or would that draw attention to me? The figure handed a clipboard through the hatchway. The steward signed it and handed it back with a joke. Then he shut the door. What was I worrying myself for? I sat back in the seat, buckled my belt and closed my eyes.

By the time we were over the Massif Central I was making plans. The first thing to do upon arrival was to send Jean-Marc a postcard to tell him to look in the projector because that was where I had left the slide. He could decide what to do with it, it did not concern me now. I was out of it. Joel LeBatard was starting anew. I would put some dinars down on a room in the old town and then sally forth and get a job. I licked my lips. Perhaps I would get a beer first and then look for a job. One of the Arab women sailed past like a black spectre on her way to the toilet. Just two eyes, hidden behind a black mesh, and painted toenails and sandals poking below the hem. A bizarre mix of traditional and contemporary. If they all dressed the same in Tunis I would have no distraction.

The hostess came by with a trolley. 'Monsieur?'

'Just water.'

She handed me a plastic cup and a small bottle of Evian and looked up. 'And mademoiselle?' she asked.

'Orange juice,' Mathilde replied as she slipped into the seat at the side of me. I stared at her. She took the orange juice and then turned to me. 'Well, you could at least say "hello".'

'What are you doing here?' I gasped.

'Flying to Tunisia, the same as you.' She took a sip at her orange juice. '*Santé.*'

'Where did you come from? I didn't see you get on.'

'You wouldn't. You were the last on. I thought for a while that you were going to miss it.' She laughed. 'That would have been funny wouldn't it? Me charging off to Tunisia on my own.'

'But... but I walked all down the plane.'

'Yes, you walked straight past me.'

'Not possible.'

'And then I walked past you.' She opened her bag and pulled out a corner of black cloth. 'Horrible things. God knows how they live in them. I couldn't wait to take it off.'

'But–'

'That's where I've just been – to the toilet. I go in as a Tunisian begum and come out as a French mademoiselle.' Her eyes were bright with amusement and success. 'Oh stop staring,' she said, 'or I'll cover myself up again and go and sit back up at the front.'

'But... What...?'

'Yes?' She pulled out a mirror, licked her finger and dragged it along her eyebrows.

'How did you know I would be on the plane?'

'Simple. Yesterday afternoon the lady at the travel agency rang me up about my credit card. It didn't take me long to work out that you were running away. Again. So I collected the ticket and made sure that I got here before you.'

'But why?'

She leaned in to me and whispered, 'Did you think I would let you get away with it? After all we've been through?'

I looked out of the window. 'I see.'

'No you don't. You never do.' I accepted that remark as her natural feminine desire to be obscure. 'So what are you going to do in Tunis?'

'Have a beer.'

'Long way to go for a beer.'

'Have another beer. Get drunk. Forget.'

She shook her head in pity. 'You really are a case, Joel. I've got a much better idea.' She dragged a large envelope out of her bag and from it she unfolded an illustrated brochure. 'Village Grand Soleil,' she read. 'First we go to Zarzis and register my title to Papa's olive grove.' She tapped the brochure. 'Then I go and see these people and ask them how much they are going to pay me to use my land for their road.'

Little girl's dreams.

'And how much do you think they will pay?'

'I shall start at a million francs.' The figure knocked the breath out of me. 'Oh do shut your mouth.'

'A million francs! They won't pay that.'

'If they don't, then none of the affluent residents of their village will be able to get to and from their houses and the company will go bankrupt. It's quite simple.'

'They won't fall for that. You're out of your mind.'

'They've sold nearly a hundred of them already.'

'They'll just ignore you and continue driving straight through your olive grove.'

It's your job to stop them. I am sure you can recruit and organise. A bulldozer for the road, perhaps; a crowd of locals with smelly goats. Should be easy.'

'But a million francs! They won't pay.' It was preposterous.

'Their insurance company will pay. It will have to, in order to secure the value of the mortgage they gave the developers. If they don't, they lose the lot.'

'I suppose you know all about insurance and mortgages?'

She smiled. 'Yes I do. Rather like you know about guns and hitting people.' She dropped the brochure onto the fold-down table in front of me. 'Don't you think it would be rather fun to ask these people for a million francs?'

I allowed my eye to wander across the photographs of chalets and plans of roads and shops. They would have one hundred rich and powerful tenants leaning on them for a rapid solution. A million francs? She was delving in her handbag again.

'Do you think I can't do it?' she said. 'I can climb along the facade of a building two storeys up, can't I?'

I nodded slowly. 'Oh yes, you could do it.' I was certain of that.

'But I'll need you, Joel. It'll be a synergy.' Another word from her university days I supposed. 'Now, how are we going to get you off the plane, have you thought about that?' I had, but in the shock of seeing her I had forgotten all about it. 'I didn't have time to read the paper this morning but it looks as if that *crapule* Reinhardt has stirred something up.'

'They won't have had time to notify the airports and ports. That trick only succeeds in thrillers.'

'Hold this.' She handed me a French passport. 'It's Papa's.' She was burrowing in her bag again. 'Bloody thing,' she muttered and yanked out the burkha and stuffed it under the seat. 'Ah, got them.' She held a pair of nail scissors in her hand. She took back the passport and opened it at Josef's photograph. It was strange seeing his face staring unblinkingly at me from the page. 'We only need to change this. They only look at the name and the picture.' She snipped through the middle of the image and gently prised it away from the page, leaving the two fixing rivets standing proud. 'Hold those.' She gave me the two halves of the photograph. 'And don't lose them.'

She pulled the brochure across the table and we studied it avidly as the hostess passed back up the aisle. Then she produced two passport-sized photographs. They were the two pictures of me that she had kept from the photo booth in La Samaritaine.

'Why did you keep those?'

I think my question embarrassed her as much as the possible answer nonplussed me.

'Oh, I don't know. I thought they might come in useful.' Her smile was girlish. She laid the two halves of Josef's photograph over one of mine and using the rivet holes as templates, she carefully drew in the circles. I was fascinated. With great precision she made a diagonal cut and edged the scissors around to cut the two holes for the rivets.

'That's pretty clever,' I said.

'Watch this then.' She flexed the photograph onto the page and it snapped under the rivets. She tidied the corners with the point of the scissors. *'Voilà.'* She handed me the passport.

'Where did you learn to do that?'

'I am head of our company's fraud investigation department. It's second nature to me.'

Josef Paul Sikorski,' I read. 'How does that help us?'

'When they check the records they might find a Joel LeBatard embarking but they won't find him arriving in Tunisia.'

Josef Paul Sikorski. How does that help me? I thought.

'Are you in this with me, then?' She tapped the brochure.

A million francs, and the girl. What more could a man want? I nodded. 'But it's obvious I am not your father. I'm too young.'

'You can be my brother. Monsieur Josef Sikorski and his sister, Mathilde.' She smiled.

So I don't get the girl after all.

'What's the matter?' she asked.

'You want me to act as a brother figure to you?'

'Until we get to the hotel.'

'And then?'

'And then I will expect you to act as my lover.'

That was more like it. A million francs and the girl. Bogart would have been proud of me. I lifted my plastic cup to her.

'Here's looking at you kid.'

With an insolent backhand swipe she swatted the water into my face.

'Will you stop calling me "kid"!'

A word to my readers

After reading *The Chinese Transfer* you told me
that you also wanted to know what happened to
the minor characters in the book.

If authors were obliged to develop and expand
the lives of all of their characters, their
work would be never-ending.

However, I value your observations and so in
writing *Rue Amélie* I incorporated characters
and incidents that an alert reader of
The Chinese Transfer would be
capable of recognising.

Did you discover them?

Martin Lloyd
2009

The Trouble with France

Martin Lloyd's new international
number one blockbusting
bestseller

"...makes Baedeker's look like a guidebook..."

When Martin Lloyd set out on his holiday to Suffolk why
did he end up in Boulogne? What caused Max the Mad
Alsatian to steal his map and what did the knitted
grandma really think of his display of hot plate juggling?
The answers to these and many more mysteries are to be
found in THE TROUBLE WITH FRANCE

THE TROUBLE WITH FRANCE contains no recipes and
no hand drawn maps. It does not recount how somebody
richer than you went to a part of France that you have
never heard of, bought a stone ruin for a song and
converted it into a luxurious retreat which they expect
you to finance by buying their book.

Nor is it the self satisfied account of another ultra fit
expedition cyclist abseiling down Everest on a penny
farthing but Martin Lloyd attempting an uneventful ride
on a mundane bicycle through an uninteresting part
of France... and failing with outstanding success.

THE TROUBLE WITH FRANCE is destined to be a worldwide
success now that Margaret's Mum has been down the
road and told her friend Pat about it.

Published by Queen Anne's Fan ISBN: 9780 9547 1500 7

NOW IN ITS FIFTH IMPRESSION

MARTIN LLOYD

The Trouble with Spain

FROM THE BESTSELLING AUTHOR OF
THE TROUBLE WITH FRANCE *COMES*
THIS EAGERLY AWAITED SEQUEL

"...makes Munchausen look like a liar..."

Still smarting from his brutal encounter with Gaul as detailed in his much acclaimed book, THE TROUBLE WITH FRANCE, Martin Lloyd drags his bicycle over the Pyrenees to pursue the twin delights of sun and breakfast.

What factor will defeat his proposed headlong plunge into raw hedonism? Will it be his profound and extensive ignorance of Spanish history or perhaps his coarse insensitivity to the culture of the peninsula?
Or would it be the damning condemnation that he is just too lazy to learn the language?

Read THE TROUBLE WITH SPAIN and you will discover nothing about bull fights and enjoy no colourful descriptions of sensual flamenco dancing but you will learn why you cannot train goldfish to be guard dogs and you will clearly understand why even Martin Lloyd's trousers ran away from him.

CAUTION
This book contains moderate use of humour, some expressions in foreign language and a short but ultimately frustrating scene in a lady's bedroom.

Published by Queen Anne's Fan ISBN: 9780 9547 1501 4

Hunting the Golden Lion

a cycle safari through France

Having recklessly declared in a previous book that it
must be possible to cross all of France staying only
in hotels called the HOTEL DU LION D'OR,
Martin Lloyd is challenged by his critics to prove
his assertion in the only way possible – by doing it.

Surely it will be a straightforward and leisurely ride
through France? As long as the hotels are no more than
a day's cycle ride apart, of course. And if your bicycle
has been constructed this century, and if you remember
to take with you all that you need... and if your name isn't
Martin Lloyd.

Is this why, on the the first day of his safari,
he is standing in his pyjamas on a pavement
a thousand miles from home,
clutching a broken bicycle
with a bleeding hand?

Published by Queen Anne's Fan ISBN: 9780 9547 1506 9

THE PASSPORT

The History of Man's Most Travelled Document

SECOND EDITION, REVISED
AND ENLARGED
with 246 pages and 80 illustrations

The passport is a document familiar to many, used and recognised worldwide and yet it has no basis in law: one country cannot oblige another to admit its subjects simply by issuing a document. But the state, by insisting on the requirement to hold a passport, provides for itself a neat, self-financing data collection and surveillance system.

This well illustrated book tells for the first time the story of the passport from its earliest origins to its latest high-tech developments. Handwritten documents adorned with wax seals, modern versions in plastic covers, diplomatic passports and wartime safe conducts, all drawn from the author's collection, complement the exciting exploits of spies and criminals and the tragic real life experiences of refugees.

Whether recounting the birth of the British blue passport of the 1920s or divulging the secrets of today's machine readable passport, Martin Lloyd has written an informative and engrossing history book which is accessible to everyone.

"...a lively and thoughtful book..."
SUNDAY TELEGRAPH

Published by Queen Anne's Fan ISBN: 9780 9547 1503 8

Martin Lloyd has recorded THE PASSPORT as a talking book for the blind. RNIB catalogue no: TB 14107

The Chinese Transfer

Martin Lloyd

The

Chinese Transfer

a thriller romance that you will not
want to put down

"...this is storytelling as it used to be... "

Paris in the 1970s – student demonstrations, union strikes
and oppressive heat. Coach driver Simon Laperche is sent
to Orly Airport to pick up a Chinese group and take them
to their hotel in the city. A run of the mill job. He could
do it with his eyes shut. It was a pity about the guide,
but then, he could not expect to please everybody.

Abruptly, things go wrong. The plane is diverted to Lyons
and Laperche is ordered to drive his coach south to
meet it... and he has to take that infuriating guide
with him. Unknown to them both, a terrorist unit has
targeted their group and is intent upon its destruction.

Stalked by the terrorists, the driver and guide continue
to bicker as they struggle to bring their group safely to
Paris. Will the mutual respect which eventually begins
to grow between them prove strong enough
when the test comes?

Published by Queen Anne's Fan ISBN: 9780 9547 1502 1

Every
Picture

"... a tender and engaging love story..."

When Jennifer Pye bumped into Richard Ennessy on his first day at art college she did not know that he was a viscount and he did not tell her. Why should he? How was he to know that their paths would cross and recross and that he would end up falling in love with her?

And once that had happened, he then found it impossible to tell her the truth for fear of losing her. At the very moment that they finally admit their feelings for one another, the relationship is abruptly wrenched asunder as their lives take a violent and unpredictable turn, casting their two destinies onto divergent courses.

Would they ever meet again?

Published by Queen Anne's Fan ISBN: 9780 9547 1505 2